"Good writers are always beginners, unprofessionals, driven by desire: ears open, vision wiped clean. They find their home in *The Paris Review*." —Hilary Mantel

"Is *The Paris Review* good? It is good. It is damn good. . . . The magazine is fucking exceptional." —Roxane Gay, HTMLGIANT

"America's greatest literary journal." —Josh Tyrangiel, *Time*

"The enduring lion of American literary magazines." —Bruce Weber, *The New York Times*

"In a world where literature seems like an afterthought, the *Review* commands attention. It isn't topical in a current events sort of way, but it feels completely urgent and contemporary." —Elizabeth Taylor, *Chicago Tribune*

"We were so absorbed in *The Paris Review* that we almost forgot about the internet. . . . We love the new *Paris Review*." —*n+1*

"It is without doubt—and with apologies to the wonderful *Granta*, its closest competitor—the King of the Little Magazines. . . . An indispensable part of the literary culture." —David Mattin, *The Guardian* (London)

"An American treasure with true international reach." —Richard Rayner, *Los Angeles Times*

"The most prestigious of American literary journals." —Trevor Butterworth, *Financial Times*

"Elegant, edgy, and surprising, an unusual but cohesive mix of writing characterized by intelligence and precision and, frequently, humor. —Maud Newton, maudnewton.com

"Whatever is going on over at *The Paris Review*, it's working like my new MacBook Air. Super slickly sexy in a way that makes me wonder if I have enough in me to keep up with it, no cords attached, with barely a mutter of effort to show that it *is* hard at work."

—Rachael Ringenberg, erstwhiledear.com

"Our favorite literary magazine."   —Libby Molyneaux, *L.A. Weekly*

PENGUIN BOOKS

THE UNPROFESSIONALS

Since its founding in 1953, THE PARIS REVIEW has been America's preeminent literary quarterly, dedicated to discovering and publishing the best new voices in fiction, nonfiction, and poetry. The magazine introduced readers to the earliest writings of Jack Kerouac, Philip Roth, T. C. Boyle, V. S. Naipaul, Ha Jin, Jay McInerney, and Mona Simpson, and published numerous now-classic works, including Roth's *Goodbye, Columbus*, Donald Barthelme's *Alice*, Jim Carroll's *The Basketball Diaries*, and selections from Samuel Beckett's *Molloy*. The first chapter of Jeffrey Eugenides's *The Virgin Suicides* appeared in the *Review*'s pages, as well as early stories by David Foster Wallace, Jim Crace, Lorrie Moore, Denis Johnson, Edward P. Jones, Rick Moody, Ann Patchett, Jim Shepard, and Jeanette Winterson.

LORIN STEIN is editor of *The Paris Review*. His criticism has appeared in *Harper's*, *The London Review of Books*, and *The New York Review of Books*. His translations include works by Grégoire Bouillier, Michel Houellebecq, and Édouard Levé. He lives in New York.

the
UNPROFESSIONALS

new AMERICAN WRITING FROM

the PARIS
REVIEW

edited by LORIN STEIN

PENGUIN BOOKS

PENGUIN BOOKS

An imprint of Penguin Random House LLC
375 Hudson Street
New York, New York 10014
penguin.com

"False Spring" from *10:04*, a novel by Ben Lerner. Copyright © 2014 by Ben Lerner.
"Human Snowball" from *My Heart Is an Idiot* by Davy Rothbart.
Copyright © 2012 by Davy Rothbart.
Reprinted by permission of Farrar, Straus and Giroux, LLC.
"Foley's Pond" by Peter Orner. First published in *The Paris Review*.
Copyright © 2012 by Peter Orner.
Reprinted by permission of Little, Brown and Company.
Excerpt from *The Turner House*, a novel by Angela Flournoy.
Copyright © 2015 by Angela Flournoy. Reprinted by permission of
Houghton Mifflin Harcourt Publishing Company. All rights reserved.

LIBRARY OF CONGRESS CATALOGING-IN-PUBLICATION DATA
The unprofessionals : new American writing from
the Paris review / edited by Lorin Stein.
pages cm
ISBN 978-0-14-312847-2 (paperback)
1. American literature—21st century.   2. American essays—21st century.
I. Stein, Lorin, editor.   II. Paris review.
PS536.3.U57 2015
810.8'006—dc23
2015011761

Printed in the United States of America
1   3   5   7   9   10   8   6   4   2

Set in Sabon LT Std
Designed by Spring Hoteling

CONTENTS

NONFICTION

PREFACE

Since 1953, *The Paris Review* has been known for discovering new writers. No little magazine has a better record of spotting original talent, from Philip Roth and Adrienne Rich to David Foster Wallace. That record of discovery is what first drew me to the *Review* as a reader, and it's why I joined the magazine as editor in 2010. The same is true for my colleagues. We relaunched the *Review* five years ago because we thought it had an important job to do—one more important now than ever before.

Why more important now? Because the other literary magazines we'd grown up on had folded, or else had faded from the scene (nobody forced them on you, nobody argued about them). The most adventurous new journals specialized in politics, criticism, history, humor, design—all kinds of things but fiction and poetry. The few glossies that still published stories stuck mainly to familiar voices, with very little space for unknowns. The book business was in crisis, having lost the local reviewers and booksellers who once paved the way for new work. Social media—often held up as a new kind of literary community—had in fact turned young writers into publicists, creating an echo chamber of empty praise. As Sarah Manguso writes in "Short Days," "The difference between today's under-thirty writers and its over-forty writers is that the former, like everyone their age, already know how to act like famous people: people whose job it is to be photographed." In many MFA programs, the novel had largely displaced short stories and poetry, reflecting the demands of a diminished marketplace. Where this happened, it often meant less close reading, less real criticism, lower standards, and less regard for artistic, as opposed to commercial, success. In the eyes of many students, and their teachers, success meant leaving school with a six-figure advance.

Young writers, in other words, were encouraged to think of themselves as *professionals*: to write long and network hard. And yet, with a few exceptions (which we excerpted in the *Review*, when we could), the new work that interested us most was in the short forms—stories, essays, poems—where every sentence, every hesitation counts. These pieces gave us that sense of interiority overheard that we miss in so much contemporary writing. And they made sense of the world we knew. Their narrators were at home in prose or verse as if in a native language. They didn't turn away from "inappropriate" feelings or refuse to face the changes that technology and corporate surveillance, for example, have made in our everyday lives. Rejecting the idea of literature as a specialized and inauthentic realm—an historic district of the mind—these writers attended to the landscape the way they found it. They spoke the vernacular of our time.

And they gave the *Review* new life. In the last decade, our circulation has tripled: the *Review* has more readers now than ever before in its sixty-year history. Clearly, there is a demand for the intensity and perfection found only in small things. As Ottessa Moshfegh put it in a recent interview: "A good short story can break my heart in a way a novel just can't. Novels require so much human tinkering. The author's fingerprints are all over the place. When I read a short story, a good one, the author disappears for me. Short stories are spiritual in that sense. As though out of thin air, they appear."

The writers in this volume range in age from their late twenties to their early forties. A few are famous; a few have become well known in the last five years; most will be new to you, as they were to us. They come from all over the country; a few are recent arrivals on our shores. Yet for all their differences, they share a commitment to realism c.2015, when one of the hardest things to represent believably is a voice that speaks on the page, one individual to another. That commitment, that complicity, has little to do with the writing profession as it's generally taught and practiced, and everything to do with why we read.

LORIN STEIN

the UNPROFESSIONALS

A DARK AND WINDING ROAD
Ottessa Moshfegh

*M*y parents kept a small cabin in the mountains. It was a simple thing, just four walls, and very dark inside. A heavy felt curtain blotted out whatever light made it through the canopy of huge pines and down into the cabin's only window. There was a queen-size bed in there, an armchair, and a wood-burning stove. It wasn't an old cabin. I think my parents built it in the seventies from a kit. In a few spots the wood beams were branded with the word HOME-RITE. But the spirit of the place made me think of simpler times, olden days, yore, or whenever it was that people rarely spoke except to say there was a storm coming or the berries were poisonous or whatnot, the bare essentials. It was deadly quiet up there. You could hear your own heart beating if you listened. I loved it, or at least I thought I ought to love it—I've never been very clear on that distinction. I retreated to the cabin that weekend in early spring after a fight with my wife. She was pregnant at the time, and I suppose she felt entitled to treat me terribly. So I went up there to spite her, yes, and in hopes that she would come to appreciate me in my absence, but also to have one last weekend to myself before the baby was born and my life as I'd known it was forever ruined.

The drive to the cabin is easy to imagine. It was a drive like any drive to any cabin. It was up a dark and winding road. The last half mile or so was badly paved. With snow on the ground, I would have had to park in a clearing and walk the rest on foot. But the snow had melted by the time I got there. This was April. It was still cold, but everything had thawed. Everything was beautiful and dark and powerful the way nature is. I brought all my favorite things to eat and ate them almost immediately upon arrival: cornichons, smoked trout, rye crackers, sheep feta, cured olives, dried cherries, coconut-covered dates, Toblerone. I also brought up a nice bottle of Château Cheval Blanc, a wedding gift I'd hidden and saved for three years. But I found no corkscrew, so I resorted to the remnants of a bottle of cheap Scotch which I was surprised and relieved to discover on a shelf in the closet next to a dried-out roll of fly tape. Later, after dozing in the armchair for quite a while, I went outside in search of firewood and kindling. Night had fallen by then and I had no flashlight, hadn't even thought to bring one, so I sort of grappled around for sticks in the glare from my headlights. My efforts amounted to a very brief but effective little fire.

I've never been outdoorsy. My parents rarely brought us up to the cabin as children. There was barely room enough for a young couple, let alone bickering parents and two bickering sons. My brother was younger than me by just three years, but those three years seemed to stretch to a wide chasm of estrangement the older we got. Sometimes I wondered if my mother had strayed, we were that different. It wouldn't be fair to call me a snob and my brother trash, but it wouldn't be far from accurate. He called himself MJ, and I went by Charles. As a child I played clarinet, chess. Our parents bought MJ a drum set, but he wasn't interested. He played video games, made messes. At recess I'd watch him throw fake punches at the smaller kids and wipe his snot on his sleeve. We didn't sit together on the bus. In seventh grade I won a scholarship to an elite private high school, started wearing ties, played rugby, read newspapers, and spent all my time at home in my room with my books. I turned out successful, but nothing special. I became a real-estate lawyer, married my law-school girlfriend, bought a pricey condo in Murray Hill, nothing close to what I hoped I'd do.

MJ was a different type of man. He had zero ambition. His friends lived in actual trailer parks. He dropped out of the public high school his junior year, shot dope, got a job in the warehouse of an outlet store, I think, unpacking boxes all day. I'm not quite sure how or if he makes a living now. He used to show up at Christmases unshowered in a ratty hooded sweatshirt, would pass out on the couch, wake up and eat like a wild boar, burping and laughing, then disappear at night. He was talented physically, could easily lift me up and spin me around, which he did often just to taunt me when we were teenagers. He had terrible cystic acne in high school—big red boils of pus that he squished mindlessly in front of the television. He didn't care how he looked. He was a real guy's guy. And I was always more my mother's type. We shared a certain refinement which I'm sure was annoying to my brother, since he called me a faggot every chance he got. In any case, I hadn't seen him in several years, since my wedding, and I hadn't been up to the cabin since my wife and I first started dating. We'd spent an awkward night up there together one spring, a lifetime ago, but that's not a very interesting story.

I rolled a joint in my car with the lights on and smoked it sitting in the armchair, in the dark. There was no cell-phone service up there, which made me nervous. I don't know why I continued to smoke marijuana as long as I did. It almost always sent me into an existential panic. When I smoked with my wife, I had to feign complete exhaustion just to excuse myself from going out for a walk, which she liked to do. I was so paranoid, so deeply anxious. When I got high I felt as though a dark curtain had been pulled across the world and I was left there alone to waver in its cold, dark shadows. I never dared to smoke by myself at home, lest I throw myself from our twelfth-story window. But when I smoked that night at the cabin, I felt fine. I whistled some songs, tapped my feet. I whistled one difficult tune in particular, a Stevie Wonder song which is melodically complicated, and after a few rounds I could really whistle it beautifully. I remembered what it was like to practice and get good at something. I thought of how great a dad I would be. "Practice makes perfect," I'd tell my child, a truism, maybe, but it now seemed suddenly endowed with great depth and wisdom. And so I felt wonderful about myself, forgetting the strange world outside. I even thought that after my child was born, I'd still come up to the cabin once or twice a month, just to keep the secret of how great I am. I whistled some more.

Around nine o'clock, I pulled my sleeping bag out and unrolled it on the bed which was covered in old blankets and dust and mouse poop, and slept with no trouble at all. In the morning I guzzled a liter of mineral water and drove on the dark and winding road back to Route 11, where there was a Burger King. I ate breakfast there. In addition to my breakfast sandwich and coffee, I purchased several Whoppers which I figured I could heat on the wood-burning stove for lunch and dinner, should I decide to stay another night. I also bought a six-pack of beer, a family-size bag of Cool Ranch Doritos, and a pound of Twizzlers from the gas station. And I bought the local newspapers and a magazine called *Fly Tyer* to stare at while I chewed. On my cell phone I found one missed call from my wife. I ignored it.

Back at the cabin I shook the dust off the blankets covering the bed because I wanted to lie down in the light from the window and read *Fly Tyer* and eat Twizzlers. Something flesh colored caught my eye amid the blankets. At first I thought what I'd seen was my wife's old diaphragm—a Band-Aid–colored thing which I'd always hated looking at. Then I thought it might be an old prosthetic arm, or a doll. But when I pulled another blanket back, I saw it was a dildo. A large, curved, Band-Aid–colored, rubber dildo. My first instinct of course was to pick it up and smell it, which I did. It only smelled faintly of rubber, anonymous. I set it on the sill of the window and went outside to collect more firewood. I was determined to start a real fire. Was I perturbed to find the dildo? It only peeved me the way one is peeved when one hears his neighbors banging pots through the walls. And it seemed at the time more like vandalism than evidence of any kind of sexual activity. It seemed like a prank. Outside I was happily surprised to find a large store of dry logs in the crawl space under the cabin.

Once I'd gotten the fire roaring, I sat down and cursed myself for having forgotten to buy a corkscrew from the gas station, since late morning by the fire seemed like the perfect time to sip my wine. I swore aloud. The friend who had given me that bottle was an old college classmate. I'd slept with his girlfriend one weekend senior year while he was visiting his parents, and I never told him. His girlfriend's name was Cindy and she was half Pakistani and liked poppers and farted in her sleep. She was the last girl I slept with before my wife. So that bottle to me meant more than good wine. There was no way I was sharing it with my wife. I considered driving back down to the gas station, but there was no guarantee they'd have a corkscrew. Plus I was too scared to leave the fire burning unattended. There was no fire extinguisher, and the plumbing was shot. Not being able to wash my hands was the only real drawback to the place. I relieved myself outdoors, watching the smoke tuft out of the metal chimney like a choo-choo train. Afterward I used sanitizing gel on my hands and sat in the armchair again.

I'd gotten lucky the night before, but after I smoked that joint that morning and saw my fire burning, heart still banging with fury about the impenetrable wine, Cindy's brown legs hanging off the bed, I knew I was in trouble. My thoughts turned to the primitive longings of early man, and I searched in my heart for some remnant of primal wantonness, and since I was looking, I found it. I rolled another joint and smoked it and removed my shirt and fed the fire apprehensively and sat on the bare floor of the cabin and growled and rocked like a baby and crawled around on my hands and knees. But the floor of the cabin was filthy. I found a broom and swept. Whoever was going up there and doing the dil-doing had no regard for cleanliness, I thought to myself. I cleaned until I was hungry, and fed the fire again and put one of the Whoppers on the iron stove. The special sauce melted and the bun burned on the bottom, but when I bit into it, it was all just chewy and lukewarm and reminded me of my elementary-school cafeteria and that low-quality food that I so desperately wanted to comfort me, but didn't.

The cabin hardly looked any cleaner after all that sweeping. In fact, I probably stirred up more dust than I swept out the door. I sneezed and drank a few beers and relieved myself again and used more hand-sanitizing gel and sat in the armchair. I smoked another joint. That last one was a mistake, since after just a few minutes I was picturing my unborn son crying over my grave fifty years into the future, and I felt the gravity of his woe and resentment toward me, and I despised him. Then I imagined everything bad he'd say about me to his own children after my death. I imagined my grandchildren's bitchy faces. I hated them for not worshipping me. Had they no idea of my sacrifice? There I was, perfectly wonderful, and nobody would see that. I looked up and saw a bat hanging from the rafters. I went to a very dark place. The oceanic emptiness in my gut churned. I pictured my old body rotting in my coffin. I pictured my skin wrinkling and turning black and falling off my bones. I pictured my rotting genitals. I pictured my pubic hair filling with larvae. And after all that, there was infinite darkness. There was nothing.

Just as I considered hanging myself with my belt, there was a knock on the door of the cabin, and a girl's voice called out, "MJ?"

The only girlfriend of MJ's I'd ever met had the odd name of Carrie Mary. I always thought Carrie Mary must have been slightly retarded because she had that kind of fat double chin and weak smile and the sort of waddle that some retarded people have, and she wore her hair in small pigtails all over her head, fixed with childish bows. I think my parents were too polite to question the relationship, but when MJ brought her home one Thanksgiving, I confronted him. "Are you taking advantage of Carrie Mary because she's mentally disabled?" My brother did not answer me. He simply took the log of goat cheese I was spreading on melba toast and threw it at the floor and stepped in it with his dirty tennis shoe. He tracked that goat cheese all around the house, and later that night I heard my brother fucking Carrie Mary. He sounded like a growling bear when he fucked her. I'd never heard anyone grunt like that before. It was so authentic. It scared me. I couldn't look him in the eye for days.

But the woman at the door was not Carrie Mary. I composed myself and received her in a manner I thought was perfectly casual. "How do you do? I'm Charles." I was very high. Shirtless, I folded my arms across my belly like a straightjacket.

"He here?" she asked, seeming to notice neither my greatness nor my awkwardness. She was a local—long, dyed, purplish hair, big gray sweatshirt, tight jeans, dark lipstick, no coat on. She looked like the kind of girl who works at a Store 24 or some pizza parlor or bowling alley, takes a lot of flak from the patrons, eleventh-grade education. "Is MJ around?" she asked, sniffling from the cold. A chilling perfume, like vodka and honey, cut through the air. I thought I'd die.

"No," I said. It seemed imperative that I come off casual. "Haven't seen him."

She bit her lips in disappointment, rubbed her hands together. I could see she was wearing a full face of makeup. Chalky powder caked over her cheeks, rouge, blue eye shadow. She looked young, twenty maybe. I tried to ask for her name.

"And to whom do I have the pleasure?" is what I said, and immediately I heard my voice echo through the trees like some nervous pervert or dweeb, like someone who's never had a conversation before.

"Is he coming back soon?" she asked. "MJ?"

"Yes, MJ," I said before I could even understand her question.

"Cool if I wait for him? My brother can't pick me up till four."

I nodded. She stepped closer to me, and for a moment I thought she wanted me to embrace her, so I lifted my arms awkwardly, then put them down. She was generous not to stare at my gut, my nipples.

"Can I come inside?" she asked.

"Sorry," I said, and turned to give her room to walk through the doorway.

I don't know why I kept up the lie about MJ. I certainly wasn't in the mood to entertain this young woman, whose name I soon learned was Michelle, but spelled somehow with an *x* because, as she put it, her family was European. Perhaps somewhere in me I felt that keeping her company would be a further affront to my wife, which was the entire point of my trip, after all. I admit I was grateful to have something come in and disturb the journey of my thinking. The first thing she did was light a cigarette and pace around and point to the dildo and blow a ring of smoke and say to me, as though she were asking me the time of day, "You a fag?"

"No," I replied, disgusted. And then for some reason—maybe I wanted to school her, blow her mind—I said, "I'm not a fag— I'm a *homosexual*." I pronounced the word very carefully, elongating the vowels and punctuating the *u*, which I thought was a pretension quite in keeping with my statement.

"For real?" she said, flicking her cigarette and gazing down at my crotch. "How do you know MJ?" she asked. I put my shirt back on.

"A friend," I said.

"What kind of friend?" she asked.

"A very dear friend," I replied. The words just came out of me. I sat in the armchair and crossed my legs. Michelle seemed to read my mind and offered me a cigarette. She looked at me suspiciously. I smoked as faggily as I could, bringing the cigarette to my puckered lips, sucking my cheeks in, then flinging my arm out, hyperextending the elbow as I exhaled to the side. I had her fooled, I knew. I was like a purring cat.

"You come up here a lot?" she asked. "To see MJ?"

"From time to time," I replied, swinging my foot. "When we can both get away."

The girl kept sniffling. She threw her cigarette out the open door and closed it, went and knelt by the fire, warmed her hands.

"Where'd he go?" she asked. She was uneasy, but she wasn't the type of girl to get offended. I was familiar with girls like her—

tough, blue-collar teenagers. They were around when I was an undergrad, off campus. There was one like Michelle who worked as a bartender in a small pool hall my friends and I went to because we thought it was quaint. That girl was beautiful, could have been a movie star if she'd wanted to, but she just chewed gum and had dead eyes and seemed immune to all manner of flattery or abuse. That's what Michelle was like. She seemed immune. And for that reason, I felt impelled to hurt her.

"He went out," I said, "to buy a corkscrew." I pointed to the Château Cheval Blanc on the floor next to my overnight bag.

She picked up the bottle, smeared her nose on her sleeve. She was pretty. A cold face with small features like a child's, no wrinkles, no expression. She held the bottle by its neck and swung it around, squinted at the label. "You like wine?" she asked. She was being polite, making conversation. I was afraid she'd drop the bottle and break it. I tried to sound relaxed.

"I love wine. Red, white," I said, "rosé." I tried another word. "Blush."

"MJ didn't tell me you were going to be here," she said, putting the wine down. "We'd had a time set and everything," she shrugged, flipped her hair.

"He'll be back," I said. "We'll sort it out."

She nodded and sniffed and crossed her arms and looked down.

"Are you hungry?" I asked her. The second Whopper was still in the bag on the counter by the sink. I pointed.

"No thanks," she said.

"I'm a vegetarian myself," I said. "MJ likes that kind of food." I was feeling very clever, very bold. "That's what I love about him—childish tastes." With this statement I felt I had surpassed a misrepresentation and graduated to fraud, from novice to expert. "He just likes to play. Play and play. I suppose that's what you two do together?"

She sat on the bed, folded her legs up Indian style. "We smoke," she said. "Crystal?" She pulled a small glass pipe from her pocket,

a crumpled ball of foil, displayed them to me on the palm of her
hand like a fortune teller or a blackjack dealer, then laid them on
the blanket beside her.

"Aha," I said. I must have looked like a grandfather to her.
She was perched on the bed there like a bird, hair flipping magi-
cally with a flick of the wrist in the quivering light from the small
window. We passed a minute or two of long, dramatic silence. I
felt I was in the presence of some great power. Then it suddenly
occurred to me that MJ might show up.

"Maybe I should go," I said. "Leave you two to it." She didn't
try to stop me. I collected my things. I put my boots on. But I
couldn't leave the girl in there alone. This was my cabin, after all.
I sat back down. She looked at her phone for a while.

"No reception," she mumbled, biting her lips. She yawned.

There was one thing about my brother I loved. He was loyal. He
would punch me, and he would insult me, but he would not betray
me. Despite all our differences, I believe he understood me. When
we were younger, seven and ten, I suppose, our mother worked at an
after-school daycare at a church and would let us play in the backyard where there was a swing set and a sandbox and a bush with
berries on it we were warned not to touch. But I liked to collect the
berries. I filled my pockets with them and flushed them down the
toilet when I got home. MJ and I barely spoke all afternoon. He was
a little kid. He dug in the sand and pissed in it, spat, threw rocks
at squirrels, shimmied up the posts of the swing set, threatened to
throw a shoe at my head. I mostly sat on a swing or under a tree. I
was too smart to play any games.

As the weeks passed, we got bored and started taking walks
through the neighborhood. It was a wealthy suburb—pretty Dutch
Colonials, some big Victorians. Those houses are worth in the
millions now. We just strolled around, peering into windows. MJ
liked to rifle through mailboxes, or ring doorbells, then run away,
leaving me standing there with my hands in my pockets. But nobody ever came out of those houses. MJ must have known nobody
would. He dared me to do things, stupid things, but I was a cow-

ard. "Pussy brains" is what MJ called me. I barely cared. He could say what he liked. He could do whatever he wanted to me. I knew, when the time was right, I would get back at him.

One afternoon we found an empty house and hoisted each other in through an open window. MJ went straight to the basement, but I just stood frozen in the kitchen, waiting, afraid to call out to him, heart tearing through my chest. When MJ came back up he had a hammer in his hands. "For squirrels," he said. He opened the refrigerator. Inside it were the most delicious foods I'd ever seen. There was a roasted ham in there, an assortment of cheeses, and there was a pie—blueberry, I think. Something came over me in that moment. I pulled the poisonous berries from my pocket and smushed them inside the pie, up under the crust. MJ gave me the thumbs up. That was the first time we broke into a house together. I stole a chip of Roquefort that day. We went back the next day and I stole the rest of it. This went on, I think, for months until our mother enrolled us in the aftercare. I still have a Buffalo nickel that I stole from inside an old rolltop desk in one of those houses. Many other things we stole and threw away—scribbled notes, address books, a fork, a pack of cards, a toothbrush, things like that. Sometimes I'd sit at one woman's vanity, smell all her perfumes and lotions, stare at my face in the mirror while MJ mucked around in the kid's room. I'd douse my cheeks with a powder puff. I'd lie on the unwieldy water bed. I'd sniff things, lick things, put everything back in its place.

Twenty years later, I still felt that the good things, the things I wanted, belonged to somebody else. I watched the waning light play in Michelle's somber eyes. She returned my gaze for a moment. It was clear the curtain had fallen for her, too. We shared a moment of recognition, I think, alone there in the darkening cabin.

"I don't think MJ's coming," she said finally. She looked at me straight in the face, shrugging. "If he does come—" she began.

"We'll say we couldn't wait. We'll say 'you snooze you lose,'" I agreed, as she uncrinkled the foil.

We shared a wonderful afternoon together. We seemed to be

playing our roles, the two scorned lovers. When she picked it up off the windowsill, I had the sense we were accomplishing great things. I let her do whatever she wanted to do to me that day in the cabin. It wasn't painful, nor was it terrifying, but it was disgusting—just as I'd always hoped it would be.

NO ART
Ben Lerner

Tonight I can't remember why
everything is permitted or,
what amounts to the same thing,
forbidden. No art is total, even

theirs, even though it raises
towers or kills from the air,
there's too much piety in despair,
as if the silver leaves behind

the glass were politics
and the wind they move in
and the chance of scattered
storms. Those are still

my ways of making and
I know that I can call on you
until you're real enough
to turn from. Maybe I have fallen

behind, am falling, but
I think of myself as having
people, a small people
in a failed state, and love

more avant-garde than shame
or the easy distances.
All my people are with me now
the way the light is.

MISTER LYTLE: AN ESSAY
John Jeremiah Sullivan

When I was twenty years old, I became a kind of apprentice to a man named Andrew Lytle, whom pretty much no one apart from his negligibly less ancient sister, Polly, had addressed except as Mister Lytle in at least a decade. She called him Brother. Or *Brutha*—I don't suppose either of them had ever voiced a terminal *r*. His two grown daughters did call him Daddy. Certainly I never felt even the most obscure impulse to call him Andrew, or "old man," or any other familiarism, though he frequently gave me to know it would be all right if I were to call him *mon vieux*. He, for his part, called me boy, and beloved, and once, in a letter, "Breath of My Nostrils." He was about to turn ninety-two when I moved into his basement, and he had not yet quite reached ninety-three when they buried him the next winter, in a coffin I had helped to make—a cedar coffin, because it would smell good, he said. I wasn't that helpful. I sat up a couple of nights in a freezing, starkly lit workshop rubbing beeswax into the boards. The other, older men—we were four altogether—absorbedly sawed and planed. They chiseled dovetail joints. My experience in woodworking hadn't gone past feeding planks through a band saw for shop class, and there'd be no time to redo anything I might botch, so I followed instructions and with rags cut from an undershirt worked coats of wax into the cedar until its ashen whorls glowed purple, as if with remembered life.

The man overseeing this vigil was a luthier named Roehm

whose house stood back in the woods on the edge of the plateau. He was about six and a half feet tall with floppy bangs and a deep, grizzled mustache. He wore huge glasses. I believe I have never seen a person more tense than Roehm was during those few days. The cedar was "green"—it hadn't been properly cured. He groaned that it wouldn't behave. On some level he must have resented the haste. Lytle had lain dying for weeks; he endured a series of disorienting pin strokes. By the end they were giving him less water than morphine. He kept saying, "Time to go home," which at first meant he wanted us to take him back to his house, his real house, that he was tired of the terrible simulacrum we'd smuggled him to, in his delirium. Later, as those fevers drew together into what seemed an unbearable clarity, like a blue flame behind the eyes, the phrase came to mean what one would assume.

He had a deathbed, in other words. He didn't go suddenly. Yet although his family and friends had known for years about his wish to lie in cedar, which required that a coffin be custom made, no one had so much as played with the question of who in those mountains could do such a thing or how much time the job would take. I don't hold it against them—against us—the avoidance of duty, owing as it did to fundamental incredulity. Lytle's whole existence had for so long been essentially posthumous, he'd never risk seeming so ridiculous as to go actually dying now. My grandfather had told me once that when *he'd* been at Sewanee, in the thirties, people had looked at Lytle as something of an old man, a full sixty years before I met him. And he nursed this impression, with his talk of coming "to live in the sense of eternity," and of the world he grew up in—Middle Tennessee at the crack of the twentieth century—having more in common with Europe in the Middle Ages than with the South he lived to see. All of his peers and enemies were dead. A middle daughter he had buried long before. His only wife had been dead for thirty-four years, and now Mister Lytle was dead, and we had no cedar coffin.

But someone knew Roehm, or knew about him; and it turned out Roehm knew Lytle's books; and when they told Roehm he'd have just a few days to finish the work, he set to, without hesitation and even with a certain impatience, as if he feared to displease some unforgiving master. I see him there in the little space, repeatedly microwaving Tupperware containers full of burnt black coffee and downing them like Coca-Colas. He loomed. He was so large there hardly seemed room for the rest of us, and already the coffin lid lay on sawhorses in the center of the floor, making us sidle along the walls. At least a couple of times a night Roehm, who was used to agonizing for months over tiny, delicate instruments, would suffer a collapse, would hunch on his stool and bury his face in his hands and bellow "It's all wrong!" into the mute of his palms. My friend Sanford and I stared on. But the fourth, smaller man, a person named Hal, who'd been staying upstairs with Lytle toward the end and acting as a nurse, he knew Roehm better—now that I think of it, Hal must have been the one to tell the family about him in the first place—and Hal would put his hands on Roehm's shoulders and whisper to him to be calm, remind him how everyone understood he'd been allowed too little time, that if he wanted we could take a break. Then Roehm would smoke. I remember he gripped each cigarette with two fingertips on top, snapping it in and out of his lips the way toughs in old movies do. Sanford and I sat outside in his truck with the heater on and drank vodka from a flask he'd brought, gazing on the shed with its small bright window, barely saying a word.

Weeks later he told me a story that Hal had told him, that at seven o'clock in the morning on the day of Lytle's funeral—which strangely Roehm did not attend—Hal woke to find Roehm sitting at the foot of his and his wife's bed, repeating the words "It works," apparently to himself. I never saw him again. The coffin was art. Hardly anyone got to see it. All through the service and down the street to the cemetery it wore a pall, and when people lined up at the graveside to take turns shoveling dirt back into the pit, the hexagonal lid—where inexplicably Roehm had found a spare hour to do scrollwork—grew invisible after just a few seconds.

There had been different boys living at Lytle's since not long after he lost his wife, maybe before—in any case it was a recognized if unofficial institution when I entered the college at seventeen. In former days these were mainly students whose writing showed promise, as judged by a certain well-loved, prematurely white-haired literature professor, himself a former protégé and all but a son during Lytle's long widowerhood. As years passed and Lytle declined, the arrangement came to be more about making sure someone was there all the time, someone to drive him and chop wood for him and hear him if he were to break a hip.

There were enough of us who saw it as a privilege, especially among the English majors. We were students at the University of the South, and Lytle was the South, the last Agrarian, the last of the famous "Twelve Southerners" behind *I'll Take My Stand*, a comrade to the Fugitive Poets, a friend since youth of Allen Tate and Robert Penn Warren; a mentor to Flannery O'Connor and James Dickey and Harry Crews and, as the editor of *The Sewanee Review* in the sixties, one of the first to publish Cormac McCarthy's fiction. Bear in mind that by the mid-nineties, when I knew him, the so-called Southern Renascence in letters had mostly dwindled to a tired professional regionalism. That Lytle hung on somehow, in however reduced a condition, represented a flaw in time, to be exploited.

Not everyone felt that way. I remember sitting on the floor one night with my freshman-year suitemate, a ninety-five-pound blond boy from Atlanta called Smitty who'd just spent a miserable four years at some private academy trying to convince the drama teacher to let them do a Beckett play. His best friend had been a boy they called Tweety Bird, whose voice resembled a tiny reed flute. When I met Smitty, I asked what music he liked, and he shot back, "*Trumpets.*" That night he went on about Lytle, what a grotesquerie and a fascist he was. "You know what Andrew Lytle said?" Smitty waggled his cigarette lighter. "Listen to this: 'Life is melodrama. Only art is real.'"

I nodded in anticipation.

"Don't you think that's *horrifying*?"

I didn't, though. Or I did and didn't care. Or I didn't know what I thought. I was under the tragic spell of the South, which you've either felt or haven't. In my case it was acute because, having grown up in Indiana with a Yankee father, a child exile from Kentucky roots of which I was overly proud, I'd long been aware of a nowhereness to my life. Others wouldn't have sensed it, wouldn't have minded. I felt it as a physical ache. Finally I was somewhere, there. The South... I loved it as only one who will always be outside it can. Merely to hear the word *Faulkner* at night brought gusty emotions. A few months after I'd arrived at the school, Shelby Foote came and read from his Civil War history. When he'd finished, a local geezer with long greasy white hair wearing a white suit with a cane stood up in the third row and asked if, in Foote's opinion, the South could have won, had such and such a general done such and such. Foote replied that the North had won "that war" with one hand behind its back. In the crowd there were gasps. It thrilled me that they cared. How could I help wondering about Lytle, out there beyond campus in his ancestral cabin, rocking before the blazing logs, drinking bourbon from heirloom silver cups and brooding on something Eudora Welty had said to him once. Whenever famous writers came to visit the school they'd ask to see him. He was from another world. I tried to read his novels, but my mind just ricocheted; they seemed impenetrably mannered. Even so, I hoped to be taken to meet him. One of my uncles had received such an invitation, in the seventies, and told me how the experience changed him, put him in touch with what's real.

The way it happened was so odd as to suggest either the involvement or the nonexistence of fate. I wasn't even a student at the time. I'd dropped out after my sophomore year, essentially in order to preempt failing out, and was living in Ireland with a friend, working in a restaurant and failing to save money. But before my departure certain things had taken place. I'd become friends with the man called Sanford, a puckish, unregenerate back-to-nature person nearing fifty, who lived alone, off the electric grid, on a nearby communal farm. His house was like something Jefferson could have invented. Spring water flowed down from an old dairy tank in a tower on top; the refrigerator had been retrofitted to work with propane canisters that he salvaged from trailers. He had first-generation solar panels on the roof, a dirt-walled root cellar, a woodstove. He showered in a waterfall. We had many memorable hallucinogenic times that did not help my grades. Sanford needed very little money, but that he made doing therapeutic massage in town, and one of his clients was none other than Andrew Lytle, who drove himself in once a week, in his yacht-sized chocolate Eldorado, sometimes in the right lane, sometimes the left, as he fancied. The cops all knew to follow him but would do so at a distance, purely to ensure he was safe. Often he arrived at Sanford's studio hours early, and anxiously waited in the car. He loved the feeling of human hands on his flesh, he said, and believed it was keeping him alive.

One day, during their session, Lytle mentioned that his current boy was about to be graduated. Sanford, who didn't know yet how badly I'd blown it at the school, or that I was leaving, told Lytle about me and gave him some stories I'd written. Or poems? Doubtless dreadful stuff—but perhaps it "showed promise." Toward the end of summer airmail letters started to flash in under the door of our hilltop apartment in Cork, their envelopes, I remember, still faintly curled from having been rolled through the heavy typewriter. The first one was dated, "Now that I have come to live in the sense of eternity, I rarely know the correct date, and the weather informs me of the day's advance, but I believe it is late August," and went on to say, "I'm presuming you will live with me here."

That's how it happened, he just asked. Actually, he didn't even ask. The fact that he was ignoring the proper channels eventually caused some awkwardness with the school. But at the time, none of that mattered. I felt an exhilaration, the unsettling thrum of a great man's regard, and somewhere behind that the distant on-rushing of fame. His letters came once, then twice a week. They were brilliantly senile, moving in and out of coherence and be-tween tenses, between centuries. Often his typos, his poor eye-sight, would produce the finest sentences, as when he wrote the affectingly commaless "This is how I protest absolutely futilely." He told me I was a writer but that I had no idea what I was doing. "This is where the older artist comes in." He wrote about the Muse, how she tests us when we're young. As our tone grew more intimate, his grew more urgent too. I must come back soon. Who knew how much longer he'd live? "No man can forestall or evade what lies in wait." There were things he wanted to pass on, things that had taken him, he said, "too long to learn." Now he'd been surprised to discover a burst of intensity left. He said not to worry about the school. "College is perhaps not the best preparation for a writer." I'd live in the basement, a guest. We'd see to our work.

It took me several months to make it back, and he grew an-noyed. When I finally let myself in through the front door, he didn't get up from his chair. His form sagged so exaggeratedly into the sofa, it was as if thieves had crept through and stolen his bones and left him there. He gestured at the smoky stone fire-place with its enormous black andirons and said, "Boy, I'm sorry the wood's so poor. I had no idea I'd be alive in November." He watched as though paralyzed while I worked at building back up the fire. He spoke only to critique my form. The heavier logs at the back, to project the heat. Not too much flame. "Young men always make that mistake." He asked me to pour him some whis-key and announced flatly his intention to nap. He lay back and draped across his eyes the velvet bag the bottle had come tied in, and I sat across from him for half an hour, forty minutes. At first he talked in his sleep, then to me—the pivots of his turn to con-sciousness were undetectably slight, with frequent slippages. His speech was full of mutterings, warnings. The artist's life is strewn with traps. Beware "the machinations of the enemy."

"Mr. Lytle," I whispered, "who is the enemy?"

He sat up. His unfocused eyes were an icy blue. "Why, boy," he said, "the *bourgeoisie*!" Then he peered at me for a second as if he'd forgotten who I was. "Of course," he said. "You're only a baby."

I'd poured myself two bourbons during nap time and felt them somewhat. He lifted his own cup and said, "Confusion to the enemy." We drank.

It was idyllic, where he lived, on the grounds of an old Chautauqua called the Assembly, one of those rustic resorts—deliberately placed up north, or at a higher altitude—which began as escapes from the plagues of yellow fever that used to harrow the mid-Southern states. Lytle could remember coming there as a child. An old judge, they said, had transported the cabin entire up from a cove somewhere in the nineteenth century. You could still see the logs in the walls, although otherwise the house had been made rather elegant over the years. The porch went all the way around. It was usually silent, except for the wind in the pines. Besides guests, you never saw anyone. A summer place, except Lytle didn't leave.

He slept in a wide carved bed in a corner room. His life was an incessant whispery passage on plush beige slippers from bed to sideboard to seat by the fire, tracing that perimeter, marking each line with light plantings of his cane. He'd sing to himself. The Appalachian one that goes, "A haunt can't haunt a haunt, my good old man." Or songs that he'd picked up in Paris at my age or younger—"Sous les Ponts de Paris" and "Les Chevaliers de la Table Ronde." His French was superb, but his accent in English was best—that extinct mid-Southern, land-grant pioneer speech, with its tinges of the abandoned Celtic urban Northeast ("boyned" for burned) and its raw gentility.

From downstairs I could hear him move and knew where he was in the house at all times. My apartment had once been the kitchen—servants went up and down the back steps. The floor was all bare stone, and damp. And never really warm, until overnight it became unbearably humid. Cave crickets popped around as you tried to sleep, touching down with little clicks. Lots of mornings I woke with him standing over me, cane in one hand, coffee in the other, and he'd say, "Well, my lord, shall we rise and entreat Her Ladyship?" Her ladyship was the Muse. He had all manner of greetings.

For half a year we worked steadily, during his window of greatest coherence, late morning to early afternoon. We read Flaubert, Joyce, a little James, the more famous Russians, all the books he'd written about as an essayist. He tried to make me read Jung. He chopped at my stories till nothing was left but the endings, which he claimed to admire. A too-easy eloquence, was his overall diagnosis. I tried to apply his criticisms, but they were sophisticated to a degree my efforts couldn't repay. He was trying to show me how to solve problems I hadn't learned existed.

About once a day he'd say, "I may do a little writing yet, myself, if my mind holds." One morning I even heard from downstairs the slap-slap of the old electric. That day, while he napped, I slid into his room and pulled off the slipcover to see what he'd done, a single sentence of between thirty and forty words. A couple of them were hyphened out, with substitutions written above in ballpoint. The sentence stunned me. I'd come half-expecting to find an incoherent mess, and afraid that this would say something ominous about our whole experiment, my education, but the opposite confronted me. The sentence was perfect. In it, he described a memory from his childhood, of a group of people riding in an early automobile, and the driver lost control, and they veered through an open barn door, but by a glory of chance the barn was completely empty, and the doors on the other side stood wide open, too, so that the car passed straight through the barn and back out into the sunlight, by which time the passengers were already laughing and honking and waving their arms at the miracle of their own

survival, and Lytle was somehow able, through his prose, to repli-
cate this swift and almost alchemical transformation from horror
to joy. I don't know why I didn't copy out the sentence—embarrassment at my own spying, I guess. He never wrote any more. But
for me it was the key to the year I lived with him. What he could
still do, in his weakness, I couldn't do. I started listening harder,
even when he bored me.

His hair was sparse and mercury-silver. He wore a tweed jacket
every day and, around his neck, a gold-handled toothpick hewn
from a raccoon's sharpened bone-penis. I put his glasses onto my
own face once and my hands, held just at arm's length, became big
beige blobs. There was a thing on his forehead—a cyst, I assume,
that had gotten out of control—it was about the size and shape of a
bisected Ping-Pong ball. His doctor had offered to remove it several
times, but Lytle treated it as a conversation piece. "Vanity has no
claim on me," he said. He wore a gray fedora with a bluebird's
feather in the band. The skin on his face was strangely young-seem-
ing. Tight and translucent. But the rest of his body was extraterres-
trial. Once a week I helped him bathe. God alone knew for how
long the moles and things on his back had been left to evolve unseen. His skin was doughy. Not saggy or lumpy, not in that sense—
he was hale—but fragile-feeling. He had no hair anywhere below.
His toenails were of horn. After the bath he lay naked between
fresh sheets, needing to feel completely dry before he dressed. All
Lytles, he said, had nervous temperaments.

I found him exotic; it's probably accurate to say that I found
him beautiful. The manner in which I related to him was essentially anthropological. Taking offense, for instance, to his more
or less daily outbursts of racism, chauvinism, anti-Semitism, class
snobbery, and what I can only describe as medieval nostalgia,
seemed as absurd as debating these things with a caveman. Shut
up and ask him what the cave art means. The self-service and
even cynicism of that reasoning are not hard to dissect at a distance of years, but I can't pretend to regret it, or that I wish I had
walked away.

There was something else, something less contemptible, a voice in my head that warned it would be unfair to lecture a man with faculties so diminished. I could never be sure what he was saying, as in stating, and what he was simply no longer able to keep from slipping out of his id and through his mouth. I used to walk by his wedding picture, which hung next to the cupboard—the high forehead, the square jaw, the jug ears—and think, as I passed it, "If you wanted to contend with him, you'd have to contend with *that* man." Otherwise it was cheating.

I came to love him. Not in the way he wanted, maybe, but not in a way that was stinting. *Mon vieux.* I was twenty and believed that nothing as strange was liable to happen to me again. I *was* a baby. One night we were up drinking late in the kitchen and I asked him if he thought there was any hope. Like that: "Is there any hope?" He answered me quite solemnly. He told me that in the hallways at Versailles, there hung a faint, ever-so-faint smell of human excrement, "because as the chambermaids hurried along a tiny bit would always splash from the pots." Many years later I realized that he was half-remembering a detail from the court of Louis XV, namely that the latrines were so few and so poorly placed at the palace, the marquesses used to steal away and relieve themselves on stairwells and behind the beautiful furniture, but that night I had no idea what he meant, and still don't entirely.

"Have I shown you my incense burner?" he asked.

"Your what?"

He shuffled out into the dining room and opened a locked glass cabinet door. He came back cradling a little three-legged pot and set it down gently on the chopping block between us. It was exquisitely painted and strewn with infinitesimal cracks. A figure of a dog-faced dragon lay coiled on the lid, protecting a green pearl. Lytle spun the object to a particular angle, where the face was darker, slightly orange-tinged. "If you'll look, the glaze is singed," he said. "From the blast, I presume, or the fires." He held it upside down. Its maker's mark was legible on the bottom, or would have been to one who read Japanese. "This pot," he said, "was recovered from the Hiroshima site." A classmate of his from Vanderbilt, one of the Fugitives, had gone on to become an officer in the Marine Corps and gave it to him after the war. "When I'm dead I want you to have it," he said.

I didn't bother refusing, just thanked him, since I knew he wouldn't remember in the morning, or, for that matter, in half an hour. But he did remember. He left it to me.

Ten years later in New York City my adopted stray cat Holly Kitty pushed it off a high shelf I didn't think she could reach, and it shattered. I sat up most of the night gluing the slivers back into place.

Lytle's dementia began to progress more quickly. I hope it's not cruel to note that at times the effects could be funny. He insisted on calling the K-Y Jelly we used to lubricate his colostomy tube *Kye Jelly*. Finally he got confused on what it was for and appeared in my doorway one day with his toothbrush and a squeezed-out tube of the stuff. "Put *Kye* on the list, boy," he said. "We're out."

Evenings he'd mostly sit alone and rehash forty-year-old fights with dead literary enemies, performing both sides as though in a one-man play, at times yelling wildly, pounding his cane. Allen Tate, his brother turned nemesis, was by far the most frequent opponent, but it seemed in these rages that anyone he'd ever known could change into the serpent, fall prey to an obsession with power. Particularly disorienting was when the original version of the mock-battle had been between him and me. Him and the Boy. Several times, in reality, we did clash. Stood face-to-face shouting. I called him a mean old bastard, something like that; he told me I'd betrayed my gift. Later, from downstairs, I heard him say to the Boy, "You think you're not a *slave*?"

There was a day when I came in from somewhere. Polly, his sister, was staying upstairs. I loved Miss Polly's visits—everyone did. She made rum cakes you could eat yourself to death on like a goldfish. There were homemade pickles and biscuits from scratch when she came. A tiny woman with glasses so thick they magnified her eyes, her knuckles were cubed with arthritis. Who knew what she thought, or if she thought, about all the nights she'd shared with her brother and his interesting artist friends. (Once, in a rented house somewhere, she'd been forced by sleeping arrangements to lie awake in bed all night between fat old Ford Madox Ford and his mistress.) She shook her head over how the iron skillet, which their family had been seasoning in slow ovens since the Depression, would suffer at my hands. I had trouble remembering not to put it through the dishwasher. Over meals, under the chandelier with the "saltcellar" and the "salad oil," as Lytle raved about the master I might become, if only I didn't fall into this, that, or the other hubristic snare, she'd simply grin and say, "Oh, Brutha, how *exciting.*"

On the afternoon in question I was coming through the security gate, entering "the grounds," as cottagers called the Assembly, and Polly passed me going the opposite way in her minuscule blue car. There was instantly something off about the encounter, because she didn't stop completely—she rolled down the window and yelled at me, but continued to idle past, going at most twenty miles per hour (the speed limit in there was twelve, I think), as if she were waving from a parade float. "I'm on my way to the store," she said. "We need [*mumble*]…"

"What's that?"

"BUTTAH!"

I watched with a bad feeling as she receded in the mirror. Back at the cabin, Lytle was caning around on the front porch in a panic. He waved at me as I turned into the gravel patch where we parked. "She's drunk!" he barked. "Look at this bottle, beloved. Good God, it was full this morning!"

I tried to make him tell me what had happened, but he was too antsy. He wore pajamas, black slippers without socks, a gray tweed coat, and the fedora.

"Oh, I've angered her, beloved," he said. "I've angered her."

As we sped toward the gate, he gave me the story. It was as I suspected. The same argument came up every time Polly visited, though I'd never seen it escalate so. They had family in a distant town with whom she remained on decent terms, but Lytle insisted on shunning these people and thought his little sister should, as well. It had to do with an old scandal about land, duplicity involving a will. A greedy uncle had tried to take away his father's farm. But these modern-day cousins, descendants of the rival party, they weren't pretending, as Lytle believed, not to understand why he wouldn't see them—I think they were genuinely confused. There'd been scenes. He'd stood in the doorway and denounced these people, in the highest rhetoric, "Seed of the usurper." They must have thought he was further gone mentally than he was, that when he uttered these curses he had in mind some carpetbagger from olden days, because the relatives just kept coming back, despite never having been allowed past the porch steps. Now Miss Polly had let them into the vestibule, nearly into the Court of the Muse. Lytle viewed this as the wildest betrayal. He'd been beastly toward them, when he rose from his nap, and Polly had fled. He himself seemed shaken to remember the things he'd said.

"Mister Lytle, what did you say?"

"I told the truth," he said passionately. "I recognized the moment, that's what I did." But in the defensive thrust of his jaw there quivered something like embarrassment.

He mentions this land dispute in his "family memoir," *A Wake for the Living*, his most readable and in many ways his best book. That's perhaps an idiosyncratic opinion. There are people who've read a lot more than I have who consider his novels lost classics. But it may be precisely because of the Faustian ego that thundered above his sense of himself as a novelist that he carried a lighter burden into the memoir, and this freedom thawed in his style some of the vivacity and spontaneity that otherwise you find only in the letters. There's a scene in which he describes the morning his grandmother was shot in the throat by a Union soldier in 1863. "Nobody ever knew who he was or why he did it," Lytle writes, "he mounted a horse and galloped out of town." To the end of her long life this woman wore a velvet ribbon at her neck, fastened with a golden pin. That's how close Lytle was to the Civil War. Close enough to reach up as a child, passing into sleep, and fondle the clasp of that pin. The eighteenth century was just another generation back from there, and so on, hand to hand. This happens, I suppose, this collapsing of time, when you make it as far as your nineties. When Lytle was born, the Wright Brothers had not yet achieved a working design. When he died, Voyager II was exiting the solar system. What do you do with the coexistence of those details in a lifetime's view? It weighed on him.

The incident with his grandmother is masterfully handled:

She ran to her nurse. The bullet had barely missed the jugular vein. Blood darkened the apple she still held in her hand, and blood was in her shoe. The enemy in the street now invaded the privacy of the house. The curious entered and stared. They confiscated the air... To the child's fevered gaze the long bayonets of the soldiers seemed to reach the ceiling, as they filed past her bed, staring out of boredom and curiosity.

Miss Polly passed us again. Apparently she'd changed her mind about the butter. We made a U-turn and trailed her to the cabin. Back inside they embraced. She buried her face in his coat, laughing and weeping. "Oh, sister," he said, "I'm such an old fool, god*damn* it."

I've wished at times that we had endured some meaningful falling-out. In truth he began to exasperate me in countless petty ways. He needed too much, feeding and washing and shaving and dressing, more than he could admit to and keep his pride. Anyone could sympathize, but I hadn't signed on to be his butler. One day I ran into the white-haired professor, who shared with me that Lytle had been complaining about my cooking.

Mainly, though, I'd fallen in love with a tall, nineteen-year-old half-Cuban girl from North Carolina, with freckles on her face and straight dark hair down her back. She was a class behind mine, or what would have been mine, at the school, and she could talk about books. On our second date she gave me her father's roughed-up copy of *Hunger*, the Knut Hamsun novel. I started to spend more time downstairs. Lytle became pitifully upset. When I invited her in to meet him, he treated her coldly, made some vaguely insulting remark about "Latins," and at one point asked her if she understood a woman's role in an artist's life.

There came a wickedly cold night in deep winter when she and I lay asleep downstairs, wrapped up under a pile of old comforters on twin beds we'd pushed together. By now the whole triangle had grown so unpleasant that Lytle would start drinking earlier than usual on days when he spotted her car out back, and she no longer found him amusing or, for that matter, I suppose, harmless. My position was hideous.

She shook me awake and said, "He's trying to talk to you on the thing." We had this antiquated monitor system, the kind where you depress the big silver button to talk and let it off to hear. The man hadn't mastered an electrical device in his life. At breakfast one morning, when I'd made the mistake of leaving my computer up-stairs after an all-nighter, he screamed at me for "bringing the en-emy into this home, into a place of work." Yet he'd become a bona fide technician on the monitor system.

"He's calling you," she said. I lay still and listened. There was a crackling.

"*Beloved,*" he said, "*I hate to disturb you, in your slumbers, my lord. But I believe I might freeze to DEATH up here.*"

"Oh, my God," I said.

"*If you could just ... lie beside me.*"

I looked at her. "What do I do?"

She turned away. "I wish you wouldn't go up there," she said.

"What if he dies?"

"You think he might?"

"I don't know. He's ninety-two, and he says he's freezing to death."

"*Beloved*...?"

She sighed. "You should probably go up there."

He didn't speak as I slipped into his bed. He fell back asleep instantly. The sheets were heavy white linen and expensive. It seemed there were shadowy acres of snowy terrain between his limbs and mine. I floated off.

When I woke at dawn he was nibbling my ear and his right hand was on my genitals.

I sprang out of bed and began to hop around the room like I'd burned my finger, sputtering foul language. Lytle was already moaning in shame, fallen back in bed with his hand across his face like he'd just washed up somewhere, a piece of wrack. I should mention that he wore, as on every chill morning, a Wee Willie Winkie–style nightshirt and cap. "Forgive me, forgive me," he said.

"Jesus Christ, Mister Lytle."

"Oh, beloved..."

His having these desires wasn't the issue. I couldn't be that naïve. His tastes in that area were more or less an open secret. I don't know if he was gay or bisexual or pansexual or what. Those distinctions are clumsy terms in which to address the mysteries of sexuality. But on a few occasions he'd spoken about his wife in a manner that to me was movingly erotic, nothing like any self-identifying gay man I've ever heard talk about women and sex. Certainly Lytle had loved her, because it was clear how he missed her, Edna, his beautiful "squirrel-eyed gal from Memphis," whom he'd married when she was young, who was still young when she died of throat cancer.

Much more often, however, when the subject of sex came up, he would return to the idea of there having been a homoerotic side to the Agrarian movement itself. He told me that Allen Tate propositioned him once, "but I turned him down. I didn't like his smell. You see, smell is so important, beloved. To me he had the stale scent of a man who didn't take any exercise." This may or may not have been true, but it wasn't an isolated example. Later writers—including some with an interest in not playing up the issue—have noticed, for instance, Robert Penn Warren's more-than-platonic interest in Tate, when they were all at Vanderbilt together. One of the other Twelve Southerners, Stark Young—he's rarely mentioned—was openly gay. Lytle professed to have carried on, as a very young man, a happy, sporadic affair with the brother of another Fugitive poet, not a well-known person. At one point the two of them fantasized about living together, on a small farm. The man later disappeared and turned up murdered in Mexico. Warren mentions him in a poem that plays with the image of the closet.

The point—the reason I risk being seen to have "outed" a man who trusted me, and was vulnerable when he did—is that you can't fully understand that movement, which went on to influence American literature for decades, without understanding that certain of the men involved in it loved one another. Most "homosocially," of course, but a few homoerotically, and some homosexually. That's where part of the power originated that made those friendships so intense, and caused the men to stay united almost all their lives, even after spats and changes of opinion, even after their Utopian hopes for the South had died. Together they produced from among them a number of good writers, and even a great one, in Warren, whom they can be seen to have lifted, as if on wing beats, to the heights for which he was destined.

Lytle himself would have beaten me with his cane and thrown me out for saying all of that. To him it was a matter for winking and nodding, frontier sexuality, fraternity brothers falling into bed with each other and not thinking much about it. Or else it was Hellenism, golden lads in the Court of the Muse. William Alexander Percy stuff. Whatever it was, I accepted it. I never showed displeasure when he wanted to sit and watch me chop wood, or when he asked me to quit showering every morning, so that he could smell me better. "I'm pert' near blind, boy," he said. "How will I find you in a fire?" Still, I'd taken for granted an understanding between us. I didn't expect him to grope me like a chambermaid.

I stayed away two nights, and then went back. When I reached the top of the steps and looked through the back-porch window, I saw him on the sofa lying asleep (or dead—I wondered every time). His hands were folded across his belly. One of them rose and hung quivering, an actor's wave; he was talking to himself. It turned out, when I cracked the door, he was talking to me.

"Beloved, now, we must forget this," he said. "I merely wanted to touch it a little. You see, I find it the most *interesting* part of the body."

Then he paused and said, "Yes," seeming to make a mental note that the phrase would do.

"I understand, you have the girl now," he continued. "Woman offers the things a man must have, home and children. And she's a lovely girl. I myself may not have made the proper choices, in that role..."

I closed the door and crept down to bed.

Not long after that, I moved out, both of us agreeing it was for the best. I re-enrolled at the school. They found someone else to live with him. It had become more of a medical situation by that point, at-home care. I drove out to see him every week, and I think he welcomed the visits, but things had changed. He knew how to adjust his formality by tenths of a degree, to let you know where you stood.

It may be gratuitous to remark of a ninety-two-year-old man that he began to die, but Lytle had been much alive for most of that year, fiercely so. There were some needless minor surgeries at one point, which set him back. It's funny how the living will help the dying along. One night he fell, right in front of me. He was standing in the middle room on a slippery carpet, and I was moving toward him to take a glass from his hand. The next instant he was flat on his back with a broken elbow that during the night bruised horribly, blackly. His eyes went from glossy to matte. Different people took turns staying over with him, upstairs, including the white-haired professor, whose loyalty had never wavered. I spent a couple of nights. I wasn't worried he'd try anything again. He was in a place of calm and—you could see it—preparation. His son-in-law told me he'd spoken my name the day before he died.

When the coffin was done, the men from the funeral home picked it up in a hearse. Late the same night someone called to say they'd finished embalming Lytle's body; it was in the chapel, and whenever Roehm was ready, he could come and fasten the lid. All of us who'd worked on it with him went, too. The mortician let us into a glowing side hallway off the cold ambulatory. With us was an old friend of Lytle's named Brush, who worked for the school administration, a low-built bouncy muscular man with boyish dark hair and a perpetual bowtie. He carried, as nonchalantly as he could, a bowling-ball bag, and in the bag an extremely excellent bottle of whiskey.

Brush took a deep breath, reached into the coffin, and jammed the bottle up into the crevice between Lytle's ribcage and his left arm. He quickly turned and said, "That way they won't hear it knocking around when we roll it out of the church."

Roehm had a massive electric drill in his hand. It seemed out of keeping with the artisanal methods that had gone into the rest of the job, but he'd run out of time making the cedar pegs. We stood over Lytle's body. Sanford was the first to kiss him. When everyone had, we lowered the lid onto the box, and Roehm screwed it down. Somebody wished the old man Godspeed. A eulogy that ran in the subsequent number of *The Sewanee Review* said that, with Lytle's death, "the Confederacy at last came to its end."

He appeared to me only once afterward, and that was two and a half years later, in Paris. It's not as if Paris is a city I know or have even visited more than a couple of times. He knew it well. I was coming up the stairs from the metro into the sunshine with the girl, whom I later married, on my left arm, when my senses became intensely alert to his presence about a foot and a half to

my right. I couldn't look directly at him; I had to let him hang
back in my peripheral vision, else he'd slip away; it was a bargain
we made in silence. I could see enough to tell that he wasn't young
but was maybe twenty years younger than when I'd known him,
wearing the black-framed engineer's glasses he'd worn at just that
time in his life, looking up and very serious, climbing the steps to
the light, where I lost him.

XY
Nick Laird

When he slide it in the slot and press
the buttons in their order, wait,
he's empire-building. Damn straight.
He's Genghis Khan. Yes ma'am. I guess
he is embarrassing. I guess he must.
Maybe he goes in for all-in wrestling
but not for alternative medicine.
Maybe nothing beats the nothingness.
Maybe he takes the antihistamine
and it doesn't stop him operating.
Simple physics, Little Richard.
If he lives here on an ad hoc basis
I'd say that's his lookout and his business.
Then I'd say, here, take my card.

LELAH
Angela Flournoy

S he stuffed fistfuls of her underwear into trash bags while the Detroit city bailiff leaned against the wall and fiddled with his phone. The other bailiff waited outside. Lelah saw him through the front window. He did calf raises on the curb near the dumpster, his pudgy hands on his hips.

She'd always imagined the men who handled evictions as menacing—big muscles, loud mouths. These two were young and large, but soft looking, baby-faced. Like giant chocolate cherubs. It had never come to this before. Lelah had received a few thirty-day notices but always cleared out before the Demand for Possession—a seven-day notice—slid under her door. Seven days might as well have been none this time around; before Lelah knew it, the bailiffs were knocking, telling her she had two hours to grab what she could, that they would toss whatever she left behind into that dumpster outside.

It was the end of April, but it felt like June. The bailiff leaning on the wall carried a gray washcloth in his back pocket, and he swiped it across his brow from time to time. He pretended not to be watching her, but Lelah knew better. He had a plan ready if she snapped and started throwing dishes at him, if she called for backup—a brother or cousin to come beat him up—or if she tried to barricade herself in the bathroom. He probably had a gun. Mostly, all Lelah did was put her hands on the things she owned, think about them for a second, and decide against carrying them to her Pontiac. Furniture was too bulky, food from the fridge would expire in her car, and the smaller things—a blender, boxes full of costume jewelry, a toaster—felt ridiculous to take along. She didn't know where she'd end up. Where do the homeless make toast? Outside of essential clothing, hygiene items, and a few pots and pans, she focused on the sorts of things people on TV cried about after a fire: a few photos of herself taken over the years, her birth certificate and Social Security card, photos of her daughter and grandson, her father's obituary.

The second bailiff stopped his calf raises when Lelah walked outside with another box. She imagined that the neighbors peeked at her through their blinds, but she refused to turn around and confirm.

"I'd give you a hand, but we can't touch none of your stuff," he said. Lelah used her shoulder to cram the box into the backseat.

"I know you're thinking, like, if we're not allowed to touch your stuff, then how are we gonna dump everything at the end."

Lelah did not acknowledge that she'd heard him. She took a step back from her car, checked to see if anything valuable was visible from the windows.

"We hire some guys to come and do that part," he said. "Me personally, I'm not touching none of your stuff. I don't do cleanup."

The bailiff smiled. A few of his teeth were brown. Maybe he was older than he looked.

Back inside the apartment, the other bailiff, the sweaty one, sat, legs splayed, on her sofa. At the sight of Lelah he stood up, leaned against the wall once more. What to take, what to take, what to take? It all looked like junk now. Cheap things she'd bought just to keep her apartment from looking barren. She snatched her leather jacket from its hook on the hallway-closet door. That's it, she thought. Leave now, with an hour and a half to spare.

Some people in Gamblers Anonymous, a place she hadn't been in months, claimed the tiny ball, spinning and spinning around on its wheel, was the reason they loved the game.

If Lelah were playing, she would never stand here, so far away from the wheel and the top half of the board, a position where she'd end up asking strangers to put her chips where she wanted them to go. If she were playing, she'd request the orange chips. She could almost feel them, the click and dry slide of them in her palm. But she couldn't play right now. She'd spent the last of her cash on lunch, and she didn't know whether she'd be approved for unemployment, so she couldn't spend the $183 in the bank.

"No more bets," the dealer said. He waved his hand over the table. People settled back onto their stools.

The ball landed on double zero. There were a few cheers, but mostly groans. It was a crowded night in Motor City Casino.

"The one time I take my money off those zeros they come up," the light-skinned woman next to Lelah said. "I been splitting the zeros all night."

"I know, I saw you," Lelah said. "That's how it always goes. That means you'll hit soon."

"Shit, I hope so," the woman said. Her fake eyelashes made her look drowsy, like a middle-aged blinking baby doll. "All I know is that I'll be back to splitting these zeros from now on."

She told herself she'd come to Motor City to eat. Her twenty-five complimentary tickets for the buffet were the only tangible benefit of thousands of games of roulette. That and a VIP card. She had anticipated a strange stare, or at least a smirk, as the valet helped her out of her overflowing car, but he hadn't seemed to notice. Or maybe she wasn't the only homeless gambler in Motor City tonight.

It was a low-stakes table, five dollars to get on the board. The woman with the eyelashes split the zeros again with twenty-five dollars' worth of lavender chips—an amount Lelah considered risky seeing as how double zero just came up. She said nothing though. Camaraderie was appreciated, outright advice was not.

Lelah knew she was an addict. She'd more or less known four years ago when she had to ask Brenda, her cubicle mate at the phone company, to lend her two hundred dollars, just until payday.

That two hundred had bloomed to a thousand in a year's time, and after she had paid Brenda back she had found other coworkers to befriend and borrow from. A few hundred from Jamaal, a sweet, chubby twenty-year-old with dreadlocks who worked on the third floor and maybe had a crush on her; sixty dollars from Yang, an older Chinese woman who used to sell pork buns from her cube before management forbade all sales except for the Girl Scout variety; twelve hundred from her supervisor Dwayne, a fifty-year-old widower with a potbelly and a gold-plated left incisor who absolutely had a crush on her but insisted he wanted nothing in return for the loan. "Now that my Sheila's gone I got nothing and nobody to spend on," he'd said.

Dwayne proved to be a problem. He waited by her Pontiac in the parking deck after her shift a few weeks after he'd loaned her the money, and as Lelah approached the car she realized his pants were undone, and that little brown bump Dwayne was rubbing his thumb over so quickly was not the knuckle of his other thumb, but in fact the head of his lonely widower penis. They fired Dwayne, but at the grievance meeting HR brought up the money she'd borrowed going all the way back to Brenda. They claimed she'd borrowed more than five thousand dollars over the four years, but that didn't sound right to Lelah. She could only account for about three thousand, and she'd paid back everybody but Dwayne. "Jesus, you could've told us you were pumping little old ladies for cash before we got in here," her union rep had said. She had been suspended without pay for over a month now and was still waiting to see if she would be terminated.

When it came to playing roulette, she followed her own code. She never bet all inside, or all out; she spread her chips around the table, she never begged the dealer to let her play out her last chip, and she didn't make loud proclamations, speak directly to the little white ball as if it gave a damn about her, or beg the chips to behave any particular way.

"No more bets."

The pit boss, a busty redheaded woman in a pantsuit, whispered something in the dealer's ear, looked hard at the people gathered around the table, then walked a few paces away.

The ball landed on twenty-seven.

"Aw hell," the woman splitting the zeros said. Lelah always played twenty-seven. Brianne was born on the twenty-seventh of February, as was her brother Troy. Now was a smart time to move on to the buffet, she knew, but she couldn't take her eyes off the dealer. He swept up all of the chips, a jumble of sherbet-colored winnings for the casino, because no one bet on her number.

It was awkward, being at a table but not playing at the table. You had to smile, look indifferent and simultaneously interested enough to justify taking up space. She stood up. Took off her jacket.

Several chips covered number twenty-seven this turn. Too late for them, Lelah thought. The woman put the rest of her lavender chips—Lelah estimated twenty—between zero and double zero again. She looked up at Lelah and winked.

"No more bets," the dealer said.

"I knew it! I knew it! I knew it!" The woman next to her jumped up from her stool. The ball was on double zero. Lelah congratulated her as the dealer slid her a small fort of chips, more than five hundred dollars.

If she were a seasoned gambler, this woman would stay put and ride this upswing out. This was what Lelah would have done. But the woman asked the dealer to give her the chips in twenties and stood up to go.

"For you," she said to Lelah. She handed her a blue-and-yellow twenty-dollar chip.

"For me, for what?"

"You said I'd hit and I did."

"You would've anyway, I can't," Lelah said.

"Like hell you can't," the woman said. Then she leaned in closer, whispered, "Roulette ain't a spectator sport."

Lelah closed her fingers around the chip.

"Well, thank you. Here," Lelah looked past the woman toward a cocktail waitress, put up a hand to get her attention. "At least let me buy you a free drink. I can afford a free drink."

"No, I need to run out of here with my money before I get pulled back in." She dropped her remaining chips into her purse, a sturdy, designer-looking purse, Lelah noticed, and headed toward the cashier.

This happened to Lelah sometimes in the casino, a stranger high off a big win gave her money just for bearing witness, and each time she felt like crying. Because a stranger could be so generous, when she'd never once thought to do that after a win. Because she wanted the money so much. Because, truthfully, it didn't take much to make Lelah feel like crying. But feeling like crying was not the same as actually crying, and Lelah was up twenty dollars.

She'd been down to less than twenty bucks and pulled ahead before. There was a red convertible sitting on top of the Wheel of Fortune slots, and though she despised slots as an amateur, vulgar game, she imagined winning so much at a table that they gave the damn thing to her; just put a ramp over the front slots so she could climb up, drive her new Corvette down, and pick up the rest of her winnings at the cashier. Or maybe she'd only get a few hundred, but it would be enough to buy her some time, so she'd resist the urge to try to flip the money. No, she'd run out of there, hundreds in her pocket, and check into a nice hotel. Yes, a nice hotel would be a good start, and then she'd take a day or two to figure out what to do next. This was a lot more plausible than the car scenario, she knew; she just had to strategize.

She figured she should eat first, before they ran out of the good stuff at the buffet, then she'd come back and try to make the chip last. Split it into ones at the five-dollar-minimum table, spread it around.

As she piled the green beans onto her plate, she thought she saw half a dozen people she recognized. The woman near the pop fountain with the red sequin hat was definitely someone Lelah had seen before; she always wore that hat and she kept rolls of quarters for the slots in her fanny pack. Lelah kept her eyes on the food.

She knew she should return to the table where the woman won the chip for her, but every open seat there made it so you could see the craps table behind it. Lelah couldn't risk being distracted. She chose a five-dollar-minimum roulette table near the bar. It was bad form to take up a seat when you had so little money to play, but Lelah was determined to make this money grow.

She put ten outside on black, two on twenty-seven, and three in the corner between seven, eight, ten, and eleven. The dealer spun the ball and it landed on eight. This brought her to fifty-four dollars, a much more reasonable amount to work with. She took off her jacket.

Lelah never kept a strict count of her money after every play. The exact amount wasn't as important to her while in the thick of the game as much as the feel of her stack of chips. Could she cover them with her entire palm, or did she have tall enough stacks that her hand sat on top of them, and the colors—the orange ones she preferred, persimmon, in fact—still peeked between her fingers? Yes, this was the thing to measure by. Let the dollar amount be a pleasant surprise. She kept playing inside and out, sometimes black, sometimes red, a few corners, a few splits, but always straight up on twenty-seven.

Her tablemates came and went. She registered their movements—new faces and body shapes—but not the particulars anymore. The camaraderie seduced her in the beginning, it helped her warm up to the task at hand, but after a while, if she didn't go broke, she'd slip into a space of just her and her hands and the chips that she tried to keep under them. A stillness like sleep, but better than sleep because it didn't bring dreams. She was just a mind and a pair of hands calculating, pushing chips out, pulling some back in, and running her thumb along the length of stacks to feel what she'd gained or lost. She never once tried to explain this feeling in her GA meetings. She couldn't even share with them the simplest reasons for why she played. They were always talking about feeling alive or feeling numb. How the little white ball made them feel a jolt in their heart, or maybe how the moment of pulling on an old-fashioned slot handle for the first time in a night was better than an orgasm. Lelah did not feel alive when she played roulette. That wasn't the point, she'd wanted to say. It wasn't to feel alive, but it also wasn't to feel numb. It was about knowing what to do intuitively, and thinking about one thing only, the possibility of winning, the possibility of walking away the victor, finally.

"You want to change some of those for twenties?" the dealer asked.

He's talking to me, Lelah realized, and she looked down for the first time in at least ten plays. Her hand rested on a cluster of persimmon stacks about six inches tall. Three hundred dollars, give or take, she could feel it. Jim, the dealer, stared at her.

"Sure," she said. "How about one hundred in twenties, one eighty in fives, and whatever's left in ones again."

Jim obliged, and Lelah slid a cobalt five-dollar chip back to him for his assistance.

She had enough for a hotel room now. She knew she should leave. Slide her chips into her purse like that generous woman did and make a beeline for the cashier. But her watch said eleven P.M. Just another half hour and she could be up six hundred dollars. She could find a place to stay for a week with six hundred dollars, maybe two weeks if she settled for a shitty motel. She could flip the money into something worth leaving with. Not could, she *would*. She put sixty on black, ten on double zero because it hadn't hit yet, forty on the third twelve of the board, and twenty on twenty-seven.

No matter how still Lelah's mind became as she played, she was never careless; her purse stayed in her lap and her cell phone was tucked in her front pocket. Vernon was the one to tell her that more than two decades ago, back when they'd taken trips off base in Missouri to the river-boat casinos. "The same guy sitting next to you shooting the shit all night will steal your wallet in a heart-beat," he'd said, and she'd nodded. This was toward the end of their marriage. Neither of them was interested in winning money, but Vernon had an engineer's knack for figuring things out, breaking systems down into their parts. They conceived Brianne after one of these trips, and although they weren't exactly in love anymore, Lelah believed they had created their daughter in hope.

"No more bets." The ball landed on fourteen. She put money on the same spots again, just half as much.

It wasn't Vernon's fault she'd ended up a gambler—she would never say it was. A few years after the divorce and her return home, Lelah started going to Caesars in Windsor on her own, and that's when the feeling found her. The stillness she hadn't even realized she'd needed up until then.

"No more bets."

Lelah looked down. Her shiny red twenties were gone. Cobalt and persimmon were left—it felt like forty dollars. Forty dollars was like no money at all so she might as well let it play. Straight up on twenty-seven twice and it was gone, and with it, the stillness. She heard the slot bells first, then noticed the stink of cigarette smoke in the air, and found herself part of a loud and bright Friday night in Motor City once again.

SHORT DAYS
Sarah Manguso

A great photographer insists on writing poems. A brilliant essayist insists on writing novels. A singer with a voice like an angel insists on singing only her own, terrible songs. So when people tell me I should try to write this or that thing I don't want to write, I know what they mean.

You might as well start by confessing your greatest shame. Anything else would just be exposition.

It can be worth forgoing marriage for sex, and it can be worth forgoing sex for marriage. It can be worth forgoing parenthood for work, and it can be worth forgoing work for parenthood. Every case is orthogonal to all the others. That's the entire problem.

I wrote my college-application essay about playing in a piano competition, knowing I would lose to the kid who had played just before me. *Even while I played, knowing I would lose*, I wrote, *still I played to give the judges something to remember.* I pretended my spasms of self-regard transcended the judges' informed decisions about the pianists who were merely the best. I got into college.

I assume the cadets are gay, but then I see they are merely unafraid of love. They are preparing to go to war, and with so little time to waste, they say what they mean.

At faculty meetings I sat next to people who had sold two million books. Success seemed so close, just within reach. On subway benches I sat next to people who were gangrenous, dying, but I never thought I'd catch what they had. That's the trouble with the idea of success: it mutates hope into hardness.

What's worse: Offending someone or lying to someone? Saying something stupid when it's your turn, or not saying anything? Tell me which, and I'll tell you your sex.

The trouble with comparing oneself to others is that there are too many others. By using all others as your control group, all your worst fears and all your fondest hopes are at once true. You are good; you are bad; you are abnormal; you are just like everyone else.

Some people ditch friends and lovers because it's easier to get new ones than to resolve conflicts with the old ones, particularly if resolving a conflict requires one to admit error or practice mercy. I'm describing an asshole. But what if the asshole thinks he's ditching an asshole?

There exist almost no role models for women—or for men.

Most bird names are onomatopoeic—they name themselves. Fish, on the other hand, just have to float there and take what's given.

I used to taunt people when I was afraid I loved them too much. Now I just avoid them. Ten years, in one case, and counting.

In a dream, my friend and I begin the act and both immediately want it to be over, but we have to continue, impelled by some obscure reason never revealed in the dream. I wake wondering whether we could ever enjoy it. I think about it all day, really dedicate myself to it. I think about it for two more days, and that's how I fall in love with my friend.

In the morning I wake amid fading scenes of different characters, different settings, all restatements of that first desire, a ghost who haunts me as the beauty he was at sixteen.

Like a vase, a heart breaks once. After that, it just yields to its flaws.

My friend learns Chinese and moves to China, but it is an imperfect Mandarin, useful for grocery shopping, not for falling in love. When her heart is broken she is obliged to ask, *Why won't you fuck me?*

My most careful friend sends me a long letter about a social date with another family. She does not mention the difficulty of having long been in love with the other father. The letter is a proxy for the love letter she'd rather have sent to him.

Biographies should also contain the events that failed to foreshadow.

Facility means "prison" (building), "lifelessness" (art), or "grace" (athletes). Within a gesture of apparent perfection, a mortal heart must beat.

I remember a girl who was famous in school for having woken from a drunken blackout and said to whoever was there, *Are you my judges?*

In real life, my healthy boyfriend said he envied my paralytic disease—that I'd earned the right to a legitimate nervous breakdown. A few years later he was in an accident and became paralyzed from the neck down. That's just bad writing.

It isn't so much that the genius makes it look easy; it's that he makes it look fast.

Of a page of perfect prose I read in a dream, I remember only this: *"Thank you," she said. Her simple answer concealed the truth.*

The man who had me in a phone booth married quickly after the affair ended. His novel had everything in it—the phone booth, the shame, the sash he sewed to wear over the surgical appliance in his belly. In the novel it covered a plaster leg cast. The front page of his Web site is a glowing glass phone booth standing alone in snow. The book got bad reviews. He has two children.

I never joined Facebook because I want to keep my old longings exactly as they were. Don't Facebook people wonder where their desires have gone?

We like stories that are false and seem true (realist novels), that are true and seem false (true crime), that are false and seem false (dragons and superheroes), or that are true and seem true, but we seldom agree on what that is.

When I run out of things to write I just kindle a little flame inside my chest and let it burn a little more of my anger, which is inexhaustible. Would you like me better if I lied and called it love?

I never expect writing to accumulate quickly, and when it does, I expect to produce nothing of value for days or years, but in Hollywood, people just write as fast and as well as they can.

The fastest way to revise a piece of work is to give it to someone whose opinion you fear. That night, revise it, praying you'll finish in time to give him the new version before he wakes up.

Having a worst regret betrays a belief that one misstep caused all your undeserved misfortune.

I can't write long forms because I'm not interested in artificial deceleration. As soon as I see the glimmer of a consequence, I pull the trigger.

My teacher cried while I listened. None of his books had ever made money, not even the famous one, he said. He'd spent his life trying to write perfect books, and when he tried to make money, he couldn't. I didn't think I'd ever feel as old as he seemed at that moment, but here we are.

The difference between today's under-thirty writers and its over-forty writers is that the former, like everyone their age, already know how to act like famous people: people whose job it is to be photographed.

I wish I could ask the future whether I should give up or keep trying. Then again, what if trying, even in the face of certain failure, feels as good as accomplishing? What if it's even better? And here we are again.

Horror is terror that stayed the night.

I can't bear to think of my dead friend, but I don't mind rereading a few things that have nothing to do with him and that always move me to tears. The grief reservoir empties to a manageable level. In this way I can mourn him without having to think about him.

I knew a few people who approached the act as a perfectible art. I knew some great perverts too. Others were in love. Desire relinquished them all.

I used to believe courage was a man in uniform killing another man in uniform—and it is. But a mother's brain washes itself. Her courage terrifies. To her, it is as easy as walking into the next room.

Shame needs an excuse to feel ashamed. It apologizes for everything, even itself.

I've never seen a ghost and I don't believe in them. I might see one tonight, but even then I wouldn't believe in ghosts. I'd believe in *that* ghost.

Just before the poetry reading starts, I ask the overgrown boy sitting next to me why he likes poetry, what happened to him, and he says, *I went to war.*

The affair is over, but at least things have gone somewhere, if only into oblivion.

The dark owns everything, but our sun comes out often enough that we think the universe is half dark, half light.

When the worst comes to pass, the first feeling is relief.

HUMAN SNOWBALL
Davy Rothbart

....

*O*n February 14, 2000, I took the Greyhound bus from Detroit to Buffalo to visit a girl named Lauren Hill. Not Lauryn Hill, the singer who did that song "Killing Me Softly," but another Lauren Hill, who'd gone to my high school, and now, almost ten years later, was about to become my girlfriend, I hoped. I'd seen her at a party when she was home in Michigan over the holidays, and we'd spent the night talking and dancing. Around four in the morning, when the party closed down, we'd kissed for about twelve minutes out on the street, as thick, heavy snowflakes swept around us, melting on our eyebrows and eyelashes. She'd left town the next morning, and in the six weeks since, we'd traded a few soulful letters and had two very brief, awkward phone conversations. As Valentine's Day came near, I didn't know if I should send her flowers, call her, not call her, or what. I thought it might be romantic to just show up at her door and surprise her.

I switched buses in Cleveland and took a seat next to an ancient-looking black guy who was in a deep sleep. Twenty minutes from Buffalo, when darkness fell, he woke up, offered me a sip of Jim Beam from his coat pocket, and we started talking. His name was Vernon. He told me that when midnight rolled around, it was going to be his hundred-and-tenth birthday.

"*A hundred and ten?*" I squealed, unabashedly skeptical.

Happy to prove it, he showed me a public-housing ID card from Little Rock, Arkansas, that listed his birth date as 2/15/90.

"Who was president when—"

"Benjamin Harrison," he said quickly, cutting me off before I was even done with my question, as though he'd heard it many times before. I had no clue if this was true, but he winked and popped a set of false teeth from his mouth, and in the short moment they glistened in his hand, it seemed suddenly believable that he was a hundred and ten, and not just, like, eighty-nine. His bottom gums, jutting tall, were shaped like the Prudential rock and were the color of raw fish, pink and red with dark gray speckles. The skin on his face was pulled taut around his cheekbones and eye sockets, as leathery and soft-looking as some antique baseball mitt in its display case at Cooperstown.

I found myself telling Vernon all about Lauren Hill and explained how nervous I was to see her—surely he'd have some experience he could draw on to help me out. I told him I thought I was taking a pretty risky gamble by popping up in Buffalo unannounced. Things were either going to be really fucking awesome or really fucking weird, and I figured I'd probably know which within the first couple of minutes I saw her. Vernon, it turned out, was in a vaguely similar situation. After a century plus of astonishingly robust health, he'd been ailing the past eighteen months, and before he kicked off he wanted to make amends with his great-granddaughter, whom he was the closest to out of all of his relatives. But, he admitted, he'd let her down so many times—with the drinking, the drugs, and even stealing her money and kitchen appliances—that she might not be willing to let him past the front door. Twice he used my cell phone to try calling her, but nobody answered. So much for sage advice.

We both got quiet and brooded to ourselves as the bus rolled off the freeway ramp and wound its way through empty downtown streets lined with soot-sprayed mounds of snow and ice. Buffalo in winter is a bleak Hoth-like wasteland, and the only sign of life I saw was a pair of drunks who'd faced off in front of an adult bookstore and begun to fight, staggering like zombies. One of them had a pink stuffed animal and was clubbing the other in the face with it. A steady snow began to fall, and I felt a wave of desperate sorrow crash over me. Whatever blind optimism I'd had about the night and how Lauren Hill might receive me had been lost somewhere along the way (maybe at the rest stop in Erie, Pennsylvania, in the bathroom stall with shit smeared on the walls). The trip, I realized now, was a mistake, but at the same time I knew that the only thing to do was to go ahead with my fucked-up plan anyway and go surprise Lauren, because once you're sitting there and you've got a needle in your hands, what else is there to do but poke your finger and see the blood?

At the Greyhound station, a sort-of friend of mine named Chris Hendershot was there to pick me up in a shiny black Ford Explorer with only four hundred miles on the odometer but its front end and passenger side bashed to shit. "You get in a rollover?" I asked him, after hopping in up front.

"Naw, I just boosted this bitch yesterday in Rochester, it was already like this. Who's your friend?"

"This is Vernon. He's gonna ride with us, if that's cool. In a few hours it's gonna be his hundred-and-tenth birthday."

"No shit?" Chris glanced in the rearview and nodded to Vernon, in the backseat. "Fuck if I make it to twenty-five," he said, gunning it out of the lot.

Chris was the kind of guy who always made these sorts of claims, hoping, perhaps, to sound tougher, but really he was a sweetheart with a swashbuckler's twinkle who was rarely in serious danger and probably had decades of fun times ahead of him, if he could stay out of prison. He had pale white skin, a rash of acne on his neck, and his own initials carved into his buzz-cut hair in several places. He looked Canadian and sounded Canadian and was indeed Canadian—he'd grown up on the meanest street of Hamilton, Ontario, and, as he'd told me more than a few times, he and his older brother had stolen seventy-six cars before getting finally caught when Chris was nineteen. Chris did the time—three years—while his brother skated. Then Chris moved in with an uncle in Cincinnati and got a job as an airline reservationist, which was how I'd met him a couple of years before. He had a gregarious nature, and after we'd found ourselves in deep conversation while I was buying tickets over the phone, he'd come to Chicago a few weekends in a row and stayed on my couch while pursuing his dream of becoming a stand-up comic. The problem was that he was absolutely sorry as a stand-up comic, just woefully bad. I saw him perform once, at the ImprovOlympic at Clark and Addison, and it was one of the hardest, saddest things I've ever had to watch—someone's dream unraveling and being chopped dead with each blast of silence that followed his punch lines. But where I would've been destroyed by this, Chris was over it by the next morning, and freshly chipper. He told me the lesson he'd learned was that he needed to focus on his strengths, and he knew himself to be an ace car thief. Before long, he'd moved to Buffalo and was working at his older brother's "mechanic" shop. When I called and told him I was coming to town and explained why, he told me he actually knew Lauren Hill, because for a while he'd been a regular at Freighter's, the bar where she worked, though he doubted she knew him by name, and anyway, he said, he wasn't allowed in there anymore because he'd left twice without paying when he'd realized at the end of the night that he'd left his cash at home. "I'll tell you one thing," he said. "That girl's beautiful. Every guy who wanders into that damn bar, they leave in love with her."

Vernon had asked if he could roll with us for a bit while he kept trying to reach his great-granddaughter. If nothing else, he suggested, we could drop him off later at the YMCA and he'd track her down the next morning. He sat quietly in the backseat, looking out the window while we cruised toward the east side of town, running every sixth light, Chris catching me up on some of his recent escapades, half-shouting to make himself heard over the blare of a modern-rock station out of Niagara Falls, Ontario, that slipped in and out of range. "Hey, check this out," he said. He reached beneath the driver's seat and passed me a fat roll of New York Lottery scratch tickets. "You can win like ten grand!" he cried. "Scratch some off if you want."

"Where'd you get these, man?"

"Get this—they were in the car when I got it! Just sitting in the backseat! I already scratched off some winners, like forty bucks' worth." He passed me a tin Buffalo Sabres lighter from his coat pocket, its sharp bottom edge gummed with shavings from the tickets he'd scratched. "Go on," he said, "make us some money."

I tore off a long band of tickets and handed them back to Vernon, along with a quarter from the center console, and Chris cranked up the volume until the windows shook and piloted us through his frozen, desolate town toward Lauren Hill's apartment, singing along to the radio, while me and Vernon scratched away: "*You make me come. / You make me complete. / You make me completely miserable.*" I looked up and saw him grinning at me and nodding his head, as if to ask, Doesn't this song fucking rock? I grinned and nodded back, because yes, in a crazy way it kind of did. A barely perceptible but definitely perceptible drip of hopefulness had started to seep back into the night.

No one was home at Lauren's place; in fact, the lights were out in all six apartments in her building even though it was only seven-thirty.

Chris cracked his window and flicked a pile of my losing scratch tickets through like cigarette butts. "She's probably at the bar," he said. "She works every night, and she's there hanging out even when she ain't working. We'll go find her." He whipped the Explorer around the corner and we fishtailed a bit in the gathering snow.

A mile down, five tiny side streets spilled together at a jagged-shaped intersection, and from its farthest corners, two squat and battered bars glared across at each other like warring crabs, panels of wood nailed over the windows and painted to match the outside walls and one neon beer sign hanging over each door—Yuengling and Budweiser—as though they were the names of the bars.

Chris pulled over and pointed to the bar with the Yuengling sign. "That's Freighter's," he said. "See if she's in there. And if she is, see if you can call off the dogs so I can get in there, too."

I jumped out and took a few steps, then had a thought and went back to the truck and asked Vernon if he wanted to come in with me. I was nervous to see Lauren and afraid she would find something creepy and stalker-like about me taking a Greyhound bus a few hundred miles to make an uninvited appearance on Valentine's Day. If I rolled in there with Vernon, it seemed to me, any initial awkwardness might be diffused.

Vernon was a little unsteady on his feet, either from the whiskey or the quilt of fresh snow lining the street paired with his ludicrously advanced age, so I held him by the arm as we crossed the intersection. A plume of merriment rose in my chest that was six parts the gentle glow of heading into any bar on a cold, snowy night, and four parts the wonderful, unpredictable madness of having a hundred-and-ten-year-old man I'd just met on the Greyhound bus as my wingman. I heaved open the heavy door to Freighter's, letting out a blast of noise and hot, smoky air, and once Vernon shuffled past, I followed him in.

Inside, it was so dark and hot and loud it took me a few seconds to get my bearings. People shouted over the thump of a jukebox and the rattle of empty bottles being tossed into a metal drum. Directly overhead, two hockey games roared from a pair of giant TVs. It smelled like someone had puked on a campfire. All of which is to say, just the way I liked it and just like the 8 Ball Saloon back in Michigan where Lauren had worked before moving to Buffalo for school.

A hulking, tattooed guy on a stool was asking me and Vernon for our IDs. I flashed him mine, while Vernon pulled out the same fraying ID card he'd showed me earlier. The doorman plucked it from his hand, inspected it, and passed it back, shaking his head. "Nope," he shouted over the din. "I need a driver's license or state

ID." At first I laughed, thinking he was just fucking with us, but then I saw he was serious.

I leaned to his ear and protested, "But he's a hundred and ten years old! Look at the guy!"

The doorman shook his head and pointed at the exit. It was useless to try to reason with him over the din, and I figured once I found Lauren, she'd help me get Vernon and Chris in.

"Wait in the truck," I shouted in Vernon's ear. "I'll come get you guys in a few minutes."

He nodded and slipped out into the cold. I took a few steps further in. The place was packed, mostly older, rugged-looking dudes—factory workers, construction workers, bikers, and their equally rugged-looking girlfriends—with a sprinkling of younger indie kids and punk rockers mixed in. All of a sudden I caught sight of Lauren Hill behind the bar and my heart twisted like a wet rag—she had her back turned to me and was getting her shoulders thoroughly massaged by a tall, skinny, dark-haired guy in a sleeveless shirt, dozens of tattoos slathered on his arms. My first thought was to immediately leave, but I also knew that would be silly—this was surely just some guy who worked with her, not a true threat. The guy finished his little rubdown and they both turned back to the bar. Lauren's beauty made my stomach lurch. She had long, straight hair, dyed black; big, expressive eyes; and her usual enormous, bright smile. I made my way over, feeling stupid for having spent the last eight hours on buses without the foresight to dream up a single witty or romantic thing to say when I greeted her.

I edged between a few guys at the bar and pulled a ten-dollar bill from my back pocket. When Lauren came close, I called out, "Can I get a Bell's Amber?"—a local Michigan brew that wasn't served in Buffalo—my spontaneous, wilted stab at a joke. Even Chris Hendershot could've conjured up something funnier.

She looked at me and the smile drained off her face. "Davy? Oh my God, what the hell are you doing here?" There was no way to hug across the bar; instead, Lauren offered what seemed to me a slightly awkward and tepid two-handed high five.

I slapped her hands and said, "I came here to surprise you," feeling suddenly lost in space.

"Oh, that's so awesome," she said, sounding possibly genuine. "But what are you doing in Buffalo?"

"No, I came to Buffalo because I wanted to see you." I shrugged and heard the next words tumble out of my mouth, even as I instantly regretted them. "Happy Valentine's Day!"

Just then, a bar-back rushing past with a tub full of empty glasses crashed into her, knocking her a couple of feet to the side. Now she was within shouting range of a few guys further along the bar, and they started barking out their drink orders. She leaned back toward me and hollered, "I'm sorry, Monday nights are always like this, and we're short a guy. Can you come back later? It'll be less insane."

"Sure, no problem," I said, putting both hands up idiotically for another slap of hands, but she'd already turned and was cranking the caps off a row of Yuenglings. I slowly lowered my hands, waited another fifteen seconds or so until she happened to glance my way, and gave her a little wave. She flashed a polite smile in return, and I whirled and slunk out the door, utterly defeated, making a promise to myself not to come back later in the night unless she called my phone in the next few hours and begged me to. It was just past eight o'clock. I'd give her till midnight.

"Should we come inside?" Chris asked as I climbed in the backseat; Vernon had made it back to the car and was up riding shotgun.

"It's kind of busy in there. Let's get some grub and come back later."

"Well, how'd it go?" asked Vernon, once we were moving again.

"Not too bad. I don't know. Not too good, either." I told them what had gone down. They both tried to reassure me that Lauren was probably really excited I was in town, but that it's always hard when someone pops in to see you and you're busy at work. I granted them that, but it still seemed like she could've maybe flipped me the keys to her apartment, in case I wanted to take a nap or chill out and watch a movie until she got home. Or really had done anything to give me the sense that she was happy I'd rolled in.

"Don't worry, man," Vernon said. "Trust me, it'll be cool." This from the guy who was now using Chris's cell phone—and had been the whole time I was in the bar—to try to reach his great-granddaughter, to no avail. He was hoping we could stop by her house, which was on the west side of town, about a twenty-minute drive.

"I'm down," I said. "Chris?"

"Rock 'n' roll." He pumped up the Green Day song on the radio, zoomed through side streets to the on-ramp for an expressway, and looped the Explorer back toward the lights of downtown, slapping the steering wheel along to the music. Vernon tore off a few scratch tickets for himself, passed me the rest of the roll, and we both went to work.

Each losing ticket I scratched out socked me a little blow to the heart. Why didn't scratch cards just have a single box that told you if you'd won or not? Why the slow build, all the teasing hoopla of tic-tac-toe game boards and wheels of fortune? You kept thinking you were getting close and then, once again: loser. All of the unanswered questions made my head hurt: Had I blown things by coming to Buffalo and putting unfair pressure on Lauren Hill? Should I simply have come on any day other than Valentine's Day? Had she meant all the things she'd said in her letters? Some of it? None of it? And what would be the best way to salvage the night when I went back to the bar? (Because, face it, I was headed back there later whether she called me or not.) A small heap of losing tickets gathered at my feet.

"Holy shit!" cried Vernon from up front. "I think we got a winner!"

"How much?" said Chris, suddenly alert, punching the radio off.

"Wait a second. Did I win? Yeah, I did. Ten bucks!"

"Not bad." Chris nodded enthusiastically. "That's yours to keep," he told Vernon. "You guys just keep on scratching."

"You bet your goddamn ass," said Vernon, still believing a bigger payday was near.

His minor stroke of glory made me glad, but to me, winning ten bucks instead of ten grand was like getting a drunken kiss on the corner of the mouth from a stranger at the bar that you'll never see again. What I really wanted was to spend the night in Lauren Hill's arms, kissing her and holding her tight; to wake up with her at dawn, make love once or twice, and walk hand in hand through the woodsy park I'd glimpsed by her apartment, which by morning, I imagined—if it kept snowing the way it was now—would be transformed into a place of quiet and exquisite majesty. That was my wish. Anything less I'd just as soon chuck out the window.

From the outside, Vernon's great-granddaughter's house looked like a haunted mansion out of *Scooby-Doo*. It sat on a wide section of an abandoned half-acre lot overgrown with weeds, brambles, and the remaining debris from houses that had been leveled on either side. Across the street, TVs flickered dimly from the windows of a low-rise housing project, and at the end of the block a closed-down liquor store with both doors missing gaped like a sea cave, open to the elements. As we pulled up in front, Vernon looked back at me and said, "Hey, would you come inside with me?" It was my turn to be wingman.

I followed him up the front walk and up three stairs to the porch, and he lifted the enormous, rusted horseshoe knocker on the front door and let it land with a heavy thud. We waited. I watched snowflakes touch down on the Explorer's windshield and instantly melt. The knocker squeaked as he lifted it again, but then, from somewhere deep in the house, came a woman's voice, "I hear you, I'm coming."

Her footsteps padded near and Vernon edged back until he

was practically hiding behind me. "Who's there?" the woman
called.

I looked over to Vernon, waiting for him to respond. He had
the look of a dog who'd strewn trash through the kitchen. "It's
your granddaddy," he said at last, weakly.

"Who?"

"Vernon Wallace." He kicked the porch concrete. "Your great-
granddaddy."

The door opened a couple of inches and a woman's face appeared, eyebrows raised, hair wrapped in a towel above her head.
She was in maybe her early fifties. Through a pair of oversize
glasses, she took a long look at Vernon, sighed, shook her head, and
said, "Granddaddy, what're you doing up here in the wintertime?"
As he cleared his throat and began to respond, she said, "Hold on,
let me get my coat." The door closed, and for a half-minute Vernon
painted hieroglyphics with the toe of his old shoe in a pyramid of
drifting snow, looking suddenly frail and ancient. Exhaust panted
from the Explorer's tailpipe out on the street, and I could make out
the hard-rock bass line rattling its windows but didn't recognize
the song.

After a moment, the door opened again and the woman stepped
out and joined us on the front porch, hair still tucked up in a towel.
Over a matching pink sweat suit she wore a puffy, oversize, black
winter coat, and her feet, sockless, were stuffed into a pair of unlaced low-top Nikes. She gave Vernon a big, friendly hug, and said,
"I love you, Granddaddy, it's good to see you," and then turned to
me and said, "Hi there, I'm Darla Kenney," and once I'd introduced
myself she said, "Well, it's good to meet you, I appreciate you bringing Vernon by." She turned back to face him and crossed her arms.
"What you been drinking tonight, Granddaddy?"

He flinched slightly but didn't respond.

"Listen," she said, "I love you, but I ain't got no money. You
know my whole situation. You're gonna have to stay with your
friend here, 'cause I can't just invite you in."

Vernon nodded deeply, unable to meet her gaze. "I was just hoping we could spend time together."

"We can!" she said. "But not tonight. I got all kinds of shit to deal with tonight. I can't even get the damn car started. You got to learn to call people ahead of time so they know you coming." She softened. "How long you gonna stay in town for?"

Vernon shrugged. "A week or two?"

"Okay, then. Look, you give me a call tomorrow, or the next day, and we'll go for a drive, we'll play cards at Calvin's. He know you're in town?"

Vernon shook his head.

Darla looked past us, to the Explorer out on the street, its motor revving, Chris Hendershot behind the wheel, slapping his hands on the dash and crooning to himself. "That your friend?" she asked me.

"Yeah. That's Chris."

Darla tugged her coat closed and fought with the zipper. "Hey, listen," she said. "I got cables. Think I can get a jump?"

Ten minutes later, Chris was shouting instructions to me, banging under the hood of Darla Kenney's '84 Lincoln Continental with a wrench while I pounded the gas and jammed the ignition. Is there any sound more full of frustration and futility than a car that won't start when you turn the key? Click-click-click-click-click. All I could think of was Lauren Hill's dismayed expression in the bar when she'd first seen me.

"Okay, cut it!" Chris shouted. I felt his weight on the engine block as he bobbed deep within. A ping and a clatter. "Now try."

Click-click-click-click.

"Cut it!"

I heard Chris disconnecting the jumper cables, and then he dropped the hood with a magnificent crash. "I'll tell you what's happening, ma'am," he said to Darla, who stood in the street, looking on, still in her unlaced sneakers and coat with a towel on her head. "Your battery cable's a little frizzy, down by the starter relay. We get this in the shop, it's nothing—ten minutes, you're on your way. Tonight, though, no tools? Ain't gonna be easy." He passed her the jumper cables and put a consoling hand on her shoulder. "I'm really sorry. Usually I can get anything moving." I was touched by his level of kindness—if this was how sweetly he treated a woman he'd just met, it was hard to imagine there was anything he wouldn't do for his friends.

I climbed from the car and joined Chris and Darla. Vernon was sitting in the Explorer, keeping warm up front, scratching off lotto tickets.

"Well, it was nice of you to try," said Darla. She looked back and forth between us. "How do you guys know my granddaddy, anyhow?"

I wasn't sure how to answer. "Well, we met on a Greyhound bus once; we were seatmates." The word "once" tossed in there made it seem like this was years ago.

But Darla saw through it. "Oh, okay, when was that?"

"Well. Tonight."

She weighed this for a second. "Is he staying with you guys?"

"I don't know," I said. "I think he was saying something about the Y." The way my awesome surprise had gone over with Lauren Hill, I'd probably end up in the next bunk.

"I stay with my brother," Chris piped up. "But we got a cot at the garage, right around the corner. It's heated. I mean, that's where we work. Shit, he can stay in my room and I'll stay on the cot."

"We're not gonna leave him on the street," I said. I meant to be reassuring, but realized a second later that my words could be taken as an accusation.

Darla toyed with the clamps of the jumper cables in her hands; the metal jaws, squeaking open and shut, looked like angry, puppet-size gators shit-talking back and forth. As little as she seemed to want to deal with Vernon, she also seemed aware that he was her responsibility as much as anyone else's, and she wasn't ready to ditch him with two white kids he'd met an hour before. "Here's the thing," she said. "He can't stay at my house, and I got no money to give him right now. But I've got a tenant that owes me four hundred fifty dollars—I was gonna stop there tonight anyhow. We get some of that money together, I'll give my granddaddy half and put him up a week at the Front Park Inn."

Me and Chris nodded. "That'll work," I said. Fuck the Y—maybe at the Front Park Inn there'd be an extra bed for me.

Darla went to the Lincoln, heaved open the back door, and tossed the jumper cables on the floor behind the driver's seat. She turned back toward us. "Can I get a ride over to this house with you guys? It's really close, like ten, fifteen blocks from here. Larchmont, just the other side of Lake Avenue."

"Ain't no thing," said Chris.

I asked Darla if she wanted to get dressed first, at least pull on some socks, but she was already climbing into the backseat of Chris's Explorer and sliding over to make room for me. "We're just going and coming right back," she said. "Come on, hop in."

The snow kept falling. On the way to her tenant's house, Darla filled me in on a few things while Chris blasted music up front. It both irritated and charmed me that he kept the radio going max force no matter who was in the car with him. Even when he'd stayed with me in Chicago all those weekends, every time we were in my truck he'd reach over and crank the volume. Vernon rode shotgun, dozing, the dwindling spool of lotto tickets in his lap.

Darla had four children, she told me. She'd had the same job—quality control at a metal-stamping plant—for almost thirty years, and as she was careful with her money, she'd been able to buy homes for each of her children in nearby West Buffalo neighborhoods. "Nothing fancy," she said, "but a roof over their heads." One daughter had split up with her husband two years before and moved to Tampa, Florida. Darla rented out one half of their house to a friend from work, and the ex had stayed on in the other half, though Darla had begun to charge him three hundred bucks a month in rent, which was more than fair, she said, and less than what she could get from somebody else. But her daughter's ex, whose name was Anthony, and who was, overall, a decent, hard-working man, had fallen behind—he still owed her for January, and now half of February. It was time for her to pay a visit, Darla said.

She coached Chris through a few turns. We crossed a big four-lane road and the neighborhood deteriorated, making Darla's street look regal by comparison. Every third house was shuttered or burned-out. On a side street I glimpsed four guys loading furniture out of a squat apartment building into a U-Haul trailer. "Okay," said Darla, "take this right and it's the first one on the right."

We pulled up in front of a tiny, ramshackle house with cardboard taped over a missing window and its gutters hanging off, dangling to the ground. Still, the dusting of snow softened its features, and there were hopeful signs of upkeep—Christmas lights draped over a hedge by the side door and a pair of well-stocked bird feeders, swinging from low branches in the front yard, which had attracted a gang of sickly but grateful-looking squirrels.

"I'll be back in a couple minutes," said Darla, stepping gingerly down to the snow-filled street. She closed her door, picked her way across the lawn to the side of the house, knocked a few times, and disappeared inside.

Chris's cell phone rang and he answered it and had a quick, angry spat with his older brother. He'd explained to me that he'd been in hot water with his brother all month. His brother had a rule that anytime Chris boosted a car he was supposed to get it immediately to their shop to be dismantled (or at least stripped of its VIN) and resold. Chris admitted that he had a habit of keeping stolen cars for a while and driving around in them to impress girls. A couple of weeks before, another guy who worked with them had landed a cherry-red PT Cruiser in Pittsburgh, and Chris had whipped it around Buffalo over Super Bowl weekend while his brother was out of town. His brother found out, of course, and had been hounding him about it ever since. Now he seemed to be giving Chris grief for driving the Explorer; I could hear his brother on the other end of the phone, shouting at him to bring it back to base. "Fuck that motherfucker!" Chris shouted, hanging up and slamming his phone on the dash. "Who the fuck does he think he is?" To me, there was something ecstatically rich and appealing in someone who acted so gangsta but sounded so Canadian; at the same time, I could see in the rearview mirror that Chris's eyes had gone teary, and I felt a guilty and despairing tug of responsibility for dragging him around town and sticking him deeper into his brother's doghouse.

The shouting roused Vernon from his mini-nap, and without missing a beat he resumed work scratching off the squares of each lotto ticket. A heaviness had settled over him. He inspected a ticket after scratching it off, sighed greatly, and let it slip from his fingers.

In the front yard of the house next door, a band of ragtag little kids wrestled in the snow and hurled snowballs at parked cars and each other, shouting, "I'ma blast you, nigga!" The oldest of them, a boy around ten, was trying to rally the rest of them through the early stages of building a snowman. I powered my window down a few inches so I could hear his pitch. "Start with a giant snowball," he said breathlessly, as he worked on packing one together, then placed it on the ground. "Then we keep rolling this thing, and rolling it, and rolling it, until it's as big as a house, and then we'll have the biggest snowman in all of Buffalo!" The other kids dove in to help him, and they slid around the yard, accumulating more snow, then breaking off chunks accidentally as they pushed in opposite directions. Everyone shouted instructions at everyone else: "Roll it that way!" "Get those Doritos off it!" "You're fucking it up!"

Lauren Hill had been about the same age—nine or ten—when her dad was killed by a drunk driver. She'd told me the story in the most recent letter she'd sent me; her mom had appeared at the park where Lauren was playing with her friends and pulled her away and told her the news. Even though that had happened in summertime, I couldn't help but picture a fifth-grade Lauren Hill building a snowman with her neighborhood pals, her mom galloping up, crazed and wild-eyed, and dragging her away to a sucky, dadless future in a grim apartment complex near the Detroit airport, populated by creepy neighbors and a steady stream of her mom's low-life live-in boyfriends. When you first got involved with any girl who'd been punctured by that kind of sadness, I'd learned, you had to be extra cautious about flooding them with goodness and light. A gentle and steady kindness appealed to them, but too much love straight out of the gate was uncomfortable, even painful, and impossible to handle. I felt like an idiot for coming to Buffalo and freaking Lauren out.

"Hey, Vernon," I said, leaning between the front seats. "Did you ever get married?"

"Yes I did. Wanda May. Fifty years we were married." He paused, passing a scratch-off to Chris. "I think this one wins a free ticket." Then, to me, with a sudden touch of melancholy, "She died in 1964."

"Damn. That's way before I was born."

Vernon slipped his whiskey bottle out, touched it to his lips, and gave me a look. "You want some advice?" he said.

"Definitely."

"You should marry this girl you came to see. Marry her right away. Tomorrow, if you want. You don't know how much time you get with someone, so you might as well start right away."

"The problem is, it's not up to me. She gets a say."

"It's more up to you than you think."

I let that sink in, watching the kids in the neighbor's yard. Their snowman's round trunk had quickly swelled from the size of a soccer ball to the size of a dorm fridge. It took all of them, pushing and shouldering it together, to keep it rolling across the lawn. Finally they ran out of juice and came to a stop, slumping against their massive boulder of snow, tall as the oldest boy. There seemed to be two opinions about what to do next. The boy in charge wanted to go down the street and recruit his older cousin and some of his cousin's friends to keep pushing. But one tiny girl pointed out that the snowman had already gotten too big for them to add a middle and a top. Also, she suspected that if the boy's cousin and his friends glimpsed the half-built snowman, all they'd want to do is destroy it. "We made it, we should get to knock it down," she said.

Vernon passed his bottle to Chris, who took a long gulp and passed it back to me. I drained the last of the whiskey down and watched as the kids gave their big, round heap of snow a pair of stick arms, then collaborated on the face—two deep holes for eyes, a Dorito for a nose, and, strangely, no mouth.

By now, Chris and Vernon were watching them, too. "You want some more advice?" Vernon asked.

"Yes, I do."

"Okay. Don't outlive your wife."

The oldest kid pulled off his red knit cap and plopped it on top of the snowman's head, and at last the whole crew of munchkins stood back to silently admire their handiwork. It was surely the saddest, fattest, strangest, and most beautiful snowman I'd ever seen.

After a few long moments, there was the sound of voices, as Vernon's great-granddaughter Darla banged her way through the side door of the house she owned. The towel on her head had been replaced by a black baseball cap, and she was trailed by two others in heavy coats with their hoods pulled up. Her appearance seemed to somehow release the kids in the neighbors' yard from their spell. The oldest boy let out a mighty cry and charged the snowman—he plowed into its shoulder, driving loose its left arm and a wedge of its face, before crashing to the ground. The other kids followed, flailing with arms and feet, and even using the snowman's own arms to beat its torso quickly to powdery rubble.

Darla and her two companions crossed the yard toward us.

Vernon turned to me and Chris. "That's how long I was married, feels like," he said, eyes blazing. "As long as that snowman was alive."

We took on two new passengers—Anthony, the ex-husband of Darla's daughter who owed Darla all the back rent, and his shy, pregnant girlfriend, Kandy. They squeezed in back with me and Darla, and we circled around the block and headed back the way we'd come. Our next destination was a Chinese restaurant where Anthony worked as a dishwasher, on the east end of town, not far from Lauren Hill's bar. Anthony told us that his car was dead, too; apparently, one of the few operational vehicles in all of Buffalo was Chris's Explorer, which he'd driven off the lot of a body shop in Rochester the night before.

Anthony and Darla continued a conversation they must have started in the house. Anthony—dark skinned, small and compact, with a thin mustache, roughly forty years old—spoke softly, but had a thoughtful, commanding presence. He was explaining why he hadn't quit his job, even though he hadn't been paid in a month. "Here's the thing about Mr. Liu," he said. "Last winter, business got so slow, sometimes there was no customers in there, he could've sent me home. But he knows I got bills, and I'm scheduled to work, so he gave me the hours and found shit for me to do. You know, shovel the parking lot, clean out the walk-in cooler. Sometimes he paid me just to sit on a stool in back and watch basketball. Now his wallet thin for a minute, how'm I just gonna walk out on him?"

"What if he goes out of business?" Darla asked. "He gonna pay you those paychecks?"

"That's what *I'm* saying," said Kandy. She sat on the far side of the backseat, deeply ensconced in the hood of her jacket; it was hard for me to get a good look at her, but she seemed no older than me or Chris, and was maybe seven months pregnant.

"We talked about that," said Anthony. "First of all, we ain't goin' out of business. It's slow every winter, Mr. Liu just had some extra costs this winter. Second of all, he do go out of business?

Mr. Liu told me he's gonna sell the building and all the equipment
an' shit, and he'll have plenty enough to pay me what he owe."

The general plan, it seemed, was for Anthony to ask his boss
for at least a portion of his paycheck so he could turn the money
over to Darla, who might then have enough to support Vernon
during his visit and buy him a ticket home to Little Rock. My
own plan was to get some shrimp lo mein and ask Chris for a ride
back to Freighter's. I wondered if bringing Lauren a carton of
Chinese food would be a sweet gesture or just seem demented.

Chris had been quiet since the phone call with his brother,
but now he dropped the music a few notches, glanced back at
Kandy, and said, "You having a girl or a boy?"

"A boy," she peeped.

"What you gonna name it?"

"Floyd."

"That was her granddaddy's name," Anthony offered.

Chris nodded. "I like that name. Question is, he gonna take
after his mom or his dad?"

"Not his dad, I hope," Anthony said cryptically.

"Well, I'll tell you what," said Vernon. "I'm sick of these scratch
tickets." Over the seat, he handed back what remained of the roll.
"Here ya go. I'm too old for this shit." His night, like mine, was not
going the way he'd hoped. He reached for the radio, turned the volume back up, and sank into his seat, eyes out the window.

This was a song I knew: "What It's Like" by Everlast. Chris
slid us back onto the Kensington Expressway, and the swirling
snow gusted this way and that, rocking the SUV like a baby plane
in turbulence. I closed my eyes and let myself sway.

> Then you really might know what it's like.
> Yeah, then you really might know what it's like . . . to have
>   to lose.

Mr. Liu's Chinese restaurant anchored a shambling commercial
strip between a Popeyes and a defunct video store. It was called the

Golden Panda, though just the right letters had burned out on the neon sign in its front window to leave THE GOLDEN AN. "Look!" I cried, rallying from the darkness, "it's the Golden AN!" Everyone stared at me flatly. "You know, from *Sesame Street*?"

"Wait a second," said Chris. "I know this fucking place. My brother loves this place. He always gets takeout here. It's so fucking *nasty* but he loves it." He looked at Anthony in the rearview mirror. "I mean, no offense."

Vernon and Kandy hung back in the Explorer while me, Chris, and Darla followed Anthony inside. The place had an odd, foul, but unidentifiable smell. It had just closed for the night, and a pretty Chinese girl in her late teens was blowing out red candles on each table that I supposed had been set out for Valentine's Day, and loading an enormous tray with dirty dishes. "Hey, Anthony," she said, tired but friendly. "If you came for dinner, you better let my mom know, she's shutting down the kitchen right now." She flipped a switch for the overhead fluorescents, and as they flickered on, the restaurant's interior grew more drab and dingy.

Anthony asked the girl if her dad was still around, and the girl told him he was. "Hey, Mary, these are my friends," he said, and told us he'd be back in a minute.

"Hi, Anthony's friends," she said. "You can have a seat if you want."

"Oh," said Anthony. "Did you hear back yet?"

"Not yet," said the girl. "The admissions office, they were supposed to call or e-mail everybody last week, but they never called me. So that's not a good sign. That reminds me, I need to check my e-mail."

"Well, look, if it don't work out, you just keep on trying." Anthony pushed his way through a blue silk curtain at the back of the dining area and disappeared down a hallway.

The three of us found a table that the girl had already cleared and sat down. Darla lowered her voice and said, "That's a fine young man right there. You know, that baby, Floyd, that's not even his baby. But he's gonna raise it and take care of that baby like it is." She shook her head. "I still call him my son. And that baby will be my grandson." Then, in a near whisper, "I hate putting the squeeze on him, but that ain't right he ain't getting paid." She eyed Mary, the owner's daughter, and said, under her breath, "This ain't the plantation. This is Buffalo!"

"I'm sure the guy'll give him some cash," I said.

As if on cue, a sudden, jarring eruption of shouting rose from deep in back. It was Anthony's voice, but the only word I could make out was "motherfucker." Soon a second voice joined the fray—Mr. Liu, no doubt, shouting back. And then a woman's voice jumped in, yelling in Chinese, followed by the sound of pots and pans clattering to the floor. Mary set down her tray and rushed through the blue curtains, and Darla said, "Oh no," and leapt up and dashed after her.

Chris gave me a dismal look and sank his head to the table. "Today's retarded," he said, sounding truly pained, his voice cracking a bit. "You know what sucks?"

"Yeah," I said, as the shouting in back increased. "That old man out there, Vernon, he thinks I should marry Lauren Hill tomorrow, but I don't think she wants anything to do with me, and you know, she's probably fucking this dude at her work."

"Yeah, that does suck," said Chris. "And I'll tell you what else sucks. I am really, really, incredibly fucking hungry."

"Maybe it'll all boil over back there and mellow out," I suggested, and again, Anthony's timing was splendid—he came ripping through the curtain just then, shouting and cursing, Darla at his heels, tugging at his sleeve and begging him to chill out.

"Get your fucking hands off me!" he said. "Fuck that motherfucker. I'll kill that slant-eyed faggot." He stopped in his tracks, turned, and screamed full force, "Fuck you, Mr. Liu! Suck my fucking dick, you little bitch!" From in back somewhere, Mr. Liu was shouting in return. Anthony kicked over a chair, and said, "Come get some of this! You want some? Come out here and get some!" Darla grabbed his shoulders and steered him toward the front door. "Fuck this place," Anthony said, deeply aggrieved, shoving her arm away. He fought his way outside.

"Come on," said Darla to me and Chris, holding the door open. "Time to go."

Back in the Explorer, Anthony was still shouting. We sat in the lot, trying to calm him down. Kandy seemed inappropriately entertained, a strange smile on her face as she pleaded with him to explain what had happened.

"That fucker," he said, jaw clenched, breathing hard through flared nostrils. "I told him he better pay me, not the whole month he owes me, just like two weeks, and he's, like"—here Anthony mocked Mr. Liu's Chinese accent—"'I no have your money. Give me more time.' And I said, 'Fuck that. Pay me.' So then he's, like, 'I can't afford you no more. I hafta let you go.'" Anthony rubbed his face. With great anger, sadness, and shame, he said, "I didn't come all the way down here tonight to get my ass fired." He had tears in his eyes.

I saw that Darla, beside him, had tears in her eyes, too. She put her arm around Anthony and soothed him. "Okay, it'll be all right. It'll all be all right." I caught Chris's gaze in the rearview mirror. Even his eyes were wet. Strangely enough, I realized, mine were, too. I thought of the kids we'd seen building the snowman— how blissfully carefree they'd seemed—and felt a mournful gulf open up inside me. Whatever lumps those kids were taking as they sprouted in their bleak, tundra-like ghetto had nothing on the disappointments and humiliations of adulthood.

Kandy took Anthony's hand and said, "Listen, baby. You need to take a few deep breaths. I got to show you something."

"Five fucking years," said Anthony. "You know how many times I coulda gone somewhere else? My cousin in Syracuse, he's roofing now, twenty bucks an hour. That job coulda been mine." He blasted the back of the front passenger seat with his fist and Vernon bolted upright. "Sorry, Vernon," said Anthony. He looked at the empty front room of the Golden Panda. "Five years. Chinese people don't know shit about loyalty."

"It'll be all right," said Kandy. Her odd smile broadened. "Vernon, come on, will you just tell 'em?"

Vernon turned the radio off and looked around, gathering our attention, wide-eyed and mysterious. Then he melted into a smile, held up a scratched-out lotto ticket, and said, "We just won two thousand dollars."

Darla immediately screamed and slapped her hands to her cheeks in astonishment. Chris's eyes bugged out of his head. Anthony turned to his girlfriend, Kandy: "Say what?"

Kandy laughed. "It's true! I scratched it off!"

Vernon handed the ticket to Chris. "Really, how it is, *you* won two thousand dollars. We were just the first ones to find out."

Everyone grew suddenly quiet, watching Chris as he brought the ticket close to check it out. He nodded slowly, gave a low whistle, and flipped it over to read the fine print on back. "Looks like ... redeem anywhere," he said softly, to himself. "They just print you a check right there. Damn. Two grand." He twisted around, looked back at all of us, and laughed. "Shit, this ain't a funeral," he said. "If I won, we all won. What the fuck, we're splittin' this fucker!"

Wild, joyous whoops of celebration filled the SUV, and all at the same time Vernon, Darla, Anthony, and Kandy hugged Chris and rubbed his shaved head. Everyone began shaking back and forth and the whole Explorer rocked side to side.

"Chris," I said. "You are a great American."

He was giggling, giddy at this sudden turn of events and all of the combined adulation. "Fuck you, dude. I'm Canadian!" Then he sobered up. "Okay, when I say we're splitting it, what I mean is, I get half, and the rest of you split the other half."

Everyone settled down a little, doing the math in their hands, and then murmured agreeably—this seemed like a more-than-fair arrangement, without asking Chris to be unreasonably generous.

Chris went on, peering back toward the restaurant, where

Mr. Liu's daughter, Mary, had emerged to gather the last of the dishes. "Look, Anthony," he said, "I know the last thing you wanna do right now is go back in there. But yo, I got an idea. And I *need* some fried wontons."

A minute later, there were nine people clustered in the cramped, pungent kitchen of the Golden Panda—me, Chris, Old Man Vernon, Darla, Anthony, and Kandy, along with Mr. Liu, his wife, and their daughter, Mary, who sat on a milk crate, pecking away at a laptop. Mr. Liu had small, round glasses and graying hair and wore an apron over a dirty white T-shirt and baggy, brightly patterned swim trunks. He was bent over an industrial-size sink, wiping it out with a blue sponge, still tense, it seemed, from his confrontation with Anthony, who stood behind Vernon, glowering at the floor.

I could guess that Chris was aiming to broker a truce between the two of them, but didn't see the tack he planned on taking even as he dove right in. "Mr. Liu," he said. "I have been a customer of your fine establishment here for a couple of years. My brother, Shawn, he's been coming here for longer than that. I love the food you have here. It's kind of nasty sometimes, but it's good nasty. It's filling. I especially like the pork fried rice. And I like how you give fortune cookies even on to-go orders."

"Thank you," said Mr. Liu, with a heavy accent, standing straight. "I see you in here before. I think I know your brother." His wife, tiny and anxious, wearing a Buffalo Bills hoodie and a hairnet, said a few rapid words in Chinese to Mary, and Mary gave a one-word response without looking up.

"I recently came into some money," Chris went on. "And knowing me, I'll spend it, it'll be gone, and that'll be that." He took a breath. "I've got an idea, though. It'll be a good thing for me, and maybe it'll help you, too. Here's what I'm thinking—I want to come here tomorrow and give you ... let's say ... eight hundred bucks, cash money."

Mr. Liu crossed his arms, not quite sure where Chris was going with this.

"I'm thinking I give you eight hundred up front," said Chris, "and me and my brother eat here free for the rest of the year." He explained that they wouldn't take advantage of the arrangement—they'd only come by once or twice a week. Basically, Chris said, he was offering to pay in advance for a year's worth of meals. But he had a few conditions. "I want you to hire Anthony back. He's been loyal to you, you gotta be loyal to him. And you gotta pay him at least half of what you owe him right now in back wages."

Mr. Liu and Anthony glanced up toward each other without actually letting their eyes meet. Mr. Liu said to Chris, "I want Anthony to work. But not enough customers."

"Well, for one thing," Chris said, "you guys need to have delivery. A Chinese place without delivery, that's like a dog with no dick. That's why my brother always sends me down here to pick up. In snowstorms and shit. I hate that shit. You have delivery, you'll double your sales. Anthony can wash dishes and go on runs, both. You need a delivery car, I can even help you find one, for a good price."

Mr. Liu spoke to his wife in Chinese, translating Chris's appeal. She responded at great length, gesturing at Anthony, Mary, and at Chris. I couldn't help but marvel at Chris's command of the situation. My image of him as a failed comic and petty criminal could barely accommodate the ease and confidence he now seemed to possess. At last Mrs. Liu fell silent, and Mr. Liu turned and said to Anthony, "Okay. You want to work here?"

Without unclenching his jaw, still staring down, burning holes in the tile, Anthony nodded.

"Good," said Chris. "Now hug it out, you two. Seriously. Go on. It's part of the deal."

Shyly, like two bludgeoned boxers embracing at the end of twelve rounds, Anthony and Mr. Liu edged near each other and slumped close in a kind of half hug, patting each other quickly on the back, but not without an evident bit of emotion.

Darla started clapping, and I found myself joining in, unexpectedly stirred; soon Kandy, Vernon, and even Mrs. Liu were clapping, too. Chris was beaming. "That's good," he said. "That's perfect." I had goose bumps. My only sorrow was that Lauren wasn't there to witness the moment.

Chris laughed, growing comfortable in his role as peace-maker. "Now, before we hit the bar to celebrate—and drinks are on me tonight—there's just one more part of the deal."

Mr. Liu eyed him nervously.

"If it's not too inconvenient," Chris said, "I was hoping we could all dig into some grub. Golden Panda leftovers, I don't care. I could eat a horse, this guy's been on a bus the last twenty-four hours"—he pointed at Vernon—"and this girl's eating for two," with a sideways nod toward Kandy. "What do you say?"

"No problem," said Mr. Liu.

All of a sudden, his daughter Mary shrieked and leapt to her feet like she'd been stung on the butt by a bee. She let out some rapid birdsong to her parents in Chinese, and Mr. Liu took the laptop from her hands and inspected the screen while Mrs. Liu threw her arms around Mary and began to sob into her shoulder. Mary looked at Anthony, tearing up herself, and cried, "I got in! I got in! Medaille College e-mailed me! Anthony, I got in!"

A half hour later, well fed, all nine of us were crammed into Chris's Explorer, speeding toward Freighter's. I sat up front in the passenger seat; behind me sat old Vernon Wallace, his great-granddaughter Darla, and Anthony and Kandy. Squashed way in back, and squealing like kindergarteners with every pothole we bounced over, were Mr. Liu and his wife and daughter. Chris was driving, phone clamped between his ear and his shoulder, talking to his older brother. "Shawn, just meet us there. It's good news, I'm saying, though."

I could hear Chris's brother chewing him out on the other end, calling him a moron, a loser, and a punk. All of the merri-ment and gladness quickly drained from Chris's face. "Yes, Shawn. Okay. Okay, Shawn. Yes, I understand." He closed his phone and tossed it up on the dash, shaking his head and biting at a thumbnail. In the back, full of jolly banter, no one else had caught the exchange.

"Fuck that, dude," I said to Chris. "Shake it off."

"It's not that easy," he said, hurt and sinking. He mashed on the gas pedal and we veered right, back tires sliding out a little, and bolted through a light that had just turned red. A few blocks down, the five-way intersection with Lauren's bar came into sight. I felt supremely nervous, but fortified by the size of my brand-new posse.

Chris clouded over with a look of fierce intensity. He reached for his phone again, dialed his brother, and propped the phone to his ear, battle-ready. Then, without warning, a siren whooped in the night, and a blinding strobe of red and blue lights filled the SUV. "Yo, man," said Anthony, "you just blew right past that stop sign." I twisted around and saw, through the back window, a cop car right on our tail, flashers twirling giddily, high beams punching the air, one-two, one-two.

"No fucking way!" Chris cried, as the phone slipped from his shoulder to the center console and tumbled to the floor at my feet. "What the fuck do we do?" He kept rolling forward, while everyone in back began shouting instructions. I was pretty sure that only Vernon and me knew the truck was stolen. A forlorn tide rose in my chest.

I could hear Shawn's voice on the phone, saying Chris's name. I plucked it up and said, "He's gotta call you back," and folded the phone closed.

"Okay," said Chris frantically. "Here's what we're gonna do. I'm gonna pull over up here, and then all of us, we're just gonna scatter in every direction. Just fuckin' haul ass into the alleyways, all these side streets, into the bushes. They can't get more than one or two of us."

"Are you crazy, boy?" said Darla. "You think my granddaddy's gonna take off running? You think *I* am? I ain't got nothing to hide from. Cops can't fuck with me."

From the way back, Mary said, "You know, there's always

policemen at the restaurant. I know a ton of 'em. I got my friend out of a speeding ticket once."

"I'm not worried about a damn ticket," Chris said.

Anthony sat forward and got close to Chris's ear. "Nobody's running," he said. "Chris—listen to me—you got warrants?"

"No."

"Is this shit hot?"

Chris nodded. "Burning."

"Okay. Listen, just pull over and talk to the guy. Just act like it's nothing. Play it cool, like everything's cool. I'm telling you, I've seen dudes talk their way outta way worse."

"I'm not going down tonight," said Chris. He was so deeply spooked, it made me remember the time I'd suggested he incorporate his time in prison into his stand-up routines and he'd told me with a grave, distant stare that there was nothing funny about being in prison.

"That's right," said Anthony. "You're not going down. Now pull over and talk to this man."

Chris pulled to the curb and turned off the radio. He reached slowly for his shoulder belt and clanked it into its buckle.

"The guy's coming!" Mary called from in back.

I watched the cop's cautious approach. He wielded a powerful flashlight and shined it at each of our windows, but they were so fogged up from all the bodies in the car, I doubted he could see much. He took position just behind Chris's window and tapped on the glass with gloved fingers.

Chris lowered the window. "Hello there, sir, good evening," he said, laying on a healthy dose of Canadian politeness.

"License and registration." I couldn't see the cop's face, but he sounded young, which to me seemed like a bad thing. Seasoned cops, I'd found, were more likely to play things fast and loose; rookies went by the book.

"Here's my license," said Chris, passing over his New York State ID. "As far as the registration, I don't have any. I just bought this thing yesterday at an auction in Rochester. I know I shouldn't be driv-

ing it around till I get over to the DMV, that's my bad." Fat snowflakes spiraled in through his window and tumbled along the dash.

"You know you ran a light back there?"

"Yes, sir. I believe I ran a stop sign just now, too. I was talking
to my brother on the phone and I got distracted. That's my bad.
I'm really sorry about that."

Chris was handling things as well as he possibly could, I
thought. But once the cop checked the plates, we'd be doomed. If
I bailed and ran, it occurred to me, maybe the cop would chase
after me and Chris could peel away. My heart jangled, and my
fingers crawled to the door handle, ready to make a move.

"You been doing any drinking tonight?" asked the cop.

"Not really, sir," said Chris. He ejected a bark-like laugh.
"Planning to, though. We're just going up there to Freighter's."
He hitched his thumb toward me. "Even got a designated driver."

The cop bent his head down and poked his flashlight at me. He
had dark, close-cropped hair, and was maybe in his mid-thirties. I
dropped my hand from the door handle. Then he leaned through
Chris's window a shade more and played his light over our bizarre
array of passengers—four generations of black folk in the backseat,
and a Chinese family in the trunk. His face crinkled up in utter baf-
flement. Either we were human traffickers with a payload of Asians
or a tour bus covering the last leg of the Underground Railroad.

I heard Mr. Liu's daughter call out from the back, "Officer
Ralston?"

He ducked his head further into the Explorer. "Who's that?"

"Mary. From the Golden Panda."

"Oh!" said the cop. "Mary! Hey, is that your dad?"

"Yeah. Guess what? I got into Medaille College! We're all
going out to celebrate. These are our employees and some of our
regulars. You might know some of them."

"But you're not old enough to drink."

"Don't tell the bouncer!" Mary giggled, playfully—even
masterfully—redirecting the conversation. "I'm just gonna have
a glass of wine."

The cop said, "All right, then," and withdrew his head from inside the truck. He handed Chris back his license. "I'll tell you what," he told Chris. "No more driving with your head up your— you know. Especially when the roads are this bad. You all take care." He doused his flashlight and headed back to his cruiser.

Chris zipped his window up. "Wait for it," he said tersely. "Wait for it."

The cop's flashers went dark, and a moment later his squad car swished past, hung a left at the next side street, and disappeared. Chris turned to look at all of us and broke out into relieved, maniacal laughter. "Holy shit!" he said. "What just happened? This is a magical night!"

Even as everyone began cheering and dancing around in their seats, slapping each other on the back, a cold ball pitted itself in my stomach. It was time to go see Lauren Hill.

"Fuck no, you can't bring all these people in here," the massive bouncer at Freighter's told me, shouting over the music. He eased from his perch and barged forward, using his bulk to crowd us back toward the door. He pointed at Vernon. "That dude didn't have an ID earlier. And this little fucker right here"—he jabbed Chris in the chest—"he's eighty-sixed for life." He took a look at Mary. "She's underage, I'll put money on that. Get these clowns out of my face. Try Cole's, across the street. They'll serve anybody."

I said in his ear, "I'm Lauren Hill's boyfriend. And these are my friends."

"Darrell is Lauren Hill's boyfriend," said the bouncer. "Get your Rainbow Coalition the fuck outta here."

Darrell? Who the *fuck* was Darrell? "Just let me go find Lauren," I pleaded.

"Knock yourself out," said the bouncer. "But these people got to wait outside."

I hustled everyone back through the door, into the freezing night. "Just give me two minutes," I said. "I'll be right back."

I rushed in, my neck hot, blood crashing through my veins. In the three or four hours I'd been away, the Freighter's crowd had gone from tipsy to riotously drunk. Two old bikers had their shirts off and were holding a tough-man contest, affectionately slugging each other in the gut. A pair of young punk rockers dry-humped in a booth. People were screaming along to a song on the jukebox and hooting at hockey highlights on the TVs. At a table in the middle of the room, a man in a winter coat dumped a humongous boot-shaped glass of beer over his own head. I was desperate to be that drunk.

The crowd tossed and turned me like a piece of driftwood, until finally I reached the bar and stood a few feet from Lauren Hill, staring at the back of her neck and her bare shoulders as she mixed a row of drinks at the rear counter. I felt like a vampire, dying to taste her skin. Lauren turned toward me, and the whole scene seemed to grind into slow motion and go mute. I waited for the moment of truth—the expression on her face when she saw that I was back. She set the drinks down in front of the guys next to me, and as she looked up she saw me and smiled—a jolting, radiant, zillion-watt smile. The room's roar slammed back in and the world returned to normal speed. "There you are," she shouted. "What do you want to drink?"

"I made some friends," I shouted back. "Can you help me get 'em in?"

"Just tell Greg I said it was cool."

"I think you better come with me."

She looked around. The other bartender had left and she was now the only person serving drinks, but there seemed to be a momentary lull. "Okay," she said. "Really quick." She ducked under the bar and followed me through the raucous crowd to the front door.

"Come outside for a second," I said. I blasted the door open and we spilled out onto the sidewalk, where a stocky, young white guy in a powder-blue FUBU sweatshirt and Timberland boots was talking to Chris and Mr. Liu while the rest of the crew looked on.

"All the food we want, all year long?" the guy said.

"My guests," said Mr. Liu.

"Rock on!" The guy wrapped his arm over Chris's shoulders, pulled him close, and rubbed his head with his knuckles. "I love you, ya little fuckhead," he said, laughing. "You are just full of surprises." This, I realized, had to be Chris's older brother, Shawn. Chris scrapped his way loose and looked up at me with a magnificent gleam.

"Davy! Let's get our drink on," Chris hollered. "They gonna let us in or what?"

"Yes, sir," I said. "But wait, you guys, everyone come here, I want you to meet someone. This is Lauren Hill." The whole group gathered close, joining us in a tight little huddle. "Lauren," I said, "these are my new friends." I went around the circle, introducing her to each of them, and as I introduced them, they each gave her a friendly hello. "This is Mr. and Mrs. Liu, they own the Golden Panda on Fillmore Avenue. And Mary, their daughter, she just found out she got into college tonight! This is Anthony, and this is Kandy—they're having a baby soon." I pointed to Kandy's stomach. "That's little Floyd in there. And this is my Canadian friend Chris I was telling you about, a man of many talents. And, Shawn, right?"

He nodded. "That's right. You're Davy?"

"Yup." I explained to Lauren that Shawn was Chris's older brother.

"And evil boss," said Shawn with a grin.

"But how'd you meet all these people?" Lauren said, a bit dazzled.

"Hold on." I continued around the circle. "This is Darla Kenney. She lives over on the West Side, in Front Park. And here's her grandfather, actually her great-grandfather, Vernon Wallace. Hey, wait a second, what time is it?"

Shawn glanced at his cell phone. "Ten to midnight."

"In ten minutes," I told Lauren, "it's gonna be Vernon's hundred-and-tenth birthday!"

"No way!" she said.

"It's true!" said Darla.

Lauren looked at me with wide, whirling eyes, really taking me in, as beautiful a girl as I'd ever seen in my life. "You were only gone a couple hours," she said. "This is crazy. This is awesome." She shivered.

"Let's go inside and have a drink," I said.

"Let's drink!" Chris echoed.

Lauren reached for the door, glowing. "Okay, all of you come on in, I'll pour a round of birthday shots. Let me tell Greg what's up." Then she paused, giving Chris an odd look. She seemed to recall his status on the Freighter's blacklist. "Except you," she said, pointing at him. "I'm sorry, but ... you just can't skip out on a tab. Not three or four times. Not here. Not in Buffalo."

"I just, sometimes I leave my wallet at home," Chris sputtered.

"I'm sorry," said Lauren.

"Wait," said Anthony. "What if we pay off everything he owes? Can he be forgiven then?"

Lauren thought about this. "Not forgiven. But if he pays every dollar he owes, plus a twenty-*five* percent tip, then he's allowed back in."

"Done," said Shawn.

"All right, then," Lauren said. She hauled open the door and grasped my hand and led me through. My heart thrummed.

For a moment she leaned close to Greg the bouncer and explained the situation. At last he nodded and Lauren waved everyone past, into the mad melee inside. She squeezed my hand as we swept across the room to the bar and whispered in my ear, so close I could feel her hot breath, "Thank you for being here." The universe had finally, improbably—almost unbelievably—become perfectly aligned.

Our whole crew stood in a crushed knot against the bar. Lauren ducked under and popped up on the far side. "What'll it be?" she shouted, spreading out a constellation of shot glasses.

"It's Vernon's night," said Chris.

Vernon peered around, the tallest of us, soaking it all in like an ancient willow admiring an orchard of saplings. "Knob Creek!" he declared.

Lauren found the bottle and poured nine Knob Creeks, plus a shot of Dr. Pepper for Mrs. Liu, who asked for root beer instead, and, at Kandy's request, a shot of Molson Ice. As Lauren passed them out, I saw Greg, the bouncer, waddling quickly in our direction. I had the gut-shot feeling that everything was about to go from wildly festive to ferociously violent in the next several seconds. But instead, Greg howled, "Let me get in on that!"

Lauren saw the confusion in my face. "Greg loves to be a bad-ass," she said, "but he's just a big softie. He goes to those Renaissance fairs. He swings swords around and wears dresses!"

"They're called kilts!" Greg bellowed, grumpy and happy at the same time. Lauren handed him a shot of whiskey; in his massive paw it looked the size of a thimble.

Lauren slipped under the bar again and pressed herself against me. We all raised our glasses, mashed tightly together, and looked around at one another, everyone's face filled with a golden glow. Darla and Vernon had their arms around each other, as did Anthony and Kandy, and Chris and Shawn Hendershot, and Mr. Liu, Mrs. Liu, and Mary. I put my arm around Lauren's waist and pulled her close.

Later in the night, much later, I ended up telling Lauren that I loved her, and she told me she loved me, too. And the next afternoon, when we woke up, hung over but in fine spirits, we went for the walk I'd fantasized about, through a city transformed by almost two feet of snow. Every tree, every bush, every fire hydrant, and every garbage can was laced with soft, gentle beauty, like we'd crossed through a portal into some distant, magic land. In a few weeks, of course, Lauren Hill was no longer with me, she was with that dude named Darrell, the other bartender at Freighter's, and Mr. Liu's restaurant, I learned, went out of business just a few months after that. Vernon made it to late summer, Darla told me later, then simply lay down on a park bench in Little Rock and died. But don't you see, none of that mattered, none of that mattered, none of that mattered. Because you can take away Lauren Hill, you can take away the love we had for each other, but you can't take away the feeling I had that night at midnight, as I squeezed her hand and looked around at my new, glorious tangle of friends, letting my eyes briefly catch their eyes and linger on each of their faces, the whiskey in each shot glass sparkling like a supernova. If there's ever been a happier moment in my life, I can't remember it.

"To Vernon!" someone cried out.   .

"To Vernon!" we shouted in chorus.

The Knob Creek went down like a furious, molten potion. I turned and looked at Lauren. She was smiling at me, sweet, soulful, and open.

"Happy Valentine's Day," I said.

"Happy Valentine's Day," she said.

And we kissed.

LIFE'S WORK
Brenda Shaughnessy

The round white knob
on the dresser drawer—
a pull, it's called—is loose,
becoming unscrewed
from itself. To tighten it,
I must empty the drawer
of the clothes nobody's ever
worn and nobody ever
will, find the screwdriver
I don't think I've ever used,
or even have anymore,
with both hands, one
outside the drawer to steady
the pull and one inside
to screw it. We used to say
that all the time to joke
we'd given up: "Screw it!"
But we hadn't. Given up
that is. Now here I am,
still at it. When I bake muffins,
bran with raisin puree instead
of sugar, I'm chapped
when no one eats them.
These details make it seem

like real life, this one spent
managing and wrangling
as much as mothering, writing
lists and e-mails instead of poems.
Home is where we stay safe
and warm, yet keep it hot
and ever wanting it
to be a beautiful story as well
as real and aware of pain,
a story where a little jumble's
okay but things should
aim to cohere as best they can
and with that modest goal
I try to attend to things
like drawer pulls. I don't
want it to fall off and get
lost forever. A couple twists
of the screwdriver and I can
feel how the slightly spongy
wood gives, compresses,
and now the knob is tight.
The dresser, however,
is on a bit of a slant, so
that drawer tends to fall
open on its own anyway.
Whenever I walk past it
I'm always pushing it
closed with my knee.

LETTER FROM WILLIAMSBURG
Kristin Dombek

*T*here are many kinds of prayer. There is a kind of prayer that's like breathing. There is a kind of prayer that's like talking to your best friend all day long. There is a kind of prayer in the face of beauty that lifts your hands up because it would be harder to keep them down. There is a kind of prayer for meaning that is answered by the one who wrote the book of the whole world and your life, so that the prayer is like waking up and finding yourself a character in the most elaborate of novels, as you've always suspected: authored, written into a world of meaning, a world meaningful because it was created by someone. There is a kind of prayer that is only a listening, the soft voice of God saying your name, saying "come to me, come to me." There is the prayer of failure, and the answering voice that forgives you. There is the death prayer, your whole body crying "why" and the voice again, telling you that you will see your loved one again in heaven.

And there is one more kind of prayer. In this one, you are tired of wrestling with God—with the problems of evil and suffering and the way that anyone who doesn't believe in him is going to hell. You're trying not to masturbate, or think about girls, or about having sex with multiple people at the same time, but you're masturbating and thinking about girls and about having sex with multiple people at the same time anyway. So you give up. You nearly stop believing. You don't even have the words to ask

God to come back, or be real; you slip down into the region below speech. And then he comes. He fills the bedroom with a presence that is unmistakably outside of you, the peace that passes understanding, a love that in its boundlessness feels different in kind from human love.

When God came into my teenage or college bedroom in that way, unasked and unmistakable, the next morning I would wake up changed. I'd go out into the world and give away everything I could. Wouldn't drive past a broken-down car without stopping to help, was kind and grateful even with my parents, couldn't stop singing, built houses for poor people, gave secret gifts to my friends, things like that. Sometimes it lasted for weeks; once, when I was in my early twenties, it lasted for nearly a year. It is called being on fire for God. It's like you've glimpsed the world's best secret: that love need not be scarce.

It has been fifteen years since I stopped believing, and I have been able to explain to myself almost everything about the faith I grew up in, but I have not been able to explain those experiences of a God so real he entered bedrooms of his own accord, lit them up with joy, and made people generous. For a long time it puzzled me why, if I made God up, I couldn't make up this feeling myself.

Like most women in Williamsburg, Brooklyn, I have spent thousands of hours and dollars on yoga classes attempting to manufacture unconditional love and moral bliss by detaching from my ego and my desires and also, not coincidentally, working on the quality of my ass. Because in the back of my mind, what I have been wondering (is this what the other women are wondering while we sit in lotus position on purple foam cubes, meditating in our jewel-toned leggings and tattoos?) is this: Isn't there some human who can make me feel this way, instead?

After I stopped believing in God, I would sometimes wake in a panic at being alone without supernatural support. So I memorized

Richard Wilbur's poem "Love Calls Us to the Things of This World," to say to myself in the morning. When I woke with someone in my bed, I would recite it to him or her:

> The eyes open to a cry of pulleys,
> And spirited from sleep, the astounded soul
> Hangs for a moment bodiless and simple
> As false dawn.
> > Outside the open window
> The morning air is all awash with angels.

Wilbur is talking about laundry dancing on a clothesline outside the window in the morning, white sheets and smocks that one mistakes for angels. It is because one wants to see the laundry as spiritual that "The soul shrinks // From all that it is about to remember, / From the punctual rape of every blessed day, / And cries, / 'Oh, let there be nothing on earth but laundry.' " Most people I recited the poem to found it a little melodramatic, but it calmed me down.

A few years ago I was living in a loft with a man and two cats and it started to happen again. In the morning, in the split second between sleep and waking, I would almost accidentally start to pray. I'd feel sunlight through the slits in the blinds, register that the alarm on my iPhone was going off, start hitting the bed and the windowsill and digging under myself to find it and tap its little snooze "button." There were cats on either side of my head, and my human husband, to the right, was snoring hairily on his back, his hands curling and uncurling on his chest like the paws of a tickled kitten. But despite how many of us there were in the bed, I felt alone and too small to survive, too permeable, too disorganized, and trapped in something I didn't have the words to describe. And something in me stretched up in a physical way toward the place where God used to be. I'd wake up and remember:

there is no God. But I wanted to give up anyway, as if in doing so I could be rescued.

There was a red armchair in the corner of the living room, and some days it was as far from the bed as I could get. The first few times I sat in the red chair it was just a comfortable place to think and cry. Then I would find myself in it for whole afternoons. I began to eye the chair, to tell myself not to sit in it. Then I'd tell myself I was just going to sit in it for a little bit. Then hours later the chair would still have me. The cats would sit a few feet from the chair and watch me warily—concerned, but mainly, I believed, judging me. One day when I left for work, I got only to the subway platform and turned back, and the second day, only to the street corner. I told the man about it, and the third day he walked me out and went down in the elevator with me and out the front door, but as soon as he was out of sight I snuck back upstairs to sit in the chair. I remember that for months I could not drive a car but I cannot remember why I could not drive a car.

I do remember the shape of the sentences that were running through my head while I was in the red chair, though not the words that were in them. They all went something like this: Is it this or that. Is it my job or my marriage. Is it my marriage or my mind. Is it him or is it me. It was him or me, him this or him that, and then always, But what if it's me this, me that. The sentences were all made of impossible twos. Knowing that the dilemmas did not make sense only made it worse; there was not even the smallest movement of my mind I could trust.

It took several years to get out of the red chair, and to do it I had to leave the loft, the man, and the cats, too. I moved into another loft and took very little furniture with me. Soon I met a man at the bar across the street. He was gentle with me but angry at the world's rules. He made what little money he needed by less-than-legal means, and owned only five short-sleeved T-shirts, four long-sleeved T-shirts, two pairs of jeans, and a pair of Converse with holes in the soles. We saw other people and talked all about it, which made for a rare kind of understanding between us. The first woman he and I slept with together was tall and thin with long, expensive black hair. When we laid her down on the floor of my new loft and undressed her, we found, tattooed across her abdomen, just above her neatly waxed pussy, the word *Freedom*.

I'd found Freedom on a South Williamsburg street corner at two in the morning, unlocking her bicycle from a lamppost. She was in a filmy white blouse over shorts and thigh-high stockings, and when I said hello, she started kissing me. I said would you like to meet my boyfriend; do you have a problem with facial hair. He was not really my boyfriend at the time but that's how it was clearer to talk in certain circumstances. She locked up her bicycle and walked inside the bar to meet him, and she didn't mind the beard. I said do you want to go home with us and she said yes. We walked up the six flights of factory stairs to my loft. We undressed one another and all ended up on the floor rather than on any comfortable piece of furniture. She and I were making out and he was kind of stroking his beard and watching us. And then he moved in and started eating her pussy, at which point she started saying these two sentences: "I want to steal you. I'm gonna steal you and take you home. I want to steal you. I'm gonna steal you and take you home." I was stroking her hair and kissing her neck and when she started saying that I said, "No, you're not gonna steal him, no you're not, just relax and let him make you come." And I held her so he could.

Actually, he didn't make Freedom come; I did. I reached inside her and did what I've only ever done before in secret, that is, away from the world of men, and he watched me. He'd never seen this, the way women can fuck each other; it is quite something to have a man who loves you watch you do it.

The next morning he and I ate egg-and-biscuit sandwiches, drank coffee, and went over the details of the previous night and morning. Then we talked about our childhoods, our dead parents, and other people we were seeing at the time. He was obsessed with a Mississippi girl who had trouble coming and I offered some strategies. I told him about something sad that had happened to a man I was seeing. We moved on to discussing which of our friends were fighting, or having problems with love or sex, or depressed.

This man had also spent time in a chair, in a dark room, staring at a wall. We tried to remember how it happens, the giving up: how the mind turns on itself and pinions the body to furniture and then convinces you that it is the furniture that has pinioned your mind. The furniture, or the girlfriend, or the husband, with their supernatural ability to cause your feelings. But it is so hard to remember the demonic logic of the place. For our friends we should remember, when they think they're stuck with sadness forever and we're trying to shine some small light on the way out. But mainly it is a blank, like women with babies say labor was.

At one point we stepped outside for cigarettes and were quiet for a moment. It was spring and a new sun was shifting light across the brick buildings on every corner of the intersection. The air felt kind and the neighborhood good, down under the Williamsburg Bridge, just across the river from Manhattan. But it was more than just a nice day: there was a peace immanent and tangible as a body, some kind of giant embrace in the air, and it was most definitely not coming from my mind. I didn't tell him about it or ask him if he felt it. Because I knew this presence, or I'd known it before. It was the one I'd been wondering about, and we'd made it ourselves, but it didn't belong to us, any more than we belonged to each other. Between us, on days like this one, there began to be a very strong sense, quite often, that anything might happen next, a feeling like the opposite of anxiety, the opposite of a panic attack, whatever you would call that.

The second woman who came home with us had only four sentences, but she said them over and over again. The first one was to me: "You're so beautiful. You're so beautiful." Eventually, she started kissing me. After a while, she broke away from me and said, "You guys are strange. You guys are strange." She was from another country, and the limited sentences were in part because of this, but it was also as if she were, in the very process of seducing us, passing back and forth between two worlds. When she was in one, she would forget about the other. I said, "Do you want to be here, what do you want?" And she looked at me, quiet, and then, with the ferocity of a small puppy, leaned in to kiss me again for a while, and began to undress me. Then she stopped and leaned back and said, "You guys are strange," and I said, "But, you decided to be here." This went on for a while. Later, in the middle of things, she started asking me, "Do you really like me or are you just doing this for him?" And I'd say, "I really like you." She'd suck his cock or I'd eat her pussy and then she'd turn to me and say, "Do you really like me or are you just doing this for him?" And I'd be like, "I really like you." And then, hours later, she started saying to me, "You're a boy. You're a boy. You're a boy." And I'd say, "No I'm not, sweetie." And he would say, "No she's not," and point out various parts of my body. "You've been all up in there." And she'd be quiet for a moment, and then say it again: "You're a boy." And I'd say, "No I'm not. I'm a girl."

I understand the trouble she was having very well. The first threesome I was in, before all this, I kept saying to the guy, over and over, "Your girlfriend is gay." I really did. The first time you feel yourself actually attracted to two people at the same time, in the same place, something very deep is shaken. You want to name the new thing, but you need new syntax to do it. Then you find yourself saying sentences like, "Just relax and let him make you come," or, "Don't be nervous, I can tell she really likes you, and I'll help you pick out a wine she'll love." The opposite of the red-chair and dark-room sentences. Sentences that in the speaking give you a feeling that is different in kind from ordinary human love, at least ordinary romantic love. If you try to find the word for this thing that is the opposite of jealousy, you end up at cheesy polyamory Web sites, where it is called *compersion*: when you feel happiness for another's happiness, even and especially when it doesn't involve you. Then your friends think you're delusional or stuck in the seventies, and you're basically relegated to having "your song" be George Michael's song "Freedom," which is why when we undressed the first woman who came home with us and found that word tattooed above her pussy, we looked at each other in wonder and a kind of fear.

A few months later, he moved in. The first time I laundered our clothes together I began to gather his underwear, and I didn't recognize it—it must have always come off in his pants, or we were usually drunk—and I thought, Who is this man. When I brought the clothes back from the laundrymat, as he calls it, hot and smelling of "meadow breeze," I put them on my bed and began to fold them, two black T-shirts, two navy T-shirts, one red T-shirt, two long-sleeved T-shirts, and two pairs of jeans, and I started sobbing and couldn't stop, as if doing a man's laundry was the most dangerous thing in the world.

The third woman we brought home had taken some care to lay the groundwork with each of us. With me she would talk about open relationships she'd been in, send me links to articles about unusual arrangements she'd heard of, talk to me about how much she understood. Him, she sexted. When we were together on my couch, there was a moment when she was sucking his cock with real enthusiasm and he was entirely absorbed, away from me, but I was stroking her hair and watching her and it would be the thing she talked about afterward, how much she felt I cared about her during that blowjob. There was a moment when I grabbed his hand and put his fingers inside of me and, for a while, it was just the two of us, together. There was another moment when he turned away and moved on top of her to fuck her and it was only them, but I was there. There is always a time when they turn away from you, together, and you panic, but if you can watch, just on the other side of the panic is a new kind of knowledge. We had come to think that this might be some part of why God forbade eating of the fruit of the tree of the knowledge of good and evil:

eat it and you can no longer believe that your happiness comes from him or me, God or me, him this or her that, or me this or me that. People who are good at monogamy must know these things already.

We have structured our most common sacred relations in twos, but we cannot explain the feeling of God without resorting to threes, or at least the religion I grew up in couldn't. God the Father made and ordered the world, watched and evaluated us from afar, and punished. He was, in fact, a trap; he loved you more than anyone ever could, but only if you only loved him and no one else. There was no place to hide from him, except in Jesus, who drew close, in the flesh, to talk about real love, fuck with the Father's rules, suffer to save us, and retreat to heaven, allowing us to figure out for ourselves what we wanted to do. And then the Holy Spirit, who did not judge and didn't seem to care about these sacrificial games, who just pitched a tent in the air around you and filled it with this wild joy. The one who watched, the one who did, the one who felt. The one with power, the one who suffered, the bliss.

A few months after I first did his laundry, he left in much the same way he'd come, without really asking. He left his clothes in a dirty pile on my bedroom floor. He'd found a girl he wanted to be with, without me, or I'd begun to feel like giving up, or it's hard to do what we were doing and live under one roof. It was his thirty-third year and he wandered through Brooklyn, sleeping and eating where he could, full of new love, and homeless.

People often ask me what it's like to believe in God so completely and then stop. It is like leaving someone you love, or falling in love: when living in one world becomes more difficult than the difficulty of leaving without knowing if the new world will be better, you leave.

I thought about it for years before I did it, but it happened all in a moment. I was sitting in my bed, in my basement room in my college house, and I thought, I have no idea if there's anything else that is true but this can't be true. I closed my eyes and kind of threw myself off a cliff into an empty space. When I opened my eyes, I saw my bookshelf and my rug and my cat and I saw that I had been right. There was a world outside the world I'd known. I have never been so relieved in all my life. And the first thing I wanted to do, but I did not do it, was pray.

OVER THE COUNTIES OF KINGS AND QUEENS CAME THE SECOND IDEA
Rowan Ricardo Phillips

After a long night swimming
In the dry dark of a book
I heard outside my window
A sound that changed my window.

Each of the planets unseen sang
As though in the grooves
Of a record I loved.
Saturn, Jupiter, Venus, Mars,

A scratch where the Earth
Where the Earth should be
Where the Earth should be
And is.

I stared out into the darkness
For some sign of the cold consoler,
That perched spinning
Night nurse who tends

To the sleeping sun
Destined to rise irresponsibly
Over the counties
Of Kings and Queens.

What are we during these
Archaic moments
Of mind-made Shangri-la
But bees trapped in amber,

Storyless and beheld,
By the amber god
Who makes it so
And the living god

Who undoes it?

FALSE SPRING
Ben Lerner

*B*efore I pressed the up button on the elevator, I saw my reflection in the shiny metal doors and said to myself, maybe even mouthed some of the words, Take the elevator back down and leave this building and never return; you don't have to do this. I had been worrying about this appointment for well over a month—ever since it had been scheduled—had worried about it so much and so vocally that Dr. Andrews had offered to medicate me; as I stepped out of the elevator, I patted the inside pocket of my coat to confirm the presence of the pill.

The receptionist I handed my form to was a young woman—she looked eighteen to me, though surely she was older—who could have been a swimsuit model or hired to dance in a club in the background of a music video. She was not unusually beautiful, but her proportions, visible through her black pantsuit even while seated, were consistent with normative male fantasy; I thought it was inappropriate to cast her in this role, whoever in human resources was doing the casting, but then felt as awkward about that thought as I did about automatically taking in the dimensions of her body. I found it difficult to meet her eyes and I tried not to blush as I handed her the credit card; my exorbitantly priced insurance didn't cover anything.

She gave me a second piece of paper to which she had stapled my receipt and told me to wait until I was called. I managed to look her in the eyes as I thanked her, but the knowledge in them was terrible, as if to say, Take a good look, pervert. When I sat down, I took the pill from my pocket and was about to ingest it, but then wondered—although it would be unlike Andrews to make this kind of mistake—if it might alter the sample. I was turning it over in my fingers when a nurse called my name and asked me to follow her.

She led me to a separate room and said on its threshold that the only thing I needed to remember was to wash my hands carefully and not to touch anything that could be potentially contaminating. She handed me a small plastic container labeled with my name and various numbers and repeated slowly, as though to a man-child, Make sure your hands are very clean, or you'll have to do it over, and then told me what to do with the container when I finished. She smiled at me without any embarrassment or awkwardness, a charity, and disappeared around the corner. I entered the room and shut the door behind me.

On the one hand, I was being medicalized, pathologized, broken into my parts, each granted a terrible autonomy; on the other hand, I felt trace amounts of what could only be described as excitement, reminiscent of the first time a classmate, Daniel, lent me, at age eleven, a pornographic magazine; the combination made me a little nauseated.

I hung my coat on the metal coat hanger and looked around me. In the middle of the room was something like a dentist's chair, peach-colored plastic upholstery and a strip of medical paper down its middle that the good nurse must replace between patrons, patients; I was not sitting in that chair. In front of the chair was a television with a DVD menu on the screen. Wireless headphones I resolved not to use were on top of the TV. Toward the back of the room was a sink with a dispenser of liquid soap and a little placard reminding me to wash my hands thoroughly. On the back wall was a contraption, vaguely reminiscent of one of those drive-through bank deposit boxes, where I could submit the container, transferring it to technicians on the other side of the wall, who could thereby receive it without our having to face one another. Bank,

medical office, pornographic theater—it was a supra-institution. It
took me a minute to realize I could hear voices through the wall,
make them out clearly: a woman was talking about her daughter's
boyfriend, how he was a keeper; a man was on the phone ordering
lunch in Spanish, something with white rice, black beans. If I could
hear them, surely they could hear whatever transpired in the room;
I resolved to use the headphones.

I went to the sink and washed my hands, then washed them
again. Then I walked to the chair, took the remote control from
the armrest, and started looking at the menu on the screen. The
TV was hooked up to some sort of service where you could select
from a huge number of movie titles organized alphabetically, but
also by ethnicity: *Asian Anal Adventures, Asian Oral Fetish, Asian
Persuasion*, etc.; *Black Anal Adventures, Black Blowjobs, Black
Cumshot Orgy*, etc., although after the ethnically specific menu,
you had the option of searching compilations by activity alone:
Best of whatever. I was surprised by the extremity of some of the
videos, and surprised to see them indexed racially; I guess I had
expected magazines. I was embarrassed to choose, but was not in
a position to deny that audiovisual assistance would aid expedi-
ency. I looked down at the remote control to see how it worked,
exactly, and then remembered: I'm not supposed to touch anything
that could contaminate the sample. What could be more contaminating than this remote control, which had been in how many sul-
lied hands?

After a few seconds of panicky deliberation, I just pressed
play—which started *Asian Anal Adventures*, even though that's not
at all my thing; *not* choosing seemed less objectionable somehow
than having to express a positive preference among the available
categories—and put the remote control and the plastic container
down and walked back to the sink and washed my hands. Then I
returned to the screen and undid my jeans and was about to try to
get the whole process going when I realized my pants were even
more potentially contaminating: I'd been on the subway for an hour;
I couldn't remember the last time I'd laundered the things. I shuffled

back to the sink with my pants and underwear around my ankles and began to worry about how long I was taking, if there was a time limit, if the nurse was going to knock on the door at some point and ask me how it was going or tell me it was the next patient's turn. I did the shuffle back to the screen and hurriedly donned the headphones, but then it occurred to me: contact with the headphones was no different than contact with the remote control. I thought about putting an end to this increasingly Beckettian drama and just trying to go on, but then I imagined getting the call that the sample wasn't usable, and so again shuffled—now wearing the headphones, now hearing the shrieks and groans of the adventurers—back to the sink to wash my hands once more. Above the sink there was mercifully no mirror.

Why, I wondered as I dispensed yet more soap, would my hands compromise the sample anyway? It's not like I'm going to be touching the actual sperm; surely I can just be careful not to introduce my hand in any deleterious way. At this point it was academic: I was finally in a position to proceed directly from cleansing my hands to deploying them—after basically hopping back to the console— onanistically.

It was time to perform, a performance about which I had more anxiety than any actual sexual encounter, which is why Andrews had given me Viagra, which, at that moment, I'd wished I'd taken. It was too late now; he said it could require hours to take effect and, besides, there was my fear, probably ridiculous, of some sort of chemical contamination. And wasn't it bad for people with cardiac conditions? Had he failed to think of that as well? Doesn't it induce vasodilation? I felt angry, like an angry old man. But rage at Andrews wasn't going to help my situation—his face wasn't the most efficacious mental image to be conjuring now.

I dreaded the prospect of abandoning the masturbatorium and having to tell the nurse, after twenty minutes of self-pollution, that I just couldn't do it, but that dread was of course nothing compared to telling Alex, my best friend. Alex had recently proposed impregnating herself with my sperm, not, she had been at immediate

pains to make clear, in copula, but rather through intrauterine in-
semination, because, as she'd put it, "fucking you would be bizarre." What would happen when I told her I'd failed to provide a
sample? I would either have to try again tomorrow, the pressure
doubled, or back out of the whole project, straining, if not ruining,
our friendship, or be forced to have them extract it through some
horrible procedure, assuming that's something they can do. For six
weeks I'd talked about my performance anxiety with Alena, a
woman I was seeing, and she'd laughed at me, assured me I'd be
fine. For several days before providing the sample, abstinence was
required; during that period, Alena, through a carefully calculated
configuration of double entendres and supposedly incidental contact and theatrical smoking, had tried to ensure that I was, as she
put it, "primed."

And, thankfully, I was: the whole thing was over with almost
comical speed, the brief experience dominated by the involuntary
afterimage of the young receptionist, as the receptionist had, I believed, foreseen. The relief was profound. I dressed and delivered
the sample to the other side of the wall and fled the institution as
quickly as possible.

Walking west with the destination of the park in mind, I tried
to imagine the process I'd begun: the lab would evaluate volume,
liquefaction time, count, morphology, motility, etc., and report
back to me about my viability as a donor. The fertility specialist
Alex had consulted had suggested we just skip this step, that, since
sperm was specially prepared for IUI, and since we had no particular reason to believe my sperm was abnormal, excepting the fact
that I'd never to my knowledge impregnated anyone despite high-
risk behavior, we should just proceed to IUI and see if it might be
successful. But I hadn't really decided if I was prepared to be a
donor or a father, especially since Alex and I were still trying to
figure out how much I'd be merely the former and how much I
would be the latter, and this test seemed like it might help the conversation, either by ending it (if my sperm were so dysfunctional
as to require male fertility treatments I wasn't willing to do, for

instance, or as to render IUI unbearably protracted—it only had around a 10 percent success rate in any particular instance to begin with, given Alex's age), or by demystifying some of the process. Trivial as it may sound, I had been so allergic to the idea of actually delivering the sperm that I thought forcing myself to go through the semen analysis would rob that dimension of the process of its psychological significance. I didn't want to say no to Alex just because I couldn't face the prospect of jacking off to porn in a medical office. While I tried to figure out if I thought completing the test had actually changed any part of my thinking, I was almost struck by a downtown bus at the intersection of Sixty-Eighth and Lexington.

Eventually I reached the park and walked into it only far enough to find a bench and sit down and watch the nannies, all of whom were black or brown, push around white kids in expensive strollers. I imagined trying to explain all of this to a future child, whom I pictured as Alex's second cousin: "Your mother and I loved each other, but not in the way that makes a baby, so we went to a place where they took part of me and then put it in part of her and that made you." That sounded okay. I pictured myself beside her bed, stroking her brown hair. "Really," I would explain, "everyone gets help making a baby, it's never just a mom and dad, because everybody depends on everybody else. Just think of this apartment where we are now," I'd say—although I probably wouldn't live in the same apartment as the child—"where did the wood come from and the nails and the paint? Who planted the trees and cut them down and shipped the wood and built the apartment, who paid for those things and how did the workers learn their skills, and where did the money come from, and so on?" I could have that conversation, I assured myself, as I watched a Boston terrier (originally bred for hunting rats in garment factories, only later bred for companionship) tree a squirrel: I'll narrate our mode of reproduction as a version of "it takes a village." But then my voice went on speaking to the child without my permission: "So your dad watched a video of young women whose families hailed from the world's most populous continent get sodomized for money and emptied his sperm into a cup he paid a bunch of people to wash and shoot into your mom through a tube."

"Wasn't the tube cold," I heard in Alex's niece's voice, a six-year-old we'd babysat together more than once.

"You'd have to ask her."

"Why didn't you two just make love?"

"Because that would have been bizarre."

"Can IUI be used for gender selection?" Now she sounded like a child actress.

"Sperm can be washed or spun to increase the odds of having male or female offspring, but we didn't do that, sweetie; we wanted it to be a surprise."

"How much does IUI typically cost?"

"Great question." Alex had recently been laid off. "According to the rate sheet, and because they recommended some injectable medications for your mom, and because we did some ultrasounds and blood work, probably five thousand a pop." I regretted saying, even though I hadn't said anything, "a pop."

"What was the annual per capita gross national income of China at the time of ejaculation?"

"4,940 U.S. dollars, but I think that's an unreliable measure of quality of life and I'd dispute the relevance of the fact, Camila." I had always liked the name Camila.

"What if you have to do IVF to make me?"

"That's more like ten thousand."

"Average annual cost of a baby in New York?"

"Between twenty and thirty thousand a year for the first two years, but we're going to live lightly."

"After that?"

"I don't know. Ask your phone." A teenager had sat down on the bench beside me and was texting; I absorbed her into the hypothetical interrogation.

"How are you going to pay for all of this?" she asked me.

"With a book advance. You're overfocused on the money, Rose."
It was my maternal grandmother's name.

"Is that why you've shifted from a modernist valorization of difficulty as a mode of resistance to the market to the fantasy of coeval readership?"

"Art has to offer something other than stylized despair."

"Are you projecting your artistic ambition onto me?"

"So what if I am?"

"Why didn't Mom just adopt?"

"Ask your mother. I guess because that's equally or more ethically complicated most of the time and because, independent of culturally specific pressures, some women experience a biological demand."

"Why reproduce if you believe the world is ending?"

"Because the world is always ending for each of us and if one begins to withdraw from the possibilities of experience, then no one would take any of the risks involved with love. And love has to be harnessed by the political. Ultimately what's ending is a mode."

"Can you imagine the world if and when I'm twenty? Thirty? Forty?"

I could not. I hoped my sperm was useless.

"Cutting and other modes of self-harm and parasuicidal behavior are endemic in my age group." I pictured the teenager pulling up her sleeve, showing me the red crosshatching.

"You're misusing *endemic*."

"The average cost for a month of inpatient treatment is thirty thousand dollars." This observation was in Andrews's voice.

"She will be surrounded by love and support."

"How will you work out your level of involvement so that neither I nor Mom resent you for it?" The teen.

"As we go along."

The conversation didn't stop so much as recede beneath the threshold of perceptibility. Maybe to distance myself from the morning's anxiety, I removed the blue pill from the inside pocket of my coat and tried to crush it, which I couldn't do, but with two hands I succeeded in breaking it in half. I absentmindedly tossed the halves onto the sidewalk in front of me, at which point a nearby pigeon approached it, no doubt accustomed to being fed by tourists from this bench. What is the effect of sildenafil citrate on stout-bodied passerines? I stood and tried to shoo the bird away; it startled, but then turned back and quickly ate a half before I managed to intervene.

Two days after providing a sample of my reproductive cells for analysis, I was in the basement of the Park Slope Food Coop bagging the dried flesh of a tropical stone fruit, trying not to listen to one of my louder coworkers as she explained her decision to pull her first-grader out of a local public school and, despite the cost and the elaborate application process, place him in a well-known private one.

The Park Slope Food Coop is the oldest and largest active food cooperative in the country, as they tell you at orientation. Every able-bodied adult member works at the coop for two hours and forty-five minutes every four weeks. In exchange, you get to shop at a store with less of a markup than a normal supermarket; prices are kept down because labor is contributed by members; nobody is extracting profit. Most of the goods are environmentally friendly, at least comparatively, and, whenever possible, locally sourced. Alex had been a member when I moved to Brooklyn and it wasn't too far from my apartment, so I'd joined. Despite being frequently suspended for missing shifts while traveling, and despite complaining all the while about the self-righteousness of its members, its organizational idiocy, and the length of its checkout lines, I'd remained a member. Indeed, for most of the members I knew, except Alex, who rarely complained about anything ("you do my complaining for me"), insulting the coop was a mode of participation in its culture. Complaining indicated you weren't foolish enough to believe that belonging to the coop made you meaningfully less of a node in a capitalist network, that you understood the coop's population was largely made up of gentrifiers of one sort or another, and so on. If you acknowledged to a nonmember that you were part of the coop, you then hurried to distinguish yourself from the zealots who, while probably holding investments in Monsanto or Archer Daniels in their 401(k)s, looked down with a mixture of pity and rage at those who'd shop at Union Market or Key Food. Worse: the *New York Times* had run an exposé about certain members sending their nannies to do their shifts, although the accuracy of the reporting was disputed. The woman now holding forth about her child's schooling was almost certainly a zealot.

And yet, although I insulted it constantly, and although my cooking was at best inept, I didn't think the coop was morally trivial. I liked having the money I spent on food and household goods go to an institution that made labor shared and visible and that you could usually trust to carry products that weren't the issue of openly evil conglomerates. The produce was largely free of poison. The coop helped run a soup kitchen. When a homeless shelter in the neighborhood burned down, "we"—at orientation they taught you to deploy the first-person plural while talking about the coop—donated the money to rebuild it.

I worked in what was known as "food processing" on every fourth Thursday night: in the basement of the coop, I, along with the other members of my "squad," bagged and weighed and priced dry goods and olives; we cut and wrapped and priced a variety of cheeses, although I tended to avoid the cheese, as it required some minimum of skill. In general the work was simple: The boxes of bulk food were organized on shelves in the basement. If dried mangoes were needed upstairs, you found the ten-pound box, opened it with a box cutter, and portioned the fruit into small plastic bags you then tied and weighed on a scale that printed the individual labels. Then you took the food upstairs and restocked the shelves on the shopping floor. You were required to wear an apron and a bandanna in addition to your plastic gloves. Open-toe shoes were prohibited, but I'd never owned a pair of open-toe shoes. For better or for worse, most people were sociable and voluble, like the woman talking now—this seemed to make the shift go faster for my comrades; for me, the talk often slowed time down.

"It just wasn't the right learning environment for Joseph. The teachers really tried and we believe in public education, but a lot of the other kids were just out of control."

The man working on bagging chamomile tea immediately beside her felt obliged to say, "Right."

"Obviously it's not the kids' fault. A lot of them are coming from homes—" The woman who was helping me bag mangoes, Noor, with whom I was friendly, tensed up a little in expectation of an offensive predicate.

"—well, they're drinking soda and eating junk food all the time. Of course they can't concentrate."

"Right," the man said, maybe relieved her sentence hadn't taken a turn for the worse.

"They're on some kind of chemical high. Their food is full of who knows what hormones. They can't be expected to learn or respect other kids who are trying to learn."

"Sure."

It was the kind of exchange, although *exchange* isn't really the word, with which I'd grown familiar, a new biopolitical vocabulary for expressing racial and class anxiety: instead of claiming brown and black people were biologically inferior, you claimed they were— for reasons you sympathized with, reasons that weren't really their fault—compromised by the food and drink they ingested; all those artificial dyes had darkened them on the inside. Your child, who had never so much as sipped a high-fructose carbonated beverage containing phosphoric acid and E150d, was a more sensitive instrument: purer, smarter, free of violence. This way of thinking allowed baby boomers in particular to deploy the vocabularies of sixties radicalism—ecological awareness, anticorporate agitation, etc.—in order to justify the reproduction of social inequality. It allowed you to redescribe caring for your own genetic material—feeding Joseph the latest in coagulated soy juice—as altruism: it's not just good for Joseph, it's good for the planet. But from those who, out of ignorance or desperation, have allowed their children's digestive tracks to know deep-fried, mechanically processed chicken, those who happen to be, in Brooklyn, disproportionately black and Latino, Joseph must be protected at whatever cost.

Noor interrupted my reverie of disdain: "Remind me, do you have kids?"

"No." Noor was bagging the mangoes. I was tying, weighing, and labeling the bags.

"I couldn't," she said, "deal with navigating New York schools."

How would Alex, or Alex and I, deal with it, if we reproduced? If I had enough money for private school, was I sure I wouldn't be tempted? I was eager to change the subject. "Did you eat junk food growing up?"

"Never in the house, but with my friends—all the time."

"What did you eat at home?" Noor was from Boston and was in graduate school now, I'd learned on our previous shift.

"Lebanese food. My dad did all the cooking."

"He was from Lebanon?"

"Beirut. Left during the civil war."

"And your mom?" I realized I'd been labeling the mangoes incorrectly, had entered the wrong code into the electric scale. I had to do them over.

"She was from Boston. Secular Jew. I guess my family on that side is Russian, but I never knew those grandparents."

"My girlfriend's mom is Lebanese," I said for some reason, perhaps to distance myself mentally from Alex and the topic of fertilization. Alena's mother was also from Beirut, but who knew if Alena was my girlfriend. "Do you still have a lot of family in Lebanon?"

She paused. "It's a long story. I have kind of a complicated family."

"We have more than two hours," I exclaimed with mock desperation, but then, because Noor looked upset, or at least grave, I moved on quickly: "Nobody in my family could cook, so we—" But then she did begin to speak, both of us keeping our eyes on

our work. She spoke quietly enough that we wouldn't be overheard by the others, who were now discussing the merits of Quaker
pedagogy.

My dad died three years ago from a heart attack and his family is largely still in Beirut, Noor said, although not in these words.
I've always thought of myself as connected to them, even though I
barely saw them growing up. My dad had a really strong sense of
Lebanese identity and I did, too. They tried to raise me bilingually
and I did learn a fair amount of Arabic as a little girl and then took
lessons at a mosque and then studied it in college pretty intensely,
am basically fluent now. My dad was a very secular Muslim, as
much a Marxist as anything else, and one of his parents had been
Christian, but in the U.S., maybe as a kind of reaction against all
the racism and ignorance, he decided to join a mosque in Boston,
but it was really more of a cultural center than a mosque. I grew up
going there a lot and developed a sense of difference from most of
my classmates, and in high school and then in college I was active
in Middle Eastern political causes and majored in Middle Eastern
studies at BU. I spent a couple of summers traveling in the Muslim
world—that's when I got to know Beirut and that part of the family. I was really involved in the BU Arab Students Association, although that could be complicated sometimes because my mom
was a Jewish American, even if not at all religious, and it was tense
with my mom because she always felt I was only interested in my
dad's history, had kind of identified with him at her expense. My
mom and I always had problems. Anyway, about six months after
my dad died, my mom started dating—*dating* was the word she
used—another guy, an old friend of hers named Stephen, some
kind of physicist at MIT, whom I'd always known a little because
we'd played with his kids occasionally when we were younger; he'd
since been divorced. My mom told my brother and me at dinner
one night, said she knew it was going to be hard for us, but hoped
we'd understand. We said we understood, although we were both
weirded out, and my brother in particular was furious it was so
soon, although I think he only expressed his fury to me.

I wasn't living at home, Noor said, I was a senior in college and lived with friends, so I didn't see Stephen very much, but my brother said Stephen was coming around all the time, and they were always going out together, and my brother and I both were pretty upset at the speed and we were both suspicious—how could we not be—that their romance had a history, that it must have started when my dad was still alive, although I tried to tell my brother it was probably just a way of dealing with her grief, that it probably wasn't serious, but every time I talked to my mom she seemed to be with Stephen. Well, about a year after my dad died I was planning to go to Egypt for three months because I'd been offered this fellowship at the American University in Cairo for recent Arab American graduates, and I was also planning to visit Lebanon, and a few days before my flight my mom called me and asked if I could meet her for lunch, and it was immediately obvious to me from her tone on the phone that she was going to tell me she was remarrying—I knew it right away—and I knew she wanted to tell me in a public place because she thought it might temper my initial reaction, and then she would ask that I help her tell my brother, who was going to freak. I was surprised that I wasn't angry, maybe in part because my parents had so clearly been estranged in the last years of their marriage, but I felt sad and a little sick and we met at some overpriced French place in the Back Bay that was to neither of our tastes.

At this point in Noor's story, a voice came over the PA asking if dried mangoes were out of stock—"are *we* out of dried mangoes"—or could somebody from food processing bring some up. This was unavoidably my job, no matter how reluctant I was to interrupt her narrative. I told Noor I would be right back, made a kind of pouch out of my apron that I filled with some of the small, labeled bags, and took them upstairs. As always, I was embarrassed to emerge into the semipublic space of the shopping floor with a bandanna in my hair and sporting a pastel apron. The aisles were mobbed—the coop had fifteen thousand active members and a shopping area of six thousand square feet, not to mention a checkout system of radical, willful inefficiency—and I had to fight my way to the bulk section where I deposited the mangoes. I didn't get cell-phone service in the basement, and now my phone vibrated in my back pocket, indicating I'd received a text, a one-word query from Alex: "results?"

Back in the basement I saw another member had usurped my place beside Noor; he must have finished whatever he was bagging and then taken over my job. I was usually quiet and passive in the coop, however critical my internal monologue, but this time I said, Excuse me, but I'd like to have my job back so I can continue my conversation with Noor. He said sure without a trace of resentment, and I resumed tying, labeling, weighing. The problem was that my butting in had drawn a few other members' attention, and Noor wasn't going to resume her story if they were listening. We worked in silence, which communicated to others that we knew they were listening, which further piqued their interest. An excruciating ten minutes passed in which Noor was quiet and I imagined possible conclusions to her story: Stephen turned out to be a virulent Islamophobe, and/or he worked for the FBI and tried to use her to infiltrate the BU Arab Student Association, or maybe the Lebanese part of her family had cut everybody off over rage that her mom had remarried.

When our coworkers had finally struck up their own conversations and forgotten about us, Noor picked up her narrative without my having to ask: So there we were at this French restaurant. As soon as the waiter had taken our order, Noor said to me, I said to my mom, You're going to marry Stephen, aren't you, and she laughed nervously and said that Stephen and she had in fact discussed marriage, that maybe that could happen someday, but that wasn't why she had asked me to lunch, at which point I assumed with a kind of numb terror that she was going to tell me she had cancer or something. But instead she said to me, Noor, your father and I made a decision when you were a baby and I've always wondered if it was the right decision. Your father was sure and insisted that we had an agreement, but since he's died I've been thinking it over and now I feel that we were wrong. Your father, my mom said to me, Noor said, although not exactly in these words, was not your biological father. I got pregnant by another man but your father and I were in love and he wanted a child and so we got married, deciding that we would raise you as our child and that's what we did, and your father, as you know, loved you tremendously and thought of you as his own child always. There had been so much turmoil and cutoff and exile in his family I just think we wanted you not to have any sense of not fully being our child or not fully being in your home. We had a lot of fights when you were in elementary school because I regretted not telling you, but at that point his position was that it was too late no matter if we had initially been wrong, because you would feel betrayed and confused and it would be psychologically damaging. We consulted a therapist who agreed with him. But in the last year I have been thinking about this constantly, Noor's mother said to her, and thinking about my own mortality, and I just feel I have to tell you, however disturbing this news might be. I also have been in therapy with someone who has helped me understand that telling you this is important for our own relationship. What I want to be clear about is that your father loved you as much as a father could love a daughter and whatever decision we made we made, rightly or wrongly, out of a sense of what would be best for you. She'd clearly memorized, Noor said to me, the last part of her speech.

"Jesus," I said.

It gets crazier, Noor said, smiling. A waiter put a salad in front of me and I remember staring into the salad trying to take in what my mom had said as she waited for me to respond. I remember we were both sitting there in silence not eating, waiting for my response to form. I felt like I was bracing for some impact because I simply couldn't feel anything, and then my mom went on: Noor, she said, now more quietly, I imagine your first question is going to be who your biological father is—which actually was not my first question, Noor said to me—and part of why I wanted to tell you all of this, part of why it felt absolutely necessary, and part of why I've been so involved again, I think, with Stephen—

"Jesus," I repeated. I was working as slowly as possible so as not to let finishing the mangoes interrupt the story again. Noor slowed down the rhythm of her work along with me, which led to her slowing down the story.

Right, Noor said to me. It's because, my mom said, Stephen is your real dad, and then corrected herself: your biological father. I had dated him before I met your father and although it was clear to both of us that our relationship, at least our romantic relationship, wasn't going to last, and even though we were being careful, I got pregnant and your father, I mean Nawaf—Nawaf was the name of the man I considered my father, Noor said to me, and it was horrible to hear my mom say his name, since she'd always said "your father" or "dad"—Nawaf wanted a child badly, Noor's mother said to her, and we were falling in love and so we decided to get married and have a family. We told Stephen our decision and Stephen at that point in his life didn't want anything to do with a child but he said he would respect our decision and that he wouldn't ever say anything. And Stephen, as you know, eventually had his own family. It's funny, Noor said to me, I still didn't feel anything; I put my hands on the table on either side of my plate and I remember waiting and waiting for the impact and the only thing that happened is my hands seemed to fade.

"Fade?"

"I mean they started to pale," Noor said, raising her gloved hands from her work as if to show me. "I had always thought of my skin as dark because my father's skin was dark, because I took after him, because I was Arab, and as I sat there looking at my hands, without feeling anything, it was like I could see my skin whitening a little, felt color draining from my body, which it probably was, because I was in shock, but I mean I started seeing my own body differently, starting with my hands."

"What did you say to your mom?" I asked. Noor was olive-skinned. Did she look different to me now than earlier in our shift?

"I said," Noor said, "that I had to go to the bathroom and just walked right out of the restaurant. It was kind of funny," Noor laughed, "that I told her I had to go to the bathroom, since she could just see me walk right out of the front door, it wasn't like she thought I was coming back. Anyway," Noor's tone shifted a little, indicating she was going to draw her story to a close, "you had asked me about my family in Lebanon—it's complicated now because I don't know if I can call them my family exactly."

"Do they know the story?" I asked.

"Not unless my dad told them, which I can't imagine him doing. My mom doesn't think so."

"Did you see them when you were living in Cairo?"

"I didn't end up going anywhere. I spiraled into a big depression and when I climbed back out of it, I applied to grad school and moved here."

"Do you"—I wasn't sure how to put the question—"do you still consider yourself Arab American?"

"When I'm asked, I say that my adoptive father was Lebanese. Which I guess is true. I still believe all the things that I believed, it hasn't changed my sense of any of the causes. But my right to care about the causes, my right to have this name and speak the language and cook the food and sing the songs and be part of the struggles or whatever—all of that has changed, is still in the process of changing, whether or not it should. Like, somebody wanted me to give a talk at Zuccotti Park about Occupy's relation to the Arab Spring and I didn't feel qualified, so I said no. There are a lot of people I haven't been able to bring myself to tell because, even if they don't want to, they'll treat me differently."

"I can't imagine what any of this must have felt like, must feel like," I said. I wanted to say that it's not the sperm donor that matters, that the real father is whoever loved and raised her, but before I could figure out how to articulate my position tactfully, I was distracted by a vision of Alex in the future, falling in love with

someone, maybe moving out of the city with "our" child. Would I
be thought of as the biological father, just a donor, not at all?

Since she'd fallen quiet, and I felt I should fill the silence, I
opted to say something about the connection between storytelling
and manual labor, how the latter facilitates the former, the work
creating a shared perceptual pattern, but the way she nodded indicated she'd ignored me.

"A lot of the time I still feel like I'm waiting for the impact,
feel the same way I felt at the restaurant. My mom and Stephen
live together now, by the way. They didn't marry. We're all trying
to work things out. What I would say is that it's a little like—have
you ever kept talking to somebody on your cell phone not realizing the call was dropped, gone on and on and then felt a little
embarrassed?"

I said that I had.

"I have a friend who was really wronged by his older brother
but had never confronted him about it. The details don't matter.
But one day he got the courage to do it, to confront him on the
phone. He'd been building up the courage for years. And he called
his brother up and he said, I just want you to listen. I don't want
you to say a word, just listen. And his brother said okay. And my
friend said what it had taken him such a long time to say, was walking back and forth in his apartment and saying what had to be said,
tears streaming down his face. But then when he finished talking,
only when he finished talking, he realized his brother wasn't there,
that the call had been lost. He called his brother back in a panic
and he said, How much of that did you hear, and his brother said, I
just heard you say you wanted me to listen and then we got
disconnected. And my friend for whatever reason just couldn't do it
again, just couldn't repeat what he had said. My friend told me this
and told me that now he felt even more confused, more alone, because he'd had this intense experience of finally confronting his
brother, and that experience changed him a little—it was a major
event in his life, but it never really happened: he never did confront
his brother because of patchy cell-phone service. It happened but it

didn't happen. It's not nothing but it never occurred. Do you know what I mean? That's kind of what it felt like," Noor said, "except instead of a phone call it was my whole life up until that point that had happened but never occurred."

Although I felt Noor had been speaking for hours, only forty-five minutes of our shift had passed. As we were finishing the last of the mangoes, someone came from checkout and asked if anybody had ever worked at the register; one of the cashiers had had to go home early and they needed another person. Noor said she had done checkout before and discarded her gloves and bandanna and apron and, after smiling good-bye to me, went upstairs. I spent the rest of the shift bagging dates and trying not to look at the clock.

When my shift was over I left the coop, buying a couple of dis-alienated bags of mango first, and, since it was unseasonably warm, decided to take a long walk. I walked on Union Street through Park Slope and my neighborhood of Boerum Hill and through Cobble Hill and beyond the BQE until I reached Columbia Street, a walk of a couple miles. I turned right on Columbia—the water was on my left—and walked until it became Furman and then continued a mile or so until I could descend into Brooklyn Bridge Park, which, except for a few joggers and a homeless man collecting cans in a shopping cart, was entirely empty. I found a bench and looked at the magnificent bridge's necklace lights in the sky and reflected in the water and imagined a future surge crashing over the iron guard-rail. I thought I could smell the light, syrupy scent of cottonwoods blooming prematurely, confused by a warmth too early in the year even to be described as a false spring, but that might have been a mild olfactory hallucination triggered by memory. Across the wa-ter, a helicopter was carefully lowering itself into the downtown heliport by South Street, a slow strobe on its tail.

I breathed in the night air that was or was not laced with anachronistic blossoms and felt the small thrill I always felt to a lesser or greater degree when I looked at Manhattan's skyline and the innumerable illuminated windows and the liquid sapphire and ruby of traffic on the FDR Drive and the present absence of the towers. It was a thrill that only built space produced in me, never the natural world, and only when there was an incommensurability of scale—the human dimension of the windows tiny from such distance combining but not dissolving into the larger architecture of the skyline that was the expression, the material signature, of a collective person who didn't yet exist, a still uninhabited second-person plural to whom all the arts, even in their most intimate registers, were nevertheless addressed. Only an urban experience of the sublime was available to me because only then was the greatness beyond calculation the intuition of community. Bundled debt, trace amounts of antidepressants in the municipal water, the vast arterial network of traffic, changing weather patterns of increasing severity—whenever I looked at Lower Manhattan from Whitman's side of the river I resolved to be one of the artists who momentarily transformed bad forms of collectivity into negative figures of its possibility, a proprioceptive flicker in advance of the communal body. What I felt when I tried to take in the skyline—and instead was taken in by it—was a fullness indistinguishable from being emptied, my personality dissolving into a personhood so abstract that every atom belonging to me as good belonged to Noor, the fiction of the world recalibrating itself around her. If there had been a way to say it without it sounding like presumptuous coop nonsense, I would have wanted to tell her that discovering you are not identical with yourself, even in the most disturbing and painful way, still contains the glimmer, however refracted, of the world to come, where everything is the same but a little different because the past will be citable in all of its moments, including those that from our present present happened but never occurred. You might have seen me sitting there on the bench that midnight, my hair matted down from the bandanna, eating an irresponsible quantity of unsulfured mango, and having, as I projected myself into the future, a mild lacrimal event.

A PLACE AS GOOD AS ANY
Jana Prikryl

Outside the funeral of the politician who died young
I waited for you. Rolled in my hand like a baton

were tissues from the mourners inside
that I was meant to throw away,

a few with your scribbled notes to me.
How they'd found me in that crowd I couldn't say,

or if the bottle blonde was your wife
or whether I had a husband.

We sat near enough to barter
knives and forks—the scraps of dinner theater.

The blonde was climbing into your lap,
playing with the buttons on your jacket.

Then all of us rose and circulated, more like a whirlpool
than musical chairs. You on the far side of the banquet.

That's when you wrote me those notes, one by one,
congealing into typescript in my hand.

At times I looked toward your place
and we locked eyes like opponents in chess.

Your hair was still so thick and dark
I didn't worry if I looked older.

When I waited for you outside, clutching the tissues
and pulling up tufts of grass, your friend's shoulder

presented itself. He said you lived in this town
and couldn't be spotted leaving with me.

I nodded, ducking back into the paneled saloon
where he'd blacked out and was sprawled on linoleum.

He agreed to drive me to the film festival.
You'd be there in the dark with strange women and men,

absorbed in pictures more honest than these
if I ever found you again.

WILLIAM WEI
Amie Barrodale

I once brought a girl home because I liked her shoes. That was the only thing I noticed about her. I live in a really small apartment. A lot of my clothes end up piled on my mattress or draped over the open door of the microwave. I guess the girl with the pink high heels woke up in the middle of the night and didn't remember where she was. She went out naked in the hall and closed the door behind her. She said that she had asked me, and I told her that was the way to the bathroom, to go out the front door. I don't remember doing that. I remember I woke up with the cops in my house, asking me if I knew this girl. I said of course, she was the girl with the pink high heels. They thought that was really funny. After that, I didn't drink for about five months. I was mostly celibate, except for my upstairs neighbor, until she moved away. She was this Indian girl. She liked to do it from behind, in this one position. That was the only thing she wanted to do. The other things were boring, she said. When I went to the shower, she got up on all fours to masturbate.

I was alone for a while after that. I got rid of everything in my apartment. I worked ten- and twelve-hour days. Each night, I went to hot yoga. They had a studio between my home and work, on the fifteenth floor of this building, so that, across from you, while you were sweating, you could look in at people living their lives, and see all these slow-moving domestic scenes, like a man standing in front of a microwave. After yoga, I liked to walk home. I liked the cold. I bought a Mediterranean style salad from the same place every night. The woman who worked there was Lebanese and studying to be a doctor. I ate my dinner in front of the TV, watching *Sans Soleil.*

It was a weeknight around ten P.M. the first time she called. I let it go to voice mail, because I wasn't expecting any call, but when I went to get the message, it was just quiet for a while, and then the person hung up. At that time, I slept on an army-style cot. I ate on it, too, lying down with the food under my face, in the posture of a dog. This was the posture I was in several days later, the fourth time she called, and I answered.

"Who's this?" I asked. She said, "It's Koko." "Koko? I don't know any Koko." "I saw you at a party; it was a long time ago." "Oh, so I gave you my number?" "No, I got it from one of your friends." "I don't understand." "He told me your name is William." "Who was he?" "I can't tell you that. He said I couldn't tell you that. He said he was only telling me because he's worried, you don't go out anymore. He said you just lie around watching the same movie and eating the same food." "That's a lie," I said. She said, "He said you do hot yoga." "I don't even know what that is," I said, "hold on." I reached out an arm and put the movie on pause. I put the container of salad under my cot and propped myself up on my elbows. "What do you look like, anyway? Maybe I remember seeing you."

"I'm about forty-eight years old."

"No," I flipped over onto my back and put an arm over my eyes, "I can tell from your voice you're younger."

"I'm attached to a breathing machine."

"Okay, fine—don't tell me, look, I've got to go."

"What do you mean?"

"Just that kind of joke—I mean, everybody says stuff like that. Why can't you just tell me what you look like?"

"Okay," she said. She sounded shy now. She thought around and said, "I guess I'm normal looking."

"What's normal?"

"I'm twenty-five. I have my hair cut into bangs."

"Uh-huh."

"I don't want to say any more than that."

It was weird, because I looked at pornography pretty frequently at this point. It was even a problem, so that I would spend an hour looking for the most disgusting pictures I could find. Maybe disgusting is not the word. For example, I liked a short video where an older man was fucking a girl in the ass while he put a Blow Pop inside her. Then he stopped and put it into her ass. Then he put it into her mouth, and he started to fuck her again. But somehow this conversation...

We talked for a long time, more than an hour, until I got sleepy, so I started to fall asleep with her on the phone. The next night, around the same time, she called me again. I was really happy she did that. We had a nice conversation. She told me this story, how she used to prank call a math teacher of hers in junior high. She did it so much, she figured out how to reprogram his outgoing message, using his two-digit remote-access code. She redid his outgoing greetings, said things that were explicitly sexual. Her teacher didn't understand technology or remote-access codes. He assumed someone was breaking into his house each day to rerecord his message. It filled him with fear and paranoia. He bought a dog. He had an alarm installed and got a prescription for sleeping pills. It was a long time—nearly a year—before the police identified Koko and got to the bottom of the mystery. I loved that. I have stories like that, too. I told her the thing I did to my video teacher at an arts festival, and the things I used to say to my science teacher and to the owner of this antique store called J. & B. Lowther. I said, "Why don't you come over here right now?" and she told me she lived five hours away by train.

She had a business selling old clothing on the Internet. She was a night owl. She stayed up until sunrise pretty frequently, working on her business. All the clothes had to be cleaned, pressed, tried on, photographed, and entered into her Web site. By this time I had seen a lot of photos of her body. She used herself as a model, and the way she did it was very artistic. I'm not just saying that because I cared about her; I worked with major fashion houses, so I know what I'm saying. She really was artistic about how she did it, even though she always chopped her own head off. She made it look exciting and interior, like she was a party of one. In fact, she had a lot of admirers on the Internet. It wasn't just gross men; it was women in fashion, too. That's how it happened we were at the same party.

"What party was it?" I asked. "I don't think there was any party."

"They had set up a small stage on the roof, with that carpet rubber as a stage. That foam stuff they put under carpets."

"I remember that. That was a terrible party."

"You looked really drunk."

"I think I was really sad; I wish you had come and talked to me."

"You were talking to some other girls. You were always talking to lots of girls. I didn't think you'd want to talk to me."

"I'm sure I wanted to."

I knew that she drank, and most nights she was talking to me, she was drunk and taking pills, but I didn't think anything about it. She never slurred, or got sloppy, but she did seem sometimes to check out. It was like her heart would go dead. It was one time when she was like this that she told me she had had other romances on the telephone. I said I didn't care about that. She said, "You don't understand; I'm a sociopath."

"What's that mean?"

"Hold on."

She was gone for a while, and when she came back, she said, "All I mean is, what if when you see me, you think I'm ugly?"

"I'm not going to think you're ugly."

"You've never even seen my face. I could be completely deformed."

"I don't care," I said. "I'd love you even if you were deformed."

I guess that was a mistake. After I said it, she got really quiet.

Then she said something weird. She said, "All my life, I've been looking for my man. I think I finally found you." I think that was the moment, for both of us, when we realized it wouldn't happen. It was the next day, I think, that she started to tell me something about her mother being sick, but I could tell she didn't want to talk about it. Besides, I had already bought a ticket.

On the train, I kept telling myself to just be myself. I had a prescription for a low-milligram antianxiety medication, as well as a mild beta-blocker, and I kept going into the bathroom to take more—I wanted to get the mixture right. After I took a pill, I'd check myself in the mirror, and I'd always be surprised at what I found. I kept expecting to find a monster.

At the station I checked my phone, and she'd left me this message where she just said my whole name, William Wei. She sounded completely freaked out. I knew her pretty well by this time. I could tell from how she sounded, it took everything in her not to run.

She was waiting across the street from the terminal. Just standing there, in front of her old car. She had on a green army coat and paint-splattered corduroy pants; her features were something like I pictured—wide eyes, Frida Kahlo—but she was more beautiful than I expected her to be.

When I got over to her car, before I could say anything, she said, "Are you nervous?"

"Are you?"

"We'll go to my house and relax."

In the car ride, she kept switching the tapes in her tape deck, and peering at me while she did it. I could tell she didn't like what she was seeing, but I didn't know what to do. I thought she had already seen me. I thought I was the one who was permitted to feel some disappointment.

She lived on the top floor of a converted flour mill. The sleeping area was the size of an ordinary bedroom, divided from the main area by ten-foot industrial shelves full of record albums—the inventory from her brother's store. He was itinerant and sometimes wrote to her, asking her to sell so many feet of albums. Her bed was a queen-size mattress on the floor. She pointed to the rotary phone beside it and lifted her cat to introduce him by name. Then she led me through the center portion of the loft, past a sliding-glass door that connected to another apartment, a place rented to someone named Douglas. He was gone for the weekend, and so I didn't think much about him.

I don't think I will describe her kitchen or her work area, except a photo on the fridge. It was of an old man in a top hat and tails. She told me that was Douglas. I was about to tell her a story that the photo reminded me of when she handed me a piece of banana bread, a glass of milk, and two pills.

"What're these?" I said.

"My mom sent them to me earlier in the week. Something about her bowels."

"What?"

"She can't have opiates."

"They're opium?"

"Percocet."

I ate the pills and broke the bread into pieces. What I wanted was for the two of us to go and sit by the window and listen to record albums and get soulful, but Koko turned on the TV and flipped through the stations until she found a documentary. When that was over, she got a couple more pills for us, and found a medley on a different station. We got take-out from a delivery service, and around eleven, her hair had fallen down, and her cheek was resting on her hand so the top of her head just touched my shoulder. I still have the shirt I was wearing at that time. It's hanging in my closet. I turned on my side to look at her body, and she pretended to keep watching TV.

I said, "I like your shoes."

"Those?" she lifted her head and turned to look at her feet. "Those are ballet slippers."

"I like how you are wearing them as shoes."

"Everyone does that."

"Everyone docs what?"

She shook her head lightly from side to side.

"Everyone does what?" I said.

"I travel business class," she pointed a finger in the air. "Un momento, por favor. Muchas gracias, señor."

She was singing along with the television, but I stopped her before the next line. I mean I kissed her. It was a bit like kissing a doll, or a timid old lady. I mean that she didn't kiss me back, but I don't know if you know this. That can be very attractive. Later, Koko and I were together in haze, and her shirt was off, and she told me how she often induced men to love her and then abandoned them. She said, "Didn't you notice how I forced this on you?" I said, "I don't know what you mean," and she said, "Yeah. That's what I'm telling you."

So that was where it ended. Or really, it ended in the car, the first time we looked at each other. I mean, she thought I was ugly, and I could see that. But the thing about a dark truth is it is indistinguishable from doubt. And so—since I couldn't just go home—I kept approaching the dark area. Not by anything I said, but by what I did, and by watching how she reacted. She was nice at times, but at others, when her kindness drew me in, she was sharp, and I spent the weekend confused. I kept thinking, "But she already saw my face."

The next morning I was buttoning my shirt in the mirror when Koko opened her eyes. She yawned and smiled at my reflection and said, "You have a nice face." Then she pushed herself up onto all fours and shifted her butt in the air. She rested her cheek sideways on her folded arms and said, "We should go and eat eggs."

I wonder why I didn't say anything to her then. Like, "Why are you putting your butt in the air?" I guess it was because I didn't know what was going on. I had gotten clammed up, by the stuff the night before. I was shaky from the pills.

The restaurant was walking distance away. It was one of those local-ingredients places. It had polished stone floors, and the polish was so high that when the hostess led us into the dining room, I thought there was a step up, but there wasn't one. It was just a trick of the light.

"What're you doing?" Koko said.

"I thought it was a step."

"You were like," she galloped one leg in imitation.

Everything I did made her angry. After we had our omelets, she pointed to a place between two of her teeth and said, "What's that thing there?" I have a large filling between two of my teeth about where she was pointing, so I told her that—"It's a filling"—and she said, "I can see it when you talk."

We went for a walk around the neighborhood. It was starting to feel like spring. We crossed into a residential area. On the sidewalk, one leashed dog was meeting another dog, and he got so excited he lost his footing and fell down on his side. An old suburban house was up for sale, and we let ourselves into its backyard to have a look around. One of its windows had been broken from the inside, and the pane lay in four pieces in the soil of a flower bed. I brushed my hand against Koko's, and she whipped her head around and said, "Do you want to take mushrooms?"

"What?"

"I have ten."

They were mixed into chocolates. They had been given to her by a friend, a photographer for *Playboy*. She said that several times, *Playboy*. She ate two chocolates and I ate one, and then we split a fourth. We got into her bed, and when I opened my eyes an hour later, the world was brilliant, alien, and unformed, and Koko was talking on the phone in the voice of a transistor radio.

"I'm fucked up," she said. "I'm on mushrooms. I'm on drugs."

"Yes, he's here since Friday."

"No, I don't think so. No. Not anything like that. Hold on," she pushed the phone aside and said, "I'm talking to Douglas."

I was really confused, so I went to get some air. I stood up out of the bed and went to look out the window. I stuck my head out and looked down at the alley, where a homeless man was digging through the garbage for glass bottles. I was really messed up, so I couldn't remember what to do. I was trying to remember if it was proper to throw money down at him. Somehow, I knew it wasn't right, but I couldn't figure out why, so I leaned back into the apartment and went to find my wallet. I looked for it out in the front room, and then I remembered where I left it. Yes, I was thinking, it definitely was what you did: you threw the money down. That was when I realized that Koko had put the phone down, and she was crying. She had been explaining, for how long I am not sure, that her mother had cancer. She told me that her mother had cancer of the bowels. I tried to console her; I sat beside her and put an arm around her shoulders. She let me hold her for a second, and then she stood up, and in a moment, she had her keys, and a door slammed, and she was gone. The cat was doing a little dance with its claws, that dance that's somehow associated with cat sex, and I was alone on her bed. It wasn't until recently I realized that whole thing about her mother was a lie. Besides, when I was consoling her, I wasn't really consoling her at all.

Anyway, it was a long time before she came back. The sorts of things I thought during that time, while I sat there, I can never really say. It was heavy. I think that's what people say—it was a bad trip; it was heavy. I think I can safely say it changed my life.

MARCH OF THE HANGED MEN
Monica Youn

1.

hyperarticulated giant black ants endlessly boiling out of a
heaped-up hole in the sand

2.

such a flow of any other thing would mean abundance but
these ants replay a tape-loop vision

3.

out of hell the reflexive the implacable the unreasoning rage
whose only end is in destruction

4.

the way the dead-eyed Christ in Piero's *Resurrection* will
march right over the sleeping soldiers

5.

without pausing or lowering his gaze for he has no regard
now for human weakness

6.

since that part of him boiled entirely away leaving only those
jointed automatic limbs

7.

that will march forward until those bare immortal feet have
pounded a path through the earth

8.

back down to hell because there is no stopping point for what
is infinite what cannot be destroyed

FOLEY'S POND
Peter Orner

Nate Zamost took that week off school. We wondered what he did those long days other than the funeral, which didn't take more than a few hours. The Zamosts lived in one of those houses just across the fence from Foley's Pond. Nate's sister, Barbara—they called her Babs—slid under the chain-link and waddled down to the water. This was in 1983. She was two and a half.

The day Nate came back to school, we refrained from playing Kill the Guy with the Ball at recess. We stood around in a ragged circle on the edge of the basketball court and spoke to each other in polite murmurs. We were a group of guys in junior high who hung out together. It wasn't like we weren't capable of understanding. Some of us even had sisters. But instinctively we seemed to get it that our role was not to understand or even to console but, in the spirit of funerals, to act. So we stood there and looked at our shoes and kicked at loose asphalt. Nate went along with it. He played chief mourner by nodding his head slowly. I remember Stu Rothstein finally trying to say something.

"Look, it's not like it's your fault," Stu said. "I mean how could you have known she knew how to slide under the fence?"

Nate looked up from his shoes.

"I taught her."

What could anybody say to that? Stu took a stab. He'd always been decent like that.

"Well, it's not like you told her to do it when you weren't looking."

"I didn't?"

Stu didn't say anything after that. Nobody else did, either. We let Nate's question hang there, and to this day I don't know whether he meant it or whether, out of grief, he was assuming even more guilt than he needed to. Like Stu Rothstein, Nate Zamost was a gentle guy. During Kill the Guy with the Ball, he never went for your head; he'd always go for your ankles and take you down easy. It was the rest of us who were more interested in blood than the ball itself. But who's to say what goes on behind closed doors, between siblings? Nate, like all of us, was thirteen that year. His parents went out for a couple of hours and left him in charge of his little sister.

Remembering it all now, what comes to me most vividly is my private anger toward Nate. Foley's Pond had always been a secret place and now everybody in town knew all about it. It was wedged inside a small patch of woods, between where Bob-O-Link Avenue ended and the public golf course began. The pond was said to have been created by runoff from the golf course, that it was nothing but a cesspool of chemicals. Proof of this theory was embodied by the large, corrugated drainpipe that hung out over the edge of the pond. Whatever it was that flowed from it didn't look like water. Once, Ross Berger dove into Foley's and came up with green hair and leeches on his thighs. Someone shouted, "The sludge supports life!" We all jumped in. It was like swimming in crude oil. A fantastic place, Foley's—scragged, infested, overgrown, and gloomed long before Nate Zamost's sister wrecked it. How many mob hits, feet tied to bricks, bobbed and swayed at the bottom of that fetid swamp? All the missing kids in Chicago, milk-carton phantom faces, all, all were dumped into Foley's.

After school we'd go down there and talk down the waterlogged afternoons. There is something overripe about spring in the Midwest, the wet and green world, the ground itself rotten, oozing, dripping. Foley's was protected by a canopy of trees. The sun only crept through in speckles. There was nothing beautiful about that pond, even in April, except that it was ours. Foley's in the rain, the rain smacking the leaves, how hidden we were, talking and talking and talking about God only knows what. Had we been a little older we may have drunk beers or smoked dope or brought girls so they could scream about not wanting to go anywhere near that disgusting water. We were thirteen and conspiratorial and what was said is now out of reach, as it should be.

It took them eleven hours to find her. Foley's was a lot deeper than anybody had thought. The fire department's charts turned out to be inaccurate. Police divers had to come up from Chicago. And something else that by now most people may have forgotten and newcomers would have no way of knowing. When they laid Babs on the grass in the dark, Nate Zamost's mother refused to acknowledge that the mottle of bloated flesh lit up by high-powered flashlights was her daughter, anybody's daughter. Mrs. Zamost didn't know Foley's. Ross Berger was down there twelve seconds, and he came up looking like an alien. She wouldn't even touch it. I was there, just outside the ring of lights. Mrs. Zamost didn't scream, just shook her head, and stepped backward into the dark.

Foley's is a real park now. The Park District manicured it. The trees have been trimmed. There's a wide, wood-chip path off Bob-O-Link that leads right to it. And they've installed tall bird feeders, long poles topped with small yellow houses.

THE DIFFERENCE
Ishion Hutchinson

They talk oil in heavy jackets and plaid over
their coffee, they talk Texas and the north cold,

but mostly oil and Obama, voices dipping
vexed and then they talk Egypt failing,

Greek broken and it takes cash for France not
charity and I rather speak Russia than Ukraine

one says in rubles, than whatever, whatever
the trouble, because there is sea and gold,

a tunnel, wherever right now, an-anyhow-Belarus,
oh, I will show you something, conspiring

coins, this one, China, and they marvel,
their minds hatched crosses, a frontier

zeroed not by voyage or pipeline nor the milk
foam of God, no, not the gutsy weather they talk

frizzled, the abomination worsening
opulence to squalor, never the inverse.

MARION
Emma Cline

....

*C*ars the color of melons and tangerines sizzled in cul-de-sac driveways. Dogs lay belly-up and heaving in the shade. It was cooler in the hills, where Marion's family lived. Everyone who stayed at their ranch was some relative, Marion said, blood or otherwise, and she called everyone brother or sister.

The main house jutted up from the ranchland, as serene and solitary as a ship, crusted with delicate Victorian detailing that gathered dirt in its cornices and spirals. The first owner had been a date heiress, Marion told me, adored and indulged, and her girlish fancies were evident in the oval windows that opened inward, the drained pond that had once been thick with water lilies and exotic fish. Palm fronds fell crisped from the trees that flanked the house's exterior. All the landscaping was now like an afterimage, long grown over but visible in the heights of grass, in the lines of trees that extended a path to the front door, bordered by white plaster columns.

We spent most of our time in the airy rooms of the main house. We watched the babies there, cradled them and sang, dangled glass beads on strings over their damp faces. We put together whatever puzzles were around, baroque castles or glossy kittens in baskets, starting over as soon as we had finished. I found a book on massage, with foldout graphs of pressure points, and we practiced: Marion lying on her stomach, her shirt pushed up, me straddling her and moving my hands across her back in firm circles, my palms slick and yellowed with oil. Marion had just turned thirteen. I was eleven.

My mother was going through a phase then, having night sweats and blackouts. She paid people to touch her: her naturopath, who placed warm fingers on her neck, her breast; the Chinese acupuncturist, who scraped her naked body with a plane of polished wood. I ended up at Marion's for weeks at a time, my clothes mixed in with hers, her half brother stealing small bills from me, her father, Bobby, kissing Marion and me good night square on the mouth.

One afternoon, we sat on the front steps of the main house, sharing a root beer and watching her father dig pits in the yard. Later, he would line them with leaves and fill them with apples.

"I need cigarettes," Marion moaned, passing me the bottle. I sipped the root beer with adult weariness. "Let's ask Jack for some," she said, not looking at me. Jack was Bobby's friend, visiting from Portland. He was rangy, the pale hairs on his arms neon against his tanned skin. He had been staying in the barn with his girlfriend Grady, who wore long skirts and ribbons around her ponytail. At dinner, when Grady lifted her arms to retie her bow, I saw dark hair under her arms and averted my eyes.

"It's not like it's a big deal. He'll share," Marion said, pinching a thread from the hem of her cutoffs. Marion was wearing her shorts over her favorite bright orange bikini, nubby fabric stretched tight across her breasts, her shoulders shining from sunscreen. I was wearing a swimsuit top, too, borrowed from Marion, and all day I had felt an anxious thrill from the strange feeling of air on my chest and my stomach. Marion raised her eyebrows at me when I didn't answer. "We're wearing these 'cause it's hot, okay? Don't worry so much."

Marion knew she was something pretty in that suit. Men stared at her, and she liked it. When Jack first came for dinner at the ranch, he would follow Marion with his eyes when she got up from the table. That day, when Jack watched Marion in the barn as he rolled a cigarette for her, I felt a flint of heat in my insides. When he glanced at me, I turned and hunched my shoulders, trying to relieve the strain of my breasts against the borrowed fabric. I never went out in that swimsuit again.

None of us knew then that bark beetles were tunneling in the trees, laying millions of eggs that would wipe out millions of trees. Bobby was warning of an attack so great that the United States would fold in on itself like a fist. It was the men's job to protect the women. Everyone who lived at the ranch was storing things, freezing food in huge, unbelievable quantities and clearing brush out of old Indian caves and caching water there in jugs. Bobby wanted to build a stone tower, forty feet high and circular, on top of a hill where the energy was paramagnetic and auspicious. They circled the site with silk flags and burning oils before they started construction. Marion and I watched from the hillside, slapping the mosquitoes on our legs. He was storing arms, Bobby said, for the wars, and we never quite knew if he was joking or not. Marion rolled her eyes at him all the time, but swallowed the foul-tasting Coptis tincture he gave us each morning for regular bowel movements and thick hair. "Like a pony's," he said, and twisted Marion's braid around his wrist.

Her family staked their marijuana plants on south-facing hillsides and planted them with sage and basil. They told their friends they had thirty plants, but they had five times that many, hidden all over the ranch. They sold to a dispensary in Los Angeles, and sometimes, if my mother was away for the weekend on an extreme juice fast, Marion and I were allowed to drive down with Bobby when he dropped it off. Marion's mother, Dinah, taught us to use a vacuum sealer on the plastic around the dope.

"Put on gloves," Dinah said, tossing me an old gardening pair. "If you guys get pulled over they'll sniff your fingernails for resin."

We triple-bagged the weed and packed it into backpacks. Dinah put the backpacks into big duffel bags and covered them with beach towels, swimsuits, folding chairs, and a crate of overripe pears to hide whatever smell was left. Marion and I piled into the backseat, holding hands, our bare thighs sticking and skidding on the leather seats. We drove along the winding coastal roads, through shantytowns and orchards that drooped in the heat, past dry hills and that distant purple ridge, the cows standing motionless in the middle of a field.

I had been down south before, but my mother and I had driven on I-5, not the back roads. My mother would never have stopped at the rock shop, where Bobby let us each buy a piece of agate, or the date farm, where an old man made the three of us milkshakes. They were thick and I sucked at the straw until my mouth ached. Marion finished hers first, then rattled the straw around in her empty cup. She rolled down the window, got my attention, and let the cup tip and fall out of the car. When I looked back, the cup was bouncing silently into the weeds.

"Hey," Bobby said, turning half around in his seat. He swatted at Marion, but she swung her legs out of reach. "Don't do that," he said. I was smiling, like Marion, but when Bobby's voice rose, I stopped. "Don't toss shit out of the car when it's full of pot," he bellowed, slapping his hand toward Marion. His hand glanced off her bare thigh and I saw it redden. "You wanna get us pulled over for something stupid?" he said, turning back to the road.

"God," Marion cried, rubbing her leg. "That hurt."

Bobby wiped his hands on the steering wheel. He glanced back at me in the rearview and I looked away.

"They just love to get you for stupid shit like that."

I smiled when Marion looked at me. She wrinkled up her face, jokey again, but I saw her grip her agate.

I held my own agate up to the light of the car window. It was smooth, a pale blue, banded with delicate threads of white. The woman at the rock shop said it was for grace, for flight. "Good for protection," she said, when I brought it to the counter. "Blue lace agate can help you call on angels. Also heal eczema, you know, if you get dry skin."

The agate Marion picked out wasn't smooth. It was jagged and bright. Flame agate, the woman called it. "See?" she said, lifting it, turning it in her fingers. "Looks like a coal, huh? Like a hot coal."

"What's it gonna do for me?" Marion asked, reaching out to touch it.

"Well, it's good for night vision," the woman said. "Addiction, too, but you're young for that. You know what?" she said, looking at Marion. "It's just a good earth stone. For power."

"They're all like that," Marion said. "All-protective, all-powerful, blah." She grinned at the woman. "Are there any bad stones?" she said. "Like, that give you weakness or stupidness or something?"

"Yeah, or cancer," I ventured, rewarded by Marion's quick snort.

The woman shook her head. She looked at me as if she was disappointed, and I looked away. The woman handed Marion and me little silk pouches. "Don't leave them in direct sunlight," she'd said as we left. "Drains their power."

When we stopped to get gas, I watched Bobby at the pump, pulling uncomfortably at his waistband. I realized that it was one of the first times I'd seen him wearing clothes that looked like what other adults wore: instead of his jeans he wore with no shirt, now he was dressed in athletic pants made of a shiny material, and borrowed sneakers. He stood stiffly, arms crossed over the sports logo on his T-shirt.

In the backseat Marion was tossing her agate from palm to palm. "Sorry Dad yelled," she said. "It's just tense. The drive."

"It's fine," I said. "Really. I don't care."

"He can be a jerk." Marion shrugged, and concentrated hard on catching the agate.

"Yeah."

Marion stopped. "He's really great, too," she said, narrowing her eyes. "He's a really great father," she said. We both looked up:

Bobby snapped the wipers out of the way and started dragging a squeegee wetly on the windshield. Through the water and soap, the road beyond was blurry and far-off.

"I don't think he's a jerk." I lowered my voice. Bobby was bunching up paper towels. "I would never think that."

We heard the high squeak of glass. Bobby had scraped the last of the water away, and the world outside the car was clear again: the clapboard of the small convenience store, the propane tanks, the highway, near and empty and without end.

Bobby dropped the weed off at a Japanese temple in Burbank. While the men did business, Marion and I flicked murky water at each other and watched the goldfish in the driveway fountain gape and flash in the sun.

"There are no rules," Jack said, back at the ranch. He showed us anything we wanted in the barn, let us pick up mouse bones, old tops. Potted garlands of bulbed plants, sweet succulents we pierced with our fingernails.

"Don't feel like you have to ask to touch anything," he said. He let us look through pulpy books with black-and-white photographs of dead bodies, of bloody sheets.

"Oof. That's Manson," he said, twirling his fingers. "I knew Beau before he hooked up with them. He wrote poems. Sweet, bad poems."

From Jack we learned about runes, about the Ku Klux Klan. About Roman Polanski. That men who wore rings on their thumbs were liars. When Jack excused himself to the outhouse, Marion rummaged through Grady's underwear in the bureau.

"Don't look through her stuff," I said. I liked Grady.

"He said we could touch anything," Marion said. "Whoa," she crowed, holding up a pair of black lace underwear. She stuck her fingers through a slit in the crotch and wriggled them. "Crotchless panties," she laughed, and flung them at me.

"Gross," I said. When I tossed the underwear back to Marion,

I saw her shove them deep into her back pocket. She looked at me, daring me to say something, then moved on to the *Playboys*, turning each page, discussing the women.

"This one's real skinny, but her tits are big. Like me. Men love that."

Another page, a tawny woman with an Indian cast to her face. Then the cartoons, somehow more lurid than the photographs: the bursting shirts and rounded rears, the unzipped fly.

A thirteen-year-old girl. We talked about that a lot, what the girl might have looked like, how Roman Polanski knew her, how it had happened. Did she have breasts? Did she have her period yet? We were jealous, imagining a boyfriend who wanted you so bad he broke the law. We were drifting through whole weeks, making bonfires at night, eating twenty popsicles in a row and burying the flimsy plastic wrappers all over the yard. We made a game of hiding the wrappers—rolling them into balls and wedging them in the crotches of trees, folding them into the pages of Jack's old almanacs and religious encyclopedias. We sat in the back of Bobby's pickup as he drove the gridded vineyards and released wrappers from our clenched fists like birds.

Marion was my first real friend. I never had the framed photos that girls like to give each other. I had never worn friendship bracelets, or even hated anyone else with another girl. My life seemed like something new and unasked for, Marion smiling at me in the sunshine, letting me wear her woven ankle bracelet for days at a time, braiding my hair that had grown colorless and thick, full of dust and the peculiar smell of heat. Bobby walked around wearing a sarong low on his hips, and sometimes naked, the skin on his penis mottled and pale, and so none of the other girls in the seventh-grade class were allowed to visit, but Marion liked it like that. She pierced my ears one night with a needle, holding a piece of cold, white apple behind my lobe, and there was hardly any blood at all. She helped me trace the outline of my face in lipstick on the bathroom mirror, so we could determine my face shape (heart) and the most flattering haircut (bangs, which she cut with Dinah's nail scissors). Her hot breath, blowing the small cut hairs out of my eyes.

We spent more and more time at the barn. Marion said that it didn't make sense to wait until a trip to town for cigarettes, or mentholated pastilles, when Jack would give us both for free. Marion would stare at him while he typed at his desk, on a computer he ran with extension cords to the main house, and we passed whole afternoons looking through his shelves, murmuring among ourselves, sitting Indian-style on the floor. Marion smiled at him with an intensity that made her look almost cruel. I tried to smile that same way.

Marion leaned up against his desk and told him about the boy who had a seizure and shat himself at the community pool. "The mommies got all the kids out of the water real quick after that," she said, and waited for Jack to laugh.

Marion had told me to watch him and tell her later if I thought he liked her. So I hung back, fingering the rows of books and geodes, spooning cold tomato soup into my mouth from a mug. I took note when Jack looked at the door or at Marion's slim thighs in cutoffs.

Marion started volunteering to deliver messages from Grady in the kitchen to Jack in the barn, or ice-cream sandwiches in the peak hours of heat. I wondered if he could feel us watching him.

I never told Marion about the time I saw Grady and Jack naked, stretched out side by side on a picnic table in the yard. "We're charging ourselves," Grady laughed, her eyes closed. "By moonlight." Dark hair spread across her thighs and up her stomach like a sleeping animal. Jack smiled lazily, his hand on her.

Marion borrowed Dinah's old Kodamatic and took me up into the hills, where she stripped and had me take pictures of her naked body laid out on rocks. "You'll be good at this, I know it," she said. She tied a red ribbon around her throat like she had seen on one of the girls in *Playboy*. She closed her eyes, opened her mouth, and put her fingers on her flushed chest. I thought she looked really great, but she also looked dead. When we pulled the film out of the camera, letting it dry in the sun, some faint blue shadows spread on her chest and throat.

Marion tucked the photos into a box with a twenty-dollar bill, and she cut off a piece of her hair to put in there too, tied with the red ribbon. She said that was what Jack would want, that she could tell he was courtly and would understand the significance of it. She said her father had told her how hair and teeth had tightly wound cellular structures that held power. A tooth would be better, she said, and she opened her jaw wide and let me look inside her pink mouth. She pointed at a tooth on the top row, said it was loose anyway and that she'd been working on it, tonguing it to make it even looser, pressing it as hard as she could stand with her fingers. It would be out soon, she said, and she would give it to Jack and he would know for sure.

We daubed vitamin E oil in swaths under our eyes, so that a pale glossy light caught and shone there. We looked like bright-eyed lemurs in the bathroom mirror.

"We're staying away for a few days," Marion said, looking at herself, running a finger around her lips, across the swell of them. I knew she was thinking how beautiful the curve of her mouth was, because I was thinking it, too. "You keep men on their toes. You make them miss you."

We planned our return to the barn: what bras we would wear, what we would say. Marion had written Jack's name on her body, on the bottoms of her feet, where the ink slid into the whorls. I saw it all when we changed for bed.

The women were drying branches of lemon verbena and sage on tin sheets all over the yard, and a puppy Jack had dragged home from town kept nosing the sheets over. Marion was reading *Ar-*

chie's Double Digest with her back against a rock wall, and I was pressing tiny sequins onto my nails with glue. The day was hot and I kept dropping the silver disks into the dirt. Marion picked a scab on her upper arm, put it in her mouth, chewed it for a while, then spat it out.

"That's disgusting."

"You're disgusting," she said, turning the page. "Fuck, they don't do anything but buy hot dogs and keep girls away from Archie."

The heat of the day lay on the grass like a blanket. I tried to get the puppy's attention, but some kids were tugging at it.

"Who do you think is prettier?" Marion asked, looking thoughtfully at her comic.

"Betty. I don't know. She's nicer."

"She looks too old. She dresses like your mother. Which do you think Jack would like?"

"Both," I said. I had a sequin poised over my nail but was watching Marion to see if she'd laugh. She stood up suddenly.

"Let's take photos today," she said. "I need to get them in the box."

We pedaled the old bicycles, bouncing roughly over gravel and ruts in the path. I carried the camera on my shoulder. Marion stood up on her pedals, her legs tan, flexing. We coasted to the lake, the water thrumming with dots of flies, scrims of algae ringing the banks.

"Let's make these good," Marion said, briskly.

"You should do whatever and I'll take the picture."

"No," she said, breaking up a clot of weeds with a stick and looking back at the main house. "You should be in them today."

I took off my clothes and folded them neatly on the bank. Marion put my hands on top of my head, and pulled strands of hair down in my eyes. She wedged a finger delicately between my teeth to show me how far to keep them parted.

"You look good," Marion said, her face hidden by the camera. She was taking pictures from far away, squatting in the dirt.

"You look young, really great."

Then she came close with the camera, so close she touched the lens to the tip of my nipple, then cackled and collapsed on the grass.

"It's hard," she gasped.

I started to step into my cutoffs, but Marion leapt up and came toward me. She threw her arms around my neck, loose like a child, and kissed me with her eyes open. "It's okay," she said. "Pretend I'm Jack. Look sleepy. Look sexy. Try to look like I do." We were breathing hard. "Get my tooth out," she said.

She pointed to the jagged-edged thing in her mouth that moved when she touched it.

"Do it with your hands," she urged.

Marion was smiling. Both of us were, like idiots. I tried but couldn't get a grip. Marion drew my fingers farther into her mouth. I was delirious. She picked up a rock and put it in my hands.

"Do it," she slurred, then took my fingers out of her mouth. Her hand was shaking. "Just hit it once, hard."

I looked at her; the witchy colors of twilight on her face, her eyes gone filmy and blank. Her mouth gaped, blood already threading out from the tooth.

"Just do it," she breathed.

I lifted the rock and gave a tap. "Wait," she said, recoiling. She took a deep breath. She opened her mouth, then, so I could hook my fingers on her jaw. I tapped the tooth again. "Nnnh," she said, but I hit harder and felt it give. The blood made a sudden sheet of red down Marion's chin. She just stood there, stunned, cupping her mouth with her hands and looking at me with something I would later identify as hatred.

By the time I was dressed, Marion was pedaling away.

When I got back to the house, she wasn't there. The puppy shuffled its nose against my foot. Bobby walked past with sheets of gray felt in his arms.

I knew enough not to look for her. I went instead to the main house, to the kitchen, where it was cool and dim and they had the radio playing. Dinah was cooking and Grady was milking a whitish liquid from plant stalks, pulsing her fingers along the stems. They were both flushed and generous, touching me affectionately as they passed. Grady motioned for me to come sit by her.

"You and Marion should be rubbing this on your faces twice a day," she told me. "You'll never get wrinkles, ever."

I smiled at them both, beaming when Grady applied the plant liquid in gentle, thorough circles under my eyes, around my mouth, between my brows. Dinah picked through beans, shuffled the wizened ones to the side, finding the hidden rot, while I sat at the counter and cut up some tomatoes from the garden. They had sunscald, their skin tight, and underneath was the hum of warm weight. I broke them open and the seeds dripped out over my hands.

Marion never showed up for dinner. I drifted off by myself, napping in the trundle bed I shared with her, in my underpants under the coolness of her sheets. I woke blinking and startled in the evening light. Dinah was downstairs, calling my name.

When I went into the kitchen to find her, Dinah cornered me. She grabbed me by the arm and pulled me toward her.

"Marion said you kissed her. She said you hit her." She was crying and shaking. I thought of the woman sorting the beans, the sun in her hair, and how different she looked now.

"Marion showed me her mouth. You stupid little girl."

Grady came in behind Dinah, and turned on the kitchen lights—the sudden illumination was worse, somehow, than the dark. Grady looked upset. I tried moving my shoulders but Dinah held them tight.

"You think this is normal?"

She shook a picture of Marion at me, the one of her with a ribbon around her throat and her legs spread open. I covered my mouth with my hands, but Dinah had seen me smile. She shoved her face hard against mine, so her mouth was in my hair. "I know," she said, into my ear. "Don't think I don't know who this was for."

Grady hefted my denim backpack into the bed of the pickup and bent down next to me in the passenger seat. "Don't worry," she said, but her voice was strained. "Just give it a few days. It'll be fine."

Dinah came out of the house, one of Bobby's old sweaters wrapped around her. She and Grady talked to Bobby while I sat with my head back against the seat, looking out at the yellow grasses. The fields were hazy with buckwheat and it was almost fall again. How had we missed the buckwheat? How had we not seen the smear of it in the hills?

"Just tell her mama we need a break for a while," Dinah said. "Just say we're going through some family stuff."

"Her mother's never around."

"Just say, I don't know, something. I don't care," Dinah said.

I saw Dinah stalk off in the side mirror, and Bobby got into the truck and started it without saying anything. I watched the lights of the main house recede behind us, the barn rising darkly against the sky, then disappearing. My face was wet and I was hiccupping, but I didn't feel like I was crying. I couldn't tell why my forehead was wet, too, my ears, where the water was coming from. Bobby was breathing hard, looking straight ahead as we drove the bumpy ranch roads.

"Marion's a stupid girl. You can't fuck around with teeth. She's too old. It won't grow back. I know what she was doing, and it doesn't work if you have a rotten heart. They're connected to your brain, too, your teeth, how you process pain, how you remember. Feel your teeth, how far up in your head they go?"

I ran my tongue across my gums.

"All calcium," he said.

He put his hand on my back and rubbed my bare skin up and down.

"And this, what you have here—we all used to be fish. Your spine's what's left of those aquatic skeletons."

I closed my eyes, imagining horrible fish swimming through murky, primordial waters. He told me then how the symbols were gathering around him, how it had to do with me coming into their lives, with the dreams he had of the floors of his childhood home covered with white figs, with the number of times he had found a dead deer on the ranch. His bees were disappearing, entire colonies collapsing for no reason. He found them in piles, their furred legs covered with dust and pollen. He could feel it, he said, a thrumming in the trees and all around, could feel that things were falling apart from the inside. Tonight confirmed it. He told me I shouldn't worry, that I was a light-holder and that things would be fine and that I would have to stay away for a little while. Marion would call me soon, he said. We could be friends again, but I knew it wasn't true.

"You're a sweet girl," he said, his hand on my shoulder. "You're better than all of them."

SMALLTOWN LIFT
Brian Blanchfield

One last stop, he says. And they drive to Westside Lanes.
I grew up bowling. I don't want to bowl. It was raining.
We're not going to bowl, the circus carpet dark with gum
beneath them, and he parts the curtains on the best
photo booth in town. He feeds it the three dollars, Get
in. They somehow share the short ridged stool. In here
we have to tell each other one true thing. *You first.* Click.
This is the best way I could think to have my arm around you.
Click. Click. Click.

VIRGIN
April Ayers Lawson

J ake hadn't meant to stare at her breasts, but there they were,
absurdly beautiful, almost glowing above the plunging neck-
line of the faded blue dress. He'd read the press releases, of course.
He recalled, from an article, her description of nursing her last
child only six months before her first radiation treatment. Then
he noticed she wasn't wearing a bra.

What did they have inside them: saline or silicone? And how
did these feel, respectively? He probably stared too long. (But how
could she expect people not to stare when she wore a dress cut
like that?)

She'd noticed.

Had his wife noticed? Doubtful. She noticed so little about
him these days.

"This is some place you have here," he said too quickly.

Though they weren't exactly friends, she'd come into his office
before, with her little girl, and they'd talked about her plans to spon-
sor a mobile mammography unit. They'd formed a connection, it
had seemed to him then, and their time together lingered taut as a
problem in his mind. But now she'd definitely seen him staring at her
breasts, about which she must have had extraordinarily complicated
feelings, and she was annoyed.

"What does that mean exactly?"

"I just meant you have a nice home," Jake replied.

"It's too big, isn't it?"

He didn't know how to reply: the house, miles from the road and framed, on this spring evening, by an almost otherworldly lushness of green, was in fact an old plantation estate that included detached quarters for both servants and slaves; of course it was, technically, too big, but what could he say? "It's lovely," he managed.

Dissatisfied, she turned to his wife. "Wouldn't *you* say a house this size is way too big, even for a family of five?"

Sheila, surveying the foyer, tilting her heart-shaped face up toward the high, vast ceiling, seemed actually to be considering the question. Jake was mortified.

To his relief she replied that she was sure the children loved all the space.

"Actually my children seem to crave small spaces," the hostess said. "The twins once spent an entire day inside a packing crate. When I was their age I hated tight spaces. I screamed when people shut the door to my room, which I shared with my brother and was about the size of a closet. I'm afraid we're doomed to want the opposite of what we have." She looked back at Jake and seemed in that moment to forgive him. "Well, you two should go on in and have a drink. Don't you look adorable, like newlyweds!"

People often immediately identified them as newlyweds. Jake worried over this, but when he asked Sheila if it bothered her, she laughed. She said what it really meant was that people were thinking of the two of them having good sex. Sheila's implied understanding of the difference between good and bad sex also disturbed him. The problem with marrying a virgin, he realized now, was that you were marrying a girl who would become a woman only after the marriage.

"You can let go of my hand now," she said to him at the party that night. He hadn't known he'd been holding it.

Sheila was twenty-two, and had just graduated with a degree in music from Bob Jones University. Jake was twenty-six and before

this job had worked as a reporter at a daily newspaper in Charlotte. He had loved the stink of newsprint that clung to his cubicle
and the late-night deadlines, the euphoria that came over him after filing a story. Then, at a party—she'd driven up to Charlotte
with some friends—he'd met Sheila, shyly beautiful and somehow
detached from the noise and flash of people in their twenties pa-
rading their allure. They'd been at the apartment of a friend of a
friend. When he went out on the balcony to smoke, he'd found her
sitting there in a lawn chair, in a robin's egg blue dress that glowed
against the orange sunset, staring up at him with a sense of expectation so palpable he felt late. She had seemed to him, with her
glossy auburn hair and knowing expression, unashamedly pure,
and all of the warm summer night they'd sat out on the porch of
the friend's apartment, watching people through the glass doors
and making up comic bits of conversation for them, analyzing their
gestures. He hadn't had dinner. Someone from a neighboring apartment was grilling meat and despite the smell of the steak, he stayed
by her side.

"I hate flirting," she'd said at the point in the night when people were beginning to couple off. He followed her gaze into the
living room of the apartment, at a girl striding across the room in
stilettos. "And I hate high-heeled shoes." He'd noticed, when he
came out onto the porch to smoke, the abandoned blue heels, her
bare feet. "Do you know why people like them so much?" He said
he had assumed it was because they were flattering to the leg, and
she excitedly replied, "Lordosis. You know: the arch of a woman's
back during copulation?" He watched as she slipped on her heels
and told him to pay close attention to the effect they had on her
posture. "Isn't our culture sick?" she said. He studied her ass, her
toned calves, and agreed wholeheartedly while she continued with
her criticisms, aware that she, cheeks flushed in the lamplight passing through the glass, was also aroused. She said that she wished
he would stop smoking because she didn't want him to get cancer,
and he promptly ground the cigarette he was smoking beneath his
heel. She asked him to hand over the pack, and, staring right into

his eyes, she tossed it behind her, over the railing. He didn't know whether to be irritated or impressed: she was so ethereal, but also kind of a bitch. By the time he made plans to drive the hour and a half to her town to see her the next weekend, he thought he might already be in love.

The wedding had taken place in a cathedral carved into the side of a mountain, at sunset, at the very end of summer. It was near perfect, marred only by Sheila's family having to deal with the arrival of an estranged, drunken uncle—someone had promptly called him a cab before the ceremony—and by his mother arriving just as the quartet began the first piece, in the skirt and blouse she'd worn the evening before, at the rehearsal dinner. He was quietly humiliated—he knew she'd driven down to Atlanta after dinner, to meet a man she'd been chatting with on the Internet—and annoyed by the lean look of her, her too-long, graying hair. He did not want to think of her growing old alone. But the tension faded the moment Sheila, in her ivory gown, shoulders bared, approached the altar. Though she moved toward him, he was stirred by the sensation that he was approaching her, and he felt none of the fear other married men had warned him about.

She had begun with the excuses five months ago. He'd be watching television, drinking a beer after work, when she came into the living room to announce that she needed to go out and buy some paper towels, or that she craved ice cream she'd failed to purchase last time she went out. "Let me come with you," he'd say. But she'd argue that she wouldn't be long, that she had a new CD to listen to, and this meant she wanted to be by herself. Early on he'd realized she preferred listening to new music alone, because he was unmusical, or at least compared to her. And so he let her go. Sometimes she came back right away. But a few times she'd stayed gone for hours. On Thursdays she had a late orchestra practice, and after one of these sessions didn't come home until close to two in the morning, claiming she'd had coffee with a female friend from the

orchestra and lost track of time. That evening, he'd pulled into the
drive at the same time she was dashing across the walkway, and
recalled that she'd looked especially nice for her practice, her usually straight hair in the waves she sometimes wore when they
went out. After they embraced, she reached back for his hand,
holding it thoughtfully in her own, her thumb reassuringly—too
reassuringly—massaging his palm. "Skip it," he begged, testing
her, but she seemed to look through him. She laughed as she turned
toward her car.

One afternoon, meaning to call his wife at home, he'd heard
his mother's voice speak; he'd accidentally dialed her number. He
made small talk for a few minutes. But in asking what he thought
of as harmless questions, he must have accidentally let some of
the suspicion he felt for his wife leak into his voice, because his
mother began to laugh at him. She said, "Aren't both of us a little
old for you to be calling to check up on me?"

"Checking up" on her was what she used to call his less artful
enquiries into her love life, the ones he made as a teenager.

"What did I say?" he asked her, already feeling a too-familiar
sense of frustration.

"It's not what you say," she explained, exasperated with him
in the manner of a daughter with her father. "It's your tone. You
talk to me like you've already decided I'm going to tell you something you don't want to hear. Or like whatever I'm about to say
to you is a lie."

Jake thought of her when she was in love—how, when he was
small, she would bend down to peer with such intensity into his
eyes before school, her hands reverentially skimming his hair and
cheeks before coming to rest lightly, worshipfully, on his shoulders; how, outside, walking through the cool air toward the bus
stop, he felt like a sacred being, warm with his mother's love and
the wonder of his own light. He had been too young, then, to understand the effects of romance: that she spent on him the excess
of her feelings for some man. In the lull between men she could
never touch him in quite the same way.

Now he sighed. When he hurt her he became to her every man who'd hurt her.

"What else?"

"I just hope you don't talk to your wife like you talk to me," she replied.

He wanted to trust his wife, he truly did. But he couldn't stop himself from noticing, in public, the way Sheila returned the types of male glances she'd before seemed not to notice. He'd be talking to her about some movie they'd just seen, or about work, and he would see her eyes dart away from him to study the back of a young waiter, or the shoulders of a man older than her father. Occasionally, he'd even seen his wife lock eyes with a stranger and offer this person a flirtatious half-smile—right in front of Jake—and when Jake asked if she knew that man, his way of telling her he'd caught her, she'd say, "He just reminded me of someone I used to know." Or, in a puzzled, dismissive tone, as if Jake were paranoid, "I'm just being friendly." It was upsetting not only in itself, but also because it was the kind of behavior he associated with his mother. Again he felt the unease he'd felt as a little boy, nervously cherishing the brief periods of peace they had between her lovers, all the while afraid that any of the strange men they encountered in shops, at the park, at the zoo or museum, could very well end up in their home. He understood how quickly their movie nights and pancake suppers, their reading the newspaper together on Saturday morning—her happily questioning him about what he'd read, delighting in his answers, ("Why don't you help me wrap my mind around that, Mr. Know-it-all?"), would be replaced by the drama of her infatuation, by a monster (gross and strong and idiotic they seemed to him) who wished him dead.

Now, at this party, on this spring night, in this huge old house, one room giving way to another in mazelike fashion, all of them familiarly pleasant with their cleverly mismatched furniture and Oriental rugs, like decor from a magazine, he would have to mind Sheila. Or, he wouldn't be able to mind her. He already felt her wanting to slip away from him and explore, and knew that she would.

She was as usual oblivious to his suspicion. "That woman," Sheila said, grinning, speaking of their hostess, "is so interesting. I wonder if she was that strange before she was rich."

She wore a strapless dark-blue dress. She kept rolling back her bare shoulders and stretching her arms. She seemed always to be stretching lately, especially in public.

"I doubt it," he said, deciding not to let on all he knew of her (as if he could've even *explained* what he knew). "Things like that change people."

"Do you really think people change, or just seem to change?" Sheila said, scanning the crowd. She would just as soon take the opposite position. She was like that. She never betrayed guilt about what she was doing to him, and that she behaved so normally around him made him think she either loved him so much that her feelings for other men didn't affect her feelings for him, or that she didn't love him at all. "Because I think everything is already there inside of you," she went on. "What you are. By the time childhood is over. What I think is that you just become this purer and purer version of what you already are."

"You mean *who* you already are."

"No. That's not what I meant," softly, thoughtfully, as if to herself.

He'd found out about her virginity on their third date, over pasta at an Italian restaurant, after the waiter handed them the wine list. "You know, I should probably tell you now: I don't drink. Both sets of my grandparents were alcoholics and so no one in my family drinks. But I don't mind that you do. Also, I guess I should tell you, too, that I don't have sex. Until I get married. I mean, I'm a virgin. Sex isn't just a physical thing to me, but a deeply spiritual thing that I only want to experience with my future husband, to whom I want to offer my purity as a gift. Just don't want you to get the wrong idea."

He understood that she had made this little speech before, that she offered it as both a challenge and discouragement. But he was not discouraged. In that moment he had become hypnotized by the miracle of her mouth, her hands, her chest rising with her breath. He had thoughts he'd have been too embarrassed to ever speak aloud: waking to an untouched blanket of snow, freshly cut flowers, the smell of baking bread. He thought, strangely, of women emerging from the water of the local pool, wet hair heavy against their shoulders, rivulets of water cascading down bare limbs. In grade school, on picture day, he had seen the ivory hem of a girl's new dress on the playground splattered with mud.

He found himself adjusting the cuff of his sleeve, smoothing his hair.

"I respect that very much," he told her. Even the sight of her fork spearing food now intrigued him.

She hadn't acted surprised.

Pictures of Sheila as a child revealed a bespectacled, awkwardly thin person in baggy clothes. Her parents were devout fundamentalists whose black-and-white television stayed up in the attic, and they limited their library to biblical commentary. Friendly but guarded, they watched him with eyes he couldn't read. Wariness fringed their air of puritanical optimism, and their voices slipped into warning tones creepy to him when the sun had just gone down and the beige of their living room appeared gray before the turning on of lamps. But her mother's frequent offers of snacks and tea reassured him.

"People are born with an emptiness inside them," said her father, a big bearded man who worked in construction. While they talked, he gently, rhythmically stroked the matted back of the family's aged terrier, his hand as wide as the dog. "If you don't fill it with God it grows. Emptiness begets emptiness," he said. "Nothing begets nothing."

"Love begets love," her mother said. She was a slender woman with a kind smile and dark, boyish haircut, her blouses a size too large.

"Love begets compassion," the father corrected. "And compassion begets love. Compassion is God's love."

Sheila's mother nodded emphatically. Sheila was picking at her cuticles and looked up to glance over at him, rolled her eyes. (She was like this—sometimes regarding her religion seriously, sometimes speaking of it almost as a joke she went along with.)

"Do you believe in God's love?" her father asked Jake.

Of course, Jake said; though *of course not*, he thought. His mother had dabbled in every major faith and some of the minor ones, had even flirted with the occult, and religion seemed to him an unnecessary and too often desperate exhaustion of will. The self-infatuated tone of people's voices when they spoke of their intimacy with a higher power depressed him. He would force himself not to cringe when Sheila's mother, smelling of the same linen-scented detergent her daughter used, hugged him good-bye and whispered into his ear, "God loves you." And when, a month before the wedding—breath drawn, eyes shut—he allowed Sheila's father to drown him in the water of the baptistery at their little country church, he felt nauseated.

But he liked imagining Sheila, with her red hair and look of calm curiosity, emerging from this little cave of deprivation. In her college photos—in the succession of them, from freshman to senior year—you could see her, whom he thought of as his Sheila, distinguishing herself from this world. The cave became the background that defined her. Her body grew graceful, shoulders rolled back, hair longer and even a deeper auburn, and the simplicity of her clothes elegant; but what changed most was the way she reacted to the camera. The shy, averted gaze of the adolescent gave way to a head-on stare, her eyes lit with something like impatience. Her school uniform—the long khaki skirts and white button-down blouses—seemed to emphasize her ease in her body, an ease that communicated to him latent sexual appetite. She had, with her pouty lips, what he and his friends, as teenagers, would've happily referred to as "a slutty face," and the irony of this made him laugh.

He thought, he felt, that she couldn't wait to lose her virginity to him.

She seemed to communicate this through her long legs, bared by short skirts—she wore short skirts constantly now that she'd graduated from the school, except when they visited her parents, for whom she dressed like an elementary-school librarian—and through the way she would press her breasts up against him when they kissed.

When his hands became too insistent, she'd pull her face from his, her long red hair falling into his mouth, and say, in a sweet, apologetic voice, "We need to stop now." Disentangle herself from his arms. It was almost as if he were with a high-school girl.

He didn't mind. Their future together had soon taken shape in his mind. She was pure and smart and talented—she played first viola in the county orchestra—and passionate. One evening, over the phone, she told him that when, after having just slid her bow across the strings for the first measure of the second piece in a concert, she felt the vibrations of all the other instruments in the air around her, she shivered with what she believed was orgasmic energy. The formality of her concerts became for him— from his seat among strangers in the dim auditorium, gazing up at Sheila in her black dress, in the circle of light she shared with the other players—a sort of erotic tease.

The first evening, in the hotel room, Sheila wore black-lace lingerie and kissed him enthusiastically; but as his hands and lips descended past her belly, she began to tense. She pushed his hand down, against her thigh. He tried again, and she finally pulled away from him, drawing the slightly stiff hotel sheets around her, complaining she felt sick from the plane. He knew she was scared— so much had happened: the ceremony, the flight, her first trip to London (she'd wanted to hear the London Symphony). They spent the rest of the night cuddling in the hotel bed and watching European movies that seemed to suggest people could never really comprehend their true realities; the tone of these was charmingly whimsical. He felt better. Warm. The frustration that came from her body pressed up against his was only temporarily problematic. It was sweet to him, really, that she knew so little about men.

The next day she seemed cheerful and energetic, delighting in the view from their window of the busy street—the pavement slicked with rain and the storefronts, the Londoners with their spectrum of umbrellas. The air was blustery, the gray of the city tinged toward silver. For breakfast they had beans and toast at a cafe, both of them drinking too much of the strong coffee, musing about what to do and see first.

But in the street, Sheila noticed some of the British girls' outfits—they wore tall boots and short plaid kilts—and complained that she didn't have anything that was in style here to wear. Did he mind shopping for a while? she asked. Inside one of the shops, she tried on a pair of black boots like the ones she'd admired, with several different skirts. After each change she stood in front of the dressing room, modeling for him. The last thing she tried on was a pink cocktail dress that had caught her eye on the way in. It was skintight, more daringly cut than what she usually wore. She frowned at her image in the mirror hanging against the wall and in the reflection met his eye. Did he like it? Yes, very much, he told her. He reached out and took the edge of the silky hem between his fingertips.

"You would."

A whisper; hostile. He quickly withdrew his hand. Though he was sitting in a chair beside the dressing-room door, he felt as if he were about to lose his balance, his vision of her back and reflection in the mirror momentarily blurred into one pale, many-limbed mass. But then in a casual tone she said she looked weird in pink, laughed; disappeared inside the dressing room. He wondered if he'd imagined the tone from before. They bought the clothes and shoes, and went back to the hotel to drop off the bags. She changed into the boots and a red-and-black kilt and took his hand as they stepped back out into the street. They spent the rest of the morning at the Tate.

When, in the afternoon, they returned to the hotel for a nap, he tried again. This time he was both more controlled and aggressive, coaxing her with more strategized kissing and massaging, trying to both ease and hurry her through it, thinking once they worked their way past the beginning she'd be fine. He had expected the first time would hurt her, but he hadn't yet gone inside her when her face changed. At first, he didn't see it as hate. He saw her screaming, her mouth gaping strangely open, before he heard the sound. Then she slapped his face. He did not move off her quickly enough, was too stunned, and just as he began to lean back she struck him again, this time catching his left temple, almost knocking him off balance. Before he could climb off of her she'd wriggled out from beneath him. He was shocked and ashamed. He'd never before tried to make a woman do something she didn't want to do sexually. But here was his wife, his *wife*, making him feel like a rapist. She scooted away from him—moving backward, her eyes all the while trained on his body—until she had her back against the headboard of the king-size bed. There, she looked down at him across an expanse of white sheets and hugged her knees. Tears ran down her face. "I'm sorry, but I can't," she said. "Sorry," she repeated. "I'm sorry." She looked, impossibly, as if she wanted to be held and also as if she might never want to be held again. He trembled as he made his way from the bed to the desk chair. There, naked, cold in the draft from the vent, he'd put his head in his hands and listened to her cry. He understood that while she didn't want him near her, he couldn't leave her alone in the room. He got up and switched on the TV and both of them stared at the flickering screen.

The man was the uncle who'd been sent away from the wedding, whom Jake had, because he was getting dressed, not actually seen.

When, wanting some form to which to attach his rage, he asked what the man looked like, she said he was tall and thin, with dark hair. That these adjectives might also have described Jake bothered him a little; but then that was silly, lots of men fit that description. She added that the man had had a damaged eye, that he'd been in an accident, had had reconstruction work, which caused the place where iris met pupil to look jagged, "like a starburst," she said. The abuse had consisted mostly of heavy petting, no actual penetration, but because Sheila had been raised in such a conservative household, the psychological damage was profound, insinuated the therapist. It was about contrast, Jake gathered.

She'd been twelve. The uncle and his wife didn't have children and had invited her to stay with them in the summer at their home in North Carolina, while her parents went on a mission trip to Lugansk. Apparently he'd worked from the home. His wife worked in some office, and during her absence he'd let Sheila watch movies and listen to music her parents prohibited. He had also let her drink. The wife had come home early one day and found Sheila walking through the living room in her panties.

"We'd been listening to music in the bedroom," she said. "I'd never heard Bob Dylan before, and he thought he was amazing, and I was laughing at him because back then Bob Dylan's voice seemed so bad to me. He said we were going to listen until I understood."

She had been crying intermittently, as she spoke, but now her lips turned into something near a smile. The therapist uncrossed her legs. Sheila's smile faded.

"And I'd gone out to the kitchen to get a drink. Aunt Mira looked like she was about to say hi to me, but then she didn't say anything. She just stared at my legs, like she was confused. Finally she said, 'What are you doing?' in a normal voice, and I said, 'Listening to music.' And she said, 'Where is your uncle?' And I knew we were going to get in trouble, but I couldn't think of what to say. I took too long and I guess she saw it in my face, and you could hear it coming from the bedroom—the stereo, I mean. She went after him then. Then she came back out to me, where I was still standing in the living room, not knowing what to do. I felt frozen. She looked like she wanted to say something to me, but instead she threw up. She was standing on a nice rug, and I remember how she leaned over to throw up on the hardwood floor instead of the rug.

"My parents came back the next day, and my dad went back there into the room after my aunt told them what had happened—I thought he was going to kill him—but when he came back into the kitchen where we were, just a few minutes later, he said my uncle was in a ball on the floor and wouldn't get up. I remember him saying that. My mother wanted to know if I'd asked my uncle a lot of questions. She said to my aunt that she had noticed I had a habit of being *interested*. In other people. And I thought, What does that even mean? Who's not interested in other people? Even my aunt looked at her funny. She was so tired. By then she just wanted my mom to shut up."

In the car, riding home, her mother asked if she'd let her uncle touch her, and she said no. "That was exactly how she said it. *Let*," Sheila said. "He only used his hands, he always had his clothes on, but I told her not at all. My dad didn't talk the whole time. At home he walked around with this blank look on his face. For days. And for a while he wouldn't really look at me when we talked. We never saw them again. My dad talked to my aunt on the phone every once in a while, at Christmas."

After that her mother never treated her the same. "She tried to make sure my dad and I were never alone together in the house. She thought I didn't notice, but I did. I noticed all the time. Once I came back from a sleepover and a pair of my underwear must have fallen out of my bag, in the hall, and an hour later she was in my bedroom, waving it in my face. She was almost screaming at me. It was like she thought I left it out *on purpose*."

She again broke into tears. He was baffled. He hadn't picked up on any animosity between her and her mother.

"He was so unhappy. He acted bored around my aunt, around everyone else, but when we were alone together he got happy. He said Aunt Mira hated him because they couldn't have children, even though the reason they couldn't have them had to do with her. Because of how she'd gotten hurt in the car accident they were in. He said just *seeing* me made him happy. He said I was so pretty.

"My mom hated the word. Pretty. When I was little, if I asked her if I was pretty, she'd say, 'It doesn't matter whether or not you're pretty. Beauty comes from being pure of heart.' She was right. She was trying to be a good mother. I understood that. I don't understand why I liked to hear it from him so much. I guess until then I thought I wasn't. But he said I was. He said it was too early for most people to see but that they would."

Her arms had been folded across her chest. Now she drew her legs onto the chair, clasped her hands around them.

"That night, at my aunt and uncle's, after my aunt saw me, I woke up and he was staring at me. I didn't know if it was for real or a dream. I was sleeping on the couch in the living room and Aunt Mira was over in the kitchen. The dining room was between them and I couldn't see her, but I could see the light from the kitchen reflecting into it. She'd been in there most of the night. It was weird but it smelled to me like she was cooking stuff. I didn't go in there. So she was awake. I felt so bad for her. And when I opened my eyes and saw him sitting there watching me I just shut them again and pretended to be asleep because I didn't know what else to do. He sniffed. Then he was quiet. But I could feel him watching me. He was there for so long. I wanted him to go away. But also I didn't. Nobody looked at me the way he did. I hate being looked at."

"By everyone?" the therapist said. "Or just by men?"

Now Sheila turned to Jake. She wiped her mouth with the back of her hand. Her lips were paler. She turned to the therapist. He thought that the therapist was excited. It had something to do with the way she leaned forward ever so slightly and seemed to

be trying to keep, rather than actually feeling, the patient, atten-
tive expression. She said that Sheila was doing a wonderful "job,"
that both of them were doing "wonderful jobs," but that for now
they needed to alter the dynamic in order to get the best results.

After that Sheila attended the sessions alone.

Time passed. He considered annulment but not seriously. He still
loved her and thought that with time, through standing by her,
he could show her that his love had to do with much more than
sex. He couldn't stay married to a woman who wouldn't have sex
with him *forever*. But he could wait.

He tried to throw himself into his new job—which consisted of
writing speeches and press releases, and spent a lot of time in his
office, a generous space in a wing of the hospital that had once been
used for patients. Because it had been a patient room, the office included a bathroom, which meant he could in the afternoons, after
meetings, work for extensive periods of time without having to go
into the hall. He'd long ago learned to control his emotions in order
to work, and here (despite the shut door, his solitude) she'd be reduced to a mood, to a gray film through which he saw the important matters at hand. But occasionally the mood would grow too
thick to see through; then he'd get lightheaded, sweaty. If it was already dark he'd go out and find a place to smoke about the grounds.
If it was day, since the hospital had a new no-smoking policy that
he himself had formally promoted, he'd have to retreat into the
white-tiled emptiness of the little bathroom to sit on the floor, back
pressed against the wall, and wait for calm.

He would always be waiting for something, it seemed. In certain moods the thought of it was beautiful, but more frequently he
wondered if his ideals were ridiculous. There, in the little bathroom, trying not to think of Sheila, who often couldn't quite mask
her disappointment when he came home, he began to fantasize
about female coworkers: a gamine intern; an older woman in
marketing who'd brushed up against him; Rachel Delaney, whom
he'd met at a hospital-wide meeting, who with her husband do-

nated huge amounts of money to the system, who had almost died
of cancer but appeared so well to him. Rachel Delaney especially.

She hadn't looked to him at all like the other wealthier donors, with
their tailored suits and designer shoes. Her ash-colored hair was
pulled up messily, in a big plastic clip, and she wore a cheap black
T-shirt with her skirt. The skirt was actually elegant, silk and em-
broidered, but the flip-flops worn ragged. At first, when his supervisor introduced them, during a break in the meeting, he hadn't
noticed she was pretty. He listened and nodded as she spoke, struggling to focus after what had been his fifth meeting that day. Then
she suddenly fell silent and rummaged around in her purse. She
brought out a square of dark chocolate and popped it in her mouth.
"Sorry," she said. "Chocolate's the only thing I can take to keep me
from smoking. Did you ever smoke?"
    He quit before he got married, he explained.
    "I know it's not the healthiest way, but nothing else works.
The only problem is that now I'm overweight. But when you've
gone through what I've been through you pretty much have to surrender your vanity."
    "You don't look overweight to me."
    "Too little muscle mass and too much fat. You wouldn't be
able to tell unless you saw me naked."
    Her figure was lovely, and he blushed at the thought of her
nudity. When she noticed she looked momentarily pleased, almost
smiled.
    "I identify with fat people," she went on. "I identify with the
dying, because I had cancer once and will probably get it again. I
was also addicted to painkillers and so I identify with addicts.
I've been poor, and believe me when I say I can fathom murder;
murder unfortunately is no mystery to me," she rambled on, her
eyes darting all over him before briefly meeting his own, only to
again make their nervous cycles. "My ability to sympathize is so
overwhelming that I find it more and more difficult to walk down
the street, to have simple human interactions. But because I've

got this ability—this ability to sympathize—I feel guilty for shutting it down. Which in itself becomes another, near-unbearable
type of tension. Even now I'm trying to resist what I see when I
look in your eyes. Sometimes I fantasize about bashing out my
brains against a brick wall."

At this Jake started. Looked to see if anyone else was listening.
Nobody was. Then a VP interrupted them, and she moved away to
talk to someone else. He was glad. She seemed to him mildly insane. But then, the next day, at a coffee shop, he'd had an unusual
craving for dark chocolate—he didn't even really like chocolate—
and bought a bar, thinking of her and, yes, picturing her naked.
Now he couldn't help but think of her when he smoked.

At home, his wife began to lock herself in the bedroom to do special exercises recommended by the therapist. She was, as he understood it, learning to masturbate without shame. She seemed
cheerful, even playful, when she came back downstairs. With the
exception of hugging and light kissing, they'd hardly touched since
their honeymoon, and moved about the house so politely that he
felt relieved by unexpected noise: the hum of the air conditioner
switching on, her flushing the toilet upstairs, the neighbors slamming the door to their car. And though they slept in the same bed
their bodies remained apart. But now she began to come up behind him and run her fingers through his hair, the way she used
to, before, and she no longer stiffened when he held her. He felt
relieved. When he intercepted a call about two missed therapy ap-
pointments, he felt confused, but not worried. Her explanations for
missing them—stuck in roadwork, an orchestra practice running
over—were plausible.

One January afternoon, during the first flurry of a light snow,
she called him at work, saying she needed him to come home, and
surprised him at the door in the same black lingerie she had worn
during their honeymoon. In bed, when he tentatively put his mouth
between her legs—hopeful, but still a little afraid he might at any
moment be slapped—she let him. Things were normal. Or, they

were wonderful: the warm house and bed and the snow falling outside the upstairs window.

The next day the roads were too bad for him to drive to work, and they enjoyed what he thought of as their delayed honeymoon. That evening, as he lay back on the bed, happily exhausted and amused that they'd actually somehow torn away not only the sheets but the mattress cover, she sighed with what he at first mistook for contentment, and said, "I guess that's it, then."

"What? What's it?" He sat up, confused. She'd seemed to enjoy herself even more than he expected she would, it being her first time; he was almost sure she had come.

She was not on the bed but standing beside it, leaning against the wall with her arms crossed. She'd put on one of his white undershirts. She'd gotten leaner after the wedding; at dinner she seemed to eat less than half of what she herself put on the plate.

"You know. Sex. I mean, it's fun. But I thought…" She looked away from him, over at the basket in the corner where they put their dirty clothes. She hadn't done laundry in a while, apparently, and clothes spilled over the basket. "I thought it would feel more…it just feels so…*physical.*"

Of course it felt physical. It was sex, he laughed nervously. What did she mean?

"I expected a spiritual element," she explained. "I expected it to be physical and spiritual."

He felt as if she'd struck him again; his whole body rather than just his head. "You mean you don't feel anything for me." He stared down at the mattress, the pale gray stripes exposed.

"No. No. I love you…I just…it's me. I try to look in your eyes and I can't and I know I'm supposed to, but I can't. It's fun, though. It's great. It's just me, is all. I shouldn't have said anything. I talk too much."

"Sheila." He looked up at her. She stared straight ahead now, lost in thought. "Did you stop seeing your therapist?"

She pulled her arms more tightly against her chest and looked into his eyes, shifted her gaze again to the laundry pile. "No."

She was lying, it seemed to him.

"OK," he said gently.

She climbed back onto the bed and curled up against him, her head on his chest, her red hair spilling over his arm. "I didn't mean to ruin everything," she said quietly. "I'm sorry."

He lost track of her early in the night, when as some coworkers approached from one direction, Sheila darted off in the other with the excuse of needing another ginger ale. He chatted with them— some women from the marketing department, two of whom were young and pretty and seemed girlishly aware of their party appearances, hands fidgeting with bracelets and smoothing hair, bodies moving in the formal dresses with a self-consciousness he'd never have glimpsed at work. Though he had trouble following the conversation, he managed to hide it. How much time had passed? Fifteen minutes? Thirty?

The women moved on.

In the far corner of the next room (crowded, red walls) he spotted his host and hostess talking to another couple. Rachel's husband, a bearded man with a lot of coarse blond hair, seemed to be telling a story, mock scowling and making exaggerated gestures. But while the couple grinned back, Rachel stared blankly past him, hand cupping a full glass of red wine. The room had two openings and at that moment, from the other side, a child in a white-flannel nightgown—Rachel's daughter, the one who'd come to his office—streaked from one opening to the other, a weirdly determined look on her face. Rachel began to hurry after her, yelling her name, the anger in her voice belied by the sudden pleasure in her expression. As she passed near him she met his eye and raised her brows so that he felt included in the child's mischief, the mother's pursuit. For a moment he forgot where he was going. But as she vanished from his sight he again became aware of the problem, his search.

There were many familiar faces—doctors and administrators, board members and their spouses—but also plenty of people he didn't recognize. Laughter would erupt from one cluster, and then the next. Many of them, though youthful and well preserved in the way of successful people in a mid-sized town, were much older than he. There was talk of time-shares in Europe, of healthcare legislation, of encounters with unruly patients. He smiled and nodded his way through.

Where was she? He made his way through a number of rooms, still sipping at the now watery gin and tonic he'd gotten when he first arrived. At the bar, he got another. He passed through the kitchen, where the wait staff was replacing trays with hors d'oeuvres, and moved out onto the broad back deck overlooking a little courtyard, a fountain. Out here white lights were strung up around the tree branches that grew along the walls, and people's faces were harder to make out. The early spring air was neither hot nor cold. He studied the throng of bodies, but he could not find his wife's face. He leaned against the railing and looked down into the courtyard. Below he glimpsed the little girl, now standing by the fountain that shimmered beneath the strung lights. Her pale hair, in the surrounding dimness, gleamed white by the glow of the water. She turned her face up toward the balcony, met his eye. Then, from the lower part of the house, from somewhere beneath the deck, a female voice that was not her mother's called out to her, and she darted into the shadows. He waited for a moment to see if she'd return, but she was gone.

Now he found himself drawn into a nearby conversation.

"But I heard it was inherited," a man said.

Jake didn't recognize these people from work.

"No. I went to high school with them in Raleigh. Daniel's parents were teachers and Rachel's family was on welfare after her dad died. It was vacuum parts." There was a pause, the clink of ice. "They owned factories in South America. Made a killing. But then it came out that handling the parts caused birth defects. Nowadays all vacuum parts are like that, if you notice. There's usually a warning in the little instruction manual? You're supposed to be sure to wear gloves or wash your hands after. But this was a while back and a company that used their parts ended up getting sued by a customer. The company tried to file a suit against the Delaney's company but it was proven that they knew what they were buying and Rachel and Daniel got out OK."

"I heard she had a nervous breakdown," a woman said in a low voice. "From the guilt. I heard she thinks her cancer was punishment from God, and that's why they donate all that money."

"That's ridiculous," said a man wearing thick-rimmed glasses. "That's just a rumor."

"It amazed me that she let them write about her like they did— her treatments and reconstruction. I'd feel weird when people looked at me and just knew, well..."

"You couldn't beat the promotion they got for the center from that, though. That was smart. Nothing beats the personal-narrative stuff. People eat that shit up."

"Didn't she hire the designer too? I like the paintings in the lobby there. Who is it who did those paintings?"

"The Japanese woman from Charleston?"

"No it was someone local. Smythe or Simms or..."

The conversation veered into a discussion of the prices of local art. He turned and went back inside the house.

It had been afternoon when Rachel knocked on the door to his office. At first he hadn't answered, hoping whoever it was would go away. The little girl with her was very blond and wore a black pair of galoshes, with a gold-and-white jumper. She looked five or six, her eyes the water blue of her mother's. Though it was March, Rachel wore another black T-shirt, and the same flip-flops, pale legs bare. Her long hair was pulled into the same plastic tortoiseshell clip.

"She knew you were in here," the little girl said.

"Violet," Rachel said in a warning voice. To him, "I don't mean to bother you, but I just wanted to talk about the press releases for the mammography unit and—" she was looking around his office as she spoke, and now paused. "Does it bother you to work in here?"

"Why would it bother me?"

"It's just, this was a patient room."

"So?"

"So people have suffered and died in here."

"People have died in here," the little girl repeated in a low, wondering voice.

"It's a hospital," he said in his most rational tone. He wanted them to leave, but Rachel was moving deeper in. She walked toward his window and began to speak of how this view of his must have been for a significant number of people a "last view of the world." The little girl began to pick up and examine objects on his desk: his brass paperweight, his Post-it notes, his pens. She looked at these things as if they were fantastic, turning them in her small white hands while the water-colored eyes contemplated their sides from multiple angles.

Now Rachel reached into her purse and extracted the chocolate, her back to him. He imagined her white skin beneath the thin black fabric of her shirt. He tried to think of something else but the only something else his mind would turn to was the deceased peering out of his window. His head ached. He did not feel well. He wanted a cigarette. The little girl, with a look of intense concentration, was sticking blank Post-it notes—pink, yellow, mint green—all over his paperwork and desk. Her mother still stared out his window, out at the overcast afternoon. His office smelled of chocolate.

"Could I have some of that?" he said.

She turned from the window to smile at him. She stepped close to him, his head level with her waist, his eyes drawn to her breasts. With one hand she self-consciously wrapped the sweater around her chest, and with the other handed him a square of the candy. She watched his face too long.

"I see," she said softly.

"See what?"

She reached out, as if to touch his cheek, but retracted her hand. He felt, still, as if she were touching him. She might have been touching him all over with the water-colored eyes: they wanted each other. Then she averted her gaze, broke the spell. "Violet, Mr. Harrison is tired and we need to get out of his hair now. Come back another time."

"Wait."

He quickly began to sift through the contents of his desk drawers for something that might interest the child. Found himself handing over pens, an old Rolodex, a small green clipboard bearing the logo of a pharmaceutical company. The child accepted these things with the air of one accepting precious gifts. Suddenly he had the feeling that all things in his office were sacred, were less and also more than what they were.

"That's all she can carry," the mother said, smiling. "Say thanks."

"Thank you," the child said to him, arms full of his things.

Gone.

He was very tired. He lay his head down on his desk, face buried in arms.

The upstairs of the house appeared smaller than he expected. Smaller and plainer. But that was probably because the hall was narrow and all of the doors shut. Would he really have to go around opening all these doors? And what would happen if someone saw him up here? They'd think he was being nosy.

What he imagined was opening the door to a bedroom, a guest room perhaps, to find a couple embracing on a made-up bed. He imagined lamplight, auburn hair, her back turned to him. Some man fumbling with the zipper at the back of her dress.

He felt lightheaded. He'd forgotten to eat anything. They could go to a diner, he thought, as soon as the party ended, after he found her. What he expected, as much as he expected to catch her with a man, was to go through all these rooms and find them empty, then go back down and run into her, find she'd been searching for him at the same time he'd been searching for her, and they'd simply kept missing each other, as they did sometimes after having drifted apart in the mall, at bookstores.

The first two doors opened to darkness, the hall light skimming the outlines of an office in one room, a treadmill and weightlifting equipment in the other. Without thinking he opened a smaller door he should've known led to a linen closet.

The next door he opened brought him face to face with his hostess.

He started.

She showed no surprise, only amusement for, he guessed, his embarrassment, his getting caught. The child was with her.

"Strawberry," the child said to him.

They sat on a plain white cot. The room had polished hardwood floors and ivory walls bearing soft ellipses of light from two standing lamps on either side of the room. The only shadows that broke the light came from their bodies, for there was no furniture. Rachel's sweater lay in a black lump beside her, on the cot, her bare arms and shoulders exposed, the thin blue straps of the dress, perhaps because he was looking down at her, seeming to barely cover her nakedness. He quickly turned his eyes to the child in her white-flannel gown, etched faintly with caramel-colored flowers, he saw now. Her blond hair looked mussed and after she said *strawberry* for the second time, she frowned.

"He doesn't know what we're playing," Rachel said to her. "He just thinks you're being weird. Tell him what we're playing."

"Word association," the little girl said to him. In a very serious voice, "I say a word, and you say the first word that comes to your mind, and then I say the first word that comes to my mind when I hear your word, and then you say—"

"He gets the point, Violet."

"Strawberry," the girl said again, insistently.

"Milk," he replied.

"Now Mommy."

"Cow."

"Hamburger," Violet said. To Jake, "Hamburger comes from cows. People kill the cows and then they eat them. They made me eat cows but I didn't know what it was," she said sadly. "I didn't know."

"Please don't start again, Violet," her mother said. "No one meant to taint you. No one knew how you'd feel about it." To Jake, "Her nanny doesn't know how to talk to sensitive children."

"I ate cows," the little girl persisted gravely.

"This is not the time for us to talk about that," Rachel said. "It's time for me to talk to Mr. Harrison now. Time for you to go."

"But I want to sleep in here with you tonight."

She latched on to her mother's bare arm and began to whimper. When Rachel gave her a threatening look, the child let go of her mother. She got up from the cot, stomped her small bare feet past Jake at the door, and in the dim hall burst into a sprint. He watched her open the door that faced theirs from the opposite end, flooding the space with light. Briefly he glimpsed a huge, high-ceilinged room with a Ping-Pong table, beyond it a sofa and a big-screen television flashing the bright pastels of a cartoon. He heard the shrieks of children. Then the door slammed shut and the hall seemed twice as dark as before.

"Close the door behind you," Rachel told him.

When he turned back to face her, she was already pulling down the straps of the dress. Her blue eyes reflected what seemed to him one moment panic, the next anticipation. In the soft light and emptiness, the room might have been any room or every room he had ever known, and she had always been in this place that was also herself, waiting. The muted laughter from the party could no longer be heard. Faintly, the music he had not noticed below announced itself through the floor.

PORN
Dorothea Lasky

All types of porn are horrific
I just watched a woman fuck a hired hand
In her marble kitchen while her friends looked on
The title of the movie was *Divorce Party*
And throughout his big cock, her skinny thighs
Her friends shouted, Nah girl, now you're free

But no she's not she's in a movie
And now I am crying
Because the man looks like an ex-boyfriend
Or my half brother
My boss
A monster
Someone who left me in the dark
Someone who darkened me
A million times over

I've only fucked 7 guys in my whole life
But I've watched more porn than you ever will
Hours and hours
A woman and a dog
Three women
A hairy fruit
Four bending over backwards

Vomit sex
The underplay
Of tendril
In motion

I watch porn
Cause I'll never be in love
Except with you dear reader
Who think I surrender
But who's to say this stanza is not porn

Calculated and hurtful
All my friends say I'm free
And yes, maybe I am
But are you free
No, you'll never be
I've got you in my grasp
I've got you right here in my room
Once again

JIMMY
Atticus Lish

*T*he white looked like a long-legged biker, as if, instead of being inside these razor wire–topped walls, he should be leaning back on a chopper going down the highway, with his long legs extended and his boots on the chrome footrests. When he walked, he rose up on his feet like the piston in a motor—up and down—chin always up, an eighth Cherokee, last name Turner. Jimmy Turner.

They told him you could get transferred anywhere in the gulag system, from state to state, and wind up in the shoe. They said you've declared war on the state of Indiana, we've declared war on the United States. This organization is bigger than the United States. We go to the outside, two thousand, three thousand miles away. This is a structure. We're like al-Qaeda. They give us life, double life, life without. The state has our commanders in max segregation units, no human contact, twenty-four hours a day, and they're still calling shots as far as politics, operations, whatever the case might be. The state takes everything they can and we're still going on like magic.

We control the drugs, we control the individuals. People fear us, in here and on the street. We control the nicotine, they said.

Jimmy, smoking a cigarette under the blue sky, nodded.

He hadn't always been here, he had started his bid in Rikers. I built up to it, he told his social worker. I passed through there,

Rikers, doing skid bids. I had a life more or less. I didn't see my opportunities.

What about your behaviors do you need to watch out for?

The drugs. Definitely the drugs.

The social worker was an obese blonde woman whose facial features were confined inside a small area in the center of her face.

I ain't like these other guys, he told her and glanced to check if her features relaxed and spread apart slightly.

Positivity, he said.

Jimmy grew up wearing a plaid shirt, standing brooding silent with his mouth shut, the trace of a mustache over his lip, waiting for Patrick to say, Let me have the spanner. Then Jimmy would take the spanner out of the red toolbox and hand it to him, in the basement of someone's house in the neighborhood, down with the boiler and the risers.

A woman teacher at Cardozo told him in front of the class, You're not registered as Jimmy Murphy. I don't know what to tell you.

Why am I registered as Turner? he asked his mother.

Their house was full of curios, bedding, scratch tickets, yard equipment, and vinyl records. Wearing a robe, his mother sat in the lace-curtain living room, her feet up.

She turned her carved-from-a-mountainside face toward him and said, Come here, I'll tellya a story. She had a bag on and the story was about something else completely.

The rooms upstairs were a mess of clothes and junk. You could open a drawer in a broken dresser and find a stack of Polaroids of people and scenes you did not recognize, then look at yourself in the mirror and wonder who you looked like. A seventies barbecue, sunshine and green fields and motorbikes. You might recognize your mother as one of the faces cut off by the camera, eyes bright, lifting a beer, fifty pounds younger.

Patrick was bigger than his real father, who had spent his life in prison and was now dying of AIDS in Morristown.

I'll give you carfare if you want to go to see him, if you should want to do that, his mother said. I wouldn't stop you. Don't ask me to go, though. That, I'm not up for.

She pressed her hand to her eyes and checked her palm for tears.

Jimmy became a union man in rubber coveralls, boots, and a World War I helmet, going down into the ground for the city. He's made his bones, his mother said at the bar. Patrick had a shot with him.

Good luck down there, lad.

What began as grounds for celebration became his daily life. The irrelevant sun rose over his windshield as he drove to work, Led Zeppelin playing on the stereo.

He had a confined-space certificate. You could feel the rock being pulverized seven times per second. Under the noise frequency, an Irish voice and a West Indian voice sounded identical. They ate their lunches underground, by lantern light, Jimmy's blackened hands leaving fingerprints on his white bread.

After work, his eyes hurting in the daylight, he put the Zeppelin on again, a mysterious version in another language of the great underground music of the drill. The excavation site was in Midtown Manhattan, by the river. He drove through the flickering channel formed by the suspension cables of the bridge and headed back to the rusted fences and dilapidated houses to a bar where there were union stickers on the wood and the brogue was distinct.

Drinking opened tunnels in his head that led into the third tomb of the night.

He watched an amateur video of guys doing stunts on bikes, set to hip-hop by a white DJ crew. They did wheelies, burnouts, endos. The backdrop was a heavy tree line. Jimmy put his hand in the plastic bowl of Doritos. The guy whose house it was came in from the kitchen and sat down in his chair and said to the TV, She's making hot dogs. A helmeted rider tilted his bike forward, elevating his rear wheel, and drove past the camera balanced on his front wheel. Dismounting, he pointed to the Wheelz logo on the back of his jacket. That's dope, the guy whose house it was said. In the kitchen, you could hear a woman boiling water.

The TV was an enormous sleek cabinet-sized piece of equipment. The three men watching it were Jimmy, a plumber, and the guy whose house it was. The plumber was the intermediary. To Jimmy, he had said, Why don't you come out? We'll hang out, smoke a bone... He sat between them now, having placed his beer on the carpet next to his feet.

One of the riders lost control and wiped out and his bike flipped over. It landed on him and went sliding down the road.

Where do they do this? the plumber asked.

Bay Shore. That's my boy filming it. He gets money from, like, the promotion.

The guy whose house it was's woman brought out a tray of hot dogs.

There's relish, she said.

She sat down on the couch and spooned relish on a hot dog.

You want one? she said to the back of her guy's head.

The video was ending. The words *Strong Island Wheelz* scrolled by on the screen.

The woman, who had high hair and a judgmental nose and lips, had left the room. The plumber took out a flask of Captain Morgan and they all drank Dixie cups of it. The guy whose house it was lounged in his chair with his knees open, the ceiling light reflecting off his eyes. His clothing was clean, like his house. His jeans, with a loop for a hammer, appeared freshly laundered. Speaking to the ceiling, he said,

I'm getting the phattest street bike.

The plumber remarked that he used to ride in the Air Force. Vegas, Lake Havasu. I used to meet a lot of women, boy.

We oughta all ride together. He looks like a biker.

My man Jimmy's got the look.

It's how you carry yourself, Jimmy said.

Straight up.

The men regarded him, their eyes at half-mast. He took a hot dog off the tray with his silver-ringed hand, his jaw opened, and he bit it in half.

My man Jimmy over here. Look at him. Them hot dogs don't stand a chance. Don't worry about it, my man. He'll tell his old lady to cook more.

He's union?

My man's a sandhog. He's on the biggest dig in the city after the Holland Tunnel.

There's a lot of money in that.

There could be, Jimmy said.

Like with tools and shit. I bet a lotta shit walks off the job.

It could.

They never stole heavy-duty construction equipment. When Jimmy was arrested, it was for DUI. He had a couple of bags of cement in his trunk and a Ryobi that retailed at six hundred dollars. He wasn't raised to steal, Mrs. Murphy said. Up in the Bronx, the local received a call about him and in the bars they said he was going to get bounced. In the meantime, he kept working. He had his supporters. Keep your head high, Jim. He went to the rectangular building with many windows on Queens Boulevard near Union Turnpike and went through the metal detector, found his part.

His defender, a sarcastic man with a double chin, did not seem to understand that they were both Irish and what this meant or that Jimmy was a union man and what that meant. Jimmy stood outside the part waiting for him against the dirty marble wall with the other people who were milling and waiting. The defender showed up late, after the case had been called, pushing through the crowd with his briefcase.

They called me already.

I'm sorry, I had another case. The judge talks too much.

But you don't need me today. They're dropping the vandalism, aren't they?

What vandalism? That wasn't me. I'm DUI.

DUI, right. You're Turner. I thought you were Rodriguez.

The next time he got arrested, they impounded his Skylark and locked him up and he stood before the court while wearing sneakers minus the laces. In court, they referred to him as Mr. Turner. He turned to his defender: I thought you were getting me off. His defender said, Nobody can get you off. You're guilty. Right or wrong? You did it, didn't you? Yes or no? So take the plea and next time learn to call a cab.

Rikers could make you deaf. For weeks after his release, he shouted. It turned his volume up. He somehow found himself in exchanges with other men on the subway or on the street who had passed through the jail as well. They found each other by the way they spoke out in public, in the line outside the unmarked entrance in Ozone Park where Jimmy waited with the other offenders wearing sweatshirts over their heads and blowing vapor in the cold, shuffling upstairs to give his number and get his pills.

On the corner, windburned, dull eyed, they said, Oh, you a union man. There's a pride, Jimmy said. You got it made, they said. All you gotta do is keep tight. Keep it in tight! they laughed. They lived in a shelter off Centre Street and did temporary work unloading trucks for Chinese merchants who owned lighting businesses on Bowery.

When I got out after five years I would do any job, a Puerto Rican named Cat said. My sentence was for murder. I served my time, I don't care. It happened because I was seeing a woman. She was Dominican. Highly attractive to men. Everybody noticed me with her. This guy, he was a big dude, he liked her and he kept trying to pursue an interest in her. I went to talk to him. He broke my nose, hurt my pride. I came back and knocked on the door. She come out and I said get José, and as soon as he come, I had a butcher knife. I jumped on him and kept stabbing him. They gave me murder. When I served my time, I used to jump rope, go for a jog, anything to forget the time.

The following occasion, they sent Jimmy upstate for fifteen months. He knew no one, and he was tense until he fought. The staff rushed in and broke it up and he kept his head up as he was led away. Twelve hours later, they brought him back and the tension started building again. So did the schemes. The idea was to get a hold of tobacco or coffee or anything for a buzz. He clicked up with a couple guys from New York. One was German Italian, a young man through whose field mouse–colored hair you could see the scars on his scalp. What hood you claim? They played cards using sugar packs from the chow hall as chips. That's where I'm from, said Frankie. Bum-rushing Flushing. How come I ain't never heard a you? What level you at?

Prepared to fight again, Jimmy stood up. Frankie hugged him. One love, kid. Frankie from Franklin Street, all my life, since '93. Stay on point. We fight niggers all day in here.

At Krayville, all the fat blonde social worker asked him was, Are you a Nazi or an Aryan?

He named his last prison. I was with the white boys there.

He saw whites wearing flip-flops and white socks, getting patted down, sticking out their tongues, arms out like Christ, white eyes with flat, black circles like sharks, getting walked with leashes.

They went to chow together, the yard together, they moved as a unit, posted sentries when they were working out. There were politics and the politics were secret—you're out of bounds asking about it, so don't ask. In the yard, they put their towels out on the ground and did their calisthenics, following cadence called by the mob. They jogged together under the Indiana sky, past the sign that said ONE PERSON AT A TIME.

The mob taught how to be stabbed under freezing showers, to teach you not to flinch. Their workouts were secret, like Shaolin monks. They wore Chinese symbols on their chests, eyelids, meaning strength, stealth, honor. The swastika itself was a Buddhist sign. It represented the pattern of a ghost running in an ancient field. They tattooed their faces, shaved their heads, stole the hardened steel spring from the barber's clippers to carve a dagger out of the metal stock of their bunks, going over and over the same cuts tens of thousands of times, a form of meditation. The guards believe they have power. What they have is the tower, an illusion. Jimmy was given what they called artillery to put in his rectum. He carried it out on the yard and removed it and secreted it in the dirt under the picnic table.

When an incident occurred in the yard, an air-raid buzzer went off through the entire prison and out into the fields and trees beyond the walls. Wherever you were, you dropped down on your face and spread your arms out. Five hundred convicts wearing high white sweat socks up to their knees got down on their faces in the dirt. Correctional officers sprinted out across the turf toward two men attacking a third. The frenzy is unbelievable—you watch him getting hit one, two, three, four times, falling and scrambling away, trying to run and falling. One of the men flattens out—you see the knife flip out of his hand. They hit one with gas as he tries to get a last lick in, and he falls on his face. The victim pushes himself away with his sweatshirt in red flaps and his skin showing like someone bitten by a lion.

His birthday came and went in a rainy season, when the staff manned the perimeter of the vast yard wearing camouflage Gore-Tex and the inmates tramped through the mud, doing dips and chin-ups in yellow foul-weather gear. He didn't receive the card his mother had sent until three months later, after it had been opened by the prison staff and scanned beneath a laser. It contained nothing but a picture of a cake and candles. There was no money. Money's tight right now. — XO Mom

On their way to chow, they strolled by a cell with wadded bloody towels on the concrete floor. Correctional staff in rubber gloves were lifting up a man who looked like yellow plastic. Crusted and streaked blood on his shaved head, stab holes like shark bites, with rubber tubes coming out such as you would use to siphon gasoline. He had been murdered with a sword.

A shame about you-know-who, they said when they were eating.

Some days he slept for up to twenty hours, but when he opened his eyes, it was still the same calendar day, the same bus-station bathroom light was still flickering in his cell, and he was still hammered by the same sound of the place, the distant slamming and calling.

Outside came months with names like May, June, women's names, names that wore summer dresses in his mind. He popped open the bottom of his deodorant and put his finger in the space where he stashed his ball of foil. The ball of foil had been unrolled and rolled back up again many times. When it was unrolled, you could see it contained a chip of what looked like the wing of a cockroach. His cellie had a needle—a tiny tube resembling the ink tube from a ballpoint pen with a needle on the end. They dropped the blankets over the bars after lockdown and cooked up and got high.

When he was high, Jimmy sat nodding with his eyes shut, his marked-up white arms extended, folds of fat across his white belly. His cellie, shaved head gray, bulbous, and helmetlike above his tan face, sat slumped forward, his state sneakers at odd angles to his legs. Speaking with his eyes closed, his cellie said,

This time a year, we used to slaughter a half dozen hogs and everbody would come for miles. They come on bikes, trucks, ever which way. We had us a kind a moonshine a man couldn't drink. I had me nigger braids in them days. My teeth was gone be all gold all across here ...

Even high, they did not smile. Jimmy calculated that he had not smiled in over a year. He lay down and covered himself with his sheet and lay like a sack of laundry.

The Aryans were bikers, and choosing his moment, Jimmy let it be known that he had been a biker, too. Not a biker, but he had ridden bikes in Bay Shore. He'd done stunts with them, wheelies, putting them up on the front wheel—little-ass rice rockets. One time his bike had flipped over and landed on him and everybody thought he was dead. It hurt like hell, but he'd stood up and walked it off and they were all amazed. He'd ridden a Harley, one of those badass choppers with the long neck in front, him just leaned back like this, shades on, gloves on, cruising down the highway. No, he hadn't been in any chapter or nothing. He'd been a lone wolf. He had gone to, let's see, to Virginia Beach, if he remembered. He'd been out to Vegas, where the chicks went crazy for a guy on a bike. He'd been to this other place—he had a picture of it at home in a drawer—a green field, a barbecue somewhere he couldn't remember, but he could remember the good time he'd had, the freedom and the honor and the good music and what it had all meant to him.

TROUBLE IN MIND
Cathy Park Hong

A heartvein throbs between her brows: Ketty-San's
incensed another joke's made at her expense,

With characters of granite schist, she hashtags a ban
on all such jokes, then they, her so-
called friends, pipe up: Why are *you*
        making such a stink
        on race?
You're so post, you're Silicon.

Scuttle back to her spot as sidekick chum.
Her lyric's needed when they need a backup
        minor key,
to that lead's blues that got no core
        (*what* a snore).

But what core is Ketty-San, sidekick chum?
Torn like tendrils of bloody tenderloin
floating in the sea, heart
        a stage set
        about to be struck—

All nightlong, she scribbles her useless esoterica.
All daylong, mumblecored, she meeps,
meeps along.

TOAST
Matt Sumell

....

I once dated a girl who, when faced with restaurant toast, would take only one bite of each of her four restaurant-toast halves. She said she didn't want any of the restaurant-toast halves to feel neglected. "You're a very nice girl," I told her. She thanked me, then complained about the ice cubes in her orange juice.

She had this other habit, too, of putting on ChapStick before drinking her coffee. The first time I noticed it was at the zoo near the giraffes, after we patronized the Perky Bean cart in the Wild Time Food Court. She told me she does it because she likes the greasy feel of the ChapStick on her lips with the warm coffee going in. She said, "I like it so much that one time I left my coffee on the porch to go get my ChapStick out of my bag, and while I was inside I got a phone call from my mom that lasted for like twenty minutes. When I finally remembered about the coffee, all these ants had drowned themselves in it, but I drank it anyway."

I looked her up and down and up again, and then at a trash can, and then at a yellow jacket flying messy figure eights above the trash can. After a while the yellow jacket started hovering over a piece of what I think was chewed-up gum stuck in the ashtray on top of the can, almost landed, then zipped off to someplace else.

"You drank ants," I said.

"I did."

"Did they taste like anything?"

"Yes," she said. "Like coffee."

I nodded at her, then together we turned and sipped our coffees and watched the giraffes chew leaves. Later, we watched an otter jerk off.

We started dating intense-style, talking all the time on the phone and in person about this and that, our regrets and our fears for the future and lawn care and breast feeding and the wipe-wash feature on cars, but mostly about what we wanted to eat for dinner. The answer was usually, I don't know, what do you wanna eat? And the answer to that was usually, I don't know, what do you wanna eat? And so on. Eventually she would go, Hmmmm, then list off ethnic groups in the form of questions—Japanese?—and I would get really frustrated and say, Let's just go to Joe's.

Joe's was this dump on Cannery Row with mediocre food, but there was no freezer in the kitchen so it was always fresh and pretty cheap, and the first time we ate there we heard an old guy say, "Where the fuck am I? Miami? I hate glass bricks." We liked it immediately. One table was shaped like a rowboat, and one was an actual picnic bench. The silverware was mismatched, too, the floor painted-over cracked concrete, the baby-blue walls decorated with pictures of boats and big fish, and a framed newspaper article about a World War II submarine hung outside the only bathroom. It quickly became our special place, and we went at least twice a week. We even had a favorite table in the corner, and got to know one of the waitresses, Jessica, pretty well.

Then one morning she followed me into the kitchen and watched me pour myself a bowl of granola and milk and scoop a big spoonful of it into my mouth and commented, "Eating granola, huh?" I was so confounded I stopped chewing to look at her, exactly one half of me wanting to pinch her cheeks, exactly the other half of me wanting to punch her across the room. I stood quietly for a few seconds until the feelings passed, and when they did I resumed eating my granola. Realizing that I wasn't going to bother with a response, she turned her attention to the window and, noticing a cat outside, declared, "Ohhh, look! A cat!" Then a few seconds later, "That cat is cuuuute."

That afternoon, after she'd gone home, she called on the phone to ask if I'd done my laundry.

Also, one night, when she was standing still and naked and backlit by the bathroom light, I noticed a kind of white, almost invisible fur all over her body. It bothered me. I never said anything about it 'cause I didn't want to hurt her feelings, but she had no problem commenting on how my dick is browner than the rest of me. "It's like the dark circles around Indian people's eyes," she said. I pretended I didn't care, but I did, but not as much as I cared about her shoes. She always wore high heels, like even on bike rides always, and to the beach and batting cages always, and to a Super Bowl party we went to once. And believe me, it wasn't so much the height thing, which she thought it was about—it was that I got sick of hearing her clomping around everywhere like a pony. At first I just made little jokes about it, started calling her Trusty and offering her carrots all the time, said things like, "You can lead a lady to water, but you can't make her be sneaky." Soon enough, though, I was promising to shoot her if she ever broke her leg. She got upset, and I said, "It'd be real sad, but I'd have no choice. Sorry." Then I pointed my finger at her like a pistol and went, Pchoooo.

One Sunday she took an hour getting ready to go to the dog park, and I told her to giddy it the fuck up. She gave me the whole I-do-this-for-you! thing in the car on the way and I said, "Whoa now. Slow down there, Seabiscuit. If you're doing it for me, lose the fancy fuckin' footware. It annoys me."

She got real quiet then, looked out the window at passing stuff, said, "You can just drop me off wherever."

"Okay," I said. "How about in the La Brea Tar Pits? Be sure to say hi to the wooly mammoths and sabertooths for me, and the bird fossils, and I'm not even fucking kidding, man."

"Don't call me *man*!" she yelled, and when I glanced over I could see that she'd started crying, which is another thing. She could be very dramatic sometimes, but worse, the drama seemed rehearsed, like she had learned it from watching too many lady movies. She'd cry about stuff that wasn't worth crying about, and allow for all these pregnant pauses and deep breaths and whisper-say something dramatic like, "You're mean." Exhale through mouth, close eyes, shake head slowly, clomp away.

She also wrote me notes, dramatic ones declaring dramatic things like, "Miss you!" And, "You really embarrassed me last night... I work with her!" And one time, verbatim, I'm not even kidding, this:

Risk or regret.

That's the phrase associated with thoughts of you.

You are someone I invest my time in who is an impossible situation.

I think you are amazing.

I haven't felt connected to anyone the way I do with you every morning we wake up together.

Risk or Regret.

Almost every night before I go to bed.

Risk or Regret.

I didn't know what to do with that info, so I put a C+ at the top of it and gave it back. More drama. More whisper-talk. More clomping.

I felt bad about that one and followed her out of the room and told her I was only kidding and that I was sorry. She said, regular volume, "Sorry for what? Do you even know?" I said for being a jackass. "That's a start," she said. But instead of explaining that I'm a moron and don't wanna fall in love and have to fuck her forever, I just kissed her and fucked her for what felt like forever.

So there were things about each other we grew not to like,

and the sex went from three or four positions to one or two, sometimes one or none when one or both of us were tired, which was
a lot. We made each other yawn. I got to know the fillings in her
back teeth.

We started spending most weeknights on the couch watching
America's Funniest Home Videos and animal documentaries. We
were watching this one where they have slow-motion aerial footage
of a wolf chasing a mother and baby gazelle all over Mongolia for
like ten minutes, and sometime early on the mother and baby got
split up, so then it was just the wolf and the little gazelle, but the
little gazelle could really move—I mean, *really* move. So they're
zigging and zagging and leaping and then just going flat out until
the little gazelle gets tired and collapses to the ground and the wolf
eats him up, just fuckin' rips him apart, but then later on we find
out the wolf eventually starves to death anyway, and then this baby
elephant goes blind in a sandstorm but continues following his
mother's footprints using only his sense of smell, only he follows
them in the wrong direction so he dies, too, when all of a sudden I
felt her scooching closer to me on the couch and I looked at her, and
without even turning away from the TV she out of nowhere says
she wants to try anal sex. I blinked at her ear for a few seconds before saying, "Okay." And before you know it I was frenching her,
and then before you know it I was doing my high school locker
combination move on her (33-14-4), followed by my La-Z-Boy
technique, and then my eating-her-pussy maneuvers, before she
pulled me up by my hair and rolled on her side, and I stuck it in
there and moved it around for awhile. The whole time she talked
her dirty talk, every now and again dropping in half-rhetorical
questions to encourage my participation, but it didn't work 'cause I
always gave one-word answers.

"You like having your cock in my ass, Mister Bad Boy?"

"Yep."

And it went on like that, not for too long, just right up until
she started yelling don't stop. Then, after the ten seconds where I

remained perfectly still with my mouth open for some reason, I apologized and went wide-legged into the kitchen for paper towels like a gentleman.

Overall I'd say it was okay—like going through a little door into a big room. I prefer vaginas. But what was a lot of fun, though, was to pretend that she got pregnant from it, and then the next day to pretend that she gave birth to our turd baby and that we named him Francis. The day after that she broke up with me by dramatic note, which basically said, I can't do this anymore, and which I read and then put in the garbage disposal. For the next few nights I dreamt she left me angry voice mails about my laundry, and for the next few weeks I wondered what it meant and back-and-forthed about trying to win her back, exactly one half of me wanting to, exactly the other half of me not. I decided nothing and realized I suck at making decisions. My younger brother, on the other hand, doesn't. He slept with three women, decided he liked the third, and married her. This is despite our on-her-deathbed-in-the-den mother saying, "AJ, you know I love Tara, but don't you think you should have some fun first?" He squeezed her hand and told her his mind was made up. I set about the business of unmaking it five minutes later, in the kitchen, by demanding he honor our mother by fucking more girls. He looked me right in the hairdo and said, "Sorry, bro."

"Don't apologize to me," I said. "Apologize to that woman in there, because you're breaking her fucking heart. Then apologize to yourself when your marriage falls apart in ten years, but now you're balder and fatter and can't get the quality ass you can right now. Then reject the apology 'cause you don't deserve forgiveness, you divorced piece a shit!"

"You're a moron piece a shit," he said.

"I don't think so."

"I know so."

"Well here's what I know so: Mom made the mistake of not fucking enough people before getting married, and she's telling

you not to make the same mistake. She's being a good mom to
you, and you're not listening, and I don't think you're seeing,
either, because I'm pretty sure Tara's face is a dirty sneaker with
googly eyes and a wig on."

"You're eating Mom's pain pills?"

"Yeah, so?"

"I love her," he said. "Be happy for me."

"No, because I love you. And I'm telling you, as your brother
and as your friend: fuck more girls. A lot more. AJ, every day millions of people die, and with their last breaths they look at their
loved ones gathered around them and say, Oh, shit, I'm dying, I
shoulda had sex with more people. But no one ever dies saying,
Oh, shit, I shoulda had sex with less people... except maybe if
they're dying of AIDS or cervical cancer, or were raped."

"That's really dumb."

"Is it?"

"Yes," he said. "It is."

Then he walked out of the room, leaving me there alone in the
kitchen, amazed and unsettled by his calm confidence, his above-
this-ness, a little because of the drugs I ate and the weird-looking
stained-glass seahorse suction-cupped to the window. Then I
thought, Focus! Then I thought, Balls, if I can't change AJ's mind,
then maybe I can change Tara's, and that's when I started treating
her real shitty whenever possible. I also unprotecto-ed her best
friend after my mother's funeral, and that Christmas I stuck gum
under Tara's coffee table and left it there. No matter what I did,
though, she was always good-humored and forgiving about it, un-
shakable as he was, and in the weeks and months after my breakup
I thought back on all this, wondering how doubtlessness like that
happens. And I don't know. What I do know is that when I asked
my father when he was sure about marrying Mom, he said, "When
I stopped wakin' up with boners."

I still wake up with boners is the other thought I thought most
in the weeks following the breakup, and, unlike my brother, I de-

cided to use them on as many girls as possible. I decided to listen to our mother. I decided to have fun.

Of course it wasn't always. In fact, a lot of the time I felt lonely and miserable, especially in the beginning, when I realized I had no real gal-getting skills and just jerked off a lot and ate snacks in bed. It also crossed my mind that I gave up on something good, something with potential, someone who cared about and believed in me. In the end, though, I let her go, and over the next few years I changed from a mostly passive prick to a mostly aggressive one, sexing a lot of girls and I'm pretty sure contracting HPV in my throat.

I continued sport-boning broads even after best-manning my brother and Tara's not-as-bad-as-I-thought-it'd-be wedding; even after they had a daughter and named her Marie, our mother's name; even after I saw first-hand how full and rich their life together seemed. I told myself it was probably them just keeping up appearances, but when I drunkenly accused my brother of keeping up appearances he assured me that wasn't the case, then asked if I'd be Marie's godfather.

I was so surprised I hugged him and apologized for being a jerk, and told him I'd consider it a real honor. Then I found out I had to take some kind of church class and turned down the job. He ended up going with Javier, this Bible-thumping family-man fuck-faced friend of his with narrow shoulders, and when I went to the baptism at St. John's I was kinda bummed it wasn't me up there waterboarding little Marie. And after the priest hocus-pocused and abracadabra-ed her and Javier promised his promises and everyone got up to leave for the reception, I stayed seated in the pew, mesmerized by the sound of the women walking out, their high heels clicking and clonking and echoing in the almost empty and expensively built house of God.

The reception was at their place, where I proceeded to drink beers with my father, the widower, the new grandpa with the new toupee. We were alone on the couch not talking to people, including each other, until I turned to him and said, "What do you do when the grass isn't always greener. When it's brownish on both sides. Like my dick."

He squinted, sipped his beer, and said, "Leave me the fuck alone."

"Sure."

I got up and tried my best to muster up the enthusiasm to flirt with married girls in flowery sundresses, but quickly ended up back on the couch with my feet on the coffee table with green gum still stuck underneath. I checked.

I woke early the next morning, alone, around six or seven. I couldn't fall back asleep, so I lay there feeling bad and hungry for about an hour, eventually getting up and dressed and finding my keys and driving to the coast. I drove past Joe's to this other place called the Lighthouse Grill, where there were no glass bricks and where I got a pretty decent serving of restaurant toast and eggs over easy and tomatoes. I was about halfway through when this guy and his lady and their daughter were seated at the table next to mine. They looked over at me a few times, so when I wasn't chewing, I tried to look like I was thinking about something, but I wasn't, not really, just: squint. Eventually they read their menus.

Just as the waitress asked me how everything was, the ice cubes at the bottom of my glass rushed up and smacked me in the teeth, and some juice dribbled onto my chin. I wiped it with my shirtsleeve and said, "Good, thanks." Sure thing, she said, and dropped my check on the table and turned around and asked the guy and his lady and their daughter if they knew what they'd like. They did, kind of, and the lady ordered some restaurant eggs and toast, and the guy ordered calamari steak and eggs, and their daughter ordered restaurant Rice Krispies and continued drawing pictures of animals with crayons on the back of her paper placemat. I didn't think the drawings were very good, but after the waitress returned with their beverages she put both hands on her knees in an exaggerated way and said, "Oh, how pretty! Is that an elephant?" And the little girl nodded. "And what's this one, a rhinoceros?" she said. And again the little girl nodded. "And this one, here," said the waitress, pointing. "What's this one?"

"It's a giraffe!" exclaimed the little girl.

"Wow," said the waitress. "A giraffe. That's great."

But it wasn't great, it looked more like a dinosaur than a giraffe. And as much as I'd have enjoyed holding that against her, I have to admit a lot of things haven't really turned out the way I'd have liked them to, either.

BICENTENNIAL
Dan Chiasson

1.

Moving as a mind moves across a math problem,
Or an eye across a lover's body,
Or a dragonfly across the sky,
Or history, through wars and bodies,
Or a film from frame to frame,
Or the moods, strangers to each other,
Or a ferry across a lake all day,
Move with me now, for I need company—

I have this wish to get caught up in something
Precisely unlike a poem, unlike writing
For its straightforwardness, its power
That is not the power of half secrecy
But is, instead, something enormous
And potentially dangerous, and this is all,
I am afraid, will move my mind one inch
Off the small white tee where it sits and waits.

My mind sits on its small white tee and waits
For something like what others experience
When they avert a tragedy, but barely,

And all of life is refocused in that moment,
Even the parts they hated yesterday,
Or, worse than hated, felt merely a blank
Where emotion would be, a blank
Where meaning would be if only they

2.

Could find the exact site in Paris, by the Seine,
Where the princess died, and see the spot,
And remember the night she died, late
In New York in the era when my friends and I
Did copious amounts of Ecstasy at parties
And when it hit you, you simply shone.
Now everyone in that room was beautiful,
And, in the mirror, your own face was a gift

For which you owed even total strangers thanks.
This was what led you in the first place
To make the call, pool the money, and meet the guy
In an alley off West Fourth Street, returning
To the bar or party with a handful of banana-
Colored pills, heads back, and away we go,
Though that night none of us expected to go
Exactly where we were going that night.

I remember, later, in the standards bar: the weeping men
Who, by some accident of history and their bodies,
It happened, cared for her the way you would a friend,
And one man requested Oh, Lady Be Good at the bar,
And the sad, slow song rang through the bar
Until I did feel, as the song kept telling me I did,
Like a lonesome babe in the wood, adrift
Upon some serotonin raft in a wide, slow stream

3.

Of time, late, late in the night of my childhood
Before I had done anything yet I would regret.
Now it was 1976, and my body in my bed
Felt for the first time what being part of a country
Feels like, a memory of flags and songs
And foods I'd never had before,
For it was the country's birthday, the country
Was having its birthday party, in a park, by the lake.

What being part of a country felt like, in the park,
With the entire breakwater full of boats,
With ferryboats blaring music offshore,
Everyone acting as though it made them happy
To be part of the country, even those I later learned
Were hippies, including my aunts and uncles,
Whose code seemed to include, toward children,
Kindness, what it felt like being part of a country

Was to be quite specifically targeted for love,
As though a letter from a stranger had arrived
Delivering the best, the most unexpected, news.
A neighbor put me up on his shoulders
So I could see, better, the band concert,
War veterans playing French horn, the neighbor
Who moved to Boston and became a caterer
Before he moved back home into his bedroom

4.

Where his parents cared for him the year he died.
He'd been my babysitter, the only boy
Who ever cared for me, and I remember

His patience in watching me play, for he,
Too, seemed to have kindness as part of his code,
And when he died the neighbors gathered
In the small front yard and planted a lilac
Which, whenever I visit home, I go and see.

Did you know next door to our house
There used to be a small, stained-glass chapel
Attached to a dormitory, where the masses
Had a distinct "folk" flare and kindness
Radiated from the mousy students,
Almost as though it was part of their code?
The girls from Rutland or St. Johnsbury,
Or far away, like Danbury, Connecticut,
Girls that now would be approaching sixty,

Who sometimes cared for me upstairs
In their tidy dorm rooms, with crucifixes
On the corkboard, coffee mugs, and toys
They'd brought with them from home,
Which now they gave to me, so I could play.
And sometimes nuns in the convent,
Whose code, it appeared, included kindness,
Showed me the few things they brought

5.

From home to their small cell-like rooms:
One, a young nun, was a coin collector
And she showed me a Standing Liberty quarter
Engraved with the first initial of a boy
She'd dated and who'd taken her to the fair;
I had the distinct impression she still loved him,
The way that whole afternoon led up

To her getting the quarter from her drawer
And putting it on the TV tray
Next to her bed, next to the rosary,
And watched me react when she said
The word *boy*. What does *R* stand for,
Sister? Richard, she said, and I wondered
(Since I was a coin collector, too,
And knew the value of every coin)
How much less it now was worth engraved.

Now she puts the coin into the drawer, and
We move inside my mind to the Paris skyline,
Where an enormous Ferris wheel appears,
Lit by the light it generates, a wheel
That spins and spins nowhere, nowhere,
All night, whether we watch it or not,
And children having their childhoods right now,
This late in time, as though they had to stand in line

6.

Just to be born, get on, and ride, and
From the top they see the sliver of history
Fate is allowing them to see, before
They disembark and scatter, some to joy,
Some to misery, and whether they live
For a hundred years or die, as some have,
Tomorrow, this is the childhood these children
Are having, which is something I remind

My own children, all the time—I say,
You are having your childhood now,
And they say, Yes, Daddy, and I say,
Jokingly, but not really, How do you feel it is going,
And they light up and they say, Great,

Which is just what I would have said as a kid
If someone—though who would it have been?—
Had asked me this very same question:

You are having your childhood now;
Today you went to the bicentennial;
Everyone in the world was there,
And you were there: How does that feel?
That's when I say, brightening, Great,
And wait until later, much later in life,
As they must wait, for the real answer. I am having
My childhood now; that's me; I am at a party

7.

By the lake, the boats jostle for space
Inside the breakwater, a neighbor lifts me
Up to see the band concert, the French horns
Blare, the men wear their war uniforms,
The hippies are riding history, the ferries
Are playing blues for the private parties,
The mountains across the water, that's New York.
I am having my childhood right now

In this country, in 1976, that's me
Near the cannons that point to the Adirondacks,
That's me clapping when the parade
Wends by, I am in a park, by the lake,
This is the exact moment in time when I exist
As a five-year-old, in this country,
And everyone is there, at the bicentennial,
There's the mayor and the chamber of commerce,

And there's the National Guard, and the Rotarians,
And there's my daddy, though he never knew me,

My handsome daddy, happy, dancing the day away,
My tall, handsome daddy and his brand new family,
Just starting out in life, elated at the thought
They'd made it this far, to this enormous party
The country threw for itself—because who else would?—
One billion years ago, today, on its birthday.

GOD
Benjamin Nugent

W e called her God because she wrote a poem about how Caleb Newton ejaculated prematurely the night she slept with him, and because she shared the poem with her friends.

Caleb was the president of our fraternity. When he worked our booth in the dining hall he fund-raised a hundred dollars in an hour. He had the plaintive eyes and button nose of a child in a life-insurance commercial, the carriage of an armored soldier. He was not the most massive brother, but he was the most a man, the one who neither played video games nor rejoiced at videos in which people were injured. His inclination to help other brothers write papers and refine workouts bespoke a capacity for fatherhood. I had seen his genitals, in the locker room after lacrosse, and they reminded me of a Volvo sedan in that they were unspectacular but shaped so as to imply solidity and soundness. One morning when we were all writhing on the couches, hungover, he emerged from the bathroom in a towel, attended by a cloud of steam. We agreed that the sight of his body alleviated our symptoms.

"If you use a towel right after Newton uses it, your life expectancy is extended ten years," said Stacks Animal.

"If a man kisses Newton, he'll turn into a beautiful woman," I said, and everyone stared at me, because it was a too-imaginative joke.

But Newton threw his head back and laughed. "You guys

are fucking funny," he said. "That's why *I* don't feel hungover anymore."

The putative reasons we named him Nutella were that it sounded like Newton and that he was sweet. But I wondered if it was really because when you tasted Nutella you were there. You were not looking at yourself from afar.

Nutella was never angry. When we discovered the poem and declared its author God, we knew he wouldn't object. He understood that it was a compliment to him as much as to the poet. To make Nutella lose at something, to deprive Nutella of control, God was what you had to be.

We learned of the poem's existence from Shmashcock's girlfriend, who was roommates with Melanie. (That was God's real name.) She told Shmash what the poem was about, and when she went to the bathroom he took a picture of it, and though it was untitled, he mass-texted it to us with the caption "On the Premature Ejaculation of Current Delta Zeta Chi Chapter President Caleb Newton."

It was the only poem I'd ever liked that didn't rhyme. I read it so many times that I memorized it by accident.

Who is this soldier who did not hold his fire
When the whites of my eyes were shrouded
In fluttering eyelids?
I thought I knew you
Knew you were the steady hand on the wheel
The prow itself
But what kind of captain are you?
Scared sailor with your hand on your mast
Betrayed by your own body
As we are all betrayed
On your knees
Above me
Begging my forgiveness
With the muscles of a demon

And the whites of your eyes
As white as a child's?

Behind the counter at D'Angelo's/Pizza Hut, I whispered, "Muscles of a demon/And the whites of your eyes/As white as a child's" for twenty minutes because it was the perfect description of Nutella. It was as if somebody had snapped a photo of him and enlarged it until it was the very wallpaper of my mind. I loved Melanie for writing it. I also felt I was her secret collaborator, for in my head I was contributing lines. I added:

Whose hands are these?
One moment swift as a gray river
The next as still as stones

Because that was another thing about Nutella. He was a war elephant on the lacrosse field and yet capable of quietude and stillness, reading econ on the porch, his phone facedown on his knee, casting light on his groin when he received a text.

While I refined my supplement to the poem, I prepared a Santa Fe Veggie Wrap. The process demanded that I empty a plastic bag of frozen vegetables into a small plastic bucket and place the bucket in a microwave. I neglected the microwave step and emptied the bag of vegetables directly onto the wrap, with the vegetables still cold and rigid. I realized what I had done when I laid the sandwich in its basket, presented it to the girl who had ordered it, and saw the gleam of frost on a carrot rod.

Evgeny called me into the management room, which was a yellow closet straining to contain Evgeny. He said that if I kept dreaming all my days I would wind up like him, a lover of art and philosophy. He pointed to his face, with its little black mustache. I promised him that from now on my motto would be "no more spacing."

I took a pizza order and thought of all I was doing to enhance my employment prospects. Majoring in business, minoring in math, seeking internships related to data mining, building networks of contacts through Delta Zeta Chi, Campus Republicans, and Future Business Leaders. I dreamed of a consulting firm that Nutella would one day helm, staffed by brothers, known for underpromising and overdelivering, with an insignia depicting a clockface in the talons of an eagle. This would represent efficiency and superior perception. It would be pinned on each brother upon attainment of the status of partner, by Nutella, with live chamber music in an acoustically flawless arboretum of recycled glass.

When the pizza emerged on the other side of the self-timing oven, I saw that I had neglected to sprinkle on the cheese. I used American slices intended for subs, room temperature, in the hope that they would melt on the freshly heated pizza in the course of delivery.

That night, Shmash read the poem aloud in the living room, as Nutella covered his face and grinned.

"Like you all have never detonated early," he said, as if it was a dashing crime. As if this thing that we had all most likely done, and been ashamed of, was the least shameful thing in the world. I felt that all the brothers would have stormed North Korea for Nutella then, with a battering ram of wood and stone.

"That girl is a god," said Buckhunter.

"No," said Five-Hour. "That girl is God." And that was how it started.

We spied her at the dining hall the next day at lunch, by the tray carousel.

"God," shouted Five-Hour, and then we all shouted it.

She stopped and squinted. Her friends took up defensive positions on her flanks.

Shmashcock moved his arms up and down. "You are God for writing that poem," he said.

"God," we all said, and moved our arms.

She looked at Nutella, who was smiling.

"Yeah, that's me," she said. She kicked at Stacks, who was on his knees. "I guess you guys can worship me."

That night she came to the house with Nutella to hang out with us. I didn't know the nomenclature for her clothing. She wore black tights that went on her arms, green tights that came up to her knees, and a headband with tiny teeth that made the hair that passed through it poofy when it emerged on the other side. A wrist tattoo peeked from the lace at the end of her left arm-tight. It was a picture of an old mill, a rectangular brick building. It represented Lowell, she said.

"The Venice of Massachusetts," said Buckhunter. His tone was that of an Englishman in a paisley, monogrammed bathrobe, smoking a pipe.

"It's got canals," she agreed. Buckhunter cracked his knuckles and made an assertive sniffing sound.

What people often failed to realize about Delta Zeta Chi was that we were like Native Americans, in that our names referred to aspects of our personalities. Buckhunter was so named because in matters of girls he had the opposite of ADD. If a girl wandered within a certain radius of Buck, she robbed him of his faculty for reason. He couldn't assess her reactions to the things he said; he couldn't see or hear her clearly. He wanted it so bad he never got it. That was his tragedy, to be cockblocked by his own erect cock.

Like many girls before her, God said ha-ha to Buckhunter, smiled disingenuously. I got her a beer and asked her questions. My name was Oprah because there were books in my room and I asked questions.

She wanted to work in public relations, she disclosed. She liked the Batman movies but not the X-Men movies. She was into Nutella as a friend.

God and Nutella made sandwiches in our kitchen. They were like two old men who had been in a war, or had been in a dragout fight that neither had won. The poem, I supposed, had scoured away all pretense. Whereas the other girls who'd hooked up with

Nutella, the ones who wanted him after the hookup and tried to date him, he treated with politeness and indifference. They were undead bumping their foreheads against our windows. They were the opposite of God.

After God and Nutella ate the sandwiches, they made carrot-ginger cupcakes for our midpoint-between-spring-break-and-summer party. In the course of so doing, they killed many ants in the kitchen and the velvety reef of mold in the sink. I offered help with the cream-cheese frosting because I was a frosting intellec-tual. Nutella argued with God about welfare entitlements versus the free market as he held a mixing bowl steady and she washed it with the rough side of a sponge.

That night God gave Nutella a spot while he did a keg stand, holding his calves above her head, her arm-tights, now Easter-egg blue, taut against her forearms. God, we shouted. There were girls at the party so hot, their cheekbones so sharp, their heels so archi-tecturally adventurous, their eyelids so thick with dark paste, they might have been the focus of male attention at a mansion with an in-ground pool. But these girls were not encircled by the brothers of our white ramshackle house. Only God was encircled.

We took turns dancing with her until Shmash asked if she wanted a beer. She declined, pivoted her way across the dance floor to Five-Hour, and humped the air near his leg. She said something in Five's ear and he said something back, and soon they were mul-titasking, their heads stabilized to enable conversation, their lower bodies humping on, like the abdomens of dying wasps.

Five and God went upstairs, Five leading the way, and we all watched Nutella. He threw his arms around me and Shmash and Stacks, and the blond hairs on his forearms were short and dry. His elbow slid around my neck and it was like rolling on a fresh-mowed August lawn.

"I want you guys to know," said Nutella, "that everything is completely cool. Five is the best man for the mission."

We did three Delta Zeta Chi owl hoots, and the sound was soft and Celtic against the human grunts and synthesizer belches of the music, and I wished the final owl hoot would never fade, our eight arms seized up forever around our heads, our huddle rotating slowly, as all huddles do, the faces of my brothers spinning in the black light. I remembered the day my mother took me to the Boston planetarium when I was seven, how the constellations maypoled around a void.

I always woke up earlier than anyone else in the house the morning after a party because I was protective of my abs and therefore drank less beer. That morning I descended to the kitchen to make breakfast and there was Five-Hour, with the shades drawn and the song from last night's dance with God tinkling from his phone. He poured hard cider on his cereal.

"No matter what happened last night," I said, "some chocolate-chip pancakes will taste better than that." I took the bottle from his hand and poured the cider and the cereal in the almost-full garbage bag sitting on the floor by the sink. I mixed batter and chocolate chips.

"Help me," I said. "Slap some butter in a pan."

Soon there was the crackling and the smell.

"Big night?" I tried.

"Fuck you," said Five, "if you ever tell anyone else what I'm about to tell you went down."

I told him I wouldn't as long as he held the bowl so I could scoop the batter right. And he talked.

Once they were upstairs, he said, God asked him please not call her God and call her Melanie instead. She hooked her phone to his speakers and asked him to take down the Eskimo-themed poster from the swimsuit issue. In all of this he obliged. When he tried to slide off her arm-tights with his teeth, she said, "Funny not sexy," which threw him a little. Once her bra was off, she put a yarn-shop Simon & Garfunkel song on repeat and kissed him on the lips.

It occurred to him that this girl had been Nutella's breaker. Bedding her was, for a Delta Zeta Chi brother, what bedding

Shania Twain would be for a Southerner or what bedding Natalie Portman would be for a Jewish person; he was belly to belly with the most major figure in the Delta Zeta Chi culture.

He thought of how Nutella, the least spastic person in the world, a man who could take a jab to the mask in lacrosse and not flinch, had burst open from her hotness, and how that explosion had been documented in a poem that was known to all our house, if not to all Greek houses. He, Five-Hour, was a champion of knights brought in to rescue a princess from a tower the king had failed to scale. I am SWAT, he thought, I am Lancelot. The more he considered it—how God was the ultimate princess, and he, therefore, the ultimate prince, deep in a forest impenetrable to others— the smaller and softer his dick became. For he could not believe that a supra-Nutellian knight was who he really was.

By this point in the telling, Shmash was loitering in the doorway of the kitchen, presumably drawn by the smell of batter. When Five and I looked up he retreated to the living room.

Five staggered to the corner of the kitchen and pressed his forehead against the wall. I turned off the stove and pinched his cheek. His face was wet. I have never cried—not once—since I was ten, and I admire people who can do it. The criers can see the admiration in my face, and it helps them talk.

"Do I just lie?" Five whispered. "Do I just act as if I fucked her, and, if someone asks, say a gentleman never tells?"

I told him to tell the truth. To act like it was nothing to apologize for, because it wasn't. He fist-bumped me, weakly at first, but again and again, until the bumps acquired force. It was not what I had said, I think, because my advice was unremarkable. It was only that he could see the respect on my face, the respect for his tears, and respect, above all, was what he needed.

"I'm done telling Oprah about not getting it up last night," he called to the living room. "And he made pancakes."

Five minutes later everyone was in the sunny kitchen eating, brewing coffee, rinsing dirty plates, taking out the trash, crushing beer cans, talking about internships. Nutella squeezed fresh OJ wearing only his Red Sox boxers and baseball cap, and juice ran down his arms. Buck proposed a toast to Five for continuing the Delta Zeta Chi tradition of almost fucking God. Dust motes frolicked in the air as if emitted by our muscles, and the kitchen smelled like garbage, chocolate, sweat, and spring. I wondered if there would come a day when I would cry.

That night I had a dream I didn't want to have. In a white hotel room, I said to Nutella, Why not? What's the reason for us not to, you and I? What harm? I woke up spattered in cum and consoled myself as I washed my abs, hunched over the sink in the bathroom down the hall, with a different question: When ten sportsmen slept beneath a common roof, the smells of their sweat joined in a common cloud, who could escape unsportsmanlike dreams?

The following evening was Otter Night at Theta Nu. We walked to the TN house with flattened cardboard boxes under our arms. To otter, you needed a cardboard box and a wet, carpeted staircase. The theme of ottering was, look how brothers will pour buckets of water on a carpeted staircase, sled the stairs face-first, and be injured.

We ottered once a year at Theta Nu, but this Otter Night was remarkable for the presence of God, who'd been invited by Nutella. As soon as she climbed the stairs with the flattened box in her hand, we gave it up. None of us had seen a girl otter. To otter was to engage in a dick-bashing test of will. (Jockstraps were expressly forbidden.) To otter with tits was beyond imagining.

She stood at the top of the stairs, eyes closed, back straight. We shouted, drank, whispered that a girl wouldn't do it, filmed with our phones. She laid her box on the ground, looked at the ceiling above her, as if to consult a watchful parent. And then, to the ticking of a drum machine and the groans of a rapper and the groans of the rapper's woman floating above the rapper and the machine, she dove.

Her eyes flinched open every step. It was all quiet the three, four seconds of actual otter, but for the damp thump-*thumps*, and a collective fraternal gasp. At the end, she reached for the bannister to slow herself, a good move, and her landing at the bottom did not look unbearable. She came to a halt with her upper body on the soaked floor, her legs sprawled on the soaked stairs, her face in carpet, the cardboard sled tucked like a lover beneath her pummeled breasts.

"Give me a beer," she said, and I hugged Stacks, Nutella, and Shmash, and they hugged me back, and we all screamed God, God, God.

Throughout the night, God drank beer and touched guys' arms. And a weird thing happened: the brothers declined to put the moves on her.

No one steered her to the dance floor and freaked her. No one hovered beside her and asked her questions about her classes, holding his beer at chest height like a mantis to display his biceps.

The brothers were scared. Attempting her, Nutella had blown his load. Attempting her, Five had limp-dicked. And she ottered like a warrior.

But to me she was a secret collaborator. We were both Nutella poets, the way people we read in core humanities were nature poets. I wasn't scared of her at all.

When the music went "Biggie Biggie Biggie," I took her by the elbow and we took the floor. We humped the air between us; we collaborated.

When the two of us left early, hand in hand, stumbling down Frat Row to Delta Zeta Chi, she said, "I have to say, I'm surprised this is happening with you."

I asked her what she meant.

"Just a wrong first impression."

The house was abandoned, all the brothers at TN's post-otter party, hoping to show off their injuries to girls who had seen them be brave. Our feet creaked on the stairs as she followed me up. In my room I gave her the plug to hook her phone to my speakers and asked her to choose music. She filled the room with the yarn-shopness that Five had described, and I recited her poem from memory, with the lines I'd added, while she sat on my bed with her chin on her fist.

"Consider it your poem, too," she said, and I knew I was supposed to kiss her, and I did.

I had never been to Silicon Valley, but that was where I went that night. Green grass in the shadow of silicon mountains, steel gray with chalk-white caps. Silicon wolves stalked the foothills, screen-eyed. I saw myself kneeling in that grass, doing for Nutella what God was doing for me. I made the sounds I thought Nutella would make.

I put on a condom as the yarn-shop song started over. When we were about to start fucking, I asked her to recite the poem. She looked at me for a moment. Please, I said, and she recited.

I recited with her, and it worked: When we fucked, Nutella was close, because we had drawn him into the room like two lungs. He was just out of reach, something sprayed in the air, like a poem.

I only saw the blood when we were finished. I looked at her face for an answer. She sat and sucked air through her nose, wiped her face with the back of her hand.

"Were you thinking about Nutella?" she asked.

I said no in a too-deep voice.

"You're lying to me. Why did you want us to say the poem?" She started to cry. Her shoulders jumped in rhythm to her sobs. "It's cool, but at least don't lie to me."

Cry, I ordered myself. We would cry together. I pictured tide pools in my eyes. I pictured what the funeral would look like if my little sister died, her friends crying in their glasses and braces. But I'd tried to make myself cry many times, and always the same thing happened: my eyes knew I was trying to do it, and refused. I couldn't make myself cry any better than Nutella and Five-Hour could make themselves Melanie's lovers.

I waited for a minute, listening, trying to join. Finally, I leaned over and put my lips under her eye, so that I could taste her. I wanted to tell her what I tasted: sour makeup and salt.

"I'm sorry I lied to you," I said. "I thought about Nutella but also you at the same time."

She took my hands and folded them across her ribs. And then something occurred to me.

"You can't write a poem about how I said that," I said. "About anything to do with me and Nutella. Even though it was your first time, you can't write a poem about it that you show to people."

I watched her blink in the dark.

"I might not write a poem about it," she said. "But I'm going to talk about it with my friends."

"You can't," I said. "You can't tell them I thought about Nutella."

"Okay, I won't," she said, and I knew that she was now the one lying.

I pulled away from her and sat up in bed. I could see what was going to happen to me like a film projected on my wall: My life was ruined. She would tell her friends, who would tell other girls, and Shmash or Five would find out from one girl or another. Shmash and Five would be too embarrassed to tell Nutella, but they wouldn't be able to resist telling other brothers, and one night, very drunk, a brother would tell Nutella. And nothing would happen. No one would say anything to me. No one would want to take anything from me. But brotherhood would be taken, in the end. The ease with which my brothers spoke to me, the readiness with which they spilled their guts in times of humiliation—this would be withdrawn. My place among them in the consulting firm of the clock and talons.

The arboretum full of chamber music exploded, as if God had sung a note so high it shattered four stories of green windows.

I sat there hating her. She must have hated me back, because she got out of bed, put on her clothes without speaking, and left the house by the time the brothers returned from TN. I lay awake and listened to them bang around the kitchen. They chanted in unison, a single, iambic owl: uh-*ooh* uh-*ooh*. It sounded like, beware, beware.

from WINEHOUSE
Kevin Young

I'm living on borrowed wine.
Last of the light.
Only I
seem to mind.
I sleep to see
what I might find.

Yes I been black
but when I come back

I want to be anonymous
as America. As famous.
Market my words.
I been treading so long
this water into wine—
why fight? My tongue hurts.
Even with death I flirt.

And if my daddy
thinks I'm fine

I'm in love with the light. How it
spills across all it touches, burns
& blooms. I cave. I parade. I quail.

For somewhere I've set sail,
three sheets to the wind. Don't
tell my mother where I been.

I said No,
No, No.

GOSPODAR
Garth Greenwell

*I*t would have made me laugh in English, I think, the word he used for himself and that he insisted I use for him—not that he had had to insist, of course, I would call him whatever he wanted. But in his language there was a resonance it would have lacked in my own, partaking both of the everyday (*gospodine*, my students say in greeting, mister or sir) and of the scented chant of the cathedral. He was naked when he opened the door, backlit in the entrance of his apartment, or naked except for a series of leather straps that crossed his chest, serving no particular function; and this too might have made me laugh, were there not something in his manner that forbade it. He didn't greet me or invite me in, but turned his back without a word and walked to the center of what I took to be the apartment's main room. I didn't follow him, I waited at the edge of the light until he turned again and faced me, and then he did speak, telling me to undress in the hallway. Take off everything, he said, take off everything and then come in.

I was surprised by this, which was a risk for him as for me, for him more than for me, since he was surrounded by neighbors any of whom might open their doors. He lived on a middle floor of one of the huge Soviet-style apartment blocks that stand everywhere in Sofia like fortresses or keeps, ugly and imperious, though this is a false impression they give, they're so poorly built as already to be crumbling away. I obeyed him, I took off my shoes

and then my coat and began to undo the long line of buttons on
my shirt, my hands fumbling in the dark and in my excitement,
too. I pulled down my pants, awkward in my haste, wanting him
and wanting also to end my exposure, though it was part of my
excitement. It was for this excitement I had come, something to
draw me out of the grief I still felt for R., who had left months
before, long enough for grief to have passed but it hadn't passed,
and I found myself resorting again to habits I thought I had escaped, though that's the wrong word for it, escaped, given the
eagerness with which I returned to them.

   . I made a bundle of my clothes, balling my pants and shirt and
underthings in my coat, and I held this in one hand and my shoes
in the other and stood, still not entering, shivering both from cold
and from that profounder exposure I felt. *Ne ne, kuchko*, he said,
using for the first time the word that would be his only name for
me. It's our word bitch, an exact equivalent, but he spoke it almost
tenderly, as if in fondness; no, he said, fold your clothes nicely before you come in, be a good girl. At this last something rose up in
me, as at a step too far in humiliation. This is what most men
would feel, I think, especially men like me, who are taught that it   ·
is the worst thing, to seem like a woman; when I was a boy my father responded to any sign of it with a viciousness out of all pro-
portion, as though he might keep me from what I would become,
a faggot, as he said, which remained his word for me when for all
his efforts I found myself as I am. Something rose up in me at what
he said, this man who still barred my way, and then it lay back
down, and I folded my clothes neatly and stepped inside, closing
the door behind me.

   It was a comfortless room. There was an armoire of some sort,
a table, a plush chair, all from an earlier time. These spaces are
passed from generation to generation; people often spend their entire lives amid the same objects and their evidence of other lives, as
almost never happens in my own country, or never anymore. I stood
for a moment just in front of the door, and then the man told me to
kneel. I could feel him looking at me in the clinical light, inspecting

or evaluating me, and when he spoke it was as if with distaste. *Mnogo si debel*, he said, you're very fat, and I looked down at myself, at my thighs and the flesh folded over them, the flesh I have hated my entire life, and though I remained silent, I thought, not so very fat. It was part of our contract, that he could say such things and I would endure them. I wasn't as fat as he, who was larger in person than in the photos he had sent, as one comes to expect, larger and older, too; he was as old as my father, or almost, anyway nearer to him than to me. But he stood there as though free of both vanity and shame, with an indifference that seemed absolute and, in my experience of such things, unique. Even very beautiful men are eager to be admired, wherever you touch them they harden their muscles, turning their best angles to the light; but he seemed to feel no concern at all for my response to him, and it was now that I felt the first stirrings of unease.

He neither spoke nor gestured, and the longer he appraised me, the more I worried that having come all this way I would be told to leave. It wasn't the time and expense of the trip to the center I would resent, but the waste of the anticipation that had mounted in me over the several days I had chatted with him online, an anticipation that wasn't exactly desire, as it wasn't desire that I felt now, though I was hard, though I had been hard even as I climbed the stairs, even in the taxi that had brought me there. He was an unhandsome man, though in the way of some older men he seemed solid in his corpulence, thick through the chest and arms. His face was blunt featured, generically Balkan; it was clear that he had never been attractive, or rather his primary attraction had always been the bearing he had either been gifted with or cultivated, the pose of uncaring that seemed to draw all value into itself, that seemed entirely self-sufficient. He would never be called a faggot, I thought, whatever the nature of his desires.

Then, to my relief, *ela tuka* he said, come here, having decided to keep me, at least for a while. When I began to rise he snapped *dolu*, stay down, and I moved across the space on all fours, the carpeting featureless and gray and coarse. When I reached him he took my hair in his hand and lifted me up onto my knees, not roughly, perhaps merely as a means of communication more efficient than speech. I had told him I wasn't Bulgarian in one of our online chats, warning him that when we met there might be things I wouldn't understand, but he had asked none of the usual questions, seeming not to care why I had come to his country, where so few come and fewer still stay long enough to learn the language, which is spoken nowhere else, which even here, as the country shrinks, is spoken by fewer people each day; it's not difficult to imagine it disappearing altogether, the language and the country both. We'll understand each other, he had said, don't worry, and perhaps it was merely to ensure this understanding that he had taken me in hand, firmly but not painfully guiding me to my knees.

He let go of my hair once this was done, freeing his hand to move down the side of my face, almost stroking it before he cupped it in his palm. It was a gesture of tenderness, and his voice was tender too as he said *kuchko*, addressing me as if solicitously and tilting my head so that for a moment we gazed at each other face to face, and his fingers flexed against my cheek, almost in a caress. I leaned my face into him, resting it on his palm as he spoke again in that tone of tenderness or solicitude, tell me, *kuchko*, tell me what you want. And I did tell him, at first slowly and with the usual words, reciting the script that both does and does not express my desires; and then I spoke more quickly and more searchingly, drawn forward by the tone of his voice, what seemed like tenderness although it was not tenderness, until I found myself suddenly in some recess or depth where I had never been. Because I spoke it poorly, there were things I could say in his language without self-consciousness or shame, as if there were something in me unreachable in my own language, something I could reach only with that blunter instrument by which I too was made a blunter instrument, so that I found myself at last at the end of my strange litany saying again and again I want to be nothing, I want to be nothing. Good, the man said, good, speaking with the same tenderness and smiling a little as he cupped my face in his palm and bent forward, bringing his own face to mine, as if to kiss me, I thought, which surprised me, though I would have welcomed it. Good, he said a third time, his hand letting go of my cheek and taking hold again of my hair, tightening and forcing my neck further back, and then suddenly and with great force he spat into my face.

He pulled me forward then, still holding my hair, and pressed my face hard into his crotch, hard enough that it must have been as uncomfortable for him as for me, so that any pleasure we took would be an accident, as it were, or a consequence of some other aim. This is not to say that I didn't feel pleasure; I had never stopped being hard, and when he said to me breathe me in, smell me, I did so eagerly, taking great gasps. I had felt it too in his earlier act, when he spat on me it was like a spark along the track of my spine, who knows why we take pleasure in such things, perhaps it's best not to look into them too closely. He too was feeling it, I could feel his cock against my cheek thicken, then lengthen and lift; there had been no change in it during my long recitation, that catalog of desires I had named, but now at our first real touch he grew hard. He kept one hand at the back of my head, gripping my hair and holding me in place, though there was no need, as surely he knew; but with the other he reached for something, as I could tell from the shifts in his balance and weight, and when finally he pulled me back from him, he slipped it quickly over my head. It was a chain, I realized as I felt it cold against my neck, or rather a leash of the kind one uses with difficult dogs, and immediately he pulled it tight, letting me feel the pinch of it. This didn't excite me, it was part of the pageantry to which I had always been indifferent, but I didn't object; I assented, though he hadn't sought my permission or consent. And then he took another chain, this one shorter and finer, with little toothed clamps at each end, which (using both his hands, letting the leash fall free, since after all I was not an animal, I didn't need to be bound) he attached to my chest. I sucked in my breath at this, the first real pain he had caused me, but it wasn't a terrible pain, and not unexciting; a thrill ran through me at this too, and at its promise.

Dobre, he said when he had finished, good, though he was speaking of his own work now and not of me. He took up the chain again and pulled it tight, twisting his wrist to gather up the slack, which he wrapped around his curled fingers until they were nearly flush against my neck. He was putting me on a short leash, I thought, though I was thinking more of his cock, which I was eager for now, perhaps because of the pain at my chest, which was more than pain, which was excitement too, as was the tightness of the chain around my neck, in which I felt the strength of his arm keeping me from what I wanted. Whatever chemical change it is had taken hold and I was lit up with it, each cell bearing its burden of want, so that after all I did strain against the leash he had been right to make so short. It was a kind of disobedience but a kind that would please, and even as he tightened his grip on the chain I heard him laugh or almost laugh, a slow satisfied chuckle. It was a sound of approval and I glowed with it. She wants something, he said, still chuckling, and he lifted his foot to my crotch, feeling my hardness as I knelt before him, she likes it, and then he used his foot to pull my cock down, letting it go so that it snapped back up, making me flinch. Then his foot moved lower and he placed his toes beneath my balls, which he fondled roughly, flexing his ankle until there was not quite pain but an intimation of pain. He was dulling my pleasure, not removing it entirely but taking off its edge.

But he didn't take off its edge, not really, and when there was a slackening in the leash I lunged forward, like the dog he called me. There was nothing extraordinary about his cock, it was solid and sizeable and thick, but none of these to a remarkable degree, and he had shaved himself there as all men here do, which I hate, the childlike bareness of it is obscene, I can't accustom myself to it. Still, I was eager, and as I took him in my mouth I felt the strange gratitude I nearly always feel in such moments, which was gratitude not so much to him as to whatever arrangement of things had allowed me what as a child I was sure I would forever be denied. It was large enough that I didn't try to take all of it at once; eager as I was there are certain preparations required, the relaxation and lubrication of passages, a general warming up. But immediately his hand was on my head again, forcing me further, and when it was clear that the passage was blocked, he used both of his hands to hold me, at once pulling me to him and jerking his hips forward in short, savage thrusts, saying *dai gurloto*, give me your throat, an odd construction I had never heard before. This too was painful, and not only for me, it must have hurt him also, but I did give my throat, finding an angle that gave him access, and soon enough it was easier; I relaxed and there was a rush of saliva and he could move however he wanted, as he did for a while, perhaps there was pleasure for him after all. As there was for me, the intense pleasure I've never been able to account for, that can be accounted for in no way mechanically; the pleasure of service, I've sometimes thought, or more darkly the pleasure of being used, the strange exhilaration of being made an object that had been lacking in sex with R., though that had had its own pleasures, which I longed for but that had in no way compensated for the lack of this. I want to be nothing, I had said to him, and it was a way of being nothing, or next to nothing, a convenience, a tool.

He stopped moving then, taking his hands from my head and even from the chain, which fell superfluous and cold down my back. *Kuchkata*, he said, not *kuchko* anymore, the vocative that had softened the word and made it tender to my ears; no longer addressing me but speaking of the object I had become, he said, let the bitch do it herself. I obeyed it, the order he had expressed not to me but to the air, I forced myself upon him with a violence greater than his own, wanting to please him, I suppose, but that isn't true; I wanted to satisfy myself more than him, or rather to assuage that force or compulsion that drew me to him, that force that can make me such a stranger to myself, it is a failing to be so prone to it but I am prone to it. He let me do this for some time, setting my own pace, and then there came again the shift in his balance that was his reaching to the table beside him, choosing some new object. He struck me with this a moment later, not very hard but hard enough that I jerked, interrupting the rhythm I had set, so that he placed his hand on my head again, taking hold of me as if I might bolt. It was another prop of the sort I had always scorned, a cat-o'-nine-tails, a kind of short whip with several strips of leather hanging down; the one time it had been used on me before the man had been timid and I had felt nothing at all, except to despise him a little because he used it only for show. This was something else, I had been struck with force, and though I had jerked more from shock than from pain there was pain too, less in the actual blow than in the moment after, a sharp heat spreading along my back.

He said a word I didn't understand then, which from his tone I took as something like steady, the kind of mixed reassurance and admonishment one might give a startled horse, and for a moment his grip on my head softened, he flexed his fingers in something again almost like a caress. I was surprised at my response to this, which was outsize and overwhelming, gratitude at what seemed like kindness from this man who had been so stern; it was something I hadn't felt before, or not for a very long time. I began moving again, having paused at the shock of the first blow, brought back by his caress or perhaps there had been a very slight pressure from his hand, I'm not sure. I took the whole length of him, and I felt his hand rise and fall again, this time more gently, and since I had warning it didn't interrupt the motion I had fallen into, it became a part of that motion; we fell into a rhythm together, and as his strokes grew quicker and more intense so did my own. Soon enough I was in real pain, my back had grown tender, and I realized that I had begun making noises, little whimpers and cries, and they too became part of the rhythm we had fallen into, his arm rising and falling and my own movement forward and back, and with that movement the swinging of the smaller chain at my chest, the ache that had grown dull but that shifted as I swayed. Then he broke our rhythm, suddenly pulling me to him and thrusting his hips forward at the same time, his grip tight, and as he ground me against him he struck me several times quickly and very hard, so that for the first time I cried out with real urgency, an animal objection. But I couldn't cry out, the passage was blocked, and with the effort I began to choke, the mechanism failed and involuntarily I struggled against him; I tried to wrench my head away, I even brought my hands to his thighs but he held me firm. He struck me five or six times in this way, or maybe seven or eight, they were indistinct as I struggled, moving incoherently, at once pushing myself back from him and flinching at the blows. Then he was still, and though he didn't release me he drew back, letting me breathe and grow calm again. *Dobra kuchka*, he said, again not addressing me but praising me to the air, and his hands were gentle as he held me, not constraining but steadying, a comfort for which I felt again that strange, inappropriate gratitude.

I was cold as I knelt there, I had broken out in a sweat. The man too was breathing heavily, he had exerted himself also, the rest was as much for him as for me. He knew what he was doing, I thought with sudden admiration; he knew how far to push and when to ease off, and I was excited at the thought of being taken further by him, of entering territories I had only glimpsed or had intimations of. Then, still keeping one hand on my head, he reached down and very quickly removed first one and then the other clamp from my chest, at which there was a quick flare of pain, making me cry out again, and then a flood of extraordinary pleasure, not sexual pleasure exactly but something like euphoria, a lifting and lightness and unsteadiness, as with certain drugs. He returned his hand to my head and gripped me firmly again, still not moving, having grown very still; even his cock had softened just slightly, it was more giving in my mouth. And then he repeated the word I didn't know but that I thought meant steady and suddenly my mouth was filled with warmth, bright and bitter, his urine, which I took as I had taken everything else, it was a kind of pride in me to take it. *Kuchko*, he said as I drank, speaking softly and soothingly, addressing me again, *mnogo si dobra*, you're very good, and he said this a second time and a third before he was done.

He stepped back, withdrawing from my mouth, and told me to lay myself out on the gray carpet facedown, with my arms stretched over my head. It was a difficult position, the carpet was rough and there was no good place for my cock, which was still hard, having never softened, or softened only briefly, though we had been together I thought for a long time. He grunted as he knelt beside me, settling his large frame, and then he placed his hands on my back, not stroking or kneading but appraising. *Mnogo si debel*, he said again, you're very fat, pinching my flesh between his fingers, but I like you, he said, *haresvash mi*, you're pleasing to me, and I thanked him, saying *radvam se*, I'm glad of that, though a more literal translation would be something like I rejoice or take joy in it, which was closer to what I felt. His hands moved lower then, to my ass and the opening there, which he touched, still tenderly, though I flinched as he tested it, saying how is your hole and inching the tip of one dry finger inside. *Kuchko*, he said again, and again I like you, still speaking tenderly to me, so that I felt I had passed some test, that I had proven myself and entered within the compass of his affection, or if not his affection at least his regard. Then he stretched out beside me, not quite touching me, and brought his face close to mine as his hand moved lower still, between my legs, which I spread slightly before lifting up my hips for his hand, which moved beneath me, snaking between my legs to touch my cock for the first time. And you like me too, he said, feeling my hardness, which he gripped for a moment tightly before letting it go. Very much, I said, I like you very much, and it was true, I was excited by him in a new way, or almost new; seldom had I been with anyone so skilled or so patient, so that even now I had no sense of the encounter speeding toward its end. His hand was on my balls now, which he drew together and down, making a kind of ring with his thumb and forefinger, drawing them tighter before folding the rest of his hand around them. He wasn't hurting me yet but I grew tense anyway, and he sensed this, bringing his forehead to my temple, laying it there and whispering again that I was good. And then he began to tighten his grip, very slowly and with a steady pressure on all sides, causing that terrible low ache to build in my abdomen, and I pressed my own forehead into the coarse fabric of the carpet, rubbing it very slightly back and forth. I groaned then, as he continued to squeeze, and then gasped as I felt his tongue on my cheek, a broad swipe from my jaw to my temple. *Mozhesh*, he said, you can take it, and then I cried out as he gave a sudden, intenser squeeze and let me go.

Good, he said again, whispering with his forehead still pressed to my temple, as I lay there recovering, though the worst thing about that particular pain is that one recovers so slowly; the pain welled instead of ebbing, settling in my groin and the pit of my stomach and the backs of my thighs. When his weight shifted next to me I almost protested, I almost said *chakaite*, wait, I had even taken the breath with which to say it. But he hushed me, making a soothing sound to keep me in my place as he shifted his frame over mine, sliding himself over until he was resting on top of me. It helped, the weight of him, it pressed me down and pressed down the pain I still felt, that ache about which there is nothing erotic, or not for me. I've heard of men who like it, who will go to great lengths to find others who will hurt them in exactly this way, though I've never been able to fathom the pleasure they take from it. But then there's no fathoming pleasure, the forms it takes or their sources, nothing we can imagine is beyond it; however far beyond the pale of our own desires, for someone it is the intensest desire, the key to the latch of the self, or the promised key, a key that perhaps never turns. It's what I love most about the sites I frequent, that we can call out for it, however aberrant or unlikely, and nearly always there comes an answer; it is a large world, we're never as solitary as we think, as unique or unprecedented, what we feel has always already been felt, again and again, without beginning or end.

He lay on me for some time, not moving or rather moving only to press me down, to ease out my pain and my will; he spread his length along mine, reaching until his hands were at my hands, coaxing free the fingers I had curled, and his feet found their place at my ankles, and then it was as if with his whole body he eased me, stretching and relaxing me at once. It was a delicious feeling, and again I admired his skill, how well he knew his instrument, how much I would take and how to bring me back from it. It was gentle, and as he lay there he spoke to me, crooning almost, calling to me again *kuchko*, the term of abuse that had become our endearment, *spokoino*, he said, relax, be calm. And I obeyed him, I could feel myself relaxing as that fluid pain drained and as he lay on top of me, moving just slightly, pressing me down and at the same time stretching me, pulling tenderly on each of my limbs, though soon his movement became something else. He had remained hard, though my own excitement had waned, had flowed out as the pain flowed in; and now it was his hardness he made me feel, grinding it into me so that my excitement returned, not all at once but like an increasing pressure that provoked its own movement in response, a movement of my hips upward just slightly and back. It was a suggestion of movement, really, all that was permitted by his bulk on top of me, but it was enough to make him laugh again, that low, quiet, satisfied laugh I heard against my ear. *Iska li neshto?* he said, does she want something, and I did, I wanted something very much. He was moving more now, not just grinding but lifting his hips, not entirely comfortably for me, as it shifted his weight to his knees, which dug into the hollows of my own knees, pinning me more insistently down. He wasn't trying to enter me but he was moving more forcefully, rubbing the length of himself against me, and I could hear his breath quicken with the effort of it. Then he lifted himself further, and without moving his hands from my wrists positioned his cock to fuck me, though he couldn't fuck me, I thought, he was dry and had done nothing to prepare me, with his hands or his mouth, and I felt myself tighten against him as he pressed forward, moving not violently but insistently. Wait, I said, speaking the word I had almost said before, wait, I'm not ready, but he said again *spokoino*, relax, be calm, not trying to enter me now but falling back to that insistent rubbing. You're ready, he said, you want it, open to *gospodar*, speaking softly, crooningly as he rose again. *Ne*, I said, *ne*, wait, you need a condom, using the word *gumichka*, little rubber. He shifted his position at this, releasing one of my arms to wrap his own around my neck, not choking me but taking hold of me, pressing the links of the chain into my skin. We don't need that, he said, I don't like them, speaking close to my ear, intimately, persuasively, and it will hurt you more if I use one. He started moving again, pressing forward though I resisted him, you need a condom, I said, please, there's one in my pocket, let me get it, and I moved my free arm as if to lift myself up, not exerting any pressure yet but setting it as a brace at my side. *Kuchko*, he repeated, not quite sternly but with disapproval, then crooning again, don't you want to please me, don't you want to give me what I want? I did want to please him, and not only that, I wanted him inside of me, I wanted to be fucked, but there was real danger, especially in this country; many people here are sick without knowing it, I knew, and knew too that he wouldn't be gentle, that I was likely to bleed, it's necessary, I said, please, I have one, we have to use it. Hush, he said again, *kuchko*, let me in, his voice gentle but his arm tightening around my neck, my throat in the crook of his elbow, let me in, and he pressed forward with real force. For a moment I wavered, I almost did let him in; it's what you wanted, I thought, it's what you said you wanted, I had asked him to make me nothing. But I didn't let him in, I said no, repeating it several times, my voice rising; no, I said, stop, *prestanete*, still using the polite form of the verb. Open, he said, but I didn't open, my whole body clenched in refusal, and now I did try to lift myself up, but found I could hardly move at all. I was used to being the stronger one in such encounters, being so tall and so large, I was used to feeling the safety of strength, of knowing I could gather back up that personhood I had laid aside for an evening or an hour. But he was stronger than I was, and I was frightened as he held me down and pressed against me, shoving or thrusting himself. But he couldn't enter, I was clenched and dry and there was no forcing himself inside, and he grunted in frustration and said again bitch, spitting the word, bitch, what are you to say no to me, and then he pulled back on my neck and bit my shoulder very hard, nearly breaking the skin, making a ring of bruises I would wear for days.

He lifted himself off me, shoving down so that I lay flat again, saying loudly, almost shouting, *kakuv si ti*, what are you, *kakuv si ti*, and there was real anger in his voice now, not just frustration but rage, *kakuv si ti*, and then he grabbed a belt from the table, a leather strap, and brought it down hard on my back. The sharp pain of it made me cry out, a womanish cry, and as he struck me he shouted *pedal*, faggot, as if it were the answer to his question, *pedal, pedal*, each time striking me very hard as I cried out again and again, saying stop, the single syllable, returning to my own language as if to air or waking, stop, I said in English, I'm sorry, stop. It wasn't just the beating that I wanted to stop but the whole encounter, the string of events I had set in motion, the will-lessness I had assumed and that had carried me now past anything I might want, so that I said to myself what have I done, what have I done.

But then he did stop, and in the sudden silence I could hear him breathing heavily, as I was, breathing or sobbing, I'm not sure which. I had risen by then, slowly gathering myself to my hands and knees though no further, it was the most I could manage in my strange exhaustion, or not strange, I suppose; I was covered in sweat again, from exertion and from fear. It was over now, I thought, but then he spoke again, saying *dolu*, down. I didn't contradict him but I didn't return to the ground, I couldn't bear to return to the helplessness I had thought I wanted. *Dolu*, he said again, and when again I didn't obey he lifted his foot and set it on my back, pressing as if to force me down. But this I could resist, I held firm, and so he reached down, not removing his foot, and grabbed the leash or chain where it hung, I was still wearing it though he hadn't held it for some time, and as he straightened he pulled it tight, not with all his strength but enough that I felt it, and felt that he could choke me if he chose. He stepped off me then, moving behind me with the leash still in hand, and I tried to rise, lifting my chest both to slacken the chain and to rise to my feet, to stand for the first time in what seemed like hours. As I began to rise I must have shifted my knees apart, I must have moved in a way that opened myself to his foot, which struck me now hard between my legs, so that it wasn't the chain that choked me but pain as I fell forward without a sound, unable to breathe, stripped clean of the will I had been gathering back in scraps; my arms collapsed and I fell forward and curled into myself in animal response. But he didn't let me curl into myself, he fell on top of me, he pushed or shifted me until I was available to him again, so that beneath pain and sharper than it I felt fear, a rising pitch of fear and protest and a terrible shame. He positioned himself as he had before, with his knees in my knees and his hands gripping my wrists, and in my confusion and pain I'm not sure if I struggled, or how much I struggled, though I did close myself to him; at first he couldn't enter me, and again I heard him make that grunt or growl of frustration. But he was wet now, he must have spat into his palm and slicked himself with it, and when he lifted just slightly and brought himself down with his whole weight he did enter me, there was a great tearing pain and I cried out in a voice I had never heard before, a shrill sound that frightened me further, that wasn't my voice at all, and I choked it off as I twisted away from him, not thinking but in panic and pain, using all my strength. Perhaps he too was frightened by my cry, perhaps I had startled him; in any case I was free of him, I had thrown him or he had allowed himself to be thrown. He must have allowed it, I think, since he made no further attempt, though he could have done whatever he wanted; after my great effort I lay exhausted, watching him where he lay on his back breathing hard.

Bitch, he said softly several times, softly but viciously, *mrusna kuchka*, dirty bitch, get out. It was a reprieve, permission to leave, and I pulled the chain from my neck and stood, after a fashion, hunched as I was around pain. I felt nothing of what I had thought I might feel in standing, I reclaimed nothing, nothing at all re-

turned. I dressed as quickly as I could, though it seemed I was moving slowly, as if in a fog or a dream, putting my socks and my belt
in my pockets, leaving my shirt unbuttoned, watching the man
where he watched me, sitting now with his back to the wall. I
turned away from him, reaching with relief for the door and feeling
something like panic again when the knob refused to turn. Like all
doors here it had several locks and I looked at them hopelessly,
turning first one and then another and finding the door still locked,
more locked now that I had turned more latches, and this was like
a dream also, of endlessness and the impossibility of escape; stupid,
I thought, or perhaps I whispered it to myself, stupid, stupid. The
man rose then, I heard or felt him heave himself up and walk to the
door. *Kuchko*, he said, not angrily now but mockingly, shaking his
head a little, pacified perhaps by the fear that was evident as he
reached around me to unlock the door, as I pressed myself as best I
could into the wall behind me; there was nowhere to go, the corri-
dor was narrow, and it was hard not to touch him as he opened the
door, as I tried to slip myself past, feeling again what he wanted me
to feel, I think, that if I left it was because he let me leave, that it was
his will and not my own that opened the door. And then that will
seemed to change, when I stepped into the dark hall he grabbed my
shoulder, gripping me hard, not to pull me back but to spin me
around, making me face him a final time. Things happened very
fast then, I had brought my hands up when he grabbed me, to ward
or fight him off, though I couldn't have fought him off, I've never
struck anyone, really, never in earnest. Still, I lifted my hands,
palms up at my chest, and when again as at the beginning of our
encounter he spat into my face, which was why he had grabbed me
and spun me around, to spit again with great violence into my face,
I placed my hands on the naked bulk of him and pushed or tried to
push him away from me. But he didn't fall back, I hardly moved
him at all, perhaps he staggered just slightly but immediately he
sprang forward, with the kind of savagery or abandon I could never
allow myself he lunged to strike at me. Perhaps he had staggered
just slightly and that was why he missed, his aim failing as he

lunged or fell forward into the hallway, where I was already moving toward the stairway, off-balance myself, almost reaching it before his hands were on me again, both of his hands now grabbing me and throwing me forward so that I fell down the stairs, or almost fell; by luck I stayed on my feet, though I landed on my right foot in a way that strained or tore something, I would limp for weeks. And perhaps it's only in retrospect that I feel I chose how I landed, though I have a memory, an instant of clearheadedness in which I knew he wasn't finished with me, though he was naked and it was dangerous for him I knew he would follow me, and so I think I decided as I fell forward not to catch myself against the concrete wall but instead to strike the small window there, hitting the pane with my right palm hard, shattering it. The noise did what I wanted, he turned and raced for his door, and for a moment as I looked up I saw he was frightened. I ran or stumbled down the flights of stairs, and reached the door just as the hallway lights went on, some neighbor above drawn out by the sound.

I don't know what I would have done if the street hadn't been empty, how I would have explained myself or the broken glass I hurried past; it was lucky no one was passing or standing there, as people often did stand, smoking at the entrances of buildings or in a streetlamp's halo. But it was very late, the boulevard was quiet, and if in a moment someone would emerge from the little convenience store (*denonoshtno*, its window said, day-and-night), if in a moment someone would emerge to investigate I had time to get away, as I thought of it, walking one block and then another without passing a soul. I kept my head down, trying to be blank and unplaceable, trying to calm what I felt, which was pain and relief and shame and panic still, even though I thought I was clear, that I was far enough now to go on uncaught. But I couldn't calm what I felt, something rose in me I couldn't keep down, as I couldn't keep walking at the pace I had set; with each step my foot was more tender and there was something else too, a nausea climbing to my throat, I was going to be sick. I turned quickly into the space between two buildings, an alleyway lined with trash bags and refuse, among which I bent over or crouched, unable to stand. But it wasn't with bile or sickness that I heaved but with tears, which came unexpected and fluent and hot, consuming in a way I hadn't known for a very long time, that perhaps I had never known. And they came in a greater rush when I raised my hands, wanting to cover my face, though there was no one to see still ashamed of my tears; they increased when I raised my hands and saw that the right was covered with blood. In the light from the street I could see where my wrist was torn, a small deep wound where it had caught on the glass. Stupid, I thought again, stupid, at the wound or my weeping, I'm not sure which. Why should I weep, I thought, at what, when I had brought it all upon myself, and I took one of my socks from my pocket and pressed it to the wound, wrapping it around my wrist and folding the cuff of my sleeve over it, not knowing what else to do.

It was a fit of weeping violent and brief, and as my breath steadied I felt a sense of resolution, that I had been lucky and must learn from that luck; I wouldn't go back to such a place, I thought, this would be the end of it, the long-sought end. But how many times had I felt that I could change, I had felt it through all the long months with R., months that I had spent, for all my happiness, in a state of perpetual hunger; and so at the same time I felt it I felt too that my resolution was a lie, that it had always been a lie, that my real life was here, and I thought this even as I struggled to climb from the new depth I had been shown. And even as I climbed or sought to climb I knew that having been shown it I would come back to it, when the pain had faded and the fear, not perhaps to this man but to others like him; I would desire it, though I didn't desire it now, and for a time I would resist my desire but only for a time. There was no lowest place, I thought, I would strike ground only to feel it give way gaping beneath me, and I felt with a new fear how little sense of myself I have, how there was no end to what I could want or to the punishment I would seek. For some moments I wrestled with these thoughts, and then I stood and turned back to the boulevard, composing as best I could my human face.

WHY POETRY: A PARTIAL AUTOBIOGRAPHY
Craig Morgan Teicher

As if in answer to a primordial urge,
I longed for something
to which to

apprentice myself.

I could not learn
to become
my mother for obvious
reasons that were not obvious

to me, so I waited. I felt
as incorrect
playing baseball
as a bear cub moving in

with a family of turtles.
Other boys
sensed my fear

of them and, I now think,
were afraid
they were missing something
that should have

scared them: themselves.
I was always afraid of myself,

my mind, quite clearly a dangerous
place to be: I could think

about anything, any
horrible depraved thing, and

whether or not I *did*
at that tender age, I knew
I was not safe
in my head, which was

where I knew my self was.
Childishly, I assumed

only *my* head was like that,
that they hated me
for a good, educated
reason. In fact,

I now think, they knew
better and hoped

that by attacking
and shaming the fear
resident in me,

in *my* self, they might
drive away the dark
within theirs.

Instead they expressed it,
which I did not,

hence I was a good candidate
for poetry

into which one's latent
monstrousness can seep

like moisture into good wood
for decades, a lifetime.
My dark is rotting harmlessly
in my poetry.

I've saved myself
and my life and
those I love for light.

MISS ADELE AMIDST THE CORSETS
Zadie Smith

....

W ell, that's that," Miss Dee Pendency said, and Miss Adele, looking back over her shoulder, saw that it was. The strip of hooks had separated entirely from the rest of the corset. Dee held up the two halves, her big red slash mouth pulling in opposite directions.

"Least you can say it died in battle. Doing its duty."

"Bitch, I'm on in ten minutes."

"*When an irresistible force like your ass...*"

"Don't sing."

"*Meets an old immovable corset like this... You can bet as sure as you liiiiiive!*"

"It's your fault. You pulled too hard."

"*Something's gotta give, something's gotta give, SOME-THING'S GOTTA GIVE.*"

"You pulled too hard."

"Pulling's not your problem." Dee lifted her bony, white Midwestern leg up onto the counter, in preparation to put on a thigh-high. With a heel she indicated Miss Adele's mountainous box of chicken and rice: "Real talk, baby."

Miss Adele sat down on a grubby velvet stool before a mirror edged with blown-out bulbs. She was thickening and sagging in all the same ways, in all the same places, as her father. Plus it was midwinter: her skin was ashy. She felt like some once-valuable piece of mahogany furniture lightly dusted with cocaine. This final battle with her corset had set her wig askew. She was forty-six years old.

"Lend me yours."

"Good idea. You can wear it on your arm."

And tired to death, as the Italians say—tired to *death*. Especially sick of these kids, these "millennials," or whatever they were calling themselves. Always on. No backstage to any of them—only front of house. Wouldn't know a sincere, sisterly friendship if it kicked down the dressing-room door and sat on their faces.

Miss Adele stood up, untaped, put a furry deerstalker on her head, and switched to her comfortable shoes. She removed her cape. Maybe stop with the cape? Recently she had only to catch herself in the mirror at a bad angle, and there was Daddy, in his robes.

"The thing about undergarments," Dee said, "is they can only do so much with the cards they've been dealt. Sorta like Obama?"

"Stop talking."

Miss Adele zipped herself into a cumbersome floor-length padded coat, tested—so the label claimed—by climate scientists in the Arctic.

"Looking swell, Miss Adele."

"Am I trying to impress somebody? Tell Jake I went home."

"He's out front—tell him yourself!"

"I'm heading this way."

"You know what they say about choosing between your ass and your face?"

Miss Adele put her shoulder to the fire door and heaved it open. She caught the punch line in the ice-cold stairwell.

"You should definitely choose one of those at some point."

Aside from the nights she worked, Miss Adele tried not to mess much with the East Side. She'd had the same sunny rent-controlled studio apartment on Tenth Avenue and Twenty-Third since '93, and loved the way the West Side communicated with the water and the light, loved the fancy galleries and the big anonymous condos, the

High Line funded by bankers and celebrities, the sensation of clarity and wealth. She read the real estate section of the *Times* with a kind of religious humility: the news of a thirty-four-million-dollar townhouse implied the existence of a mighty being, out there somewhere, yet beyond her imagining. But down here? Depressing. Even worse in the daylight. Crappy old buildings higgledy-piggledy on top of each other, ugly students, shitty pizza joints, delis, tattoo parlors. Nothing bored Miss Adele more than ancient queens waxing lyrical about the good old bad old days. At least the bankers never tried to rape you at knifepoint or sold you bad acid. And then once you got past the Village, everything stopped making sense. Fuck these little streets with their dumbass names! Even the logistics of googling her location—remove gloves, put on glasses, find the phone—were too much to contemplate in a polar vortex. Instead, Miss Adele stalked violently up and down Rivington, cutting her eyes at any soul who dared look up. At the curb she stepped over a frigid pool of yellow fluid, three paper plates frozen within it. What a dump! Let the city pull down everything under East Sixth, rebuild, number it, make it logical, pack in the fancy hotels—not just one or two but a whole bunch of them. Don't half gentrify—follow through. Stop preserving all this old shit. Miss Adele had a right to her opinions. Thirty years in a city gives you the right. And now that she was, at long last, no longer beautiful, her opinions were all she had. They were all she had left to give to people. Whenever her disappointing twin brother, Devin, deigned to call her from his three-kids-and-a-Labradoodle, goofy-sweater-wearing, golf-playing, liberal-Negro-wet-dream-of-a-Palm-Springs-fantasy existence, Miss Adele made a point of gathering up all her hard-won opinions and giving them to him good. "I wish he could've been mayor forever. FOR-EVAH. I wish he was my boyfriend. I wish he was my daddy." Or: "They should frack the hell out of this whole state. We'll get rich, secede from the rest of you dope-smoking, debt-ridden assholes. You the ones dragging us all down." Her brother accused Miss Adele of turning rightward in old age. It would be more accurate to say that she was done with all forms of

drama—politics included. That's what she liked about gentrifica-
tion, in fact: gets rid of all the drama.

And who was left, anyway, to get dramatic about? The beloved was gone, and so were all the people she had used, over the
years, as substitutes for the beloved. Every kid who'd ever called
her gorgeous had already moved to Brooklyn, Jersey, Fire Island,
Provincetown, San Francisco, or the grave. This simplified matters. Work, paycheck, apartment, the various lifestyle sections of
the *Times*, Turner Classic Movies, Nancy Grace, bed. Boom.
Maybe a little *Downton*. You needn't put your face on to watch
Downton. That was her routine, and disruptions to it—like having
to haul ass across town to buy a new corset—were rare. Sweet Jesus, this cold! Unable to feel her toes, she stopped a shivering
young couple in the street. British tourists, as it turned out; clue-
less, nudging each other and beaming up at her Adam's apple with
delight, like she was in their guidebook, right next to the Magnolia
Bakery and the Naked Cowboy. They had a map, but without her
glasses it was useless. They had no idea where they were. "Sorry!
Stay warm!" they cried, and hurried off, giggling into their North
Face jackets. Miss Adele tried to remember that her new thing was
that she positively liked all the tourists and missed Bloomberg and
loved Midtown and the Central Park nags and all the Prada stores
and *The Lion King* and lining up for cupcakes wherever they happened to be located. She gave those British kids her most winning
smile. Sashayed round the corner in her fur-cuffed Chelsea boots
with the discreet heel. Once out of sight, though, it all fell apart;
the smile, the straightness of her spine, everything. Even if you
don't mess with it—even when it's not seven below—it's a tough
city. New York just expects so much from a girl—acts like it can't
stand even the *idea* of a wasted talent or opportunity. And Miss
Adele had been around. Rome says: enjoy me. London: survive me.
New York: gimme all you got. What a thrilling proposition! The
chance to be "all that you might be." Such a thrill—until it becomes a burden. To put a face on—to put a self on—this had once
been, for Miss Adele, pure delight. And part of the pleasure had

been precisely this: the buying of things. She used to love buying things! Lived for it! Now it felt like effort, now if she never bought another damn thing again she wouldn't even—

Clinton Corset Emporium. No awning, just a piece of cardboard stuck in the window. As Miss Adele entered, a bell tinkled overhead—an actual bell, on a catch wire—and she found herself in a long narrow room—a hallway really—with a counter down the left-hand side and a curtained-off cubicle at the far end, for privacy. Bras and corsets were everywhere, piled on top of each other in anonymous white cardboard boxes, towering up to the ceiling. They seemed to form the very walls of the place.

"Good afternoon," said Miss Adele, daintily removing her gloves, finger by finger. "I am looking for a corset."

A radio was on; talk radio—incredibly loud. Some AM channel bringing the latest from a distant land, where the people talk from the back of their throats. One of those Eastern-y, Russian-y places. Miss Adele was no linguist, and no geographer. She unzipped her coat, made a noise in the back of her own throat, and looked pointedly at the presumed owner of the joint. He sat slumped behind the counter, listening to this radio with a tragic twist to his face, like one of those sad-sack cab drivers you see hunched over the wheel, permanently tuned in to the bad news from back home. And what the point of that was, Miss Adele would never understand. Turn that shit down! Keep your eyes on the road! Lord knows, the day Miss Adele stepped out of the state of Florida was pretty much the last day that godforsaken spot ever crossed her mind.

Could he even see her? He was angled away, his head resting in one hand. Looked to be about Miss Adele's age, but further gone: bloated face, about sixty pounds overweight, bearded, religious type, wholly absorbed by this radio of his. Meanwhile, somewhere back there, behind the curtain, Miss Adele could make out two women talking:

"Because she thinks Lycra is the answer to everything. Why you don't speak to the nice lady? She's trying to help you. She just turned fourteen."

"So she's still growing. We gotta consider that. Wendy—can you grab me a Brava 32B?"

A slip of an Asian girl appeared from behind the curtain, proceeded straight to the counter and vanished below it. Miss Adele turned back to the owner. He had his fists stacked like one potato, two potato—upon which he rested his chin—and his head tilted in apparent appreciation of what Miss Adele would later describe as "the ranting"—for did it not penetrate every corner of that space? Was it not difficult to ignore? She felt she had not so much entered a shop as some stranger's spittle-filled mouth. RAGE AND RIGHTEOUSNESS, cried this radio—in whatever words it used—RIGHTEOUSNESS AND RAGE. Miss Adele crossed her arms in front of her chest, like a shield. Not this voice—not today. Not any day—not for Miss Adele. And though she had learned, over two decades, that there was nowhere on earth entirely safe from the voices of rage and righteousness—not even the new New York—still Miss Adele had taken great care to organize her life in such a way that her encounters with them were as few as possible. (On Sundays, she did her groceries in a cutoff T-shirt that read THOU SHALT.) As a child, of course, she had been fully immersed—dunked in the local water—with her daddy's hand on the back of her head, with his blessing in her ear. But she'd leaped out of that shallow channel the first moment she was able.

"A corset," she repeated, and raised her spectacular eyebrows. "Could somebody help me?"

"WENDY," yelled the voice behind the curtain, "could you see to our customer?"

The shopgirl sprung up, like a jack-in-the-box, clutching a stepladder to her chest.

"Looking for Brava!" shouted the girl over the radio, turned her back on Miss Adele, opened the stepladder, and began to climb it. Meanwhile, the owner shouted something at the woman behind the curtain, and the woman, adopting his tongue, shouted something back.

"It is customary, in retail—" Miss Adele began.

"Sorry—one minute," said the girl, came down with a box underarm, dashed right past Miss Adele, and disappeared once more behind the curtain.

Miss Adele took a deep breath. She stepped back from the counter, pulled her deerstalker off her head, and tucked a purple bang behind her ear. Sweat prickled her face for the first time in weeks. She was considering turning on her heel and making that little bell shake till it fell off its goddamn string when the curtain opened and a mousy girl emerged, with her mother's arm around her. They were neither of them great beauties. The girl had a pissy look on her face and moved with an angry slouch, like a prisoner, whereas you could see the mother was at least trying to keep things civilized. The mother looked beat—and too young to have a teenager. Or maybe she was the exact right age. Devin's kids were teenagers. Miss Adele was almost as old as the president. None of this made any sense, and yet you were still expected to accept it, and carry on, as if it were the most natural process in the world.

"Because they're not like hands and feet," a warm and lively voice explained, from behind the curtain. "They grow independently."

"Thank you so much for your advice, Mrs. Alexander," said the mother, the way you talk to a priest through a screen. "The trouble is this thickness here. All the women in our family got it, unfortunately. Curved rib cage."

"But actually, you know—it's inneresting—it's a totally different curve from you to her. Did you realize that?"

The curtain opened. The man looked up sharply. He was otherwise engaged, struggling with the antennae of his radio to banish the static, but he paused a moment to launch a little invective in the direction of a lanky, wasp-waisted woman in her early fifties, with a long, humane face—dimpled, self-amused—and an impressive mass of thick chestnut hair.

"Two birds, two stones," said Mrs. Alexander, ignoring her husband, "that's the way we do it here. Everybody needs something different. That's what the big stores won't do for you. Individual attention. Mrs. Berman, can I give you a tip?" The young mother looked up at the long-necked Mrs. Alexander, a duck admiring a swan. "Keep it on all the time. Listen to me, I know of what I speak. I'm wearing mine right now, I wear it every day. In my day they gave it to you when you walked out of the hospital!"

"Well, you look amazing."

"Smoke and mirrors. Now, all you need is to make sure the straps are fixed right like I showed you." She turned to the sulky daughter and put a fingertip on each of the child's misaligned shoulders. "You're a lady now, a beautiful young lady, you—" Here again she was interrupted from behind the counter, a sharp exchange of mysterious phrases, in which—to Miss Adele's satisfaction—the wife appeared to get the final word. Mrs. Alexander took a cleansing breath and continued: "So you gotta hold yourself like a lady. Right?" She lifted the child's chin and placed her hand for a moment on her cheek. "Right?" The child straightened up despite herself. See, some people are trying to ease your passage through this world—so ran Miss Adele's opinion—while others want to block you at every turn. Think of poor Mama, taking folk round those god-awful foreclosures, helping a family to see the good life that might yet be lived there—that had just as much chance of sprouting from a swamp in the middle of nowhere as anyplace else. That kind of instinctive, unthinking care. If only Miss Adele had been a simple little fixer-upper, her mother might have loved her unconditionally! Now that Miss Adele had grown into the clothes of middle-aged women, she noticed a new feeling of affinity toward them, far deeper than she had ever felt for young women, back when she could still fit into the hot pants of a showgirl. She walked through the city struck by middle-aged women and the men they had freely chosen, strange unions of the soft and the hard. In shops, in restaurants, in line at the CVS. She always had the same question. Why in God's name are you still married to this asshole? Lady, your children are grown. You have your own credit cards. You're the one with life force. Can't you see he's just wallpaper? It's not 1850. This is New York. Run, baby, run!

"Who's waiting? How can I help you?"

Mother and daughter duck followed the shopgirl to the counter to settle up. The radio, after a brief pause, made its way afresh up the scale of outrage. And Miss Adele? Miss Adele turned like a flower to the sun.

"Well, I need a new corset. A strong one."

Mrs. Alexander beamed: "Come right this way."

Together, they stepped into the changing area. But as Miss Adele reached to pull the curtain closed behind them both—separating the ladies from the assholes—a look passed between wife and husband and Mrs. Alexander caught the shabby red velvet swathe in her hand, a little higher up than Miss Adele had, and held it open.

"Wait—let me get Wendy in here." An invisible lasso, thought Miss Adele. He throws it and you go wherever you're yanked. "You'll be all right? The curtain's for modesty. You modest?"

Oh, she had a way about her. Her face expressed emotion in layers: elevated, ironic eyebrows, mournful violet eyes, and sly, elastic mouth. Miss Adele could have learned a lot from a face like that. A face straight out of an old movie. But which one, in particular?

"You're a funny lady."

"A life like mine, you have to laugh—Marcus, please, one minute—" He was barking at her, still—practically insisting, perhaps, that she *stop talking to that schwarze*, which prompted Mrs. Alexander to lean out of the changing room to say something very like: *What is wrong with you? Can't you see I'm busy here?* On the radio, strange atonal music replaced the ranting; Mrs. Alexander stopped to listen to it, and frowned. She turned back to her new friend and confidante, Miss Adele. "Is it okay if I don't measure you personally? Wendy can do it in a moment. I've just got to deal with—but listen, if you're in a hurry, don't panic, our eyes, they're like hands."

"Can I just show you what I had?"

Miss Adele unzipped her handbag and pulled out the ruin.

"Oh! You're breaking my heart! From here?"

"I don't remember. Maybe ten years ago?"

"Makes sense, we don't sell these any more. Ten years is ten years. Time for a change. What's it to go under? Strapless? Short? Long?"

"Everything. I'm trying to hide some of this."

"You and the rest of the world. Well, that's my job." She leaned over and put her lips just a little shy of Miss Adele's ear: "What you got up there? You can tell me. Flesh or feathers?"

"Not the former."

"Got it. WENDY! I need a Futura and a Queen Bee, corsets, front fastening, forty-six. Bring a forty-eight, too. Marcus—please. One *minute*. And bring the Paramount in, too! The crossover! Some people," she said, turning to Miss Adele, "you ask them these questions, they get offended. Everything offends them. Personally, I don't believe in 'political correctness.'" She articulated the phrase carefully, with great sincerity, as if she had recently coined it. "My mouth's too big. I gotta say what's on my mind! Now, when Wendy comes, take off everything to here and try each corset on at its tightest setting. If you want a defined middle, frankly it's going to hurt. But I'm guessing you know that already."

"Loretta Young," called Miss Adele to Mrs. Alexander's back. "You look like Loretta Young. Know who that is?"

"Do I know who Loretta Young is? Excuse me one minute, will you?"

Mrs. Alexander lifted her arms comically, to announce something to her husband, the only parts of which Miss Adele could fully comprehend were the triple repetition of the phrase "Loretta Young." In response, the husband made a noise somewhere between a sigh and a grunt.

"Do me a favor," said Mrs. Alexander, letting her arms drop and turning back to Miss Adele, "put it in writing, put it in the mail. He's a reader."

The curtain closed. But not entirely. An inch hung open and through it Miss Adele watched a silent movie—silent only in the sense that the gestures were everything. It was a marital drama, conducted in another language, but otherwise identical to all those she and Devin had watched as children, through a crack in the door of their parents' bedroom. God save Miss Adele from marriage! Appalled, fascinated, she watched the husband, making the eternal, noxious point in a tone Miss Adele could conjure in her sleep (*You bring shame upon this family*), and Mrs. Alexander, apparently objecting (*I've given my life to this family*); she watched as he became belligerent (*You should be ashamed*) and she grew sarcastic (*Ashamed of having a real job? You think I don't know what "pastoral care" means? Is that God's love you're giving to every woman in this town?*), their voices weaving in and out of the hellish noise on the radio, which had returned to ranting (*THOU SHALT NOT!*).

Miss Adele strained to separate the sounds into words she might google later. If only there was an app that translated the arguments of strangers! A lot of people would buy that app. Hadn't she just been reading in the *Times* about some woman who had earned eight hundred grand off such an app—just for having the idea for the app. You want to know what Miss Adele would do with eight hundred grand? Buy a studio down in Battery Park, and do nothing all day but watch the helicopters fly over the water. Stand at the floor-to-ceiling window, bathed in expensive light, wearing the kind of silk kimono that hides a multitude of sins.

Sweating with effort and anxiety, in her windowless Lower East Side cubicle, Miss Adele got stuck again at her midsection, which had become, somehow, Devin's midsection. Her fingers fumbled with the heavy-duty eyes and hooks. She found she was breathing heavily. ABOMINATION, yelled the radio. *Get it out of my store!* cried the man, in all likelihood. *Have mercy!* pleaded the woman, basically. No matter how she pulled, she simply could not contain herself. So much effort! She was making odd noises, grunts almost.

"Hey, you okay in there?"

"First doesn't work. About to try the second."

"No, don't do that. Wait. Wendy, get in there."

In a second, the girl was in front of her, and as close as anybody had been to Miss Adele's bare body in a long time. Without a word, a little hand reached out for the corset, took hold of one side of it and, with surprising strength, pulled it toward the other end until both sides met. The girl nodded, and this was Miss Adele's cue to hook the thing together while the girl squatted like a weight lifter and took a series of short, fierce breaths. Outside of the curtain, the argument had resumed.

"Breathe," said the girl.

"They always talk to each other like that?" asked Miss Adele.

The girl looked up, uncomprehending.

"Okay now?"

"Sure. Thanks."

The girl left Miss Adele alone to examine her new silhouette. It was as good as it was going to get. She turned to the side and frowned at three days of chest stubble. She pulled her shirt over her head to see the clothed effect from the opposite angle, and in the transition got a fresh view of the husband, still berating Mrs. Alexander, though in a violent whisper. He had tried bellowing over the radio; now he would attempt to tunnel underneath it. Suddenly he looked up at Miss Adele—not as far as her eyes, but tracing, from the neck down, the contours of her body. RIGHTEOUSNESS, cried the radio, RIGHTEOUSNESS AND RAGE! Miss Adele felt like a nail being hammered into the floor. She grabbed the curtain and yanked it shut. She heard the husband end the conversation abruptly—as had been her own father's way—not with reason or persuasion, but with sheer volume. Above the door to the emporium the little bell rang.

"Molly! So good to see you! How're the kids? I'm just with a customer!" Mrs. Alexander's long pale fingers curled round the hem of the velvet. "May I?"

Miss Adele opened the curtain.

"Oh, it's good! See, you got shape now."

Miss Adele shrugged, dangerously close to tears: "It works."

"Marcus said it would. He can spot a corset size at forty paces, believe me. He's good for that at least. So, if that works, the other will work. Why not take both? Then you don't have to come back for another twenty years! It's a bargain." She turned to shout over her shoulder, "Molly, I'm right with you," and threw open the curtain.

In the store there had appeared a gaggle of children, small and large, and two motherly looking women, who were greeting the husband and being greeted warmly in turn, smiled at, truly welcomed. Miss Adele picked up her enormous coat and began the process of re-weatherizing herself. She observed Mrs. Alexander's husband as he reached over the counter to joke with two young children, ruffling their hair, teasing them, while his wife— whom she watched even more intently—stood smiling over the whole phony operation, as if all that had passed between him and her were nothing at all, some silly wrangle about the accounts or whatnot. Oh, Loretta Young. Whatever you need to tell yourself, honey. Family first! A phrase that sounded, to Miss Adele, so broad, so empty; one of those convenient pits into which folk will throw any and everything they can't deal with alone. A hole for cowards to hide in. Under its cover you could even have your hands round your wife's throat, you could have your terrified little boys cowering in a corner—yet when the bell rings, it's time for iced tea and "Family First!" with all those nice churchgoing ladies as your audience, and Mama's cakes, and smiles all round. *These are my sons, Devin and Darren.* Two shows a day for seventeen years.

"I'll be with you in one minute, Sarah! It's been so long! And look at these girls! They're really tall now!"

On the radio, music again replaced the voice—strange, rigid, unpleasant music, which seemed to Miss Adele to be entirely constructed from straight lines and corners. Between its boundaries, the vicious game restarted, husband and wife firing quick volleys back and forth, at the end of which he took the radio's old-fashioned dial between his fingers and turned it up. Finally Mrs. Alexander turned from him completely, smiled tightly at Miss Adele, and began packing her corsets back into their boxes.

"Sorry, but am I causing you some kind of issue?" asked Miss Adele, in her most discreet tone of voice. "I mean, between you and your..."

"You?" said Mrs. Alexander, and with so innocent a face Miss Adele was tempted to award her the Oscar right then and there, though it was only February. "How do you mean, issue?"

Miss Adele smiled.

"You should be on the stage. You could be my warm-up act."

"Oh, I doubt you need much warming. No, you don't pay me, you pay him." A small child ran by Mrs. Alexander with a pink bra on his head. Without a word she lifted it, folded it in half, and tucked the straps neatly within the cups. "Kids. But you gotta have life. Otherwise the whole thing moves in one direction. You got kids?"

Miss Adele was so surprised, so utterly wrong-footed by this question, she found herself speaking the truth.

"My twin—he has kids. We're identical. I guess I feel like his kids are mine, too."

Mrs. Alexander put her hands on her tiny waist and shook her head.

"Now, that is *fascinating*. You know, I never thought of that before. Genetics is an amazing thing—amazing! If I wasn't in the corset business, I'm telling you, that would have been my line. Better luck next time, right?" She laughed sadly, and looked over at the counter. "He listens to his lectures all day, he's educated. I missed out on all that." She picked up the two corsets packed back into their boxes. "Okay, so—are we happy?"

Are *you* happy? Are you really happy, Loretta Young? Would you tell me if you weren't, Loretta Young, the Bishop's Wife? Oh, Loretta Young, Loretta Young! Would you tell anybody?

"Molly, don't say another word—I know exactly what you

need. Nice meeting you," said Mrs. Alexander to Miss Adele, over her shoulder, as she took her new customer behind the curtain. "If you go over to my husband, he'll settle up. Have a good day."

Miss Adele approached the counter and placed her corsets upon it. She stared down a teenage girl leaning on the counter to her left, who now, remembering her manners, looked away and closed her mouth. Miss Adele returned her attention to the side of Mrs. Alexander's husband's head. He picked up the first box. He looked at it as if he'd never seen a corset box before. Slowly he wrote something down in a notepad in front of him. He picked up the second and repeated the procedure, but with even less haste. Then, without looking up, he pushed both boxes to his left, until they reached the hands of the shopgirl, Wendy.

"Forty-six fifty," said Wendy, though she didn't sound very sure. "Um...Mr. Alexander—is there discount on Paramount?"

He was in his own world. Wendy let a finger brush the boss's sleeve, and it was hard to tell if it was this—or something else— that caused him to now sit tall in his stool and thump a fist upon the counter, just like Daddy casting out the devil over breakfast, and start right back up shouting at his wife—some form of stinging question—repeated over and over, in that relentless way men have. Miss Adele strained to understand it. Something like: *You happy now?* Or: *Is this what you want?* And underneath, the unmistakable: *Can't you see he's unclean?*

"Hey, you," said Miss Adele, "Yes, you, sir. If I'm so disgusting to you? If I'm so beneath your contempt? Why're you taking my money? Huh? You're going to take my money? *My* money? Then, please: look me in the eye. Do me that favor, okay? Look me in the eye."

Very slowly a pair of profoundly blue eyes rose to meet Miss Adele's own green contacts. The blue was unexpected, like the inner markings of some otherwise unremarkable butterfly, and the black lashes were wet and long and trembling. His voice, too, was the opposite of his wife's, slow and deliberate, as if each word had been weighed against eternity before being chosen for use.

"You are speaking to me?"

"Yes, I'm speaking to you. I'm talking about customer service. Customer service. Ever hear of it? I am your customer. And I don't appreciate being treated like something you picked up on your shoe!"

The husband sighed and rubbed at his left eye.

"I don't understand—I say something to you? My wife, she says something to you?"

Miss Adele shifted her weight to her other hip and very briefly considered a retreat. It did sometimes happen, after all—she knew from experience—that is, when you spent a good amount of time alone—it did sometimes come to pass—when trying to decipher the signals of others—that sometimes you mistook—

"Listen, your wife is friendly—she's civilized, I ain't talking about your wife. I'm talking about *you*. Listening to your ... whatever the hell that this—your *sermon*—blasting through this store. You may not think I'm godly, brother, and maybe I'm not, but I am in your store with good old-fashioned American money and I ask that you respect that and you respect me."

He began on his other eye, same routine.

"I see," he said, eventually.

"Excuse me?"

"You understand what is being said, on this radio?"

"*What?*"

"You speak this language that you hear on the radio?"

"I don't *need* to speak it to understand it. And why you got it turned up to eleven? I'm a customer—whatever's being said, I don't want to listen to that shit. I don't need a translation—I can hear the *tone*. And don't think I don't see the way you're looking at me. You want to tell your wife about that? When you were peeping at me through that curtain?"

"Now I'm looking at you?"

"Is there a problem?" said Mrs. Alexander. Her head came out from behind the curtain.

"I'm not an idiot, okay?" said Miss Adele.

The husband brought his hands together, somewhere between prayer and exasperation, and shook them at his wife as he spoke to her, over Miss Adele's head, and around her comprehension.

"Hey—talk in English. English! Don't disrespect me! Speak in English!"

"Let me translate for you: I am asking my wife what she did to upset you."

Miss Adele turned and saw Mrs. Alexander, clinging to herself and swaying, less like Loretta now, more like Vivien Leigh swearing on the red earth of Tara.

"I'm not talking about her!"

"Sir, was I not polite and friendly to you? Sir?"

"First up, I ain't no sir—you live in this city, use the right words for the right shit, okay?"

There was Miss Adele's temper, bad as ever. She'd always had it. Even before she was Miss Adele, when she was still little Darren Bailey, it had been a problem. Had a tendency to go off whenever she felt herself on uncertain ground, like a cheap rocket—the kind you could buy back home in the same store you bought a doughnut and a gun. Short fused and likely to explode in odd, unpredictable directions, hurting innocent bystanders—often women, for some reason. How many women had stood opposite Miss Adele with the exact same look on their faces as Mrs. Alexander wore right now? Starting with her mother and stretching way out to kingdom come. The only Judgment Day that had ever made sense to Miss Adele was the one where all the hurt and disappointed ladies form a line—a chorus line of hurt feelings—and one by one give you your pedigree, over and over, for all eternity.

"Was I rude to you?" asked Mrs. Alexander, the color rising in her face, "No, I was not. I live, I let live."

Miss Adele looked around at her audience. Everybody in the store had stopped what they were doing and fallen silent.

"I'm not talking to you. I'm trying to talk to this gentleman here. Could you turn off that radio so I can talk to you, please?"

"Okay," he said, "so maybe you leave now."

"Second of all," said Miss Adele, counting it out on her hand, though there was nothing to follow in the list, "contrary to appearances, and just as a point of information, I am not an Islamic person? I mean, I get it. Pale, long nose. But no. So you can hate me, fine—but you should know who you're hating and hate me for the right reasons. Because right now? You're hating in the wrong direction—you and your radio are wasting your hate. If you want to hate me, file it under N-word. As in African American. Yeah."

The husband frowned and held his beard in his hand.

"You are a very confused person. I don't care what you are. All such conversations are very boring to me, in fact."

"Oh, I'm *boring* you?"

"Honestly, yes. And you are also being rude. So now I ask politely: leave, please."

"Baby, I am out that door, believe me. But I am not leaving without my motherfucking corsets."

The husband slipped off his stool, finally, and stood up.

"You leave now, please."

"Now, who's gonna make me? 'Cause you can't touch me, right? That's one of your laws, right? I'm unclean, right? So who's gonna touch me? Miss Tiny Exploited Migrant Worker over here?"

"Hey, I'm international student! NYU!"

Et tu, Wendy? Miss Adele looked sadly at her would-be ally. Wendy was a whole foot taller now, thanks to the stepladder, and she was using the opportunity to point a finger in Miss Adele's face. Miss Adele was tired to death.

"Just give me my damn corsets."

"Sir, I'm sorry but you really have to leave now," said Mrs. Alexander, walking toward Miss Adele, her elegant arms wrapped around her itty-bitty waist. "There are minors in here, and your language is not appropriate."

"Y'all call me 'sir' one more time," said Adele, speaking to Mrs. Alexander, but still looking at the husband, "I'm gonna throw that radio right out that fucking window. And don't you be thinking I'm an anti-Semite or some shit..." Miss Adele faded. She had the out-of-body sense that she was watching herself on the big screen, at one of those screenings she used to attend, with the beloved boy, long dead, who'd adored shouting at the screen, back when young people still went to see old movies in a cinema. Oh, if that boy were alive! If he could see Miss Adele up on that screen right now! Wouldn't he be shouting at her performance—wouldn't he groan and cover his eyes! The way he had at Joan and Bette and Barbara, as they made their terrible life choices, all of them unalterable, no matter how loudly you shouted.

"It's a question," stated Miss Adele, "of simple politeness. Po-lite-ness."

The husband shook his shaggy head and laughed, softly.

"See, you're trying to act like I'm crazy, but from the moment I stepped up in here, you been trying to make me feel like you don't want someone like me up in here—why you even denying it? You can't even look at me now! I know you hate black people. I know you hate homosexual people. You think I don't know that? I can look at you and know that."

"But you're wrong!" cried the wife.

"No, Eleanor," said the husband, putting out a hand to stop the wife continuing, "maybe she's a divinity. Maybe she sees into the hearts of men."

"You know what? It's obvious this lady can't speak for herself when you're around. I don't even want to talk about this another second. My money's on the counter. This is twenty-first-century New York. This is America. And I've paid for my goods. Give me my goods."

"Take your money and leave. I ask you politely. Before I call the police."

"I'm sure he'll go peacefully," predicted Mrs. Alexander, tearing the nail of her index finger between her teeth, but, instead, one more thing went wrong in Miss Adele's mind, and she grabbed those corsets right out of poor Wendy's hands, kicked the door of Clinton Corset Emporium wide open, and hightailed it down the freezing street, slipped on some ice and went down pretty much face-first. After which, well, she had some regrets, sure, but there wasn't much else to do at that point but pick herself up and run, with a big, bleeding dramatic graze all along her left cheek, wig askew, surely looking to everyone she passed exactly like some Bellevue psychotic, a hot crazy mess, an old-school deviant from the fabled city of the past—except, every soul on these streets was a stranger to Miss Adele. They didn't have the context, didn't know a damn thing about where she was coming from, nor that she'd paid for her goods in full, in dirty green American dollars, and was only taking what was rightfully hers.

GRAMERCY PARK
Sylvie Baumgartel

The windows around Gramercy have eyes.
We look, they look back.
A brook cut through the swamp.
The Dutch called it *Krom Mesje*, little crooked knife.
A little body of water is a dagger, a bigger body is a kill.
The Dutch came for beavers and named us all to pieces.

Baghdad is a swamp of killing.
Gramercy is a kill two acres big.
Bombs lit the desert sky like flowers.
The Super Hornet pilot says, It's lovely,
The only part of the Iraqi girl you can see is her eyes.
It was a perfect home.

The Turks stormed Baghdad and
Decimated the Byzantines.
The winners had better arrows.
Balls of ice fell on the losers.
Inside each ball was a flower.
The flowers in the ice balls looked like eyes.

When you live on Gramercy Park,
You get two keys,
The doorman keeps them both.

LETTER FROM KENTUCKY
J. D. Daniels

John C. Skaggs was born in Green County in 1805, thirteen years after Kentucky became our fifteenth state. His son, Ben Skaggs, was born in 1835 in Bald Hollow and married Missouri Ann Carter.

Their second eldest boy, Will Franklin Skaggs, had his pick of Pleasant Poteet's granddaughters: he could have had Delilah or Myrtie Scripture, but he chose Ella Green Poteet; and their third child, after Carter C. and Elvie Omen, was Sylvia May.

Meanwhile, in Larue County, Elmina G. Dixon married Bryant Young Miller's boy, and they bore a girl they called Mary Bothena Doctor Bohanan Sarah Lucritia Miller Rock, who, mercifully, named her own son Charlie.

And Thomas Jefferson Quinley's daughter Sefronia married Edwin Russell Wheatley, and begat Mildred Lucille, who married Robert Raymond Salisbury, who called himself Butch Daniels— of whom we will not speak.

Their son married Charlie and Sylvia's daughter, and begat me: "His Majesty the Ego," as Freud wrote in 1908, "the hero of all daydreams and all novels."

This happened in Kentucky, except for the Freud part. That happened in Austria.

I was born in Kentucky and lived there for the better part of three decades.

As schoolchildren we were taught that the word *Kaintuckee* came from *Ka-ten-ta-teh*, which meant, in Cherokee, "the dark and bloody ground."

Later they said *Ken-tah-ten* meant "future land" in Iroquois. In high school, they claimed it was Wyandot for "land of tomorrow," and I recall a field trip to see a documentary with that name.

Before long historians were telling us it could be Seneca for "place of meadows," or it might be a Mohawk word, *Kentah-ke*, meaning "meadow."

And from time to time there was an expert, often but not always on a barstool, who argued that the region in its pristine state had seemed to its settlers to be nothing but wild turkeys and river canebrakes: *Kaneturkee*.

It was clear that no one had any idea what he was talking about—and, in this manner, the most valuable part of our education was received.

I flew back to Kentucky on a cold spring day aboard a paper airplane that every sneeze of wind knocked sideways. Next time I'll swim. Everyone hates flying. Even birds hate flying.

A sign in the airport said LOUISVILLE WELCOMES TOGETHER FOR THE GOSPEL NAZARENE YOUTH INTERNATIONAL 2012 PENTECOSTAL FIRE YOUTH CONFERENCE. There was nowhere to sleep. The many hotel rooms of downtown Louisville were occupied by boys and men in red T-shirts with white crucifixes ironed on. They stood in traffic, gawking.

Someone had cut down the peach tree in the front yard of my old Preston Street house. There was a scrap of vinyl siding across the front step, and plastic wrap on the inside windows to keep out the draft, and wax paper fluttering under a gap in the door.

Across the street from that house had once been the only bar where they had known what I wanted, a shot of Jim Beam and a bottle of Sterling, and Bill set it up every time he saw me coming. It was called B & B Bar, said to have been named for its owner

Bill and then for Bill again, because what kind of name is the B-Bar.

I had seen an old man get shot in front of that bar because he wouldn't give two kids his bicycle. I snorted pills off the back of the toilet in that bar with a woman I didn't understand was a prostitute: but later it became clear to me.

Blind John, still dripping rain from his trip to the ATM, offered me a hundred dollars to let him go down on me. "I think you're in the wrong bar," I said. "Maybe you are," he said.

I lost a lot of money shooting nine ball in that bar. Listen to your uncle Tim-Tom and never play pool for money against a man called Doc.

I saw a little man stab a big man with a carving knife on that bar's front steps. Later the wet knife glimmered under the streetlight on the hood of a prowl car. The big man went to the hospital; the little man went to the penitentiary. I don't know where the bar went.

I drove down to the tractor-trailer plant where my father had managed the repair shop, but the plant had closed. I had worked there twice.

The first time was in the touch-up shop with Orville, soldering brake-light wires and repainting trailers Andrew had banged his forklift into, as a summer job and as a warning from my father: this was the kind of job I was going to wind up with if I didn't straighten up and fly right. I was the only man in that garage with ten fingers.

The second time was in the decal shop as a college dropout. I had not straightened up, I had not flown right, this was the kind of job I had wound up with.

By day, Mayflower trailers, Frito-Lay trailers, Budweiser and Bud Light trailers, Allied trailers; by night, drinking Colt 45 with Allen down by the train trestles, and later Boyd crawling around on the floor with a cardboard box on his head, insisting that he was a Christmas present. I read *The Faerie Queene*—counting syllables, thinking about the number seven—and thought: One of these days I am going to jump off the Second Street Bridge.

Finley's was gone, too, nothing but a pile of bricks. At Indi's, eating the rib tips with red sauce and macaroni and cheese and mashed potatoes and gravy, I listened: "You never know. That's what I told them at his funeral this morning. I said *all right, see you later.* But I was wrong."

And I remembered my friend Allen asking me if I saw a plain white van parked across from his house down by the racetrack.

Allen said, "Tell me something, man. The van is real? I'm not paranoid? It's been parked there for days. Three days."

"I am sure that is true."

"Listen—am I crazy? Could it be the FBI?"

"Allen," I said, seated in his forest of pot plants, "let me ask you a question. What amount of drugs and paraphernalia is in your house, do you think? And what is it the FBI gets paid to do all day? I am one hundred percent certain it is the FBI. I will see you later."

I said *see you later,* but I was wrong. I did not see Allen later. Allen went to jail.

I took the Gene Snyder Freeway out to the Bible College and got off at Beulah Church and drove past AMF Derby Lanes ("all you can bowl") and Highview Church of God and Highview Baptist Church and Victory Baptist Church Camp.

An old woman with a long gray ponytail was doing yard work, cutting back bushes I had planted in front of the house where I had grown up, where I had tried to grow up. A tired black dog lay in the yard, her yard now, not mine.

It's an old story. The horse knows the way to carry the sleigh: you go back to the place, but the place isn't there any more.

I drove out of Fern Creek down Bardstown Road toward Buechel, past Cash Xpress and Mister Money, past Xtreme Auto Sounds and Ventura's Used Tires and Global Auto Glass, and past the Heart of Fire City Church, the pastor of which had once

helped us move some furniture and when it came time for my
mother to write him a check for his services he said, "Don't cheat
a blind man, sister, I can't read."

I drove to my uncle Charles's house out in Okolona, past
Latino Auto Service and the Godfather (the strip joint that once
had on its marquee THE MAYOR IS GAY PLEASE SUE SO I CAN
PROVE IT), past Liquor Palace 5 and Discount Medical Supplies,
past Furniture Liquidators Home Center, past Cash America
Pawn and Cashland, past the Mower Shop, past Los Mezcales
and El Molcajete, past Big Ron's Bingo and Cashtyme Cash Advance ("You're Good For It!"), past Moore's Sewing & Learning
Center, and DePrez Quality Jewelry & Loan, and Floors Unlim-
ited, and Chain Saw World.

I turned on the rental car's radio and the man on the radio
said, "Your gift right now, just twenty dollars a month, could help.
Seventy-three more gifts needed. People like you, doing their part.
One song left in this challenge. Standing in the gap for those who
need it. We here believe in the infallible Word of God. Unchanging
principles for changing times."

I drove past something. Then I drove past something else.

"There is an awful lot of drugs now in these small towns and big
towns both," my uncle Charles said. "You may not know the police
shot that boy you all used to play with. Said he was cooking meth
down there in his shed. They had him surrounded and he came out
alone with his pistol. Found thirty-seven shell casings when it was
all done with. What was his name?" But Charles couldn't remember the dead man's name.

"You'll stay with us tonight," my aunt Alice Carol said.

"I have a hotel room near the airport."

"Honey, everything in this town is near the airport."

"I guess I made a foolish decision."

"You've always been foolish."

My aunt was teasing me. She didn't think I was so bad. One
Thanksgiving—we were listening to the old boys jaw for hours about

hiding up a tree with my grandfather's shotgun in order to shoot a neighbor's brown dog that had killed two of their chickens, and after both barrels were empty there was nothing left but the dog's collar and its tail, which they'd helped the neighbor bury—she had turned to me and said, "If you want to be a writer, why don't you go get a pen and paper and write down all these lies?"

Standiford Field was now called Louisville International Airport and the Executive West hotel was the Crowne Plaza, but Executive Strike & Spare still stood on the other side of Phillips Lane. I walked across the street and shot nine-ball for a couple of lazy hours. It turns out it's like riding a bike—you never forget how, and especially not if you never knew how in the first place.

Overheard at the bar: "He and his friends see this old man take his wallet out at the liquor store, so they know he's got money, and they follow him home. But his wife's there. Now that's two counts. I called him and his mother says, He ain't here. I called back. I said, Santino, I heard you cut your monitor off. You know you got court this Friday? You coming? You know that's another felony? Do not shave your head again, I told him."

"It's funny what order we all remember the salad dressings in."

"My youngest daughter has excellent upper-body strength."

"I sleep very well on the floor."

I took 64 east out of Louisville through the junction. Panels of cars and blown-out tires were scattered in the breakdown lane. I passed Exit 8, the off-ramp to the Southern Baptist Theological Seminary, such as Southern Baptist theology is. The speed limit rose to seventy, and mangled deer, coon, possum, turkeys, and skunks began to appear.

Over the Kentucky River in Fayette County, I stopped and for three dollars I ate a plate of biscuits and sausage gravy that would almost have fit into a football stadium.

"Here comes Rex. Today's to-do list: raise hell with the waitresses."

"That ain't on his list. That's just normal."

I did not change to the Bert T. Combs Mountain Parkway, which is the way I would have gone fifteen years earlier if I'd been drinking beer with my friend Gary on our way to Red River Gorge before he went crazy and they put him away in Central State for the first time, but not the last.

Gary was a big boy, ugly and pale, with a nose like a peeled potato. I'm not just saying that because my ex-wife slept with him once. We all slept around. She slept with Larry, too, but I don't have anything bad to say about Larry. I myself almost slept with Larry, he was irresistible, a beautiful man. *Gary* and *Larry*—these names have been changed to protect the innocent, but not mine: I am guilty.

But before any of that happened Gary and I were good friends, and we were together in the pro-Martin faction when Lawyer Jack pulled a knife on Big Martin one night in the kitchen of the Highland House and Martin just shrugged and picked up the kitchen table and hit Jack with it.

Gary and I agreed on that dispute and on other important matters, we camped out together, we got high and talked about numerology, and it was in this way that I became important enough to him to lash out at when he fell ill.

"You blue-eyed Jew," he said to me as his mind disappeared. "You dumb piece of fuck. I'm going to stuff six dollars and ninety cents in pennies up your ass and staple it shut."

Six-ninety was 138—which was 23 times 6 (the 2 and 3 of 23 multiplied)—times 5 (the 2 and 3 of 23 added). Gary could go on for hours about the significance of these numbers to him. He had infinite bad luck, he would say, because of 138: an unlucky 13 conjoined with the sideways Möbius strip of an 8.

They wheeled him away, strapped to a stretcher.

Gary had written, "Jack looks like your dad! Whew! Happy reading!" in the copy of *On The Road* he'd given me for Christmas in 1992. I don't remember if I read it or not. It's about a road.

I didn't have a Dean Moriarty for my long car trip, but I had the man on the car radio. And the man on the radio said: "Pieces of the Divine puzzle will be played out in the coming economic Armageddon. From crisis to consolidation. I want you to pray for me today."

We sang about the blood Wednesday nights at church suppers, Thursday nights at choir practices, mornings and evenings on Sundays, and every summer at a peacock-ridden revival camp in Alabama.

The old rugged cross, stained with blood so divine. There is a fountain filled with blood. I must needs go on the blood-sprinkled way. He bled, He died to save me. How I love to proclaim it, redeemed by the blood.

They vainly purify themselves, said Heraclitus, *by defiling themselves with blood, just as if one who had stepped into the mud were to wash his feet in mud. Any man who marked him doing thus would deem him mad.*

Our pastor had a method. After his sermon, we sang "Just As I Am" over and over again—without one plea, but that Thy blood was shed for me, and so on. We would sing until someone gave in. We sang all day.

It was the same unrelenting method of the middle school phys-ed coach who, perceiving that Weak Henry was weak, hit on the technique of making the whole class do extra push-ups until Henry finished his allotted twenty. Henry couldn't make it happen. We did twenty more, thirty more, forty; and after class, Demetrius and Alonzo beat Henry in the locker room until he peed.

One morning, after an hour of "Just As I Am," my mother shrieked and fell into the aisle. My father helped her stand. His face was strange. The two of them knelt and prayed at the altar. A nice old lady wearing a white gauze eye patch smiled. I waited to see what the people who told me what to do were going to tell me to do next.

It was this child grown into a man, then, if anyone ever grows up, who now drove past Lynn Camp Baptist Church, who drove past Hazel Fork Holiness Church and Living Waters Pentecostal Church, who drove past Faith Tabernacle Pentecostal Church and Turkey Creek Baptist Church short of breath, sweating like a sinner, drowning in blood.

I played Jesus one year and Judas the next in the passion play. I taught Vacation Bible School, and visited and sang hymns to the homebound, and, all that rigamarole having been accomplished, I chased the preacher's daughter through the cornfield after Sunday evening services until I caught her.

And my father mowed the field out back of our church. He helped Deacon Jack repaint the sanctuary and he helped Deacon Willy reshingle the roof. He cooked and served at the Wednesday night church suppers and was happy to do it. But he didn't have much time for what he called *churchified* people.

"I find it difficult to believe that the Creator of the universe gives a fuck if I drink a cold beer on a sunny day," my father said. "These people can't say *sugar*, they just got to say *sucrose*. Meanwhile they don't have no more idea what God wants from me than the man in the moon. It's my own dick I'm talking about, and I can jump up and down on it like a pogo stick if I want to."

I thought I was back in Kentucky to write a magazine story about a TV show set in Harlan County. That isn't how things worked out. I wrote this letter instead.

Harlan is not *nowhere*. What you want to do is this: You drive to nowhere, then you turn left. You keep going until page eighty-eight, the last page of the atlas and gazetteer with its detailed topographical maps, which has apparently been paginated on the assumption that Harlan is the last place you're going to want to go.

In Harlan, in the morning, a woman walked across a restaurant and closed my notebook and said, "You can work all day, honey. Eat your biscuits while they're hot."

And the woman at the hotel's front desk said, "If you're like those other people, you're going to want a zero balance."

"I guess I am like other people."

"I know all you government men like to keep a zero balance."

I came out of Harlan bewildered on the Kingdom Come Parkway headed back toward Pineville, with its massive floodgates.

The man on the radio said: "I'm going to have a multitude of nations come forth from my loins. And as part of my covenant, You are asking me to mutilate the very part of myself through which You are going to fulfill Your promise. I mean, Abraham, he didn't have the biological insight that we have in our modern medical world, but Abraham knew well where babies come from. And here's God—"

I passed Daniels Mountain and Manito Hill. Out past Tin Can Hollow, I turned south on 25E. I passed Clear Creek Baptist Bible College and John's Tire Discount and an immense sign that said ARE YOU ADDICTED TO PAIN MEDICATION?

I bore south through Meldrum and Middlesboro (home of the actor Lee Majors, aka Harvey Lee Yeary, aka Colonel Steve Austin, "The Six Million Dollar Man") all the way to the corner of Virginia, Kentucky, and Tennessee, aka the Cumberland Gap.

Pale pink-and-white dogwoods and purple wildflowers lined the ascent to Pinnacle Overlook. At the gap Boone had penetrated a wall of rock and forest 600 miles long and 150 miles wide. He saw a new world, where all the old mistakes waited to be made again.

When Boone was asked if he had gotten lost in that forest, he said: I can't say as ever I was lost, but I was bewildered once for three days.

Back on 25E, heading north, I drove through crumbling hills past West Roger Hollow through Corbin into Laurel County. I drove past Magic Vapor Shop and Tri-State Flooring. I took 192 East to the Hal Rogers Parkway out past Lick Fork.

Soon I saw a barn I remembered. I saw horses and cows, trailers up on broken cinder blocks, front yards full of table legs and coffee cans. I passed Urban Creek Holiness Church. I passed Jimbo's 4-Lane Tobacco and the Federal Correctional Institution.

At Burning Springs I turned on 472 to head toward Fogertown, where barns had been reclaimed by the land, overgrown with tall trees poking through holes in their roofs. At Muncey Fork was a burnt-down house. Creeping vines were pulling down telephone poles and billboards.

All at once and with no fanfare I passed Cornett Charolais, where I had spent many pleasant Sunday afternoons with old Joe Dale and Dale Junior and Linda and Bessie—*pleasant* is a pious lie—more like bored, *bored*, not knowing what all of this would one day mean, what I would one day want to pretend it had all meant.

I wanted it to mean to me what it meant to my father: home and happiness with his foster family. I liked being sent to slop out the hogs after dinner, listening to the rustling in the dark along the fence line. I liked hiking in the rocky hills with my father, seeing that he was calm and pleased, seeing the shale and sandstone and limestone and schist and slate. I liked walking across fields and hearing him holler, "Sookie! Sook calf!"

Apart from those pleasures I had been bored and sullen, reading photocopied pages of *The Antichrist* folded inside *Sports Illustrated*, waiting to escape from that army of hayseeds. But twenty years later my father's foster mother is dead, as anyone but me might have foreseen, because she was a person and not a tree; and I would eat a photocopier in exchange for two more bowls of her soup beans and cornbread—one for me, and one for my father, to whom it would mean the world made young again.

Instead I name these places. I throw my song into the mouth of death. I break his teeth. There is no death, there is no hell.

I drove past the old Russell House Grocery, and there was what I wanted to find: the Pleasant Grove Baptist Church, established

1860. I have seen my father cry three times, and one of those times was in this church, at his foster father's funeral.

The second time I saw my father cry was while he was strangling me. He had said my friends, Scott and Allen and Gary, were no-good weirdos and long-haired faggots, and I was on the verge of becoming one too, and that if I didn't act right he was going to cut my hair himself with the lawnmower.

I dared him to, more than a little frightened that he would try it. That was just the sort of thing he was always doing: kicking in a locked door, or pushing around a far-too-young panhandler with a sign that claimed he had been a VIETNAM VETERAN.

"Step around the corner, John Henry," my father said, "I'd like to have a word with this young man in private." He nudged the kid with his boot. "Yes, I do mean you—you dilapidated cocksucker."

And afterwards, in the cab of his truck, trembling, beating his fists against the steering wheel, he said, "What's the matter with these people, Johnny? I'm a Vietnam veteran. And just look at me. I'm fine. I'm fine!"

I dared my father to cut my hair, and he picked me up by my throat and smashed me against the wall, then threw me through the doorway into my bedroom and leapt on top of me, and he was strangling me with both hands and shaking me and cursing and shouting at me before he came to his senses and started to cry.

"My family is falling apart," he said, and it was true, I was destroying our family, why couldn't I do as I was told without having impulses and desires of my own.

That is the second time I saw my father cry. The third time is private.

It's not as if my friends *weren't* no-good weirdos. Big Scott had come over earlier that afternoon, and my father had said, "Hey, gorilla." Then: "Scotty, come here, boy, you're hurt."

My father had glimpsed a bloody letter *s* above the collar of

Scott's T-shirt. He pulled the collar down and saw the still-bleeding word PUSSY, which Big Scott had cut into his chest with a razor-blade moments before sprinting over to show me.

"Who did this to you, boy?" my father said. "You can tell me."

Scott looked at my father.

"I don't believe that," my father said. "No."

I didn't want to write about my father, but I don't seem to have much choice. There is no such thing as a repressed impulse: the inside and the outside are the same side.

What serpent's-tooth-sharp story is this to tell about the man who helped to give me life, who saved my life when I was choking on shish kebab (thereby earning, certain tribesmen might argue, the right to choke me himself), who sacrificed his body at punishing jobs in order that I might have shish kebab to choke on?

Take, eat: this is my body, which is broken for you—and I hope you choke on it.

I visit my father in the Florida Everglades and I see a nice old man. Just this week, he mailed me his sausage-gravy recipe. ("Step Five: Buy helmet, put on, tongue smacking top of mouth may cause injury.") I am deceived: Where has this nice old man hidden the menacing ogre of my childhood?

His aim was to protect me from the darkness all around us, using the darkness inside himself. All that darkness had to be *good for something*, didn't it? That was what the darkness was *for*, wasn't it?—not only for tormenting him and, using him as its instrument, everyone he loved?

It's nothing to get upset about, it isn't even me it happened to, that person died in 1995, he died again in 2003 and again at the beginning of this sentence. He's been dying for most of act 5, scene 2. Maybe someone ought to stab him again.

The man on the radio said, "Four famine scenarios. How to prepare for an economic crisis of Biblical proportions. The salt plan: how to turn adversity into advantage."

"Whence comest thou, Deceiver?" I said. "From going to and fro in the earth, and from walking up and down in it?"

"Be a blessing to others in times of economic turndown. This book will help you get your head straight about what is happening in the world today, and it's very personal and practical at one hundred and forty-two pages."

"Leave me alone," I said to the man on the radio. "That's just the word *God*, the word the conjure man uses to wring hot tears out of the wet rag of your heart. I don't want the word *God*, but the Word of God."

The man on the radio said to me: *I ordained thee a prophet unto the nations.*

I said, "Ah, Lord God, I cannot speak, for I am a child."

But the man on the radio said: *Say not, I am a child: for thou shalt go to all that I shall send thee, and whatsoever I command thee thou shalt speak. Behold, I have put my words in thy mouth.*

I wept until I had to pull over. God had laid His burning hand on me. If you don't turn the radio off, you can't drive anywhere in this country.

CONTRIBUTORS

Amie Barrodale received the 2012 Plimpton Prize for Fiction. Her collection *You Are Having a Good Time* will be published in 2016.

Sylvie Baumgartel lives in Santa Fe, New Mexico.

Brian Blanchfield's second book of poetry, *A Several World*, received the 2014 James Laughlin Award. An editor of *Fence*, he lives in Tucson, Arizona.

Dan Chiasson has published four poetry collections, most recently *Bicentennial*. He is *The New Yorker*'s poetry critic.

Emma Cline won the 2014 Plimpton Prize for Fiction. Her first novel, *The Girls*, will appear in 2016.

J. D. Daniels received the 2013 Terry Southern Prize for Humor. A collection of his nonfiction, *The Correspondence*, will be published next year.

Kristin Dombek writes the "Help Desk" column for *n+1*. Her book *The Selfishness of Others* will be published next year. "Letter from Williamsburg" was included in the Best American Essays of 2014.

Angela Flournoy was raised in Southern California by a mother from Los Angeles and a father from Detroit. "Lelah" is a revised excerpt from her first novel, *The Turner House*.

Garth Greenwell is the author of a novella, *Mitko*, and the forthcoming novel *What Belongs to You*.

Cathy Park Hong is the author of three poetry collections, most recently *Engine Empire*.

Ishion Hutchinson, born in Port Antonio, Jamaica, is the author of *Far District* and the recipient of a 2013 Whiting Writers Award. He lives in Ithaca, New York.

Nick Laird is the author of two novels and three poetry collections. Born and raised in County Tyrone, Northern Ireland, he lives in New York City.

Dorothea Lasky is the author of four poetry collections, most recently *Rome*.

Ben Lerner received the 2014 Terry Southern Prize for Humor. He is the author of three poetry collections and two novels. "False Spring" is an excerpt from his second novel, *10:04*.

April Ayers Lawson received the 2011 Plimpton Prize for Fiction. She is a regular contributor to *Vice* and her work has appeared in *Oxford American* and *Granta Norway*, among other places.

Atticus Lish received the 2015 Plimpton Prize for Fiction. "Jimmy" is adapted from his first novel, *Preparation for the Next Life*.

Sarah Manguso is the author of two poetry collections and four books in prose, most recently *Ongoingness: The End of a Diary*.

Ottessa Moshfegh received the 2013 Plimpton Prize for Fiction. She is the author of the novella *McGlue* and the novel *Eileen*.

Benjamin Nugent is the author of a novel, *Good Kids*, and the cultural history *American Nerd*. "God" was collected in the Best American Short Stories of 2014.

Peter Orner is the author of two novels, two books of nonfiction, and two story collections, including his most recent book, *Last Car Over the Sagamore Bridge.*

Rowan Ricardo Phillips is the author of two poetry collections, *The Ground* and *Heaven*, and a work of criticism, *When Blackness Rhymes with Blackness.* He divides his time between New York City and Barcelona.

Jana Prikryl is a senior editor at *The New York Review of Books.* Her first book of poems, *The After Party*, will be published in 2016.

Davy Rothbart is the creator of *Found Magazine*, a longtime contributor to *This American Life*, and director of three films, including *Medora*. His latest book is the essay collection *My Heart Is an Idiot.*

Brenda Shaughnessy is the author of three poetry collections, most recently *Our Andromeda*. She works at Rutgers University–Newark.

Zadie Smith is the author of four novels and a collection of essays. A London native, she lives in New York.

John Jeremiah Sullivan is the Southern editor of *The Paris Review* and the author of *Blood Horses* and *Pulphead*. "Mr. Lytle: An Essay" won the 2011 National Magazine Award for best essay and a Pushcart Prize. Sullivan received a 2015 Windham-Campbell Prize for nonfiction.

Matt Sumell is the author of the story collection *Making Nice.*

Craig Morgan Teicher is the author of three poetry collections, most recently *To Keep Love Blurry* and *Cradle Book: Stories and Fables.*

Monica Youn's second collection of poetry, *Ignatz*, was a finalist for the National Book Award. Her third collection, *Blackacre*, will be published in 2016.

Kevin Young has published eight collections of poetry, most recently *Book of Hours*, and a work of criticism, *The Grey Album: On the Blackness of Blackness.*